**Readers love Kathle**

'If you like getting your history from ████████████ dry tomes then this is the book for yo████ ████y recommend it!'

'I was transported back to the age of the giant steamships criss-crossing the Atlantic, and to the ill-fated voyage of the *Titanic*. The author has done an immense amount of research and really brings this event and era to life – I truly felt as though I was there in that moment with the heroine . . . An emotional roller-coaster that will keep readers turning the pages – highly recommended!'

'Heartwarming and loved the twist in the tale. Couldn't stop reading, so some late nights for me!'

'The mark of an excellent book – when you don't want it to be finished and when you want to find out more about the subject . . . This book was an education as well as entertaining – as always well written and one not to put down until it was finished.'

'It was a highly captivating, dramatic and emotional read in places. I literally could not turn the pages fast enough, with wanting to find out what happens next and as to how it would all end.'

**KATHLEEN MCGURL** lives in Christchurch with her husband. She has two sons who have both now left home. She always wanted to write, and for many years was waiting until she had the time. Eventually, she came to the bitter realisation that no one would pay her for a year off work to write a book, so she sat down and started to write one anyway. Since then, she has published several novels with HQ and self-published another. She has also sold dozens of short stories to women's magazines, and written three How To books for writers. After a long career in the IT industry, she became a full-time writer in 2019. When she's not writing, she's often out running, slowly.

## Also by Kathleen McGurl

# The Lost Child

## KATHLEEN MCGURL

ONE PLACE. MANY STORIES

HQ
An imprint of HarperCollins*Publishers* Ltd
1 London Bridge Street
London SE1 9GF

www.harpercollins.co.uk

HarperCollins*Publishers*
Macken House, 39/40 Mayor Street Upper,
Dublin 1, D01 C9W8, Ireland

This edition 2024

2

First published in Great Britain by
HQ, an imprint of HarperCollins*Publishers* Ltd 2024

Copyright © Kathleen McGurl 2024

Kathleen McGurl asserts the moral right to be
identified as the author of this work.
A catalogue record for this book is
available from the British Library.

ISBN: 9780008591670

MIX
Paper | Supporting
responsible forestry
FSC™ C007454

This book contains FSC™ certified paper and other controlled
sources to ensure responsible forest management.

For more information visit: www.harpercollins.co.uk/green

Printed and bound in the UK using
100% renewable electricity at CPI Group (UK) Ltd

*For Cindy L. Spear*
*a wonderful writers' champion*

# Prologue

## 15 April 1912

The ship was listing badly now and it was all Arthur Watts could do to stay upright and keep hold of the precious bundle in his arms. He transferred the child to one arm so he could cling onto a railing with his other hand, and heaved himself along the slanting deck to where a lifeboat was being made ready to launch. It was his last chance. His only chance. The last lifeboat.

Lucy, thank goodness, had got away on an earlier boat. She'd been carrying little Frederick while he'd brought tiny Norah. The twins were only ten weeks old. Arthur and Lucy had been planning a new life, in America, and had saved for years to pay for their passage. And now this. They'd been fast asleep in their steerage cabin when the ship struck something – an iceberg, people were saying. When it became clear that the *Titanic* was in trouble, they'd grabbed a baby each and headed up to the boat deck.

And there, they'd been separated. 'Women and children first!' an officer had shouted, pushing Lucy through the crowd while Arthur was held back.

'Our baby, pass her our baby!' he'd yelled, but in all the noise and commotion no one had heard. He'd caught glimpses, through the masses of people, of Lucy being hauled onto a lifeboat, the boat being swung wildly out on its davits and then lowered – too fast! – into the water. He'd leaned over the side and could just see a crewman take the oars and begin rowing the boat away, while Lucy stared up at the ship, shouting something.

'I'll get on another boat!' Arthur had yelled back, but he doubted she'd heard. All around people were shouting and screaming.

Arthur had joined the masses around other lifeboats but only women were allowed through, and no one seemed to realise the bundle of blankets he clutched contained a child. His little girl. His son and wife were safe, but this little one was going to perish along with him, if he didn't take action soon. In his arms she whimpered and wriggled. 'Ssh, my pet. Daddy will do all he can to save you.'

And now this lifeboat was the last one. Men were boarding it. All the women had already gone. It was a chance for them. The last chance to save himself and little Norah. He pushed forward but there were too many people, all of them trying to clamber aboard, and already they were swinging the lifeboat out. He was being shoved and jostled and struggled to keep Norah safe in his arms.

'Where've you ladies been hiding?' an officer called out, and Arthur noticed two women in stewardess's uniform being pushed through the crowd to the lifeboat.

This was it. His final chance. He thrust the bundle containing Norah at one of the women. 'My baby. Take her, please.'

The stewardess stared at him with wide brown eyes, but she opened her arms and took the baby wordlessly. Arthur watched as she and the other woman struggled onto the lifeboat and took up seats, and the boat was hurriedly lowered into the water. It hit the sea hard, sending people falling into the bottom of the boat, but the stewardess managed to keep hold of Norah and even now was tucking the blanket she was wrapped in tightly around her.

'Thank you,' Arthur whispered, as he clung to the deck rail, watching.

Down below, a crewman in that last lifeboat shouted, 'Oars out!' and then it was moving away, the crewmen aboard pulling strongly to get away from *Titanic* before she went down.

Arthur stayed where he was. Around him, other men were rushing everywhere, shouting about launching the collapsible life rafts. There were hundreds more people still on board than the collapsibles would take. There was no point him joining them, trying to get on a raft. He'd saved his wife and children, and now he must make his peace with the world, for his time in it was coming to an end.

He looked up, gazing at the night sky with its myriad stars that shone down, reflecting off the calm sea and the numerous icebergs. It was a beautiful sight. Focusing hard on the starlight, he was able to tune out the shrieks and cries of those still aboard the ship; those who were doomed. He was going to enjoy his last moments as best he could, watching the stars, contemplating the enormity of the universe, all the while knowing that life would go on without him and those precious babies of his would grow up in time to have children and grandchildren of their own. They'd never know him, but his darling Lucy would tell them stories of the father who'd loved them so very much.

And as the ship broke in two and slipped beneath the surface of the freezing ocean, it was these thoughts that brought him comfort, even as the cold black water closed above his head.

In the lifeboat, Lucy craned her neck to try to see what was happening on the deck of the ship far above her. She thought she saw Arthur leaning over the rail, still clutching little Norah wrapped in her blanket.

'Arthur!' she screamed. 'Arthur, find another lifeboat!'

'Shut up. Right in my ear, that was.' The woman beside Lucy scowled at her and elbowed her in the ribs.

'It's my husband, up there,' Lucy replied.

'We've all got husbands still on board,' the woman snapped. 'At least you're safe.'

'But my baby, my baby,' she whimpered, unable to stop herself as she stared up at Norah in Arthur's arms.

'You've got your baby in your arms. Be thankful for that, and now shut up and let the crewman get on with his rowing in peace.'

Lucy had no choice. But she kept her eyes fixed on Arthur, and then . . . there! Through the gloomy night sky, she saw him push through the crowd towards a lifeboat that was yet to be launched. 'Go on, Arthur,' she whispered. 'Get on it.'

'Hmph. If he gets on, it'll be at the expense of some poor woman,' her neighbour said, but Lucy ignored the other woman. She watched as the lifeboat was winched down the side of the ship. A woman on it was clutching a blanketed bundle that looked identical to the one she held, the precious bundle containing Frederick. Had Arthur somehow managed to get Norah on a lifeboat in the care of someone else?

She tried to keep sight of the other lifeboat but soon it was lost to her, as the crew of her own lifeboat rowed them away from *Titanic*. The ship was low in the water now; only a few decks were still above the water line. As she watched, the lights flickered and went out, and they were left in darkness, with only starlight to see by. There was a terrible grinding, crashing noise accompanied by shouts and screams. 'A funnel's gone,' someone on her lifeboat said, and Lucy found she could watch no longer. She buried her face in the blanket that held Frederick and wept silently.

And there she stayed, not looking up again even as her boat companions screamed when the ship finally went down, taking her beloved Arthur with it. That Frederick was saved, and possibly Norah too on the other boat, was some comfort but not enough.

4

Arthur was lost. Her beloved husband, the best father any baby could have had. Gone.

In her arms, Frederick snuffled and wriggled, and she clutched him tightly against herself. His future, Norah's, her own – everything was so uncertain now. And all she could do was hold the baby and wait. Wait for what – she didn't want to think about it too closely. Rescue . . . or death.

# Chapter 1

## Jackie, 2022

Jackie picked up her pint, clinked it against Tim's glass, and grinned. 'Like old times, isn't it? Us on a night out, having a few drinks together and with a pub band to look forward to. When are they playing?'

'Starting nine o'clock, I think,' Tim said, scanning a nearby poster that advertised the pub's gigs. 'Yes, just like old times. I know it's not over, there's still loads of Covid about and no doubt there always will be. But at least we can go out again now, go on holidays, and get our lives back on track.'

Jackie nodded her agreement. It had been a long haul, for everyone. And Tim was right – the pandemic wasn't over, would possibly never be truly finished, but the restrictions had been lifted and life could continue. 'I'll still be working from home a couple of days a week. Henry said that was OK. I probably get more done from home than I do in the office. Fewer interruptions.'

'Yeah, you're lucky,' Tim said. 'Hard for me to teach PE from home, though. Imagine it: "OK, kids, now find yourself a sibling or failing that a parent who's home-working, and practise your rugby tackles on them . . ." Can't quite see it working.'

Jackie laughed. 'Well, let's hope the schools never have to close again.'

'I'll drink to that.' They both raised their glasses and took a long pull of their pints. Tim looked at Jackie quizzically. 'So, talking of school, there's only one more term and then it'll be the summer break. Any chance your boss will let you take extended leave again this year? Like you did in 2019? It'd be good to go away for a long trip. A real adventure, somewhere.'

Jackie smiled at him. 'Like what?'

'Trek to Everest base camp? Go scuba diving on the Great Barrier Reef? Cycle through France from the Channel to the Med? The world's our oyster!'

'Well, they all sound like fun.' Jackie contemplated the ideas. All pie in the sky, of course. They'd probably end up with a two-week hiking holiday in Scotland or a cycle-touring trip around the west of Ireland, given the uncertainties that were still around. But she enjoyed considering the possibilities.

'So . . . will you ask Henry?'

'Ask him what?'

'For six weeks off. The dates of the summer break are in our house diary. It's late March already, so we should make a decision and get something booked as soon as possible. I'm thinking the cycling trip through France. Or I also fancy a Dolomites hiking and backpacking trip. Staying in Europe's probably best, in case the whole Covid thing flares up again. Also, we wouldn't need to fly. We could get trains to the start and end point. That would be greener, plus there'd be less likelihood of picking up Covid before we even start. So, which is it?' He looked expectantly at Jackie.

His enthusiasm was endearing and one of the things she'd always loved about him. He'd get an idea and before you knew it everything was planned and booked. They'd done a lot of travelling and had many adventures in the thirteen years they'd been together, and all she'd ever had to do was say yes to his ideas then turn up at the start of the trip with a rucksack packed. 'Oh, Tim. I'd love to . . . but I know Henry wouldn't let me have six weeks this year. I'd be able to get three, I reckon. We can do a decent trek in three weeks.'

'Three. Hmm.' Tim took a sip of his beer. 'By the time you allow a couple of days either end to get there and back, that's not much over two weeks for the walking. I was honestly hoping for something more than that. I mean . . . after the wasted two years we've just had, surely you want to make up for that too? We're not getting any younger, are we?'

'Thirty-five is hardly old!' Jackie laughed indignantly. He was right, though. They were not getting any younger. And her biological clock was ticking, loudly. 'Talking of not getting younger – back in 2019, when we did that South America trip, we said we'd do two more big summer trips and then we'd talk about starting a family. We said back then, that 2022 would be the "Year to Start a Baby".' She made air quotes around the words, and waggled her eyebrows suggestively. 'Maybe we should be thinking about that?'

'Ah, Jacks,' Tim said, reaching across the table for her hand. 'You know I want kids. But not yet. Our lives have been on hold for two years and now I want to make up for that. A big trip this summer and next, and then I guess we think about having a family.'

'I'd be thirty-eight by then. And if it took us a while to get pregnant, I'd be over forty.'

'Plenty of people are over forty when they have their kids. A boy in my class has parents in their late fifties and he's only thirteen.'

'Bully for them,' Jackie said. It came out with more vehemence than she'd intended. 'I mean, everyone makes their own decisions about what they want, and what's best for them. It's fine for people to wait until their forties to have children if that's what they want. But Tim, it's not what *I* want. I thought this would be the year we'd go for it. I thought maybe we'd even have a child by the end of the year. We still could . . . if we tried and got lucky . . .'

She glanced up at Tim, expecting to see a cheeky smirk on his face at the idea of trying for a baby imminently but his expression was one of horror. She frowned, and he quickly recomposed his features. 'Jacks, no. Not gonna happen this year. No need to rush things . . .'

'Rush! We've been together thirteen years!'

'And they've been fab years, haven't they? All the places we've been, the things we've done. That year when we both took a sabbatical and toured the world? So many people never do anything like that.'

'We were lucky to be able to.' Jackie would never stop feeling grateful that they'd had the chances to do all the things they had.

'We made our own luck. And now, we can do it again – now that the Covid restrictions are over. And we must, Jacks! Anyway, can we even afford a baby right now?'

'If we can afford for me to take unpaid leave to go on a six-week summer trip then surely we can afford to have a baby, Tim.' She was beginning to feel exasperated with him.

'Hmm.' He rubbed his chin as though unsure of the logic. 'I just mean there's time enough for kids. Time enough to settle down and play at being parents.'

'It's hardly playing! Full-time job, so Sarah tells me.' Her best friend had given birth during a lockdown, and little Bobby was now over a year old, walking now, saying his first words. Lockdown had meant Jackie wasn't able to meet her friend's baby until months after he was born.

'Ah ha! It's Sarah who's got under your skin!' Tim said, triumphantly. 'She's had a baby so now you feel you should have one too. That makes sense.' He nodded as though he'd solved the problem and lifted his empty beer glass. 'I'll get another. You?'

'No, thanks.' Jackie still had half of hers left, and somehow she no longer felt like drinking much. On the other side of the bar, an area was being cleared ready for the band. Amps were being set up, and a young man in a black T-shirt was busy plugging in cables and setting up microphone stands. Jackie glanced at her watch. Still nearly half an hour before the band were due to play. Could they duck out early, go home and watch a bit of TV instead? Early nights with a book had become the norm during the lockdowns, and she had to admit she rather liked them. Perhaps she really was getting old.

'Suit yourself,' Tim said, and went to the bar, leaving Jackie alone with her thoughts. Their relationship had been a long one. They'd met as students, but started going out together after graduation when they'd reconnected after meeting up in a pub with mutual friends. Later that year, they'd gone camping in the Alps with the same set of friends, and had ended up sharing a two-person tent, staying up half the night talking and planning future adventures. It had only taken a few weeks before they moved in together and the rest, as they say, was history.

She'd always assumed that after a few years of living life to the full, travelling as much as their jobs and finances allowed, they'd settle down, marry and start a family. Become conventional. The year they'd turned thirty, they'd sat down and had a heart-to-heart about what they each wanted, and had agreed that they still felt too young to have children and both wanted a few more years of fun first. In Jackie's mind, the milestone, the natural turning point in their lives, had been thirty-five. That was now. But the pandemic had changed things, forcing them to stay home for two years postponing all the plans they'd had. She still wanted what Tim wanted – the fun lifestyle they'd enjoyed – but she also wanted children before it was too late, before she was very much older.

'So, Sarah's got a rug rat and now you want one,' Tim said, as he returned with another pint and a couple of packets of crisps. His tone was cheerful, as though the whole thing was a joke. It crossed Jackie's mind to be offended by this – it wasn't really a joking matter after all. They were making decisions that could affect their entire future. But she didn't want an argument. Not here, not now, on their first proper night out in what seemed like ages. She forced herself to respond with a chuckle and a shrug.

11

'Not exactly. I hate the term "rug rat". Little Bobby is the cutest thing ever. And,' she leaned forward and spoke earnestly as something occurred to her, 'when they're really tiny they're very portable, so Sarah says, and you can still do lots of travelling with small babies. We could get a camper van and go touring in that, or have a walking holiday carrying the baby in a sling or whatever.'

'Where would we park a camper van?' Tim asked.

'In the driveway?'

'Then I wouldn't be able to get my Audi out easily.' His face fell, and Jackie rolled her eyes. That car, the ageing TT he'd bought, was Tim's pride and joy. But it was a two-seater convertible, and wholly unsuitable as a family car. 'Scuba diving and hang-gliding would be out of the question, though.' Tim did at least look thoughtful, as though he was considering the possible adventures that would still be achievable with a baby.

Jackie laughed. 'Yeah, can't quite imagine doing those with a little one. But what I mean is, why don't we start trying for a baby now? We could plan a three-week trip for this summer, something I'd be able to do whether I was pregnant or not. Then next year we plan something that's possible with a small baby.'

'One two, one two.' Across the bar, the band were testing out their microphones.

'Why do they always say that? Must be something more original they could say.' Tim took a gulp of his pint. He was putting off answering her, Jackie realised. She knew him so well. She knew when he needed a bit of time to decide how to answer. They'd always had the kind of relationship where they could trust what each other had said, where neither of them ever went back on anything already agreed. She knew that Tim knew that whatever he said now would set the course of their future. It sounded dramatic, putting it like that, but it's how things had always been.

'Tell you what,' he said at last, 'how about we meet in the middle. One more adventure this summer, then after that we try for a baby. So – six more months, then we can be at it like rabbits until we get pregnant. How about it?' He raised his eyebrows suggestively, which made Jackie giggle and blush.

'Sounds good. I'll . . . come off the pill sooner though, as I know it takes a while before you can get pregnant. We'll have to use alternative methods for a bit.'

'No problem, my gorgeous girl,' Tim replied, and Jackie felt a surge of love towards this man, her soul mate, the man she knew she'd spend the rest of her life with. And if they were lucky and were able to have children quickly after the summer, by the time they reached forty they might have completed their family. Depending on how many they wanted, of course.

'Two kids? Or three?' she asked him. 'And what names do you like? I think . . . perhaps Ryan for a boy. And Amelia, or maybe Olivia for a girl.'

Tim laughed. 'You're getting a bit ahead of yourself there! Let's just see how we get on, eh? It might be harder than you think.'

'You'll be a great dad,' she replied. He was more used to stroppy teenagers than tantrum-throwing toddlers, but she was sure he'd be good at every stage.

'And you'll be an amazing mum. Now, before they start,' he nodded towards the band who were getting their instruments out and beginning to tune up, 'let's make a decision on an adventure for the summer. My preference is a walking trip, probably in Italy. Dolomites? Or end to end of the Apennines would be awesome!'

'The what now?'

'Mountain range down through the middle of Italy. We could start at the southern end, in Calabria, walk northwards. The Abruzzo region is where I'd want to spend most time. All those gorgeous medieval villages, tucked away in fabulous mountain scenery. In the summer, it'd be hot in the valleys but there'd be no snow so it'd all be passable. What do you say?'

'Sounds good! But remember, I'll only be able to get three weeks off. I'll ask for four, but I wouldn't hold out much hope.

Henry's away at the moment. Some *Titanic* memorabilia auction. He'll come back with boxes and boxes of stuff I'll have to sort through, no doubt. But yes, I'll ask him when he's back.'

'OK, well, let's see what Henry says, eh? I'll get some maps, work out some routes and all that.' Tim lifted his pint glass and clinked hers once more. 'To us, to travel, to adventure.'

'And to our future together,' she replied.

He nodded and was about to say something else, but at that moment the band started playing a raucous version of 'With a Little Help from My Friends' and there was no chance for more conversation. Still, they'd had the talk they needed, they'd agreed on plans and their future was back on track. Jackie felt both excited and contented with their decisions. Life was good. She sat back to enjoy the band, pleased now that they'd stayed. There'd been enough nights when they'd been forced to stay home reading books, and there'd be plenty more to come when they had children. It was right for them to make the most of their freedom and youth now, while they still could.

If Covid had taught them anything, Jackie thought, it was to take your chances while you could, for you never knew what was around the corner.

# Chapter 2

## Madeleine, 13 April 1912

The sun was just about to sink below the horizon, its last rays glinting across the sea, turning the sky shades of orange, red and purple. Already the evening star could be seen in the east. Madeleine Meyer had spent much of the afternoon sitting by the porthole of their little cabin. She'd thought she would read a lot on the voyage. She'd imagined strolling on deck, making friends, dining with the captain. Rebuilding her life, with her husband, Ralph, alongside her. What kind of life would it be? What purpose would it have? She still had no idea.

It hadn't been so easy. The change of scenery, their plans to tour Europe for a few months, her need to find a new purpose in life – she'd thought simply stepping on board the ship would make it all happen. But so far, she still felt as bad as she had back home in Manhattan. The last three hours, during which she'd stared at the horizon and read only a paragraph of her novel, proved it.

Perhaps this trip had been a bad idea. Perhaps they should have stayed at home.

'Darling? How's your book?' Ralph had returned to their cabin. She dredged up a smile to plaster on her face.

'It's all right. I'm not really concentrating on it, if I'm honest.'

'Maybe try a different book? There's a well-stocked library on board. There may not be much else to do on *Carpathia*, but there are plenty of books at least.'

'Perhaps I will.' She held out a hand to him, and he crossed the cabin to her, raising her hand to his lips to kiss.

He took his pocket watch out and consulted it. 'We should probably start dressing for dinner now.'

Madeleine suppressed a sigh. She really didn't feel like going to the dining room, where she would have to be cheerful and lively all evening. But she knew Ralph enjoyed dining with fellow passengers, so she had not yet suggested having room service. She needed to snap out of her low mood and make the best of things. She couldn't mope forever on what might have been. She knew she should count her blessings – Ralph, their comfortable lifestyle, the adventures that awaited them on this trip. 'Yes, all right,' she replied.

She heaved herself out of the armchair she'd been in all after-noon and took two evening dresses from the closet, holding them up for Ralph to consider. 'Which one tonight? I've worn both already on this trip. Perhaps I should have brought more.' Packing for long trips was always a problem, Madeleine thought. And she had found it harder than ever this time, since their loss.

'Oh, darling, you brought enough luggage as it is!' Ralph laughed. 'I like the blue best on you.'

'Very well. I'll wear that one.'

'Shall we sit with the Marshalls again? You seemed to be enjoying chatting with Miss Evelyn Marshall last night, and I found Charles an interesting conversationalist.'

'All right. Yes, Evelyn is a sweet girl.'

Ralph smiled encouragingly at her. Bless him, he was doing all he could to cheer her up. It had been several months since it happened – their own personal tragedy. She was taking a long,

long time to get over it, and poor Ralph was being very patient with her. Deep down, Madeleine suspected she would never get over their loss. But perhaps she would eventually learn to live alongside it.

She dressed, arranged her hair, and added a little rouge and lipstick.

'You look beautiful, my darling,' Ralph said, standing behind her where she sat at the little dressing table in their cabin. 'As lovely as you did on the day we were wed. Can you believe we'll soon celebrate our fifth anniversary?'

She smiled sadly at his reflection. 'It's gone by so fast. And yet here we are.'

Here they were – just the two of them. She'd married relatively late in life – at over thirty she'd been considering herself on the shelf until she'd met Ralph. She'd expected children to come along quickly, one after the other, to make up for lost time. As a young woman, she'd thought four would be the right number to have, and had fantasised about having a boy, then a girl, then twins. Her late marriage had made her reconsider, and she'd thought two children would be enough. One, even.

And yet . . . here they were, just herself and Ralph. And there was no chance now of having a family, after what had happened.

This trip to Europe, where they planned to spend six months or more, was intended, in part, to help her find new purpose in life. Ralph seemed happy with their life, though she knew he too had been devastated by their loss and was quietly disappointed at what it had meant for their future. But it hadn't floored him the way it had her. It hadn't left him depressed and reeling, wondering what was the point of going on.

It was different for women, she supposed. More personal. Women felt things more deeply. Or perhaps, men were simply brought up not to show their feelings as much. She'd tried to talk to Ralph, to explain how she felt, but he would brush it off, jolly her along, and she'd learned to keep her sorrows to herself.

Ralph was a journalist, and he planned to write travel articles for his paper while they were away. What Madeleine would do she had no idea, and whenever she tried to think about it, she just found herself mourning for the life – being a mother – that she would never now experience.

The dinner gong sounded, and Madeleine stood and picked up her evening purse. 'Seven-thirty already. I suppose we ought not be late.' She took Ralph's arm as they left the cabin and walked along the passageway towards the first-class dining room. It wasn't far – *Carpathia* wasn't a huge ship.

'I've had an idea,' Ralph said, as they entered the dining room. 'When we reach the end of this trip, let's sail back to New York on the *Titanic*. Treat ourselves to a little more luxury. There'll be more to occupy us on board a larger ship too.'

He was trying as always to cheer her up, Madeleine knew. She smiled up him. 'Yes, why not?'

'That's my girl. Look, there are the Marshalls. Over near the piano.'

He pointed, and they made their way towards their friends. Mr Charles Marshall stood as they approached, and Ralph shook his hand and then those of his wife and daughter, while Madeleine kissed each in turn. All took their seats. The captain was due to join them at their table tonight, but hadn't yet arrived.

'I'm glad we're sitting together again. I was looking forward all day to chatting with you some more,' Evelyn Marshall said to Madeleine. Madeleine had judged her age to be somewhere in the early twenties, but she'd found she got on better with Evelyn than she had with her mother, Josephine, whom she found a little intimidating, if she was honest. Madeleine supposed she had more in common with the younger, childless woman.

'Is it your first time crossing the Atlantic?' she asked Evelyn.

'Oh, no. We've made the trip many times, but this is our first visit to Gibraltar. What about you?'

'First time for many years.' Since before her wedding. They'd always been reluctant to book anything in case she'd got pregnant.

'What do you think of *Carpathia*?' Evelyn asked. 'I must admit I find it a little dull during the day. There's not much to do on this ship.'

'You're right.' Madeleine didn't want to admit she'd spent hours staring at the horizon that afternoon. She could have gone for a walk on deck, she realised now, and perhaps found Evelyn to keep her company. But what kind of company she'd have been for the younger woman was a different question. 'Let me tell you what Ralph and I just decided upon, on our way to dinner today. We're going to travel back to New York at the end of this trip on *Titanic*. What do you think about that?'

'Oh, how lovely! You know, my three cousins are on board *Titanic* now. I was so jealous when I heard they had tickets for its maiden voyage. If only Mama and Papa and I had been travelling westward rather than eastward we might have been on it too.'

'On what, honey?' Mrs Marshall asked.

'*Titanic*, Mama. With Charlotte, Caroline and Malvina.'

'We don't even know if the ship left port yet.'

'Ah, Mrs Marshall, I can reassure you that it did sail from Southampton on time,' Ralph said. 'I picked up a paper just before we left New York, that carried a report of the grand farewell Southampton gave it. I believe it was due to call at Cherbourg and Queenstown, and then cross the Atlantic. It must be about half-way by now. You know people on board?'

'Three of our nieces,' Charles Marshall replied. 'Silly, excitable girls, all three, but that's what the younger generation is like.' He raised an eyebrow at Evelyn, and the twitching of the corner of his mouth showed he was teasing.

'Oh, Papa. You love them,' Evelyn responded.

'I do, it's true. And I hope they are having a marvellous time on board the largest liner ever to be launched.'

Ralph leaned forward. 'Is it bigger than its sister, *Olympic*?'

'Pretty much the same size, I believe. The two of them share the honour of being the biggest, but I believe *Titanic* is the more luxurious.' Mr Marshall picked up the glass of wine a waiter had just poured for him and took a sip. 'No doubt we shall hear all about it in excruciating detail when next we meet our nieces.'

'When will that be?' Madeleine asked, but she received no answer for at that moment Captain Rostron arrived to take his place at their table. The men stood to shake hands, and it was a few minutes before all the formalities were over and everyone was seated again.

'I suppose we'd better not giggle any more, now that the captain's with us,' Evelyn said quietly to Madeleine, and she nodded. Across the table, Ralph and Charles Marshall had engaged the captain in conversation about their course, the weather conditions, and the maximum speed of the ship.

She regarded Captain Rostron as she listened to the men talk. It was the first time she'd met him. He was a small man who was probably only a few years older than herself. Perhaps he was about forty. He had a confident manner. They'd be safe with him in charge of the ship, Madeleine knew, although she couldn't have explained why she felt that way. Just that he inspired confidence. He had the air of a man who was used to being obeyed at all times.

'Will we pass anywhere near *Titanic*?' Mrs Marshall asked the captain.

'No, we are on the southern route across the ocean. *Titanic* will be on the northern route. We won't come anywhere near.' Captain Rostron smiled kindly at Mrs Marshall. 'It would be nice to think we'd pass close enough to see her, of course. A fine ship. Did you see the *Olympic* in New York? She arrived just before we departed.'

'No, we didn't see her. Our nieces are on the *Titanic*, that's why I asked. I know I'm just being silly but I thought how lovely it would be if we passed them and waved.' Mrs Marshall blushed as she said this. And so she should, Madeleine thought. Whoever heard of two ships out at sea, passing so close that you could wave at passengers on the other ship?

'Well, if we are ever in range of *Titanic*, it might just be possible to send a message to them on the Marconi equipment. There is a small charge for private messages, of course, but if you really want or need to get in touch with them, please do search out the Marconi operator tomorrow.' Captain Rostron picked up the printed menu that was propped against the salt cellar in the middle of the table. 'Ah, splendid. Confit duck this evening. One of my favourites.'

Evelyn gasped. 'How exciting, to think that ships at sea, out of sight of each other, can communicate!' She turned to Mr Marshall. 'Papa, I would love to send my cousins a Marconigram tomorrow! Please say we can!'

Madeleine smiled to see how Evelyn's eyes shone at the idea, and it seemed her enthusiasm was infectious.

'Yes, I don't see why not. You're sure it's all right, Captain?'

'Absolutely. Of course, any official messages such as weather warnings or the like must take priority but if it's all quiet in the Marconi cabin, I'm sure Harold Cottam, our Marconi operator, will be all too pleased to have something to do. *Titanic*, of course, will be fitted with much more up-to-date equipment than we have. Our range isn't terribly good, so I cannot guarantee the other ship will receive your message, or that we'll pick up any reply, but you are welcome to try if you wish.'

'I think the ladies do wish it,' Mr Marshall said with a laugh. 'I'll see about it first thing tomorrow, then.'

The first course of their dinner arrived, and the conversation eased off while they ate. A pianist had begun to play. As dinner progressed, Madeleine and Evelyn chatted about their plans once they reached Europe, while Ralph continued talking to the men.

Later, back in their cabin, Ralph hung up his dinner jacket and removed his tie. 'I'm glad you have found a friend. There's not much to do on this ship, so it's good you have someone to talk to. I hope it's helping, taking your mind off . . . everything else. Perhaps you might meet up with Evelyn during the day?'

'Yes, I think I shall. For a while, at least.'

'I'm glad to hear it, darling.'

She knew he fretted about her, and was glad that she'd made him happy by agreeing to spend more time with Evelyn. 'What about you? Will you spend more time with the Marshalls tomorrow?'

'Perhaps. But I intend visiting the Marconi operator. I was very interested in what the captain had to say about it over dinner, and I would like to learn more. Perhaps there's a piece I could write on the changing nature of communication at sea, the impact of modern technology . . .' He tailed off and stared into space.

Madeleine smiled. She knew that look. It meant he was already working out a killer first line for an article, and picturing it printed in some publication or other. She was so proud of him, of his track record as a journalist and his ability to sniff out interesting stories that sold, that people wanted to read. It was a shame for him that time on board ship was dead time, but if he'd found something to write about, that would keep him occupied and make him happy.

# Chapter 3

## Jackie, 2022

Jackie stopped taking the pill immediately after that conversation in the pub with Tim. She shyly bought a packet of condoms and put them on Tim's bedside table. He'd picked them up and sighed, but then grinned at her and insisted on 'trying one on for size' and she knew he was on board with her plan of trying for a baby later in the year, after their summer adventure. Every now and again over the following few weeks, she'd say or do something to remind him of the plan – discuss what colour to paint the little spare room she'd thought would make a good nursery, leave a catalogue open at a page showing cots or prams, or comment on an article in the Sunday paper about how best to wean a child. She was careful not to overdo it. No more than once a week, or less. He was playing along with it, rolling his eyes at her more blatant reminders but taking it all with good humour.

As the weeks went on Jackie found herself thinking more and more often about the realities of becoming parents. It really was true, the stories about biological clocks ticking and making you more and more desperate to have a baby. She was lucky, she thought, that she had Tim and he wanted children, and they'd been able to agree and plan when they would start a family.

She told Sarah. The two of them had started meeting up once a fortnight for a girl's night out, when they'd go to a pub and have a few glasses and a good old chat.

'These nights out with you are my lifeline,' Sarah said, when they were settled at a corner table, with a bottle of wine and two glasses in front of them. 'A chance to be Sarah Radcliffe again for a few hours, rather than just Bobby's mum.'

'Just?!' Jackie had said with a laugh. 'Thought you said it was a full-time job?'

'It is, and it's marvellous, but there are times, you know, when I need some me-time. You'll get this, if or when you have kids.'

'Speaking of which . . .' Jackie began, and Sarah squealed, cutting her off.

'Oh my God, you aren't, are you? What are you doing with this then?' She grabbed the wine bottle and moved it out of Jackie's reach.

'No! Not pregnant, no! Pour me a glass, for goodness' sake. All I was going to say was . . .'

'You're trying for one? Tim enjoying the process, is he?' Sarah smirked.

Jackie laughed. 'Good God woman, let me get a sentence out, will you? I was going to say, Tim and I have had a chat about it, and we've agreed to start trying for a baby—'

'Yes! Knew it!' Sarah punched the air triumphantly.

'—after our summer holiday this year.' Jackie finally managed to say.

'Oh! Why wait till then?'

'One more adventure, we agreed. Because we weren't able to travel for the last two years.'

'Tim and his adventures! What are you going to do?'

'Walking in Italy. The Apennine mountains.'

'Mmm, sounds great.' Sarah did not sound enthusiastic. Her idea of a good holiday had always been lying beside a pool in the Canary

Islands. 'We're renting a holiday home somewhere near Newquay, in Cornwall. We'll be taking Bobby to the zoo, to the beach, and to a delightful sounding place called Pixieland. A woman I work with recommended it for toddlers. He'll be eighteen months by then.'

'That sounds lovely.' Jackie meant it. She loved the idea of a simple family holiday somewhere in England, digging sandcastles on the beach, introducing her child to exotic animals at the zoo. And while she had no idea what Pixieland would be like, the name was a bit of a giveaway.

'I'd say we could swap, but your holiday sounds a bit strenuous for me,' Sarah said. 'Anyway, I'm pleased for you. You've pinned him down to agreeing to start trying in a few months' time. Well done!' She picked up her glass and clinked it against Jackie's.

'Thanks. Not much progress, I know, but it's a step. I must admit, I can't wait. It's all I can think about these days.'

'What, shagging Tim in the hope of getting pregnant?' Sarah put on a shocked face.

'Ha ha, no. Babies.'

'Uh, oh. Ticktock, eh?'

Jackie nodded.

'I was like that,' Sarah said, her tone more sympathetic now. 'I suppose it's nature's way of ensuring the species survives. I mean, if we were all fully aware of the reality of pregnancy, giving birth and sleepless nights we'd probably never do it.'

'All right, spare me the horror stories,' Jackie said. She'd heard them before, in any case. 'But you're right. I can't wait. Just got to get this trip over and done with and then . . . But what if I don't conceive quickly? What if there's something wrong with one of us, and it doesn't happen? And then I'll be forty and childless and . . .'

Sarah wagged her finger at Jackie. 'Stop it. Don't let your mind wander down that route. You won't know until you try, so no need to worry about it unless it happens. But I'm pleased for you, honestly, and anything I can do along the way to help, I will do. Just promise me . . .'

'What?'

'That even after you get pregnant, you'll still come on our nights out. You can drink mineral water. And when you have the baby, you'll still come out. I *need* these nights out, Jackie!'

Jackie smiled. 'I promise.'

'So,' Sarah said, 'tell me more about your Italian holiday plans for the summer? Last big adventure for a while? How many weeks?'

'Depends if Henry will let me take some unpaid leave. Tim wants me to ask for six weeks but there'll be no hope of that. I'm going to try for four. Might only be able to take three weeks.'

'Henry'll let you have four, won't he? You've always said what a lovely man he is to work for.'

Jackie nodded. Henry Fotheringham was a lovely man; a wealthy business owner with property in several countries and fingers in countless pies. He'd employed Jackie as part of his team of personal assistants. Her main responsibilities were organising his vast collections. He bought rare books, antique scientific equipment, war memorabilia and anything related to the White Star Line and specifically, RMS *Titanic*, with which he was obsessed. Jackie's job was to search for opportunities where he might be able to add to his collections. And then when he bought more items, she was responsible for researching them, cataloguing them and displaying the choicest items in one of his many houses. She loved the work. Especially when he bought job lots of wonderful old books and she could spend days looking through them and being paid to do so.

'He is,' she replied, 'but I don't want to take advantage of him. I don't want him to decide he can manage without me.' She'd had the job for five years now. It had started as a temporary position to catalogue a book collection Henry had bought. She'd done a good job with it, and then when she'd realised how many rooms full of other collectibles he had in his huge country house in Berkshire, where Jackie's job was based, she'd suggested she stay on to work on the rest of it. Henry had been only too pleased.

She'd realised, over time, that for him it was the thrill of buying and then owning these items that counted. He didn't have the time or the patience to look at them or catalogue them, but he did want to be able to show off the best of them.

'He'd be lost without you. Lost, I tell you! Talking of bosses, mine's been a pig lately. Do you know what she said to me last week?' Sarah launched into a long anecdote about her manager at the IT company where she worked. Jackie only half listened, the other half of her mind was occupied with wondering whether she'd continue working after having a baby (yes, she thought, she would, the job was too good to give up) and what kind of childcare arrangements they would need.

By the time they left the pub after a marvellous, fun evening full of laughter, she was a little inebriated. That was perhaps why, she later thought, she'd miscounted the weeks, and told an amorous Tim that it was a safe time of the month and there was no need to use any protection.

'You sure?' he'd said breathlessly, and she'd nodded, feeling certain that there was no way she could get pregnant right then.

But she was wrong. Two weeks later, her breasts felt sore and tender, a week after that she realised her period was late, and a week after that the morning sickness began. She took a test one morning after Tim had left for work and gasped when it revealed two blue lines, showing her for certain that a baby was on its way, despite their carefully agreed schedule. How on earth would Tim take the news? It was only May. They weren't supposed to have started a baby until September at the earliest. She'd messed up. But they wanted a baby, they'd agreed to start trying later in the year, so how bad was it really? A few months early wouldn't matter. She'd still be able to do the Italian hiking trip that they'd planned to start in mid-July.

*  *  *

Tim came home that evening bubbling with excitement. He'd trawled a bookshop after work for maps and books about the Abruzzo region of Italy, and the Apennine mountain range. 'Look, here's one with a suggested walking route,' he said, slapping down a slim book with a cover featuring a happy couple of hikers in front of a range of magnificent rocky mountains. 'I don't think it's exactly what we talked about, but we can use ideas from this as a starting point. And I have the detailed maps. Ordered them a while back and they'd just come in.' He laid out a set of walkers' maps of the area, opened one and began peering at it.

Jackie smiled. There was nothing Tim liked better than studying maps and planning routes. Unless it was walking or cycling the routes themselves. She looked over his shoulder at the map, at the town he was pointing at. 'See, we can fly to Rome and take a bus to L'Aquila, and start our hike from there.'

'Rome! Could we spend a few days at the beginning or the end in the city?' Jackie liked that idea. Combine one of Tim's adventures with a bit of sightseeing. And if she was feeling tired due to her pregnancy, she could always relax at a hotel or in cafés.

'It'd eat into our walking time, especially as you've only been able to get three weeks off work,' Tim said. He must have realised he sounded petulant for he smiled and shrugged. 'But yes, it's a good idea. Great opportunity. I know you always wanted to see Rome. We'll do it.'

'Fantastic! Just a couple of days, eh? To see the Sistine Chapel, the Coliseum, the Roman Forum, St Peter's, the Vatican museum . . .'

'They'll be busy days!' Tim laughed. 'So I'll get a route sorted out for us that takes around fourteen days. Allowing for a few days in Rome, the travelling time, the journey time to L'Aquila and a day to explore that town . . . how does that sound?'

'Perfect!' She smiled happily at him. Now was the moment to tell him the big news. 'I think we'll enjoy that a lot. All three of us.'

'Three?' He gave her a puzzled glance. 'Who else have you invited?'

In answer, she patted her tummy. 'I know we hadn't planned

it yet, but . . . we took a risk one night a few weeks back if you remember. And, well, oops!' She grinned at him and winked.

He stared at her, his mouth dropping open. And then he shook his head a little and gave her a weak smile. 'Well, that's . . . unexpected. I mean . . . wait, it's not September, is it? Did I miss the summer?'

'No! It was an accident, but now it's happened, it's all right, isn't it?' Jackie had a moment of panic. She'd seen it, a look of shock and horror had momentarily crossed his face before he'd masked it with a smile.

'Of course, Jacks. Of course, it's all right. I mean, you'll only be in the early stages still, right? Able to do the hike?' He held out his arms to her and she stepped into them, wrapping her arms around his waist and leaning against his chest.

'Yes, I should be fine. You might need to carry more of the gear than me though, as I'll be carrying the baby.'

'The baby. Our baby.' Tim's tone was gently incredulous, and she leaned back so she could look up at his face.

'I know, right? Hard to believe we made one. Just like that, first time of trying.'

'What?' Tim sounded aghast. He pushed her away from him, and she realised what she'd said.

'I mean, first chance, not even trying.'

'Jacks, you didn't . . .?'

'Didn't what?'

'Do it . . . on purpose? I know how desperate you were for a baby.'

'Of course I didn't! How can you think that? We'd made a decision, we'd agreed to wait until September, but then, like I said, we took a risk and this is the result.'

'I remember that night. You insisted it was OK, that it was a safe time of the month . . .' Tim sounded suspicious.

'I thought it was. I must have got it wrong.'

He regarded her for a moment, not saying anything. He suspected

29

her of going against their agreement, clearly. Of allowing herself to get pregnant in an underhand way. 'Tim, you do believe me, right? I would never do anything that went against something we'd decided together. Not something as important as this. It honestly was an accident. I suppose I'd had a bit to drink with Sarah that night and got my calculations wrong.' It was the only explanation she could think of.

Thankfully, he seemed to accept it, and pulled her back towards him, kissing her forehead. 'Yes, I believe you, you silly thing. Anyway, we are where we are.'

'Yes. Actually, we're lucky. Might have taken years to conceive. At least we've been spared that.'

'Indeed.' Tim let go of her and went to the fridge, pulling out a can of lager. 'Drink? To celebrate?'

'I shouldn't . . .' She patted her middle.

'Oh, of course. Arrghh, you're going to miss out on all those wonderful Abruzzo wines. You poor thing. There's nothing for it – I'll have to drink your share, while you watch me, parched, desperate for a taste, sipping warm water from a plastic bottle . . .'

Now it was Jackie's turn to groan at the picture he'd painted. Tim chuckled. 'Aw, never mind. It'll be worth it when we have a little one of our own, eh?'

'Yes!' Jackie reached for him again and snuggled into him, pleased that she'd told him, and he'd accepted it, and all was well. Now that he knew, she would make an appointment at her doctor's, get herself on their antenatal list, book a twelve-week scan, find a local National Childbirth Trust group to join, and tell other people such as their parents (who would all be delighted at the idea of becoming grandparents!) and Henry (who'd be worried she'd give up her job, but delighted for her anyway) and, of course, Sarah, who'd squeal with joy.

Despite the sickness that had afflicted her for the last few days, she was looking forward to this pregnancy progressing. By early next year, they'd be parents.

# Chapter 4

## Madeleine, 14 April 1912

The next day was Sunday, and Madeleine attended the church service held in the second-class dining room in the morning. It was taken by Reverend Anderson who was a passenger on board, and Captain Rostron also led part of it. Madeleine was not particularly religious – what benevolent God would have put her through all that she'd suffered these last few months? – but as she said to Evelyn, as they awaited the start of the service, 'It passes an hour. Might as well attend.'

'Agreed,' Evelyn said, with a smile and a sideways look at Madeleine that made her giggle a little. She hid her mouth behind her hand, as the reverend was signalling he was ready to begin.

It turned out to be a reasonable way to spend an hour. The prayers were mercifully short, and the hymns were enjoyable to sing. In the sermon, the reverend mused on the importance of making the best of things no matter what life throws at you, and it gave Madeleine food for thought. He was right. You couldn't control what happened to you. You could only control how you responded to it. And she'd reacted badly to her loss.

As she'd married relatively late in life, she and Ralph had wasted no time before trying for a baby. It had taken years to fall pregnant and when she finally did, they'd been ecstatic. At last, the baby she so longed for was on its way. She'd welcomed the morning sickness as a sign all was well. But then the bleeding started, and soon after she was diagnosed with an ectopic pregnancy. The doctor had told her that this foetus could not be allowed to continue growing; if left it could kill her. She'd undergone an operation, and then a long physical recovery from it. All of it underpinned by the knowledge that not only had they lost the baby she'd been carrying, but she'd also lost her womb and ovaries. She'd come round from the surgery and the doctor had told her they had been removed: 'At your age, my dear, you don't want to risk another pregnancy, do you?' he'd said, as she'd stared at him, disbelieving, through her tears. She'd lost all chance of ever having a baby. She'd lost all purpose in life – or so it had felt for months, until Ralph had proposed this trip to find a new direction. For both of them, he'd said. But she knew it was really for her own benefit. She hadn't wanted a new direction, though. She'd wanted a child of her own.

Sometimes she thought she'd do anything to have a child to love and bring up as her own. The need in her to hold and care for a baby was almost a physical pain at times. She thought of the toy panda she had hidden in her trunk. She'd bought it during that brief, wonderful period when she was pregnant, when she thought that, at long last, they were going to be parents, as she'd always dreamed. It was part of a fully kitted out nursery they had back home in New York. A nursery that would never now house a baby. Ralph didn't know she had the panda with her. It was silly, but she'd been unable to part with it. It was as though giving it up would mean admitting her failure to do that simple natural thing that women were designed to do. Give birth to a live, healthy child.

'We are sent trials, and we are tested, and we must endeavour to respond positively at all times no matter what, doing our best for the good of all, rather than allowing ourselves to become self-pitying. In this way we serve the Lord,' the reverend said, wrapping up his sermon. Madeleine nodded at this. She'd been sent a trial, but she had not responded positively. She had allowed herself to wallow in self-pity. But it was so hard not to, when your world had been turned upside down. Her arms ached to hold a child of her own, which she could never have. It would take her a long time to fully heal.

'Ralph should have come along,' Madeleine said to Evelyn afterwards. If he'd heard the sermon too, perhaps it would have opened the way for a conversation about how she still felt after the operation, and how they might find a way forward. Whenever she tried to raise the subject, he brushed it off as though it was all in the past, something that no longer needed discussing.

'Why didn't he?' Evelyn asked.

'He was off to find out more about the Marconi equipment on board the ship,' she replied. She remembered the conversation from last night. 'Oh, did you send your Marconigram to your cousins on *Titanic*?'

Evelyn nodded. 'Yes, first thing. Well, we visited the Marconi cabin on the top deck, and gave the operator a message to send. I don't know whether he's sent it or not yet.'

'It'll be terribly exciting if you get a reply.'

'If we don't, we won't know whether they received it until we next see them. Which will probably be many months, as we are currently travelling in opposite directions.' Evelyn shrugged.

'Well, maybe you could ask in a letter. The old-fashioned way.'

Evelyn laughed. 'Yes, I could. Our message was only saying *Hello from the mid-Atlantic!* in any case. Nothing of any importance. I suppose that's all the Marconi equipment is – a bit of fun. A novelty.'

'Hmm, or maybe more than that. I must go and find Ralph now. Perhaps he's learned more about it.' Madeleine bade Evelyn farewell and went off to find her husband. He was in the first-class library – a sumptuously decorated, wood panelled room – sitting with his pipe and the papers that were several days out of date by now. She was sure he must have read them all already.

'Had a good morning?' she asked him, as she took a seat next to him.

'Marvellous, yes. I spent a good long while with Harold Cottam, the Marconi operator. He's told me so much about how it all works. It's fascinating.'

'You weren't interrupting his work?'

'Not at all. Frankly, I think he gets bored. There has to be someone manning the equipment all day, otherwise incoming messages might be missed and they could be important. Warnings of bad weather ahead and suchlike. Although actually on this ship, as there's only himself, and he retires to bed around eleven o'clock, there are several hours overnight when the cabin is unmanned.'

'I spoke to Evelyn, and they wrote out a message to be sent to their cousins on the *Titanic*. Do you know if that has been sent yet?'

Ralph nodded. 'I'd imagine so. I think he was up to date. He wasn't sure if *Titanic* would be in range, but he says if he's not certain or gets no reply within an hour or so, he tries the message again a little later.'

Madeleine smiled. 'It's marvellous, isn't it? To think, two ships that can't even see each other can be in contact. The things they can do these days!'

'Communication, my dear, is the key to the future.' Ralph pulled out a notebook and jotted down a few words. 'And that, I think, might make for a good article. The power of long-range communication. For instance, Cottam told me he heard a few reports of icebergs, drifting further south than they usually do. Picking up warnings like that means a ship will know to keep an extra watch for them, and could avoid a tragedy.'

Madeleine felt a pang of worry. 'Icebergs? Are they likely to be a problem for *Carpathia*?'

'No, darling, not at all. We are on the southerly route across the Atlantic. But for ships further north, picking up those warnings, well . . .' He raised his eyebrows and adopted a serious tone. 'It could quite literally be the difference between life or death.'

She laughed. 'Now you're being a little overdramatic. Surely icebergs can be spotted from miles away and the ship's course altered to avoid a collision? Big white hunks of ice floating in the sea, reflecting sunlight – how on earth could you fail to see them?'

He smiled indulgently at her. 'Yes, I am sure you are right. Anyway, as I said, there's no fear of us coming across any.' Ralph pulled his watch from his waistcoat pocket. 'Now then, I must go to the saloon. It is almost noon.'

'I'll come with you,' Madeleine said, and took his arm.

It was a daily ritual on board this and other ships, for the wealthier passengers to place small bets on how far the ship had travelled in the previous twenty-four hours. Ralph enjoyed taking part. The purse was small, but it was a bit of fun.

In the saloon, passengers were milling about waiting for an officer to come and post up the results of the day's calculations on the bulletin board. Madeleine knew they worked out the angle of the sun at noon, and this, together with estimates of the ship's speed and measurements of wind speed and direction, all fed into the calculation of the daily run. *Carpathia* was not a fast ship – Madeleine had asked Captain Rostron about its maximum speed, which was just fourteen knots. Other liners managed over twenty.

And it was the captain himself who posted today's statistics on the board. 'Ladies and gentlemen, the daily run since noon yesterday is . . .' He paused dramatically, scanning the expectant faces, '307 nautical miles.'

'Hurray!' Ralph let out a little cheer. 'My money was on 315. I must be in with a shot?'

'Sorry, old man,' Charles Marshall said, stepping forward. 'I bet 310, which makes me closer.'

'And I wagered 308!' A handsome man in his thirties stepped forward.

The captain greeted him with a handshake. 'Louis! You have done well. I believe you are the closest?' He glanced at the assembled crowd but there was no one who'd placed a closer bet. 'You take the purse. Congratulations. Ladies and gentlemen, the book is now open for tomorrow's run. Please place your bets with First Officer Dean.'

'That's Louis Ogden, the man who won,' Ralph said to Madeleine. 'He's a friend of the captain.'

'Does that mean he had inside knowledge? Is that fair?' she asked.

'He only had the same information available to the rest of us. The top speed of the ship, the maximum nautical miles it can travel in a day, and his own observations of conditions,' Ralph replied.

'Besides, I shall give my winnings to charity.' Madeleine turned with a gasp to see Mr Ogden right behind her. He winked and smiled. 'Your husband's right. I had no inside knowledge. Captain Rostron is scrupulously fair in everything he does, you can be certain of that.'

'Oh, I didn't mean . . .' Madeleine began, but Mr Ogden raised a hand to cut off her apology.

'No need. Name's Louis Ogden. My wife's Augusta, she's around here somewhere.'

'Pleased to meet you, Mr Ogden. I'm Madeleine Meyer. I believe you already know my husband, Ralph.' She shook his hand.

'I do indeed. We met the other evening. He's a journalist, as I understand it? And I am interested in photography. I have my camera on board. We could make quite a team.' Louis Ogden looked at her with a wry smile. 'If only there was something exciting happening on the ship that we could write about and photograph, eh?' He spoke quietly but even so, Captain Rostron must have heard for he turned towards them with a smile.

'Ah, Louis, a quiet voyage is a good voyage. I pray for zero excitement when crossing the Atlantic. May the weather be good and the days be dull.' He clapped Ogden on the back and grinned. 'Well, I have charts to consult and courses to set. I shall see you at dinner. Good afternoon, and to you, Mrs Meyer.' He left the saloon to return to his duties.

'He's a decent man,' Ogden said, 'and I suppose he has a point about a quiet voyage being a good one. He's told me many times that he sees himself as a kind of surrogate father to all his passengers. His job is to be caring, strict but fair, doing whatever it takes to keep them safe and well while on his ship.'

'That's nice to hear,' Madeleine replied. Ogden's words had given her a feeling of security.

Ogden nodded. 'He takes his responsibilities very seriously. Not a man to get on the wrong side of, where passenger welfare is concerned.'

There was a tiny bit of excitement that evening over dinner, when a steward brought a note to the table that once more Madeleine and Ralph were sharing with the Marshall family. 'Message for you, sir,' he said, handing the slip of paper to Charles Marshall.

He unfolded it and smiled. 'Well, it seems the *Titanic* is in range of this ship's Marconi equipment after all, and has received the message we sent earlier. Our nieces have replied.'

'Ooh!' Evelyn squealed. 'What do my cousins say?'

Her father passed the note over with only a raised eyebrow as comment. Evelyn glanced at it and laughed. 'That is so like Charlotte. She has no sense of fun!' She handed the note to Madeleine and now it was her turn to be amused. The reply read simply, *Message received, love Lottie.* 'Bit of a let-down, really.'

Madeleine nodded. 'I hate to say it about your cousins, but yes. A rather dull response. But at least we know it works – this ship-to-ship radioing.'

'We already knew it worked,' Charles Marshall said. 'Ralph

here's been telling me about his visit to the Marconi operator today. There's ship-to-ship messages flying about all over the ocean, not to mention ship to shore.'

'Isn't it funny that we can't hear them?' his wife said. 'You'd think if there's so much being sent we'd hear a buzzing or something.'

'Beyond the scope of our hearing, darling,' Marshall replied.

The conversation moved on then, and the rest of the evening was uneventful.

Back in their cabin, Ralph turned to Madeleine and sighed. 'How many more days until we reach Gibraltar? Thank God for the Marshalls. Without them to chat to this voyage really would be extremely dull. Next time, we are going to take a larger, faster ship with more to do on board.'

She nodded and retired to bed, hoping that perhaps tonight she would sleep more soundly than of late, with fewer hours lying awake mourning the life she thought she was due to have.

'Wake up, Maddy. Wake up!'

Madeleine awoke with a start, to find Ralph leaning over her, shaking her shoulder. 'What is it? Are you unwell?'

'I'm fine, but—' He looked worried.

'What is it?' She was wide awake now, and sat up, staring at him. Above them, somewhere, there was a clanking, scraping sound.

'Something's wrong. Not sure what. But those noises . . . and listen to the engines . . .'

She listened hard and understood what he meant. Normally at night the engines were relatively quiet. The ship slowed down a little so people could sleep without disturbance. But now they were much louder than usual, as though the ship was at full steam. And above them, those sounds . . .

'I think they're doing something with the lifeboats . . . There's one on the deck immediately above us. Sounds to me as though they're getting it ready to launch. In the middle of the night!'

Ralph's voice quivered a little as he spoke. He was really frightened, Madeleine realised, and she felt her own heart beat a little faster.

She swung her legs out of bed. 'Come on. Let's get dressed and find out what's happening.'

'Yes.' Quickly and without speaking again they pulled on the nearest clothes and shoes. Madeleine chose her warmest coat and stoutest shoes. If there was any chance they'd be spending the rest of the night in a lifeboat she wanted to be as comfortable as possible.

Outside in the passageway, a few other passengers were poking their heads out of their cabins, peering up and down in concern. A steward passed by carrying a pile of blankets.

'Excuse me, what is happening? Is the ship in trouble?' Madeleine asked him, keeping her voice low. She understood that the last thing the crew needed was for people to panic, whatever the matter was.

'No, not at all. Go into your cabin and go back to sleep, madame.'

'But . . . what are those sounds? And why are you gathering up blankets?' Madeleine persisted.

'Back inside, please. Captain's orders.' The steward bustled past, telling others to go inside too. Most complied but Madeleine kept the door a little open, watching until he'd turned a corner.

'I'm going out on deck, see if I can find an officer,' Ralph said.

'I'm coming with you.'

Ralph opened his mouth as if about to tell her to stay in the cabin, but he must have seen the determination in her eye for he nodded and took her hand. 'Quickly, then, before that steward comes back.'

They went up the nearest stairs to the boat deck immediately above them. 'Here, let's just tuck ourselves in here,' Ralph said, pointing to a small space behind one of the funnels. Madeleine squeezed herself in alongside him, and from there they could definitely see that the lifeboats were being prepared for launch.

Crew members were removing chocks that held them in place, and swinging the boats out on their davits.

Above them the night sky was clear, with more stars shining than Madeleine had ever seen. It was a beautiful night and on a different occasion she'd have enjoyed gazing at the stars. But if the ship was in trouble, who cared whether the stars shone or not? She recalled how just a few hours earlier Ralph had been complaining about how dull the voyage was. He'd clearly spoken too soon. Despite herself, she felt a frisson of excitement. If nothing else, the crisis, whatever it was, would take her mind off her other troubles. She was worried and frightened, and yet she felt alive, properly alive for the first time since their loss.

'Excuse me,' Ralph said, emerging from their hiding place, and addressing the nearest crew member. 'Please tell me what is happening? Why are these lifeboats being got ready? Are we in trouble?'

'No, sir, *Carpathia*'s not in any trouble at all. Captain said to get these ready as a precaution. You'd be best going back below, sir.'

'A precaution against what?' Ralph asked, but the man just shrugged and got on with his work.

'Do you believe him?' Madeleine asked. 'That the ship's not in any trouble?'

'No.' Ralph was staring at the decking, a small muscle in his jaw working as though he was trying to decide what to do next.

'But how can we be in any difficulties? It's such a lovely night. Look at the stars,' Madeleine said.

Ralph glanced up, then frowned. 'Beautiful, yes, but . . .'

'What is it?'

'The Pole Star. It's . . . in the wrong place.'

'What do you mean?'

'We should be heading east, across the Atlantic. The Pole Star should be on our left, in the north. But look.' He pointed at the constellation Madeleine knew as the Plough, or Big Dipper, that she always thought looked like a saucepan, and she followed the

40

line made by the two stars at the side of the pan, as her father had taught her long ago. The next star reached was always the Pole Star, that indicated true north. It was the only bit of navigation by starlight she knew.

And tonight, the Pole Star was dead ahead.

'Why are we going north?'

'And at full steam. We're off course. Something's wrong. Something is very wrong, and I intend to find out what. We need to track down an officer.'

'Who'll only advise us to go back to our cabins.'

'Which we'll ignore. Come on.' Ralph took her hand and pulled her back to the stairs. 'Someone must tell us what's going on.'

# Chapter 5

## Jackie, 2022

A week after telling Tim about the baby, Jackie was at work in the small office she used at Henry Fotheringham's country house. It was a short, pleasant drive from the home she shared with Tim, on the western side of Reading. Henry too was spending a rare day in his office in the same building. It was too soon to say anything to him about her pregnancy, Jackie decided. She wanted to wait until after the twelve-week scan, until she was perhaps starting to show. Until then, she preferred to keep knowledge of the baby to herself and Tim, their own special secret. Every time she thought of it, of that tiny life just beginning inside her, she felt a warm glow course through her, of excitement, anticipation and pure love for the growing child she couldn't wait to meet.

In the mid-morning, Henry called Jackie in to him. 'Now then. I was at an auction of *Titanic* memorabilia a few weeks ago and was successful in bidding on one lot. It's now been delivered to us here.'

'Ooh, what did you buy?' Jackie asked. Probably more crockery and cutlery retrieved from the wreck, she thought. That was the usual kind of thing on sale at these auctions.

'I have absolutely no idea,' Henry said, sounding pleased with himself. 'A box of . . . stuff. It didn't cost much. Actually, most of it, apparently, is from *Carpathia*, not *Titanic* at all.'

'*Carpathia*?'

'Oh, come on. You know!' Henry ran a hand through his greying hair. 'The ship that went to *Titanic*'s rescue. She picked up all the survivors.'

Jackie nodded, thinking of that scene near the end of the *Titanic* film, where Rose sits huddled in a blanket after being rescued, shielding her face from her hated fiancé. That presumably was supposed to be on board *Carpathia*. 'Yes, I remember now.'

'This box of stuff came from a descendant of someone who worked on board *Carpathia*. What I'm really hoping for is a commemorative medal. All the crew were given one for their part in the rescue. I would love one to add to my collection.' Henry stared into the middle distance, as though picturing such a medal in one of his display cases, with his like-minded friends exclaiming over it.

'All right, I can easily go through the box quickly and look for such a thing, and then get on with cataloguing everything.' With a bit of luck, Jackie thought, there'd be some books in the box. More likely though, it'd be old newspapers, maybe the crew member's uniform, probably a number of items totally unrelated to *Carpathia* that just happened to have been shoved in the same box. But she always enjoyed getting her hands on a new collection of memorabilia and working her way through it, imagining the people who'd handled those items before her, wondering what kind of lives they'd led. And this was an interesting one. Most people bought *Titanic* items. She wondered about *Carpathia*. It possibly had just as interesting a story to tell. How had the captain heard about the disaster? What had prompted him to go to the rescue? How had his own passengers reacted to picking up

*Titanic* survivors from lifeboats? How had they accommodated them all? And where had *Carpathia* taken them? Jackie could already imagine herself Googling for the answers to these questions. Background information helped – she'd be more likely to be able to sort the important, interesting items from the rubbish if she understood *Carpathia*'s story.

'Thank you, Jackie. I'll have it sent to your office. Feel free to take it home to work on if that's easier for you. And if you find a medal,' Henry looked up at her, his eyes gleaming, 'be sure to let me know immediately. Or anything else of particular interest, eh? You know the sort of thing I like.'

'Of course. Looking forward to having a good rummage through. Will you be around for the next few days?'

Henry pulled a face and shook his head. 'I'm due in Nice tomorrow. Clarissa has tickets to some events at the Cannes film festival. Not my thing, as you know, but I have to go with her, look pretty on her arm and all that.'

'Oh. Poor you,' Jackie said, pulling a face. Henry laughed.

'I know. I've not much to complain about, have I? Right then, off you go, I'll get that box sent up and I'll see you again after Cannes, I hope.'

'Yep. Thank you, and have a good time in France.' She left his office and went back to her own, just along the corridor of the huge country house Henry used as a base. She was still chuckling about him being made to go to Cannes by his latest girlfriend Clarissa, an actor several years younger than himself, whom Jackie suspected would not be his partner for very much longer as they seemed to have nothing in common. Many people could only dream of going to the film festival. Henry complained about having to go. He'd have to stay in his villa just outside Nice and put up with all the parties and people and paraphernalia that came with being super-rich. Oh, it was a hard life for some!

To be fair, she told herself, Henry had never really got over losing his wife ten years before. His grown-up children led their own lives and didn't seem very supportive. He'd had a string of partners in recent years, none of them lasting long, some clearly only with him for his money. But Jackie suspected Henry was looking for something deeper and more meaningful. He'd be unlikely to find that with Clarissa.

About an hour later, there was a tap at Jackie's office door, and Lisa, another of Henry's personal assistants, pushed open the door with her hip and carried in a cardboard box, the kind that removal companies used, plain brown cardboard with 'Dad's Old Stuff' scrawled on one side in marker pen. 'Here you are,' Lisa said. 'Henry mentioned you're ready to work on this.'

'Yes, thanks!' Jackie pushed to one side the paperwork she'd been dealing with, to make space on her desk. 'You can put it there.'

Lisa set the box down with a groan. 'God knows what's in this one. He likes old tat, doesn't he?'

'Might not be tat,' Jackie said. 'Some of it usually is, but there are always a few gems in among it all.'

'Hmm. Well rather you than me going through it.' Lisa looked down at her immaculately manicured nails. 'I can't bear shoving my hands into boxes of old stuff. Could be anything in there!'

Jackie laughed. 'I know! That's what I love about it!'

'All I can say is I am glad I insisted Henry employ someone else when he started buying up those old books.' Lisa patted Jackie on the shoulder. 'Well, I must go and sort out hotels and restaurants and whatnot in Nice. I shall leave you to it. Unless you'd like me to fetch you a coffee to help get you going?'

Jackie had gone right off coffee since discovering she was pregnant so she shook her head. 'Thanks, no. Enjoy Nice, if I don't see you before.'

'Will do. And you enjoy . . . that.' Lisa nodded at the box where Jackie was already beginning to pick at the end of the packing tape that sealed the box.

'Cheers.' Lisa left, and Jackie tore off the tape with a flourish, feeling the usual flurry of excitement she always had when she started work on new acquisitions. Inside, on top, was an old newspaper. She took it out and checked the date: November 1978. That was probably when the items had been stored away in the box, though she assumed it must have been opened and looked through since then, maybe when an attic was cleared and the decision made to sell the box at auction. The auction house at least would have checked through when deciding how to list it.

She put the paper to one side, and lifted out the next item. Inside an old plastic bag from Marks and Spencer there was a neatly folded steward's uniform with a badge from the Cunard company stitched on the breast pocket. Had *Carpathia* belonged to Cunard, then? That was easy enough to check using Google and Wikipedia. She made herself a note to read up a little on *Carpathia* before she began the work cataloguing the items. But first she wanted to rummage through to see what was here. If there was one of those medals Henry had mentioned, she wanted to find it sooner rather than later. Today would be good.

Under the uniform was a pad of paper, headed with the Cunard logo and the ship's name. Then a steward's cap, and beneath that a couple of novels from the 1920s that seemed unrelated to the ship. Well, Jackie thought, it had been labelled 'Dad's Old Stuff' which could include anything. A photo in a frame, wrapped in another sheet of 1970s newspaper, came next. It showed a young woman with two small children. The photographer's details on the back showed the picture had been taken in 1910. 'Maybe you were "Dad's" wife and children,' Jackie murmured, putting the photo down carefully on her desk.

Then there was a folded bathrobe, with the Cunard logo on and *Carpathia* embroidered on a pocket. 'Liberated from a first-class cabin, perhaps?' Jackie mused.

Inside another M&S plastic bag was a collection of newspapers, brittle and stained with age. Jackie unfolded them carefully and spread them on her desk. All were from April 1912 and related to *Titanic*, their headlines screaming about her departure from Southampton on her maiden voyage, the first rumours and speculation surrounding her accident, and then extensive reporting after the details emerged. As she stacked the papers in date order, she scanned each front page. 'Friends and relatives must have had an agonising time, waiting to see whether their loved ones had died or not,' she muttered. Some of the headlines were totally incorrect, stating that *Titanic* was being towed to port, or that everyone on board had perished. Fake news, it would be called these days, and how awful for those back home whose hopes would be raised up and dashed, over and over, depending on which newspapers they read.

Henry would love these papers, she thought, as she reluctantly put them to one side to go through in detail later.

At the bottom of the box was a notebook, the kind reporters might use. It had been written in; several pages were filled with a hard to read cursive hand. On the cover someone had written the initials '*M.M.*'

'A diary?' Jackie wondered, as she opened it up, but the pages weren't dated. On the inside cover was written '*Titanic interviews*'. Now that was something very interesting. She flicked through a few pages but it would take a while to get used to the handwriting to read it properly. A job for another day when she could devote her time exclusively to it.

There was no sign of any medal. Jackie sighed. Henry would be disappointed. In truth, there wasn't much here that would interest him other than the newspapers and perhaps the notebook, depending on what it contained. He tended not to be interested in old clothes or uniforms. She sent him a quick email listing the contents of the box and letting him know that she hadn't found a medal in there. He'd keep searching, she knew. Once he had an idea of something he wanted to own, he never stopped until he possessed it. Jackie would need to trawl the internet for future sales of *Carpathia* memorabilia or for listings of the medal itself.

She glanced at her watch. Lunchtime already. She had a ready-made salad in the fridge in the little staff kitchenette, and she'd make herself a cup of tea there. And she'd stop herself brooding on whether Tim was fully ready for fatherhood, or whether there was any likelihood of her miscarrying, or whether she really would be able to manage a strenuous hike in the Italian mountains at three or four months pregnant. Life was too short to worry, she always told herself, and yet . . . she tended to do rather a lot of it.

The morning sickness was becoming worse. It was still early days for her pregnancy, but already Jackie was in a routine of getting out of bed and going straight into the bathroom. She couldn't face a cup of tea or coffee or anything to eat for the first half hour. Ginger biscuits, drinking tea in bed before getting up, all the tips she'd read up on in the *Pregnancy and Birth* book she'd bought – none of it worked.

'Get up, throw up, then start the day,' she said to Tim on Saturday morning, after she'd emerged from the bathroom. 'Seems to be how things are going to be from now on.'

'For how long?' Tim asked with a frown. 'Will you still be like this when we're camping in Italy?'

Jackie stared at him. For a moment there she'd thought he was asking how long it'd go on because he was concerned for her. Not because he thought it might adversely affect their holiday. 'I don't know. I think for most women it gets better after about eighteen weeks.'

'And how far in are you?'

'Eight weeks.'

'Oh. So . . .'

'So yes. I might still be suffering when we go away. I guess I'll just have to deal with it.'

'Poor you.' He put his arms round her and she softened. He did care. He was being sympathetic. It was just . . . that nagging doubt she'd been unable to dismiss ever since she'd seen his initial reaction to the news that she was pregnant. That little voice that said he wasn't ready for this, he didn't really want it. She banished the thought. He'd done nothing to suggest that was how he felt. Nothing at all. It was probably just her hormones making her supersensitive, seeing slights where there were none. Imagining worst-case scenarios. Surely that wasn't healthy? It wasn't good for her baby to worry so much. She needed to snap herself out of it.

She hugged him back. 'Thanks, Tim. It'll all be worth it when we have a little one in our arms, eh?'

'Certainly will. Says he who doesn't actually have to do the vomiting or the giving birth,' Tim said, and she laughed.

'I'll tell you what you *can* do towards this baby's arrival,' she said. 'The spare room. Let's start work this weekend clearing it out. I mean, it has nearly ten years' worth of clutter in it, and we need space for the baby. Sooner we get started on all that junk the better, eh?'

'Oh Christ, no. Not this weekend, Jacks. I'm off out at football this afternoon.'

'Tomorrow, then.'

Tim pulled a face. 'Rugby's on. Munster are playing Leinster. I wanted to watch the match.'

'Surely that doesn't take all day? I just thought we could do a couple of hours, make a start on going through what's in there. Some of it we can store in the loft and some of that junk is surely rubbish.'

'There's no rubbish in there!'

Jackie tipped her head on one side and smiled at him. 'I mean, those piles of sailing magazines. They're years old. Surely we can throw those out?'

'Oh right. Throw my stuff out.' Tim let go of her and went to stand by the sink, leaning back on the worktop. 'What about your stuff?'

'I've nothing in there!'

'Ironing board? That's yours.' They'd always left it set up in the spare room, unless they had visitors.

'That's bloody well *ours*, Tim! We both use it. How can you say it's mine? Just because . . . I'm a woman, is it?'

'What, are you trying to make me out to be a misogynist now? Just because I happen to remember that you brought the ironing board to our relationship, not me. You already had it when we moved in together. I used to iron on a blanket on the kitchen worktop, remember?'

Jackie blushed. She'd been too quick to take offence, when clearly none was intended. 'OK. Well, the ironing board is easily dealt with anyway – it can go back in the hall cupboard and we'll take it out as needed. But those piles of magazines? And your wetsuit that's hanging on the back of the door? And the boxes of old university lecture notes? And the other boxes, the stuff from your mum's attic that you said you'd store for her when she downsized? That was supposed to go straight up into our loft but you wanted to go through it first. But you never did.'

Tim grunted. 'Never had time to.'

'Can't we just throw it all out then?'

'No, we should go through it. There's my great-grandfather's old stuff. He was a sailor in the merchant navy. For all I know there's valuable stuff in those boxes. The kind of stuff your boss collects. I'll sort it out at some stage. What do you have in mind for that room, anyway?'

'We need to convert it into a nursery. I think we should get rid of the old bed that's in there, to make space for a cot. The bed's past its best anyway. We can get a sofa bed in the sitting room for occasional visitors. I want the room painted, probably a soft cream or something neutral like that. And I'll make some cute curtains for the window. That old chest of drawers in there will be perfect for baby clothes. We could paint it – I don't know, a duck-egg blue perhaps?'

'What's in it now?'

'Ski socks, woolly hats and gloves, thermals . . . that sort of thing.'

'So where are we going to put all that?' He had his arms folded across his chest, and he wasn't smiling any more.

She shrugged. 'I don't know. We'll have to make room in our wardrobe. Or put it in a suitcase in the loft, perhaps? It's not as though it's in use all the time.'

'Pain in the arse to have to go up to the loft every time I want a woolly hat.'

'Keep one in your sock drawer, then.'

Tim pulled a face. 'Next you'll be telling me I've got to get rid of the Audi, and replace it with a boring family car that has space for a baby car seat.'

'Well . . .' Jackie began.

'You know I love that car, Jacks.' He sounded petulant now.

'I was going to say, no you don't have to sell it. We can use my car if we're all going somewhere.' Though privately she thought it'd be a good idea to replace it. 'Anyway, the room's more important right now. Come on, Tim. Sooner or later we need to do this. Might as well be sooner.'

'Yeah. But not this weekend, all right? I have other things I want to do.'

'More important than getting ready for our baby?'

'Christ, Jacks! You're only eight weeks pregnant! We've got ages yet!' He threw his arms in the air and walked out of the kitchen. Jackie was left sitting at the table, trying not to cry. It was her hormones. Taking things too personally. Seeing insult where none was meant. Wanting to nest. And maybe he was right, and it was a bit too soon.

But still, his reaction to her suggestion had unnerved her. If he wouldn't engage with this sort of preparatory job now, did it mean he wasn't fully engaged with the idea of them having a baby at all? She'd thought he'd be excited, that he'd enjoy clearing the room out and deciding on decor schemes. The point of starting it all this early was so they wouldn't be doing it in a rush when she was heavily pregnant. Or even after the baby came, as Sarah had. She'd been too superstitious before the birth to do anything to prepare for Bobby's arrival. Poor Martin had spent his entire paternity leave buying cots, prams, nappies and baby clothes. Jackie wanted to be totally ready to welcome the baby into their home, so that both she and Tim would be free to simply enjoy the early days with their child. She imagined the moment when they'd bring him or her home from hospital and into the new nursery. Tim would be different then, she knew, once he actually had his own child in his arms. He had to be.

# Chapter 6

## Madeleine, 15 April 1912

Madeleine followed Ralph back inside, down flights of stairs and into the main passenger areas of the ship. They passed several crew members hurrying about but none would stop to talk. Twice they were told to return to their cabin, and twice Ralph said in his most imperious voice, 'I cannot, I must speak with the captain urgently.' Eventually, they found themselves near the main saloon. Inside, it looked as though all the stewards had been asked to assemble, and the Chief Steward, Hughes, was standing on a raised platform addressing them.

'Why are they all in there?' Ralph muttered.

'Ssh, let's listen,' Madeleine replied. From where they stood, half-hidden by the wedged-open door, they could just hear what the Chief Steward was saying. And his words made Madeleine clap her hand to her mouth in horror.

'We are heading north on full power,' Hughes was saying. 'All steam is being diverted to the engines, at the expense of other systems. We are taking this course because we have received a distress call from the RMS *Titanic*. She has struck an iceberg and has asked us to come at once.'

There were audible gasps and a few mutterings from the assembled crew at this, and the Chief Steward waited until silence resumed before continuing.

'Our lifeboats are being made ready just in case we need to take people off the *Titanic*. Captain Rostron has requested that we try to keep all our own passengers in their cabins overnight. If you are asked what is happening tell them only that we are safe and there is no need to worry.' He coughed, and looked at a scribbled set of notes.

'Meanwhile, there are a number of jobs we must do. Gather all blankets and position them by every gangway and in public areas. And some in the lifeboats. Provide tea and coffee for all our own hands. Have tea, coffee, soup and brandy available in each saloon in case we need to take on board extra passengers. I will need a team at each gangway later on, ready to receive such passengers, should it be necessary to do so. We must also record the names of everyone as soon as they come on board.'

One stewardess raised a hand tentatively. 'Sir, are we expecting that *Titanic* will sink, and we will have to pick up the s-survivors?' She stumbled on the last word. Madeleine didn't blame her. There were thousands of people on board the huge new liner, and it was inconceivable that it might go down. Hadn't it been billed as 'unsinkable' by its builders?

The Chief Steward fixed the stewardess with a stare. 'Captain Rostron suspects there is no serious danger, but nevertheless he wants us to be fully prepared, in case the worst happens. So, without questioning it, that is what we shall do. The doctors on board are setting up medical stations for each class of passenger. Should we need to take on more people, we must condense our steerage passengers into a smaller area to make way, and also free up as many cabins and beds in first and second class as possible.

If there are very many people to bring on board, we will need makeshift beds in the saloons and dining rooms.'

He pulled himself up to his full height and gazed around the room. 'Every man to his post, and let him do his full duty like a true Englishman. If the situation calls for it, let us add another glorious page to the history of the Empire.'

There was silence for a moment at his final words, and then an energy, a buzzing, as the gathered stewards set about organising themselves to do the tasks they'd been set. Madeleine and Ralph drew back from the door before the crew came out, and found a quiet corner out of the way.

'*Titanic*, in trouble. Can you believe it?' Madeleine said.

'I can believe it has struck ice. But I don't believe that this is anything serious. Isn't she supposed to be unsinkable? I was reading about its hull, which is divided into several compartments. If holed, two or three can fill up completely with water and she would still stay afloat. *Titanic* may be stricken but she is not sinking. I think our Captain may be overreacting.' Ralph grinned at her. 'But it is a bit of excitement on this dull ship, what? It might provide me a story to write about. It's a relief to know that *Carpathia* is not in any danger.'

She smiled at him. 'Trust you to find another story to write. I hope you are right. I hate to think that all those passengers, including the Marshalls' nieces, might be in danger.' And children too, she thought. There'd be little children among *Titanic*'s passengers.

'I'm sure they are perfectly safe. Certainly, they are having an adventure they will never forget. Well, we wished for some diversion and now we have it. Let's see what else we can find out.' He took her hand and they hurried through the ship, in no particular direction that Madeleine could see, just trying to stay out of the way of crew members who might force them to return to their cabin.

Back on the boat deck, they saw that work to ready the lifeboats was almost complete. Piles of blankets and other supplies had been put in each. Staring at one lifeboat was Louis Ogden, winner of the previous day's betting on distance travelled. His wife – Madeleine recalled her name was Augusta – was behind him.

'Ah, Mr Meyer. Any idea what's happening? Why are these lifeboats being made ready?'

Ralph looked around to see if any crew members were in earshot. 'We have heard . . .'

'What? Tell me! Fellow that was working on that boat said something about going to *Titanic*'s rescue. That's the biggest load of baloney I ever heard, as I said to Augusta. I don't believe it for a moment. We're the ones in trouble.'

Ralph put a hand on the other man's arm. 'I've just heard the same. The stewards have been briefed to make *Carpathia* ready in case we have to take on board survivors. *Titanic* has hit an iceberg. I don't believe she'll go down, I think Rostron is over-reacting, but I suppose he's doing what he thinks is best.'

Augusta stepped forward to Madeleine's side. 'Is this right? Are we . . . safe on this ship?'

'I believe so, yes. But think of those poor people on *Titanic*.'

'It must be terrifying for them.'

Louis Ogden nodded. 'They will be all right on that ship. Maybe she has some trouble with her engines or similar.' He rubbed his chin thoughtfully. 'I'm still not convinced. I think we might yet be in danger. Augusta, we should fetch your jewellery, and put on warm coats. Just in case.'

'But it's not us, it's *Titanic* . . .' Ralph said.

'If so, and assuming *Titanic* can't possibly be in any real trouble, we'll all be laughing about it this time tomorrow. But I'm taking no chances.' Ogden took his wife's arm and led her away, back to their cabin.

Madeleine stared at Ralph, who shrugged. 'It's all right, Maddy. We're safe. And it's right that the captain's doing all he can to help *Titanic*, even if it does turn out to be unnecessary. Now, do you want to try to get some sleep? I imagine it'll be hours before we're within sight of *Titanic*. Maybe not until after dawn.'

'I'm not sure I will be able to sleep. But we could go back to our cabin to rest, and keep out of the way of the crew who obviously have a lot to do.'

'Yes, let's do that,' Ralph agreed.

Their cabin was cold, and no amount of fiddling with the heating controls made any difference. 'I guess they've diverted all steam to power the engines, rather than the heating system,' Ralph said, as he wrapped a scarf around his neck.

Madeleine was lying on her bed fully dressed, with a blanket over her. She was trying to read but her mind kept drifting to the fate of *Titanic*. As the hours passed it was clear that *Carpathia* was definitely not in any danger. But it was also clear that the potential danger to *Titanic* was being taken very seriously by their captain and his officers. Preparations to pick up survivors went on all night, and there seemed to be a constant stream of stewards hurrying along the corridor outside their cabin.

'If it was all a false alarm, we'd have slowed down by now,' Ralph said at some point. 'If *Titanic* had radioed to say she was all right after all, we'd have turned south again.'

'If we were in range of her signals,' Madeleine said.

'We were in range hours ago, when we first turned north. We must be much closer now.'

Madeleine looked out of the cabin's porthole. 'There's a glimmer of light on the horizon. It's nearly dawn. Let's go up and see if we can't spot *Titanic*.'

Ralph nodded, and they quickly put on shoes and hats, and headed up to the boat deck once more. They weren't the only ones. Several other passengers were milling about, talking in urgent whispers, sharing concerns and theories as to what was going on.

Madeleine crossed to the boat rail and scanned the horizon. She could see a few dark shapes, but none of them looked like another ship. 'Are those icebergs?' she asked Ralph.

'Yes, I think so. Lots of them. We must be a long way north. And look!' He pointed high up, ahead of the ship.

She saw it – a small green light hanging in the night sky. 'What is that?'

'A flare, I think. From *Titanic*, perhaps.'

As he spoke there was a whooshing noise and a flash, and then above them a similar light shone. 'The captain's responding. Sending up rockets to let whoever sent up that flare know where we are, and that we are coming.'

Madeleine nodded at that. Whoever had sent up the green flare would be comforted to know it had been seen and help was on its way. But if it had come from *Titanic*, surely they should be able to see her on the horizon by now? A shudder of fear ran through her as she leaned over the railings, watching as the ship continued to plough on through what was becoming a field of ice floes.

The night was cold and still very dark, with little more than starlight to pierce the blackness, other than the faintest glow on the eastern horizon. Above them was a magnificent canopy of stars, more than Madeleine had ever seen before. Some twinkled brightly, low down, dead ahead, and only as she stared at them did she realise they were in fact reflections from an iceberg. 'Ralph, look!' she said, and at that moment it seemed the officers and crew had seen them too, for the ship began turning sharply to starboard.

Madeleine held her breath as the ship swung around, thankfully missing the iceberg though not by very much. And now she could see where the green flare had come from. 'Look!' She clutched Ralph's arm and pointed.

'What?' He was short-sighted and his spectacles were still in their cabin. He leaned into her, looking along the line of her arm as she kept her finger steady. 'What is it, Maddy?'

'A boat. A small row boat,' she whispered, and the horror of what that implied hit her with the force of a tidal wave. 'Oh, Ralph.'

He put his arm around her shoulders and pulled her tightly to him. The sudden move to starboard had taken the ship past the lifeboat and as they stood there keeping their eyes on it the engines came to a stop, then restarted in reverse, and the ship moved backwards, towards the tiny vessel.

Madeleine huddled close against Ralph, partly for warmth and partly for comfort, as she watched the little boat move closer, inch by inch.

'We have only one crewman and cannot work very well!' A shout came up from the little lifeboat which was very close now. And then, 'Stop your engines!'

*Carpathia*'s engines stopped then, and an officer and two crew members climbed down a rope ladder and jumped aboard the lifeboat as it drifted past. Madeleine watched as they manoeuvred it closer beneath an open gangway. A woman on board shouted something about *Titanic* but Madeleine could not make out what she said.

One by one the occupants of the lifeboat were brought on board. Some were hauled up in a sling while others climbed a rope ladder. They came in through a gangway, a couple of decks below Madeleine and Ralph. In the distance, as the sky grew lighter, Madeleine could see two or three more lifeboats slowly making their way over. And *Carpathia* was still firing rockets every quarter hour to let them know where she was.

'I'm going to go down, see if there's anything I can do to help those people,' she said to Ralph.

He nodded, but pulled her back for a moment. 'What I don't understand is, where is *Titanic*? I thought we'd find her, listing a little, perhaps unable to move. But . . .' He waved his hand vaguely in the direction of the ice field. 'She's just . . . disappeared.'

Madeleine stared at him, her eyes filling with tears. Of course there was only one place the great liner could have gone, but she did not want to voice that fear. 'We must hope that everyone on board her managed to get onto a lifeboat,' she whispered, and Ralph squeezed her and nodded grimly.

# Chapter 7

## Tim, 2022

It was Tuesday evening, and that only meant one thing for Tim. His regular weekly night out with Alfie, his old friend from school who now happened to live nearby. They'd have a pub meal out and a few pints, a couple of games of table football or pool, and they'd set the world to rights. Tim had always looked forward to these nights. There was something about people you were at school with, people you grew up with, who'd shared the same awesome maths teacher and sadistic English teacher, who'd attended your tenth birthday party and who'd been there when you got drunk for the first time aged fifteen. And for Tim, that was Alfie. For Alfie, it was Tim.

Jackie, bless her, understood this completely. She had her nights out with Sarah, and she made sure that Tim never missed a night out with Alfie, unless they were on holiday and it was impossible.

As he donned his battered leather jacket and pocketed keys, phone and wallet, Tim wondered whether he'd be able to continue with this routine once the baby came along. God, he hoped so. He needed this. He needed Alfie's company, the ease of being with someone he'd known since he was five, the camaraderie of blokes' friendship. It'd be all right, he thought. Jacks had told him once that her mate Sarah said their nights out were the one thing that kept her sane, since the birth of her little boy. Bobby, Tim thought the child's name was. He was mildly embarrassed to find he wasn't altogether sure, even though he'd seen the baby – a red-faced, squealing little bundle – several times. If he was honest, he'd never really taken to the child. He'd held him, somehow managed not to drop him, exclaimed over his cutesy little fingers and toes, and hurriedly handed him back to the nearest parent – Martin, if he remembered correctly. And then he'd wondered how he'd ever manage with a child of his own. Martin had taken Bobby back, expertly holding him against his shoulder with one hand and had grinned wryly at Tim. 'It's all right, mate,' he'd said. 'I had no clue either. But you learn quickly when you become a parent. You have to.'

It'd be different with his own, Tim thought. At least, he hoped it would. Some sort of primeval instinct would kick in, some recognition of his own genes in the tiny body, and he'd know immediately that he could love the baby, do anything for it, lay down his life for it if necessary. That's how it was supposed to be, although right now he couldn't imagine it.

'Bye, Jacks. See you later. Don't wait up, eh?' He kissed her and headed towards the door.

She smiled. 'Have a great evening. Give my love to Alfie.'

'Will do.'

Then he was out of the door, feeling the sense of freedom that always kicked in at this time on a Tuesday, and still contemplating his forthcoming fatherhood. It was coming a little sooner than he'd expected, sooner than he'd agreed to, but such was life. Full of surprises. And Jackie was right, they were getting on, and at thirty-five she was more than ready to start a family, as she'd made very clear to him.

He walked up the street, wet after an afternoon of rain, pondering how life would change. For it would change, he knew it. He wasn't stupid. He was going into this with his eyes wide open, even if, being honest, he was slightly reluctant to do so. He'd wanted a few more years of freedom and fun. Damn Covid! It had taken so much from so many. He knew that, relatively speaking, he and Jacks were the lucky ones. The ones not too badly affected by the pandemic. They'd got through it, they'd had a bout of Covid each but not too badly. For them, it had felt like little more than a mild dose of flu. And they'd been in settled, safe jobs. They'd had to make changes of course – Jacks had worked from home; he'd had to take classes of mixed ages, for children of key workers for whom schools had stayed open while other kids were taught from home. But unlike teenagers taking important exams or new graduates looking for first jobs, the pandemic hadn't happened at too bad a time for them.

All it had done was cut out a couple of years of travel for them. They'd holidayed in the UK instead when lockdown restrictions had allowed.

It occurred to him that parents of newborns must have had a tough time through the lockdowns. Imagine being unable to go out to meet your friends and support network, being stuck at home all day with a needy baby? It was a good job they hadn't had a kid just before the pandemic struck. It begged the question, was there *ever* a good time to have one? Having them young ate up your prime years when adventure was round every corner. Having them later meant you were tied down just as your finances were improving and you were more able to afford those adventures. It was a shame you couldn't put off parenthood until retirement. But even then, you wouldn't want children tying you down just when you were finally free of the tyranny of work. He shook his head wryly at this thought.

Rounding the corner at the end of the road, he crossed over and entered the Rising Sun pub where he and Alfie always met, grinning when he saw Alfie was already there, sitting on a bar stool with not one but two pints in front of him.

'Tim, me ole cocker. I got the first round in. Get your laughing gear around that, ole buddy.'

'Cheers, Alfie. Had a good week?' Tim lifted his pint and took a long, satisfying slug from it.

'Can't complain, mate. And you?'

'Pretty good.' Tim drank again. But there must have been something off about the way he'd answered Alfie's enquiry, for his friend was watching him carefully.

'Pretty good? What's up, Timbo?'

'Ah, nothing much.'

'But something? Come on, man. You can never hide anything from the Alfatron, you know that.'

Tim laughed, and shook his head. 'Alfatron. What kind of a nickname is that?'

'One that shows I am the all-powerful, all-knowing, king of the Rising Sun. There's something on your mind, Tim. I've known you long enough to be able to spot it from five miles out. Come on, spill the beans.'

Might as well tell him, Tim thought. Actually, talking to Alfie would be cathartic and might even be useful. 'It's Jacks.'

'God, she's not left you, has she?' Alfie looked horrified.

Tim shook his head. 'No, no fear of that. We're as solid as ever. No, but she's found out she's—'

'Up the duff?'

'You could put it like that, yeah.' Tim gave a twisted smile.

'Awesome, buddy!' Alfie clapped him hard on the shoulder, almost spilling his pint. He was grinning broadly. 'Always wondered which of us would be the first to have a sprog. Marianne's not keen yet. Says she wants to wait till she's thirty.'

'Advantages of a younger girlfriend, eh?' Tim said. 'Jacks is feeling the ticking of the biological clock, so she tells me.'

'And you? Your clock ticking, is it?'

In answer, Tim merely shrugged and took another pull of his

63

pint. It was going down fast. At this rate he'd be buying the next round before they'd even moved to a table.

'Uh oh. Something tells the Alfatron that Timbo's not entirely sure about being a daddy.' Alfie raised his eyebrows. 'Why, man? You'll be cool as a dad. Cooler than cool. What's up?'

'God, I dunno. Just . . . well . . .' It was time to open up. Confess his misgivings to his best mate. See what advice he had to offer. 'The pandemic, you know?'

Alfie nodded sagely. 'I remember it well, buddy boy.'

'So there were two years, right? When we couldn't go anywhere, do anything.'

'You went to Skegness, if I recall correctly . . .'

'Yeah, among other places, but I mean, we didn't leave the country.'

'None of us did, mate. None of us.'

'And now we can, and it's OK, or at least, as OK as it's likely to get. And we've planned to go to Italy this summer. Hiking, for three weeks. With a few days in Rome thrown in, sightseeing, to scratch the itch that Jacks has to see the Sistine Chapel and all that.'

'Yeah, so that's good. Sounds like fun.' Alfie was watching him carefully.

'But she's got pregnant a bit before we planned. Like, we said we'd start trying in September, after this trip. There was an accident, she says, and here we are.'

'But you can still do this holiday?'

'Yeah, but I was kind of . . . expecting—' He'd been about to say 'hoping' but stopped himself in time, '—expecting it might take us a while, and we'd be able to fit in a ski trip next winter, and maybe another long summer one next year, and—' He broke off, hating the way he must sound.

'And in the meantime, Jackie gets stressed and upset because she's not getting pregnant, and so do you, and you start wondering what's wrong, and you go for tests and take temperatures every day and do all sorts of shit, and before you know it, the whole "we must get pregnant" thing is taking over your life. No, mate. You're lucky it's happened quickly. I'm pleased for you, really, I am.'

'Thanks.'

'You don't seem happy about it. I thought you wanted a family? A five-a-side soccer team, you used to say you wanted.'

'No, I'm happy.'

'Just worried about the limitations it's going to put on your life?'

Tim nodded. 'I guess I want you to tell me it won't change anything. That life goes on, and it's good in different ways, after we have a sprog.'

'Sprog? What's all this, Tim?' Two more of Tim's friends had entered the bar behind him.

'Hi, Niall. Marco. It's nothing.' He didn't feel ready to tell these two the news, to whom he wasn't as close as to Alfie. Not yet. He hoped Alfie wouldn't say anything.

'I distinctly heard you say "after we have a sprog",' Niall said, smirking. 'Jackie got news, has she?'

'Just talking hypothetically,' Tim said, in desperation, throwing a glance at Alfie in the hope he'd back him up.

'Yeah, we were just talking about how life changes when you become a dad,' Alfie said.

'Jeez, it'd change beyond all recognition,' Marco said, waving at the barman to take his order. 'Two pints of lager please, mate. Cheers.'

'Got a mate at work who's just had one. Well, about six months back,' Niall said. 'He doesn't go out any more. Rushes home the second he clocks off. Spends his lunch breaks shopping for nappies and stuff. His life's effectively over.'

'Or a new stage of his life is just beginning, perhaps?' Alfie said.

'What is it, Alf? You thinking of starting a family?'

'No, I'm not. Just saying, becoming a dad wouldn't mean the end of your life. Just a moving on to new things. Rewarding too, I imagine, watching your kid grow up.' Alfie shot Tim a glance as he said this, and Tim groaned inwardly as the other two picked up on it.

65

'You're saying that, Alfie my lad, because Tim here has told you some juicy news. That's it, innit? Tim, you do have something to tell us, don'tcha?' Niall grinned, and Tim realised there was no getting out of it now.

'Early days, Niall, but yeah. We're gonna have a baby.'

'Knew it!' Niall slapped him on the back. 'Congratulations, my son! Let's all raise a glass to the mini-Wilsher that's on the way! When's it due?'

'Dunno, really. Months away yet. Like I said, very early days. Only found out myself a few days ago.'

'We best make the most of you then,' Marco said. 'You're on borrowed time now. We won't see hide nor hair of you once your baby comes.'

Tim grimaced. 'That's kind of what I'm afraid of. We're supposed to be off to Italy this summer, walking in the Apennine mountains, but with her pregnant I reckon we won't be able to do as much.'

'Aw, baby spoiling your holidays already! And not even born yet!' Niall guffawed. All right for him, Tim thought. None of this crowd had children, or even long-term partners. Although they were all over thirty they were all still living the same way they had at twenty. In the pub most nights, at the football on Saturdays, going on lads' holidays in places like Benidorm or Palma every summer.

'You'll just have to come up with different holidays that you can do with a kid,' Alfie said. 'When they're very little they're portable and you can still go away and do adult stuff. So my sister said. When they're toddlers it's harder and you need to take their needs into account. Then when they're bigger, they'll probably want to do the cycling and walking trips you like anyway.'

'So what, I wait ten years to get back to it?' Tim said.

Alfie shrugged. 'Not a case of "waiting", is it, mate? You'll be doing other things in the meantime. Being a parent. It's what you wanted, isn't it?'

66

'Yeah but . . .'

'But not yet! Don't blame you, Tim,' Marco put in. 'No kids for me until I'm forty, I reckon. Not till I'm too old to want to go out and have fun.'

'And only then if you can find someone to have them with!' Niall said, laughing. 'You don't have too good a track record in that respect, eh, Marco?'

'Ah, someone'll have me.' Marco pulled a 'poor me' face and they all laughed. Tim looked around at the group, enjoying the banter, enjoying being part of it all and wondering if Niall and Marco were right – perhaps there would only be a few more occasions like this, between now and the birth of the baby. Perhaps it'd all be different after. It's not that he was afraid Jackie wouldn't let him go out – of course she would, and he would encourage her to go out with Sarah. They'd surely be able to find a routine that worked for them, that gave them both time with their mates. But would he feel different then? Would he find he no longer had much in common with them? Not Alfie – he knew they'd been friends for so long that nothing would change. But these other two? Would him having a child at home mean he felt differently towards them, or they towards him? They were still joking now about Marco's inability to hang on to girlfriends for more than a couple of months. Perhaps, Tim thought, he'd already grown apart from them after so many years with Jacks.

'Beers? My round,' Niall said, and the others nodded. He went to the bar, and Marco took the opportunity to nip to the toilets.

Alfie came to stand beside Tim. 'Don't listen to those two, mate. You will find it's different when you have a kid. But in a good way. Fulfilling, my brother-in-law said, and he was a right lad, the kind you'd have thought would never settle down. He said to me the other day he can't imagine life without their kids now. You'll be like that – you and Jackie.'

'You think?'

Alfie nodded sagely. 'Yep. This'll be the best thing that's ever happened to you, trust your old mate the Alfatron.'

'Hope you're right.'

'I am, mate. It'll just take a bit of adjustment, that's all. Or, a bit of growing up, as my sister put it. And she's always right, believe me. What did your mum think about becoming a grandma?'

'Haven't told her yet. Like I said, it's early days and Jacks wants to wait until she's had a scan and is confident all is well. You know Mum. She's been a bit clingy since Dad died. More dependent on me. Jacks said we shouldn't tell her and then have to disappoint her if something goes wrong. She hasn't told her own parents yet either.'

Alfie nodded again. 'Good idea. She's a wise woman, your Jackie. She'll be a good mum.'

Tim looked away, staring out of the pub window at the passing traffic. 'Yeah, she will. That's the other thing, if I'm being honest. I don't know if . . . like . . . if I've got it in me to be a dad. Not of a baby. Teenagers are fine. I'm used to them at work. But babies, toddlers, the messy, needy ones . . .' He shuddered.

Alfie stared at him. 'Timbo, are you . . . frightened by it?'

'Guess I am, kind of.' Tim shrugged.

'So was my brother-in-law. He confided once when Sharon was out of the way. But then when their kids came along he said it was instinctive. You just got to do what feels right for the child.'

'I dunno if I have the instincts. I held a mate's baby once. He was a few months old at the time. Felt like I was gonna drop him. Had no idea what to do, and I felt nothing for it.'

'Different with your own,' Alfie replied. 'You develop a bond.'

Tim pulled a face. 'I just can't imagine that with a newborn. Give me teenagers any day. You know where you are with them – they can talk for a start, so they'll simply tell you what they need. Whereas newborns are so helpless. All they can do is—' He broke off as Marco returned from the gents and Niall from the bar.

'Here you are, chaps. A pint apiece,' Niall said, handing them

68

each a glass. 'Cheers, and here's to Tim's forthcoming incarceration with a squalling, shitting dictator.' Marco spluttered with laughter.

'I'll drink to that,' Tim said, determined not to rise to the provocation any further. Food for thought, all of it. But Alfie's was the advice he'd most listen to. Alfie had always been the wise one, the voice of reason, and he'd proved that again this evening. Though he could have done with a little more time to discuss the fear he felt at the prospect of having a small person entirely dependent on him and Jackie for everything. A small person he had no idea how to handle, or even whether he could love them the way he should.

# Chapter 8

## Madeleine, 15 April 1912

'Let me help, please?' Madeleine said to a steward who was near an open gangway, standing beside a pile of blankets, ready to receive people from the lifeboats.

The steward nodded. 'Give each person one of these. Then direct them into that room for assessment.' He pointed to an open door through which Madeleine could see a makeshift surgery had been set up, and *Carpathia*'s medical officer, Dr McGee, was awaiting patients. The steward then moved towards the gangway to help with hauling survivors inside. One by one they appeared, either climbing up rope ladders or more often, hauled up on a kind of swing seat attached to ropes.

Women were brought up first. Each had shocked, numbed expressions on their faces. Madeleine set to work, comforting them as best she could, ushering them into the warm, wrapping blankets around them and pushing cups of warm soup into their hands before directing them into the surgery for assessment.

'Excuse me, have you seen my husband? Have any men been picked up from other lifeboats?' Madeleine's heart broke as almost without exception, the women asked the same thing. She decided not to answer them directly, for she had no more information than they had. Better to concentrate on what each woman needed for her own well-being. Perhaps their menfolk would be on some other lifeboat, or picked out of the sea later. Or perhaps not. She did not want to give them false hope.

'Here, tuck this around you. Do you have any injuries? The doctor will check you over.' She put as much sympathy into her voice as she could, to make them feel they were safe now, their ordeal was over.

Except for waiting to see if their loved ones had survived.

Some people seemed to want to pour out everything that had happened to them, talking rapidly to anyone who'd listen. They spoke of panicked crowds surging towards each lifeboat as it was launched, of the moment when *Titanic* broke in two and plummeted under the surface, of people in the water clutching hold of wreckage to keep themselves afloat, of the awful screams and moans of despair, of the even more awful silence as those in the sea perished. Other survivors were mute, uncomprehending, as though they had no idea what had happened. Madeleine treated each as she would have wanted to be treated herself. Listening if they wanted to talk, asking no questions if they wanted to remain silent.

One woman had a child of about six with her, a little boy who was wide-eyed and terrified. He was dressed in a nightshirt, with a man's jacket around his shoulders. Madeleine could imagine the scene on *Titanic* – the boy's father snatching the child out of his bed, wrapping him in his own jacket, pushing his wife and child forward onto a lifeboat. 'Where's panda?' the boy kept saying, and on questioning him Madeleine realised he was missing his toy. She recalled the panda in her luggage. Perhaps she might find this child later, and give him the bear. His need for it was far greater than hers. It would be a small thing, but maybe it'd help a tiny bit. These people had lost so much.

The day gradually brightened as dawn arrived, and the little lifeboats kept coming. Some were full to bursting, riding low in the ocean and their passengers had been sitting with their feet in water, terrified they might capsize. One held only a dozen or so. Madeleine did not judge. She was beginning to get an idea from those who wanted to talk, of the confusion and terror there'd been on board *Titanic* when it became clear the ship was sinking. Some of the less full lifeboats had launched earlier, when many people still believed the ship was not really at any risk and had been unwilling to leave the comfort of the ship for a small wooden lifeboat.

Each lifeboat had a handful of men on board. An officer from *Titanic* and two or three crew members who'd been responsible for rowing the boat. They were, as one said to Madeleine, the lucky ones. 'Not many men got on the boats, miss,' one said. 'It was women and children first.'

'What happened to those who didn't get onto the boats?' she asked, keeping her voice low so other survivors nearby didn't hear.

'They was on deck when the ship went down,' the man said, matter-of-factly. 'They'll all have died. Water's too cold to survive in for long.'

Madeleine nodded to show she'd understood, and turned away to busy herself with pouring more cups of soup from an urn and to hide her distress. She couldn't allow herself to think too much about the tragedy. There was work to be done for those who lived. Later, when alone in their cabin, she'd spare a thought for those who'd died.

It put into perspective her own loss, the tragedy that had sent her spiralling into a pit of despair for so long. The long years of wondering if she would ever fall pregnant, the euphoria when finally she did and they began to think the family life they'd always dreamed of would at last be a reality. The miscarriage and surgery, and knowledge that she would never now be able to have a baby of her own. With a supreme effort she'd roused herself enough to agree to the trip, and help a little with the

72

preparations. And now they were here, and the adventure they thought they'd be having was on hold while they dealt with a terrible tragedy, something so overwhelming it forced her to stop dwelling on her own problems and instead think of the needs of others. Perhaps this was what she needed. To do something useful, something helpful and good, rather than sitting alone with her thoughts that constantly spiralled inward and downward. And yet, her yearning for a baby was as strong as ever within her, no matter what was happening around her.

She went out into the passageway to see if there was another lifeboat arriving yet. By the commotion near the gangway, it seemed there was, and the crew were busy securing it and getting the first passengers ready to be brought aboard. 'This is a full one,' the steward she'd spoken to earlier called out, and Madeleine made sure she had plenty of blankets at the ready. Further along, some survivors who'd arrived on earlier boats were milling about, watching, hoping and praying for the arrival of their loved ones. Madeleine hadn't the heart to send them away.

There seemed to be some difficulty getting one woman off, hauled up in the sling. She was carrying something, and it made it hard for her to hold on.

'Careful, she's holding an infant!' a crewman shouted, and the steward and other men responsible for bringing her on board leaned out to steady her, to stop her swinging back against the hull of the ship.

At last, she was on board. She was wearing a bulky lifejacket and coat, and indeed in her arms was a baby, tightly wrapped in a blanket. She looked dazed, hardly able to stand. This was another lifeboat that had taken on water, its occupants forced to sit with their feet in freezing water all night.

Madeleine tried to usher her into the makeshift surgery but the woman stumbled and half fell against the wall. Madeleine helped her to stand upright again. 'In here. Get yourself and your baby checked by Dr McGee.'

'Not my baby,' the woman said, staring at Madeleine with wide eyes, as though she'd only just realised what she was holding. 'I kept it warm. What do I do with it now? Will you take it, please?'

Madeleine gasped. She, hold a baby? She wasn't sure she could, not after what had happened to her own. Her arms had ached after the surgery, as though they were missing holding a child. Cautiously she pulled back the blanket that was tightly wrapped around the child, and peered at him or her. She couldn't tell whether it was a boy or girl. It was probably around three months old, she thought. Looked healthy enough.

'Please? A man thrust this baby on me as I boarded the lifeboat. I can't keep it.' The woman, who Madeleine now saw wore a *Titanic* stewardess's uniform under her coat, held the child away from her. She was close to collapse, Madeleine realised, and instinctively she put out her hands to take the baby. She could do this, she *must* do this, to help this poor woman. She was ashamed to see that her hands were shaking, almost as much as the other woman's. And she wasn't the one who'd spent a night adrift in a lifeboat on a freezing sea.

She took the bundle, surprised to feel how warm it was. The baby's little body radiated heat through the shawl it was wrapped in. A tiny face, pursed lips, eyes tightly closed as though the baby was determined to sleep through all the commotion, no matter what. Madeleine's emotions, her longing for a child that she'd tried so hard to suppress on board the ship, bubbled to the surface as she gazed at the baby's face, a small gasp escaping her unbidden. Maybe . . . if this child was orphaned, as was most likely the case, perhaps she could keep it? Maybe it could replace the one she'd lost, the baby she'd yearned for and still grieved for? They could be a family at last. A jumble of images surged through her mind of a future for the three of them, herself a mother at last . . .

She hugged the baby closer to her, smiling at the idea of watching this child grow through the years, imagining first steps, first words, being called 'Mama'. The baby had a smudge of dirt on its cheek. Madeleine lifted a hand to brush it off, but just then she was jostled from behind. Another woman grabbed the child from her, pushing her against the wall as she did so.

'My baby, my baby!' the woman moaned, burying her face into the blanket wrapped around the child. She didn't stop, didn't look at either Madeleine or the stewardess, but ran off along the passageway, clutching the precious bundle.

'Who . . . who was that?' Madeleine stuttered, staring after the woman and baby.

The stewardess shrugged. 'Must be hers.' She gulped and gazed at Madeleine. 'I was on the last lifeboat. I think the father must have . . . perished.'

'You saved that child, then.' A wave of disappointment washed over her, as she realised those brief dreams of adopting the child as her own could never be, not if the mother had survived. Immediately she berated herself for those thoughts. It was a blessing that the child had been reunited with its mother. Madeleine could not imagine the pain that woman must have felt, sitting all night on a lifeboat separated from her baby, and probably assuming the baby had perished. The agony she must have gone through. And now she had the child back in her arms, where it belonged. No wonder the woman hadn't stopped to thank the stewardess. She'd have been too overwhelmed with relief at finding her child.

Rousing herself, Madeleine turned to the stewardess. 'Come on, let's get you a blanket and some soup.' She led her into the make-shift surgery, found a seat for her and wrapped a blanket around her shoulders. She took the woman's name – Violet Jessop – for the list of survivors that the purser was compiling, and sent her to sit with her soup and wait for an assessment by Dr McGee.

Once Violet was comfortable, Madeleine walked away to take a moment to compose herself. The encounter with the baby had shaken her, bringing to the surface all those feelings of loss and regret that she'd thought she was beginning to bury at last. She imagined herself in Violet's place, clutching someone else's baby to her through the long dark hours in the lifeboat. A thought occurred to her – in that position she'd never have been able to give the baby up. She'd have wanted to keep it, to call it her own. God, she didn't even know if the baby was a boy or a girl!

And then she felt a pang of regret that someone had snatched the child right out of her arms. The baby might have become hers. If the mother hadn't spotted it right then, Madeleine could have taken the child back to their cabin, cared for it there. Maybe there'd have been some way they could have adopted it. Ralph would have agreed. He'd have understood her need for it was so intense.

She was horrified to find herself thinking such things. Was she honestly considering that she might have abducted the baby? Or was it really abduction if she'd truly believed both of the child's parents had died?

It was a good thing, she told herself, that the child's mother had recognised the baby and snatched it from her. A baby belonged with its mother. The one thing that bothered Madeleine was wondering how on earth had the woman been separated from her baby? Why had she got on a lifeboat without her child? In her place, Madeleine would never have been parted from her baby. She'd have kept a tight hold, no matter what. The chaos on board *Titanic* as it sank must have been enormous for the woman to have lost sight of her precious child.

She gave herself a little shake and set to work again. There were still people who needed her help. One by one the survivors were brought on board over the next few hours, as the dawn ripened into a cold, still day. The ship was filling up, though Madeleine had no idea how many had been rescued. Hundreds, definitely. Among them was Bruce Ismay, the director of the White Star Line. Madeleine glimpsed his face as he was ushered through to a private cabin. She recognised him from the papers, and there was a whisper quickly passed among the *Carpathia* crew and those helping, that confirmed who he was. The man looked utterly, totally defeated. In shock. He must feel to an extent responsible, she realised. Even though she knew nothing of the circumstances of how and why *Titanic* had sunk, as the director of the company that owned the ship, Ismay surely bore some responsibility. Her heart went out to him.

'Maddy? You're still here? Take a break. Come and have a cup of coffee.' Ralph had appeared at her side. Madeleine finished helping a *Titanic* crew member who was wearing a woman's coat over only a vest and realised that Ralph was right – she needed a break. She hadn't slept last night; she'd eaten no breakfast, and she'd been on her feet for hours. There were others from *Carpathia* who could take her place, both crew and passengers. Everyone from the Cunard ship wanted to do their bit to help.

'Very well. I'll take a break for a short while.' She caught hold of Ralph's hand and followed him away from the gangway. Everywhere she looked there were people with blankets draped around them, their eyes wide, calling out for friends and relatives.

'Excuse me,' one young woman said to her. She was dressed similarly to Violet Jessop. 'Have you seen my sister? In a *Titanic* stewardess's uniform? Her name's Ruby . . .'

'I haven't, no. But check with the purser – he has a list of all survivors brought on board.'

The young woman nodded. Her eyes were glazed over with fatigue and fear.

'Good luck,' Madeleine said, and pointed her to where the purser was sitting at a desk with a clipboard. 'The poor thing,' she said to Ralph.

'There are so many who've lost someone. I have been trying to find out how many we've saved.'

'I heard that many men didn't make it onto the lifeboats. I can't understand why not, once they knew the ship was going down.'

'I'm hearing that there was not capacity for everyone,' Ralph said gently. 'In addition, some boats were launched only part full. If we've picked up half of *Titanic*'s passengers and crew we'll have done well. And there were no other ships that came to the rescue. Only us.'

Half the passengers. With the other half now at the bottom of the ocean. It was a sobering thought. Madeleine bit her lip to stop the tears from falling, and followed Ralph up to one of the dining rooms where thankfully breakfast items had been laid out. There was no chance of a table, however, as the room was thronged with so many more people than usual. But they were able to pick up cups of tea and a plate of toast and marmalade. 'It'll do, Ralph. It'll keep us going.'

They found a bench under a porthole to perch on while they ate. 'Look, there's Charles Marshall,' Ralph said. 'Marshall! Any news of your nieces?'

Madeleine cringed, fearing the worst. She glanced at Mr Marshall's face which showed a curious mixture of grief and elation. 'Malvina and Charlotte have been saved. They are with my wife now in our cabin. Evelyn is waiting to see if . . . if Caroline has also been saved.'

'Oh! Mr Marshall, that is . . . good news and hopeful news. I will find Evelyn as soon as I have drunk this tea, and I will remain with her while the rest of the survivors are brought on board. Pray to God your niece Caroline has been spared.'

'Indeed. I must dash. I promised them I'd find some food.' He set off in the direction of the breakfast buffet.

'An odd family reunion, in a place it should never have been able to happen,' Ralph commented.

'To think only last night we were enjoying those frivolous Marconi messages being sent between the ships. And then it was Marconi messages that brought us to *Titanic*'s aid,' Madeleine mused.

Ralph was rubbing his chin thoughtfully. 'I must capture this story. While it's fresh and new. I must hear the survivors' stories, get them all written down. For when we get back to land everyone will disperse and stories will be lost.'

She gasped. 'You're going to question these people? Don't you think they should be left alone, to recover and come to terms with what's happened? Ralph, darling, I can see it's a scoop, it's a huge story, but please tread gently with these poor people.'

He took her in his arms. 'Of course I will. Of course. I will be discreet and sympathetic. And I wonder . . .' He moved her gently back and regarded her. 'Would you help? Would you consider interviewing some of the female survivors? They'd be more likely to open up to you.'

She stared back at him. 'Ralph, no, I . . . I'm no journalist.'

'You're a good listener. Everyone always says so. And all you need do is listen to their stories, and make a few notes that I can use. With their permission, of course.' He held her upper arms and spoke with passion. 'Maddy, this is the biggest story of our lifetimes. And we're right here, in the thick of it. The truth *has* to be told. The world will want to know the details of what happened. *Titanic*'s loss on her maiden voyage – it's a story that'll be remembered forever. It's huge. There'll be an insatiable appetite for articles about it. And *I* could be the first one to tell the full story. There's no other journalist on board. We *have* to do this, don't you see? We have a duty to do this!'

His fervour affected her. She gave him a small smile. 'Very well. I will do what I can.'

'That's my girl. I'll give you a notebook to write it all down in. I've heard they're moving the first- and second-class women survivors to the first-class library. That's where you should go.'

'Let them settle first. I must return to the gangway in case there are more arriving in lifeboats. Helping them all get safely on board has to be our first priority, Ralph.'

'Of course. Well, I shall go and see what I can find out to make a start on the information gathering. I shall come and find you later.'

Madeleine lifted her face to be kissed by him, then went back to her previous station. There were still some lifeboats waiting to discharge their passengers. She was glad to see it. The more lifeboats they picked up, the more lives had been saved.

Above her, the ship's flag had been lowered to half-mast.

# Chapter 9

## Jackie, 2022

Despite it being still early days in her pregnancy, Jackie could not help herself. She wanted to start buying things for the baby. She had collected a pile of catalogues showing prams, car seats, cots, baby gyms and other smaller items and her favourite evening pastime now was to browse through them, deciding whether to go for bright colours or subtle neutrals.

Tim had very little input to this. Now and again, she'd ask him his opinion on two different three-wheeled buggies: 'Do you like this navy one? Or the cream? I'd worry the cream would get dirty but the navy is very regimental looking, don't you think?'

He would tear his attention away from the Italian maps and guidebooks he was perusing and roll his eyes at her. 'Whatever you prefer, Jacks. Honestly, I don't mind, as long as whatever you choose is robust enough to go off-road.'

She'd chuckled at the term 'off-road', and made a note of the two options. Perhaps in another catalogue or website or shop she'd find a colour she liked that was more practical than the cream one. But it would certainly be important that the buggy would stand up to active use.

Tim's whole world revolved around sports – teaching it at the school where he worked, attending a few clubs himself such as Ju-jitsu where he was quickly working his way up through the belts, refereeing team sports at the weekends or going to matches, and in between, watching it on TV. Whatever else you said about Tim, Jackie thought, no one could accuse him of being unfit and inactive. It was one of the things that had brought them together – back at university they'd both been members of the Adventure Club, spending weekends rock climbing, canoeing, camping in the Lake District and walking up mountains.

On Saturday, he was refereeing a local youth team's soccer match, and Jackie had a few hours to herself. She couldn't help it. She wanted to go shopping for the baby. Not to buy any of the larger items – she wanted to wait and choose those together with Tim, when he felt ready to do so. But a few smaller bits and pieces, some outfits, cot blankets, cute cuddly toys for newborns – surely it wouldn't hurt to buy that kind of thing? She could tuck them away in the back of a drawer, in case Tim thought she was wrong to buy them. He wouldn't, she thought, but she didn't want to have to explain. She knew that most people would suggest buying baby gear in the first trimester of a pregnancy was far too early.

But she wanted to buy them. And so she would.

After Tim had left for the match, and she was over that morning's bout of sickness, she put on a lightweight jacket, grabbed her handbag and set out to go shopping. Even if she decided not to buy anything in the end, it'd be fun looking at everything and building up ideas of what was available. In the town shopping centre, there was a branch of Boots that had a large baby section, and a few boutique nursery stores. She intended going round all of them.

It was in Boots that it happened. She'd picked out a pack of two newborn baby sleepsuits in cream and fawn with a cute bunny logo on them, and was perusing a display of small stuffed toys that could be hung from cot railings, when she felt a sharp pain in her abdomen followed by an ominous warm dampness between her legs. 'Oh my God,' she said, clutching a hand to her middle. She scanned the store for signs to the toilets but couldn't see any. A member of staff was stocking a shelf nearby. Jackie took a step towards her and with horror realised blood was trickling down her leg, a dark stain spreading down from her crotch. 'Excuse me, I need help,' she began to say to the sales assistant, and then her legs turned to jelly, there was a buzzing in her ears, her head began to spin and the world turned black.

She woke up to find herself covered in a blanket, with a pillow under her head, and a makeshift screen erected around her, though she still lay in the aisle of the shop. The female staff member she'd approached was crouched beside her. 'We've called an ambulance for you, love. Stay still, now. Don't try to move.'

'What happened?' Her words came out as a croak. She could guess, but didn't want to have to face it . . .

'You fainted, love. You're . . . bleeding too. May I ask, are you pregnant?'

Jackie nodded. At least, she hoped she still was. But there had been a lot of blood, all very sudden, and she knew she must expect the worst. A sob rose up in her throat that she was unable to stop.

'Ah, love. I know. Been there myself.' The member of staff, who wore a name badge that read Sue, looked to be in her late fifties, and had a kind, sympathetic face.

'My first,' Jackie whispered. She wanted this woman's sympathy. She needed her to know how much this child was wanted.

'That's hard, love.' Sue took her hand and squeezed it. 'I'm going to stay with you until the paramedics come, all right? They'll probably want to take you into hospital. You might need . . .' She stopped talking and bit her lip, her eyes glazing over.

Sue was remembering her own miscarriage, Jackie thought. Recalling her own experience when she'd lost a baby. She squeezed

Sue's hand. And now it felt like it was her comforting the other women.

Sue glanced down at her and gave a weak smile. 'Ah, let me stop talking. You might be all right. Sometimes women bleed and the foetus is still OK. How many weeks along are you?'

'Ten.'

'Early days. What's your name, love? I should have asked. I'm Sue.'

'Jackie.'

'Well, Jackie, we can but hope. Are you comfortable enough? Gave me quite a shock when you fell down at my feet, I can tell you.'

'I'm all right.' She wasn't, though. She was very far from being all right.

'Josh, any sign of the ambulance?' Sue called to another staff member who was guarding the aisle, keeping curious shoppers away. Jackie appreciated their concern.

'Not yet,' Josh replied.

'I could move . . .' Jackie said. 'I'd like to get up off the floor.'

'We can put you somewhere more private if you can walk,' Sue said. 'Wrap the blanket around you. I'll help you up. See that door? Just through there, on the right, is a set of offices. We can put you in one of those.'

'OK, thank you.' Gingerly, Jackie got to her feet, feeling another rush of blood leave her. She thought she must have definitely lost this baby. She wouldn't need any medical staff to tell her that. She forced herself to hold back the tears, at least until she got off the shop floor, away from the stares of passing shoppers.

'Here we go. Well done, love.' Sue tucked the blanket around Jackie's waist, holding it in place, hiding her bloodstained jeans. On the floor, where she'd lain, were the two baby sleepsuits, crumpled and marked with blood. She must have collapsed with them beneath her.

'Oh God, sorry about those,' Jackie said, nodding down at them.

'No matter. You're what matters. Come on, take it easy and we'll soon have you sitting somewhere private.' Sue put an arm around her shoulder and led her towards the door that was marked 'Staff Only'.

Once through it, a man in a suit ushered them into an office and cleared some paperwork off a chair. 'There you are. Sue, I'll send the paramedics in here, then. Can I get you any tea?'

'I think it would help?' Sue looked at Jackie and she nodded. 'Thank you.'

The man nodded and left the room, closing the door quietly behind him. Jackie sat in the chair that had been cleared, with the blanket still wrapped around her. The seat was covered with some sort of vinyl, wipe clean, she hoped. Why she was worrying about a few things getting blood on them when her baby might have lost its life, she didn't know. And she didn't even know whether it was a boy or a girl. If she'd lost it, she'd never know now, she realised. It was that thought that made the tears finally fall, and the sobs come at last.

Sue knelt beside her and wrapped her arms around her. 'There, now. Have a good cry. I cried for days when it happened to me. Awful thing, it is. You might still be pregnant, but even if the worst has happened, you have to let yourself grieve, and it's all right to do that.'

It helped, somehow, that Sue was giving her permission to cry. And cry she did, clinging to Sue, clutching at her blouse, sobbing on her shoulder and drawing just a tiny bit of comfort from the older woman's sympathy and compassion.

Jackie didn't have to stay long at the hospital. She was given an ultrasound scan at which the technician confirmed he could find no foetus. 'Are you completely sure of your dates?' he asked. 'Because maybe you weren't quite as far along as you'd thought. We'll book you in for a follow up scan in two weeks, to be certain.'

She was sure of her dates, but even so, he was offering a shred of hope. The appointment was made and she was sent home with a stack of leaflets about how to cope with the trauma, both physically and emotionally. All the medical staff, like the staff in the shop, were quietly sympathetic, which she appreciated.

Yet she knew it hadn't really sunk in. She'd been pregnant for such a short time, but she'd already thought of the baby as a complete human, with a personality, with looks that were a perfect mixture of herself and Tim. Despite the warnings she'd had from Sarah not to allow herself to think like that. And despite the hospital staff saying there was a chance she was still pregnant if she had her dates wrong, she knew she wasn't. She felt different somehow. More . . . alone. She knew it was over. Even so, the two weeks she'd have to wait for the confirmatory scan would be long and hard, made worse by that tiny flame of hope burning within her.

She was glad she hadn't told anyone else. Only Tim and Sarah. Her parents hadn't known, so they wouldn't need to grieve for a lost grandchild. Neither had Tim's mum. And it had been too early to say anything to Henry.

She took a taxi home from the hospital, wearing a pair of hospital scrub trousers on her lower half, her ruined jeans in a carrier bag. Tim was still out at his match, or at the pub with some of the lads as he often did afterwards. That was OK with her. She was only too happy to have a bit of time at home on her own before he returned and she had to tell him the news. She could get changed, deal with those jeans – probably throw them out. Make herself a hot drink and try to relax.

By the time he came back, she'd done all that, and was curled on the sofa under a blanket, wearing a pair of pyjamas, with a mug of hot chocolate in her hand and a box of tissues nearby.

'Jacks? You all right?' he said, as he entered the room and saw her there. 'Got a cold or something? Not Covid I hope?' He dumped his kit bag on the floor and perched on the arm of the sofa, putting a cool hand across her forehead.

'Not Covid or a cold, no,' she managed to say, before the tears fell again.

'What, then?'

Wasn't it obvious, she wanted to say, but stopped herself. She bit her lip and shook her head.

'What, Jacks? Come on, tell me.' Tim slid off the sofa arm and knelt on the floor beside her, stroking her arm.

'I've lost it,' she said in a whisper.

'Lost . . . what have you lost?' Tim frowned.

'The baby.' There, she'd said it. She took his hand, ready to offer him the sympathy so many strangers had shown her. Would he cry? It was his baby too. Their own flesh and blood, now lost. 'I miscarried. In Boots.'

'Oh. Oh, Jacks, I'm sorry.' He stood up and gazed down at her. His expression was . . . not what she'd have expected. Something had flashed across his face, a look of . . . relief. Yes, his first reaction had been relief. He'd quickly wiped that look off his face and his expression was once more one of sympathy, but too late. She'd seen it. Just as when she'd told him she was pregnant he'd looked shocked, horrified almost, for a split second.

'Are you really?' she said, quietly.

'Am I really what?' He frowned once more.

'Sorry. Are you honestly sorry I've lost it, Tim?'

'Of course! I know how much you wanted this.'

'Because I could have sworn that just for a moment there you looked relieved when I told you. And surely it wasn't just *me* who wanted the baby? Didn't you want it too? I know it was earlier than we'd planned but . . .'

'Jacks, you're not being fair. Of course, I wanted it. Of course, I'm sorry you've lost it. Are you all right? I mean, what happened?'

'I bled, the staff in Boots looked after me and called an ambulance, I went to hospital and had an ultrasound scan. I've got to have another in two weeks to be certain, but I know it's gone.' She choked back a sob.

'So . . . what now?' Tim was still standing over her. She wanted him to kneel by the sofa again, put his arms around her, be as tender and caring as he'd been when he first came home and he'd thought she had Covid.

She shrugged and looked away. 'I need to recover. Get over this. And then, assuming the second scan confirms the miscarriage, in a while we try again. In a couple of months, they said. When we feel ready. And there's no physical reason why it shouldn't be successful next time. Just one of those things, they said.'

'So, back to plan A. Try for a baby after our Italian trip. That's good, then.' Tim picked up his kit bag and turned to leave the room.

'Good? *Good?* Tim, do you realise what you just said? I lost a baby not two hours ago and you're telling me it's *good?*' Jackie couldn't believe what he'd said. It had slipped out, she realised, but even so. It told her how he really felt about all this. Their original compromise had been to start trying for a baby in September, but she thought he'd come round to the idea of having one sooner. But now, that flash of relief she'd seen on his face, and what he'd just said – he clearly hadn't been as committed to the idea as she'd thought he was. The pain of that realisation shot through her with a jolt, feeling like the miscarriage all over again.

'I didn't mean . . .' he started saying, but he quickly tailed off, and raised his hands in the air, shaking his head, as though he couldn't think what he did mean. He looked pained with embarrassment at being caught out, she thought.

'I think you did,' Jackie said. 'I think deep down you're pleased to be delaying having a family a bit longer. You weren't all that happy when I got pregnant, were you? And now, you won't have to deal with me feeling sick on the Italian trip so you're delighted with this outcome. Well. I'm not. And I need a bit of support.' Tears ran down her face as she watched him, half longing for him to come to her and hold her, to make everything better and half wishing she could be left alone to grieve if he couldn't grieve with her.

'Don't be stupid, Jacks. I'm not delighted with the outcome.

You're suffering, so of course so am I. Shall I make some tea? Want lunch?'

'No. I don't want any of that.' Jackie hauled herself upright, off the sofa, wrapping her blanket around her shoulders. 'I'm off to bed. I need to rest. Perhaps . . . just leave me alone for a while, eh?'

He didn't follow her as she left the sitting room and went upstairs. At the top of the stairs she made a decision and turned left into the spare room, not right into their bedroom. They hadn't yet thrown out the old guest bed, and it was made up. She'd sleep in there, among the piles of sailing magazines and boxes of old rubbish, for the rest of the day and tonight, she decided. She wanted to be alone, to process her grief. It was clear Tim didn't feel the same way she did, and she couldn't bear to be with him at that moment. Every time she looked at him, she saw once more in her mind that flash of relief.

After all these years together, did they actually want different things from life after all? She tucked herself up under the duvet in the spare bed, and decided that now was not the time to ponder that question. Now, she needed to grieve her lost child, and later she could focus on the 'What next?'

# Chapter 10

## Madeleine, 15 April 1912

Down at the gangway, Madeleine came across Evelyn who was waiting anxiously for her third cousin, Caroline, to arrive. 'Evelyn! I heard that two of your dear cousins have been rescued. Is there any more news?'

'Not yet. Oh, Madeleine, I am so worried.' The younger woman twisted her hands around each other, pacing back and forth. 'I'm glad that Charlotte and Malvina are safe but . . . poor Caroline! The others said she was separated from them in all the confusion on deck, and that their lifeboat was launched in a hurry despite them pleading with the crewman to wait for Caroline. It's all so awful!'

'It is, yes. But there is still hope. Look out there.' Madeleine made Evelyn look through a nearby porthole. Two more lifeboats were in view, and there was another just beginning to be unloaded. 'She might yet be on any of those boats. Do not give up hope. Will you help me deal with the survivors?'

But Evelyn could not stop pacing and crying and twisting her hands. In the end Madeleine made her sit down with a pile of blankets that needed folding. 'Doing something useful with your hands, dear, might help take your mind off it all while we wait for Caroline.'

As the morning wore on, some *Carpathia* passengers came down to see what was going on. Madeleine could not believe that people had managed to sleep through it all, and were only now surfacing and wondering who all the extra people were. One woman complained loudly that the first-class lounge had been commandeered for *Titanic* survivors, and where was she going to sit for her morning coffee now? Madeleine had no time for such people. What was more important – a cup of coffee or the lives of hundreds, thousands even, from the other ship?

She was pleased to see that the majority, however, were sympathetic and offering their assistance. People were rearranging their berths, doubling up with friends to free up cabins, bringing spare clothes to be distributed as needed. In one corner, a few women were busy cutting up and sewing blankets into basic outfits for children who'd come on board wearing nothing but their nightshirts. She remembered the boy who'd lost his panda toy. There were a lot of children among the survivors. Most were with their mothers, sitting quietly in their laps, looking white and shocked. They'd have lost their fathers, she knew. Here and there, mothers comforted their children, telling them Daddy would be on the next lifeboat, just wait and see. Other mothers sat with tears running down their faces, clinging to their children, unable to answer their questions.

At least they had each other, Madeleine thought. There seemed to be no orphans. Even the baby the stewardess Violet had brought on board had been reunited with its mother. And for these poor women who'd lost their husbands, having their children safe with them would be a relief. But they had difficult times ahead.

She was busy persuading one survivor to take a mug of soup when there was a squeal from Evelyn. Looking round, Madeleine saw her friend rush forward and throw her arms around another woman who'd just been brought on board. She smiled. This must be Caroline. At least the Marshall family were now reunited, with no losses.

As a tearful Evelyn led her cousin past, Madeleine smiled and put out a hand to pat Evelyn's shoulder. 'I'm so glad,' she whispered. Evelyn seemed too choked with emotion to be able to respond, and her cousin wore that shocked, numbed expression that was becoming all too familiar.

Finally, the last lifeboat they could see came alongside and everyone was brought on board. Madeleine spotted Louis Ogden with his camera, taking a photograph of it from the deck, as the people on it prepared to climb aboard. Later, the word went around that there was to be a religious service held in the first-class dining room. Madeleine went up and found Ralph already there, waiting for it to begin. It was attended by a handful of *Titanic* survivors, and most of *Carpathia*'s passengers.

The captain spoke first, telling the congregation that they would soon be turning south and steaming back to New York to allow the *Titanic* passengers to disembark. After that they would depart again for Gibraltar as originally scheduled. He apologised for the delay to their journeys. 'Not at all, least we can do,' one man spoke up and there was a murmur of agreement from everyone.

'We are still on the spot, perhaps directly over the wreck of *Titanic*,' Captain Rostron went on. 'And so it seemed fitting and right that we hold a service while we are still here.' He looked tired. Madeleine supposed he must have been up all night, along with many of *Carpathia*'s crew.

Reverend Anderson led the service, remembering those who had been lost and giving thanks for those who had been saved. Madeleine bowed her head and prayed fervently, though she knew from what survivors had said that well over half of *Titanic*'s passengers and crew, mostly men, had been lost. It was all too much to contemplate.

'Shall we go up on deck, before the ship leaves this spot?' Ralph said to her once the service was over.

She nodded, and they made their way up. The sun was high in the sky now – it was near midday. Around the ship were numerous icebergs, some small, like floating motorcars and others the size of cathedrals. Madeleine gazed down into the water. Here and there floated pieces of wreckage, bits of wood, a deckchair or two, discarded life jackets. But not much. There was so little to show that an enormous liner had been there, and had sunk with so much loss of life.

She stood beside Ralph trying to make sense of it all, and then the engines started up and the ship began to turn.

'Oh! We are leaving!' She'd known – the captain had said so – that they soon would, but somehow turning away from the spot, the implicit admittance that no further survivors would be picked up, that there *were* no more survivors, was almost impossible to bear. Many of *Carpathia*'s passengers were out on deck now, leaning on the railings; some openly sobbed, and others silently mouthed prayers for the lost.

It was a beautiful, calm, bright morning. The wrong kind of weather for a shipwreck, Madeleine thought. It was all wrong. Everything was wrong.

As *Carpathia* picked up speed and left the ice floes behind, Ralph rubbed her back. 'Well, we have a few days now before we reach New York. And there is much to be done.'

Back in their cabin, Ralph rummaged through his suitcase and pulled out an empty notebook which he handed to Madeleine. 'Here. For you to capture the women survivors' stories. You have done what you can to bring them on board and make them comfortable. Now let them tell their stories.'

He ran a finger down the side of her face. 'This is what we can do for them now. This is what we can do for those who are lost – we can tell their stories, make sure the truth is known and they are not forgotten. This is what journalism is for, Maddy.'

Images of some of the people she'd helped that morning flitted through her mind. The child who'd lost a panda toy. The crewman wearing only a vest and a borrowed woman's coat. The stewardess, the baby she'd brought on board and the child's mother, of course. Yes, their stories deserved to be told. And all this – it was helping her a little. It was stopping her dwelling on the loss of their own baby. It was giving her something to do, a purpose, a way of being useful, and that had to be a good thing.

Ralph was right. Capturing survivors' stories was what they could do. It was all they could do. Madeleine took the notebook, wrote her initials on the front of it and promised him she'd do her best.

Madeleine stood outside the first-class library which had been set aside as a lounge for some of the first- and second-class survivors. She clutched the notebook Ralph had given her tightly, and checked for the third time that she had a sharp pencil. This was how they could play their part in the tragedy, how they might do some good for these poor people by getting the full story told, she reminded herself.

Taking a deep breath, she stepped into the sumptuously decorated room. It had wood panelling, heavy brocade curtains and an array of leather-bound books for passengers to borrow. There was a table on which were displayed a variety of newspapers – all well-thumbed and several days old now. All long out of date, as they reported the start of *Titanic*'s maiden voyage, the crowds that had waved her off from Southampton. There were writing desks, stocked with Cunard headed notepaper, pens and ink.

*Titanic* survivors were sitting on every available sofa and armchair. Some were trying to sleep, some stared into space looking shocked and lost, and others spoke quietly to their neighbours. The atmosphere was subdued and contemplative. The women were dressed in a variety of clothing – in nightwear under coats, in items donated by *Carpathia*'s passengers, or still wrapped in blankets. One or two were in evening dress. Madeleine recognised one woman – the film star Dorothy

Gibson – who was dressed in a long white satin gown and adorned with priceless jewellery.

She gazed around at them all, wondering where and how to start. She remembered that at least one newspaper had listed *Titanic*'s first-class passengers. That might prove useful for Ralph's story. She crossed to the newspaper table and thumbed through them, finding the relevant page and tearing it out. Folding it, she tucked it into the back of her notebook.

And now she could put off the moment no longer. There was a woman sitting nearby who'd been watching her, who looked as though she had a friendly face. Madeleine smiled at her and went over. 'May I sit with you?' she asked, and the woman nodded.

Madeleine pulled up a chair. 'Hello. My name is Mrs Madeleine Meyer and I'm a passenger here on *Carpathia*. My husband is a journalist. We were wondering if perhaps some of the survivors from *Titanic* might want to tell your stories. Sympathetically, of course. We believe there is a need for the wider world to know what happened, to know the personal stories behind the tragedy.'

'Oh, I'm not sure I can . . .' the woman stuttered.

Madeleine's instinct was to apologise and move away, but Ralph had told her to persevere a little. 'They may begin by saying no, but if you ask them gently again, or even a third time, they may then want to share their story.'

'May I start just by taking your name?' Madeleine made her voice as quietly sympathetic as she could, hoping that it conveyed the sympathy and compassion she felt for all the survivors.

'Yes, um, I'm Jocelyn,' the woman said, although she didn't sound too sure and she frowned as she spoke. Madeleine decided not to ask for a surname.

'Hello, Jocelyn. Perhaps you can tell me a little about what happened last night?'

'Well, I was on deck with my with my . . .' Jocelyn swallowed audibly, and Madeleine realised she was trying to say her husband.

Who was presumably lost. She nodded, and waited for Jocelyn to compose herself and continue.

'And we were so close to the iceberg, you could reach out and touch it. Bits of ice fell on the deck. Some boys had a kind of snowball fight.' Jocelyn smiled slightly at the memory. 'It was all good fun, then. No one knew that below the water the iceberg had ripped a hole in the ship.' She looked straight at Madeleine. 'That's what the officer on my lifeboat told us had happened. That the ship had been sliced all the way along, that's why we had no chance.'

'I see. And how long was it before you realised it was . . . serious?'

'Oh, maybe after an hour. No, half an hour. Oh, I don't know. One minute we were all laughing and joking, and the next they were putting the lifeboats out. Harry – that's my h-husband . . . I mean, he was my husband – pushed me forward. Said he'd get on a later boat. And then . . . it all happened so quickly. I was on the boat, we were rowing away, it was so dark I couldn't see what happened to Harry, but he's not here. I've checked everywhere. They said all the men . . .'

'If you give me your surname, I'll ask the purser. He's made a list of everyone who came on board. Just in case he's . . .'

Jocelyn stared at her. 'You think there could be a chance?' Her eyes were brimming with unshed tears.

Madeleine sighed. 'I'm sorry, I didn't mean to raise your hopes. I'm afraid there probably isn't, as you've already checked. But I can see if anyone knows anything.'

'All right. It's Harry Marchant. But if you're printing a story about us, please don't use our names. It's . . . his parents, you see. They don't actually know . . . about us. They didn't approve of me, and we . . . well, we ran away to get married, and then decided to have a honeymoon in New York.'

'I'm so, so sorry,' Madeleine said. To lose your husband so soon after marrying – that was terrible. She recalled the early days of her own marriage – that exciting, heady time when every day brought new joys, new discoveries. Her heart broke for Jocelyn, who was now crying openly, and dabbing at her face with a sodden handkerchief. 'I'm sorry if I've upset you, talking about it. Please, take my handkerchief.' She pulled a little scrap of cotton and lace from a pocket and passed it over. It seemed such an inadequate square of fabric to cope with the immense grief Jocelyn must be enduring. Embarrassed, she moved away with a promise to check the purser's list of names.

'I'll tell my story,' an imperious looking woman who dripped with jewellery said, as Madeleine scanned the room for someone else to talk to.

'Thank you,' Madeleine sat down and introduced herself.

'I'm Lady Lucille Hamilton,' the woman announced. 'We were playing bridge, and then there was an awful racket which we ignored, and then Charles, who was my bridge partner, said that the engines had stopped. Well, we're going to be late to New York if the engines have stopped, I said, and he agreed, and off he went to find out what was happening. And then we were told we had to get into a lifeboat, and I said it was all a load of poppycock, for hadn't they said the *Titanic* was unsinkable? Well, I shall be demanding my money back. It wasn't cheap you know, first class on the maiden voyage. And had we known . . .'

'Your bridge partner, Charles, did he . . .?'

'Oh, he got on the same lifeboat as I did. Women and children first, the officer was saying, but old Charles was having none of that. Between you and me . . .' Here she leaned closer and spoke into Madeleine's ear, 'I think he slipped the officer a few notes, if you know what I mean? Anyway, he was there on our boat, and a jolly good thing he was as well, for he's the one who worked out how to send up those green rockets. Had he not done that, this ship would never have found us, I'm sure of it, so it's Charles we have to thank for saving all our lives.'

'Not all lives were saved, Lady Hamilton.'

'Oh, most of the first class were. All those in the water, all those I could see anyway, they were all just steerage.'

'They're still people,' Madeleine said quietly.

'Yes, but they're not such a loss to society, are they?'

Madeleine stared at her, aghast, but the woman didn't seem to realise what she had said. 'We all rubbed along very well in our lifeboat, I must say. It was quite the adventure. The chaps that rowed it were splendid. In fact, I'm hoping we can gather everyone together before we leave this ship, and take a group photograph. I hear there's a chap among the *Carpathia* passengers – Ogden, is it? – who has a camera. If it can't be managed on the ship, then we'll do it in New York. I should like a memento of our night together and our dramatic rescue. She looked about her, and wrinkled her nose. 'I must add, these Cunard ships aren't a patch on the White Star Line ones, are they?'

Madeleine had heard enough from the other woman, and was not been able to stop herself answering back. 'Your White Star Line ship is at the bottom of the ocean. You ought to be grateful you're not there with it. If our captain hadn't responded to the distress call, I dread to think . . .' She gathered up her notebook and pencil and left the library before she said anything rude.

Taking a deep breath once she was outside the room, she considered her options. The library had been reserved for first- and second-class passengers from *Titanic*. Even after a shipwreck, it seemed the captain wanted to segregate the classes. Perhaps women from steerage would be better to interview. At any rate, Madeleine didn't feel she could stomach any more of the likes of Lady Hamilton.

There were survivors from *Titanic* in all areas of the ship. In every dining room and saloon, in passageways and sitting on staircases. And more out on the decks, huddled in blankets on deck chairs. Madeleine decided to try speaking to some women out there. She made her way to the largest open deck area and gazed around to decide who to approach. One woman sat with her arms wrapped around herself, and as Madeleine walked past, she shot out an arm and grabbed her. 'Please, can you help me?'

'I will try,' Madeleine said, as she crouched down beside the young woman. 'Would you prefer to sit indoors? There's somewhere . . .'

'Not the library with those awful women. That one who was on a lifeboat with only sixteen people. My Arthur died because of people like her.'

'I'm so sorry. What can I do for you?'

'Help me find my baby?' The woman looked at Madeleine with a pleading expression in her eyes. 'I know she was rescued. I saw Arthur push her onto a lifeboat. And now I can't find her!'

'How old is she?' Madeleine asked, gently.

'She's tiny. She's only three months old.'

'What's your name? And the baby's name?'

'I'm Lucy Watts. My baby is called Norah. Arthur was carrying her, you see, out of our cabin when it happened. I was on a lifeboat with Frederick and others, but they were pushing back the men and not letting them on, and they didn't realise he was holding a baby, I suppose.'

'But you know he got Norah onto a lifeboat?'

Lucy screwed up her eyes, as though trying to picture the scene. 'It was dark, and I was far below in my lifeboat, but I saw . . . I saw . . . he darted forward just as they were filling that boat, the last one I think, and he pushed her onto someone and I think . . . I hope and pray . . . that person took her and climbed onto the lifeboat with her. But I couldn't see any more after that as it was dark, so dark, and our crewmen were rowing us away from the ship.' Lucy sobbed, a huge guttural sound that brought with it all the despair she must have felt, watching the ship go down taking her husband with it.

Madeleine put her hand on Lucy's arm, and the young woman turned to her and threw herself against her. Madeleine wrapped

99

her arms around Lucy and let her cry, let her moan and wail and grieve for her lost husband. And for her lost baby.

After a moment, as people were staring at them, Madeleine gently held Lucy away a little. 'There, now. It's a terrible, terrible thing. Try to compose yourself as best you can. I will see if I can find out if there are any unaccompanied babies that were brought on board. I am sure you will be reunited with little Norah in no time at all. I heard there's a makeshift nursery that's been set up somewhere. You could check there for Norah.'

Lucy shook her head. 'She's not there. I left Frederick there and came out to search for Norah. I can't lose her, I can't! She's everything, she's my daughter, my darling!'

'Who is Frederick?' Madeleine asked, gently.

'My other child, my son, my other darling. I had two, don't you see? I was holding Frederick, Arthur had Norah. Oh my sweet girl, she cannot be lost!' Lucy broke down and sobbed, and all Madeleine could do was hold her once more. She thought about the baby the stewardess Violet Jessop had brought on board. The dear little mite she'd held for those few precious moments. Could that be Norah? But that baby's mother had run forward and snatched the child. Unless . . . and a terrible thought occurred to her . . . that *hadn't* been her mother? Was it possible that woman was unrelated, and the baby had been Norah? Surely not! Whatever the truth was, she knew she couldn't say anything to Lucy now. She couldn't raise her hopes like that, in case she was wrong. It would be too, too cruel.

At last Lucy composed herself enough to speak again. 'Sh-she's wearing a little bracelet. It's very distinctive, a tiny silver bangle, engraved with little flowers, her name N-Norah Frances and the date of her birth. 27 January 1912. It's on her right wrist.'

'Might it have fallen off?' Madeleine asked gently.

Lucy shook her head. 'It's a tight fit. It expands and there's a knack to removing it. Please, will you search for her? I can't lose her, not after losing Arthur!'

· 'I will, I promise.' Madeleine patted her back in what she hoped was a reassuring manner, and stood up. A steward was passing with cups of soup, and Madeleine took one and offered it to Lucy. 'Here, drink this. It might help a little.'

Lucy took it without a word, but put it on the deck beside her chair and began rocking back and forth, her arms wrapped around herself as though to make up for the lack of a child to hold.

Madeleine tapped her notebook against her hand. She had work to do. A baby to search for, and more survivors to interview. Not the first- and second-class women who were sitting in the library. What about the steerage women? Madeleine knew they'd been taken to the steerage areas of the ship. They'd have stories to tell that were every bit as valid as those of the upper classes. And maybe that woman and the baby were down there too? Madeleine tried to recall what she'd been wearing, but it had all happened so quickly she only had a vague impression of a brown coat, dark hair that hung loose over her shoulders, and . . . that was it. Not much to go on.

If she could find her and a baby wearing a bangle engraved with the name Norah Frances, that would be a wonderful outcome.

# Chapter 11

## Jackie, 2022

Jackie went back to work on Monday, despite the trauma of the weekend. Physically she felt all right, although she was tired and still bleeding. Emotionally she felt drained. But there was no point staying home with only daytime TV for company. Tim had to work, and Jackie knew that being alone with her thoughts would be far worse than being at work with plenty to distract her. Besides, she had not told Henry she was pregnant, and she didn't want to tell him she'd miscarried. He'd be sympathetic but it would be an uncomfortable conversation, for both of them. And she didn't want to lie and give some other reason for her absence.

No, all in all it was better for her to go to work.

Henry wasn't even in the office. He and his PA Lisa were away on yet another business trip. Jackie was thankful that her job was UK based. All the travelling Lisa had to do, having to stay at Henry's side at all times, would not suit her at all. And would probably be impossible when she had a child.

Jackie sighed. If she ever had a child. It felt further away than ever since the miscarriage. At the moment, the idea of trying again was unthinkable. She kept reliving that awful scene in Boots when she'd felt the baby slip away. Perhaps after the second, confirmatory scan she'd be able to look ahead, to put the miscarriage behind her. And then perhaps Tim would also feel ready to try again, more prepared this time for the reality of parenthood. She could only hope so. Until then all she could do was wait.

She arrived in her office before nine o'clock and slumped in her chair behind her desk. With no Henry or Lisa around she could work on whatever she wanted to. She opened the notebook that she used as a to-do list and glanced through the outstanding jobs. A couple of smaller tasks were high priority so she tackled those first – adding a sale of Victorian railway memorabilia to Henry's calendar, replying to an email offering a collection of first edition Dickens novels for sale.

Then, she made herself a coffee and eyed the box of *Carpathia* bits and pieces. It had been put to one side for far too long since her first rummage through. Now was the perfect time to itemise its contents, and look in detail at the newspapers and notebook that had been in it. The first part of this task wouldn't take too long – the box's contents had been a little disappointing at first glance. If the notebook contained more than simply shopping lists or the like, maybe that would help take her mind off her troubles.

She set to work, inspecting the main contents in detail, writing a description of each, and as expected, finished in less than an hour. She listed the newspapers, their dates, headlines and bylines, and scanned each article. Those written while the world awaited the facts of the disaster struck a chord with her – the waiting, fearing the worst but not knowing for certain whether loved ones had died or not.

'Notebook, you are my only hope,' she said, talking to herself as she often did when alone in an office. She opened it up to the first page and peered at the writing within. Whoever had written it had used a loopy, cursive style of handwriting that was, at first sight, difficult to read, but as Jackie kept working she became used to the style. Some pages were written in ink but most were in pencil, which in places had smudged or worn away, making it even harder to decipher.

The first page read: *Jocelyn? Snowball fight – boys. Good fun then. Sliced all along. Half an hour. Lifeboats, a later boat. Harry Marchant.*

'What does all that mean, dear notebook writer?' Jackie muttered. Who was Harry Marchant? The writer? She thought not. Something about the handwriting made her think the writer was a woman.

The next page, overleaf, said: *Running away to marry, New York honeymoon. So sad. Don't print names.*

Jackie looked back at the inside cover on which was written *Titanic Interviews*. With the reference to lifeboats on the first page, and now this page mentioning New York, she turned to her computer and searched for the Wikipedia page about *Carpathia*. 'Probably should have done this before I started, but better late than never,' she told herself. She knew, of course, *Carpathia* had been the ship that went to *Titanic*'s rescue, picking up all survivors from the lifeboats. It had then turned back to New York with its devastated passengers. Could these notes have been written while the rescue was in progress? Was it possible?

She felt a tinge of excitement as she turned to the next page and read. *Lady Lucille Hamilton. Bridge. Partner Charles – on same lifeboat. Poss bribed an officer? Sent up flares. Thinks most 1st class saved. Wants photo. Unpleasant.*

'Unpleasant? Did you not like Lady Hamilton, dear writer?' It seemed not. An intriguing detail about Charles, whoever he was, possibly bribing an officer.

'I think,' Jackie muttered, 'these are interviews with *Titanic* survivors. In which case this notebook is very interesting indeed.' Chances were all these stories would have been printed in newspapers at the time but even so, holding a notebook that was presumably used on *Carpathia* for interviews with *Titanic* victims, probably captured within days or even hours of the tragedy – that was something very special.

Who had taken the notes? Who was M.M.? Was it a member of *Carpathia*'s crew? A steward, given it had been stored in the same box as a steward's uniform? That seemed most likely.

Jackie turned to the next page. Here there were more notes – some hurriedly written as though jotted down while the interviewee spoke, and some more detailed, a story written out in full, as though the writer had sat somewhere quiet and written up what they remembered. One story in particular made her gasp.

*Lucy Watts. Norah Frances – few months. Father pushed baby onto someone. Violet Jessop? Baby bangle, silver, flowers, date of birth 27 January 1912.*

*Lucy was separated from her husband in the crush, he made her get on one lifeboat which was launched. He was holding their baby Norah and she's sure she saw him thrust the baby into the arms of someone as they got on a later lifeboat. It was dark – how could she see, from down below in the water? Still, she seemed certain. Husband is Arthur Watts, presumed lost.*

*Violet Jessop brought a baby on board – could it have been this one? Lucy searching ship for her child.*

Poor Lucy. To have saved yourself but lost your child in such a way. Jackie put a hand on her midriff. She too had lost a baby. How terrible it must be to carry a baby to term, give birth and then lose it in such tragic circumstances? And to think somehow your husband had got the child onto a lifeboat but you couldn't find her? 'Doesn't bear thinking about,' Jackie said. Her eyes prickled with tears at the losses this unknown woman from so long ago had borne. It reminded Jackie that she was not alone in experiencing loss. Had Lucy Watts ever been reunited with baby Norah, she wondered? She fervently hoped the story in the notebook was true and the father had managed to save little Norah.

She stopped reading then, opened a document on her computer and typed up the notes she'd read so far, exactly as they'd been written. It would be a lot easier to refer to a transcript than the original notes, and it meant the notebook would not need to be handled quite as often.

The following pages contained more interview notes with a woman named Nancy Smith. And then there was another page headed *Lucy Watts*. Beneath that was a note that added to the intriguing story: *Lucy was carrying a baby boy when she came on board, doctor says.*

Carrying a baby boy yet looking for a child called Norah? Were there two babies? Or had poor Lucy been confused after her trauma? Jackie was desperate to find out more. Who'd written the notes? Who was Lucy Watts and were there actually two babies? What about this stewardess – Jackie referred to the notes – Violet Jessop, who had apparently brought a baby on board that wasn't her own?

Jackie made a list of items to research, names to Google, facts to follow up on. Henry wouldn't be all that interested. He cared more for objects and artefacts, especially technical items, than human stories. But Jackie cared, and already she felt a kind of connection with this Lucy Watts who'd lost a baby. In a way, she had something in common with her.

The following pages in the notebook were a set of notes on Marconi equipment – some technical details about how it worked, the name Harold Cottam and a note saying *as discovered by Ralph*. Who was Ralph? One of the newspaper bylines, from the day after *Carpathia* reached New York, was a Ralph Meyer. Could it be the same person? Had the notebook belonged to someone connected with him?

'So many questions, not enough answers!' Jackie exclaimed. She looked again at the notes.

'Harold Cottam. That name rings a bell,' she muttered, and once more turned to Google and Wikipedia, discovering quickly that Harold Cottam had been the Marconi operator on board *Carpathia*. It was he who had picked up *Titanic*'s distress call and gone to awaken Captain Rostron to tell him. He'd been fortunate to pick it up – Cottam had been on the point of undressing for bed, listening in to wireless communications only out of interest, when he picked up the 'CQD' distress call, and *Titanic*'s plea to 'Come at once, we have hit a berg.'

It was sheer luck that Cottam had picked up the call, and quick thinking on his behalf to alert Captain Rostron who had immediately turned his ship northward in the direction of the coordinates *Titanic* had given, ordering full steam ahead. By the time *Carpathia*'s passengers awoke the next morning the ship had arrived at the spot of the disaster and survivors were being brought on board. There'd been no sign of *Titanic*, which was already at the bottom of the ocean.

Jackie spent an absorbing hour or so reading up on it, following links to various websites and searching for the names written in the notebook. One website listed known *Titanic* survivors, with a brief snippet of information about each of them. She was delighted to learn that Violet Jessop, mentioned in the notebook as having been carrying a baby when she came on board, had been a stewardess on *Titanic*. Her memoirs had been posthumously published and Jackie ordered a copy. Henry might not read it but she would. It could be useful background information.

Jackie turned once again to the notebook. At the very back the same spidery handwriting continued. *Lucy Watts's loss puts my own into perspective. She lost a living, breathing child she'd loved for months. I never met my baby, and never will. I feel a connection with this woman, and wish I could do something tangible to help her. She lost her beloved Arthur, I still have Ralph. I should count my blessings, though I fear Ralph alone will never be enough for me, and I will always wonder what kind of a mother might I have been?*

Jackie read the words several times. She guessed the writer of the notebook was Ralph's wife, and perhaps it was indeed the journalist Ralph Meyer? Perhaps he'd asked her to interview female survivors for him? And it sounded as though the writer had suffered a loss of her own – a baby she'd never met. A miscarriage, then. 'I feel your pain, unknown woman,' Jackie said, feeling tears pricking at the corners of her eyes, both for herself and for this woman long ago who, it seemed, had yearned for a child just as she, Jackie, did too. And both she and the notebook writer had been touched by the story of Lucy Watts and her missing baby. Another thing they had in common.

Somehow, she got through the day, distracting herself with research. Reading up on early Marconi equipment had been interesting and it was something she knew Henry would be interested in too. He liked antique technology and she'd trawled the usual auction sites to see if there was anything she might acquire for him. A radio set like the one which had helped save *Titanic* survivors would be right up his street, far more so than the stories in the notebook.

To her delight, she'd found something for sale of the right era, the sort of equipment used by ships in the early 20th century. She'd studied the photos and read up on it, realising for the first time the enormous part such equipment had played in the *Titanic* story. Without Marconi equipment probably no lives would have been saved, and it was even possible that the world would never have known what happened to the 'unsinkable' ship. She'd composed a quick email to Henry, outlining what she'd discovered and asking if he was interested in acquiring the equipment.

Guglielmo Marconi, she learned, was a pioneer of wireless telegraphy and the first person to realise that it could compete with transatlantic telegraph cables, if only the signal range could be sufficiently extended. The first land to land transatlantic transmission had been achieved in 1902 but for signals between ships the range was not as far. Even so, by 1912 most ships carried Marconi wireless equipment.

At last, it was time to finish for the day. Jackie switched off her laptop and put away the *Carpathia* items. There was still more to do on the notebook but that would have to wait for another time. She shrugged on her jacket and left the office, walking out through the grand entrance hall of Henry's country estate and across the gravel car park. She took her phone out of her pocket and called Tim to talk about what his plans were that evening. She didn't feel like cooking, and if he didn't either they'd need to buy a takeaway. She could pick one up on the way home.

His phone went straight to voicemail, so she left a brief message. He called back within minutes, just as she was getting into her car.

'Just wondered what you want to do for dinner tonight,' she asked. 'I'm not in the mood for cooking so . . .'

'Actually, I'm out tonight,' Tim interrupted. 'Parents' evening. Had you forgotten?'

She had, but even so, usually parents' evenings were over by seven-thirty and he'd be home for dinner. 'Will you get a takeaway on your way back from that then?'

'Er, no. Phil and Janice suggested a few of us go out for a pizza after.' Phil and Janice were two other teachers at his school, with whom Tim occasionally socialised.

'Oh . . .'

'You could come too? I think Janice is bringing her other half along.' Tim sounded as though he was hoping she'd say no. In any case, Jackie had no intention of going out and being sociable with people she barely knew that evening.

'No, sorry Tim, I'm not up to that.'

'You went to work . . .'

'Yes, and sat in an office by myself all day. Barely spoke to anyone else. Tim, I was hoping for a quiet night in, you and I, sitting in front of the TV. After—'

'Sorry, love. I'm free Thursday night. Book me in for a snuggle on the sofa then, eh? Look, I've got to go. Need to set up, ready for the parents' evening. First appointments are in half an hour. I'll be back . . . about eleven-ish, I should think. Love you, bye.'

Jackie stared at her phone. He'd hung up without even waiting for her to say goodbye. He hadn't asked how she was, how her day had been. She'd forgotten about the parents' evening, it was true, and of course it wasn't something he could get out of. But he could have made excuses not to go out for pizza after, and come home to her instead. Especially given how fragile she was feeling. She glanced at her watch. It was just coming up for six o'clock. Five hours until she'd see Tim. Five hours on her own at home, with just the TV for company. It had been all right at work – there'd been plenty to do and plenty to occupy her mind. Home was a different story. All those baby equipment catalogues were still stacked beside the sofa, reminding her of what she'd lost.

She picked up her phone again and called Sarah. The one person who would help, who knew she'd been pregnant and would understand her sense of loss.

'Hey up,' Sarah answered. 'It's Monday. What you doing on the phone to me on a Monday?' It was true, they never normally spoke on Mondays. Wednesdays were more usual, to arrange their nights out which were almost always on Thursdays.

'You free tonight? I . . . could do with a chat . . .' Jackie tried to keep her voice light. She hadn't yet told Sarah about the miscarriage.

There must have been something in her voice that alerted Sarah to her problems. 'Martin's out tonight so I can't go out, but if you can come round, I'll put Bobby to bed early and we can have some wine . . . or not, as you're . . . Oh my God. Are you all right?'

Jackie suppressed a sob. 'I lost the baby.'

'Oh, honey. Right, we'll definitely have that wine then. Come round whenever you want. I'll start on Bobby's bedtime right now.'

'Thanks, mate.'

Jackie drove straight there. She couldn't face her own, empty home. Martin answered the door to her; he had not yet gone out. Sarah must have told him the news for he wordlessly pulled her into a sympathetic embrace before ushering her through to the sitting room. 'Sarah is just finishing off getting Bobby into bed. He was worn out after his day at nursery today, so she'll be with you very soon. I'm sorry, I've got something on that I can't get out of or I'd have stayed home to babysit . . . but maybe you'd prefer to stay in anyway? I'm so sorry to hear your news, Jackie. Terrible thing.' He looked as though he was about to say something more, perhaps to ask how Tim had taken it, but at that moment Sarah came in to the room and she too immediately hugged Jackie.

'Honey, I'm so sorry. Sit down. I'll fetch that wine, unless you wanted something else?'

'Wine's good. I'll have to leave my car here though.' It was only a half-hour walk home from Sarah's anyway, or she could call a taxi.

'No problem. I'll get you a glass. Martin's just on his way out.'

A few minutes later they were alone, with Bobby sleeping upstairs and Martin gone. Jackie took a sip of the wine Sarah had poured her and told her friend the whole story, including Tim's apparent relief that fatherhood was no longer imminent for him.

'I'm sure you're reading too much into it,' Sarah said, but there was a frown line at the bridge of her nose. 'I don't think men see early miscarriage in quite the same way we do.'

'They have no idea. I think only people who've been through it can really understand.'

Sarah nodded sagely, and bit her lip. Something about the gesture made Jackie think that her friend understood only too well how it felt. 'Sarah, did you . . . have you ever . . .'

'Yes. An early one, like you.'

'Oh Sarah. You never said!'

'It was ages ago. It was so early we hadn't told anyone.'

'I'm so sorry. And how . . . how was Martin after? How did

he take it?' Jackie was almost longing to hear that Martin's reaction had been just like Tim's, that Tim wasn't acting unusually.'

'He cried his eyes out. Martin's very sensitive. Perhaps more than Tim. Or perhaps Tim just doesn't like to show his emotions.'

Jackie shook her head. 'I don't think this is Tim being macho and hiding his feelings. I think he was honestly pissed off when I got pregnant ahead of the schedule we agreed. And now, in his mind, we're back on the track we should have been following. All he can think about is this trip to Italy in July.'

'The hiking trip?'

'Yes. I'd have been able to do it pregnant although I might have wanted to cut it short, or perhaps only do part of it myself, especially if I was feeling sick or tired. Now Tim just sees the miscarriage as removal of an obstacle that stood in the way of his full enjoyment of it.'

'Ah, now, Jackie, I think you might be being a little unfair to him, there.'

'You didn't see his expression. When I told him I'd lost the baby – and remember, I'd only been back from the hospital an hour – he looked relieved. Just for a brief moment, but it was definitely relief.'

'Maybe,' Sarah said carefully, taking Jackie's hand, 'maybe it was relief that you were all right. Tim's a good bloke, Jackie. You've been together a long time. Don't write him off over this.'

'I'm not,' Jackie said, but even to herself her voice carried no conviction. *Was* she writing him off over it? Did she see this as the beginning of the end for them? After thirteen years together? Would she be able to forgive him, to forget that momentary expression on his face, that may have been accidental as Sarah had suggested? Or would she always remember it, driving a wedge between them for ever?

'Look, you had a trauma, just two days ago. You're bereaved, you're upset. And so's Tim, in his own way, I'm sure. You both need to allow yourselves to process this, to let some time pass. It's not easy. And in the meantime, be kind to each other. Be kind to yourself too. At times like this you need to put your own needs first.'

Jackie took a gulp of her wine. 'He's not been kind to me. I mean, take this evening. He had to do the parents' evening, but he didn't have to agree to go for pizza with the staff afterwards. He could have come home to be with me.'

Sarah pinched her lips together. 'Hmm. You have a point there. I think I'd have been cross about that too.'

'You see?'

'Want me to talk to him about it? Perhaps he doesn't realise . . . Or Martin would, I'm sure, if you think it'd be better coming from another man . . .'

Jackie shook her head. 'No, I don't think so. It's our problem and we need to deal with it. I'm glad I came here this evening though. You've helped.'

'I've done nothing . . .'

'You've listened. Held my hand. Been sympathetic.' Jackie gave her friend a watery smile. It had helped, simply being with Sarah, talking it through.

'You're very welcome. Any time.'

There was a cry then, from upstairs. 'Ah, no. Bobby. Probably lost his dummy. I won't be a moment.' Sarah darted out of the room and returned a minute later with a still-grizzling Bobby in her arms. 'Sorry. Think he's teething. I need to give him some Calpol and a cuddle before he'll settle again.'

'Let me hold him, while you get the Calpol,' Jackie said, holding out her arms. 'That's all right, isn't it, Bobby, for your Auntie Jackie to cuddle you for a minute?'

Bobby nodded solemnly and reached for her. She took the little boy and cradled his warm little body against her, while Sarah went to the kitchen in search of the medicine.

Jackie rocked back and forth, cooing to Bobby who was clearly sleepy but red spots on his cheeks showed that his gums must be sore. She examined her feelings as she held this child who she

113

knew so well. In a matter of months, she'd expected to be cradling her own baby, but now, well, who knew when that would happen? She'd wondered if she'd feel differently towards Bobby, having lost her own, but no. She didn't. She loved her friend's child just as much as she always had.

'Here, hold him upright a bit more,' Sarah said. She had filled a plastic syringe with a dose of Calpol and was holding it out. Bobby saw it and obediently opened his mouth to take the medicine.

'Good job he likes it,' Jackie said.

'Of course. It tastes amazing, and always does the trick.' Bobby had swallowed it and now was closing his eyes, already looking on the point of sleep. 'Want to put him back in his cot?'

'Sure.' Jackie followed Sarah upstairs and into the room they used as a nursery. A dim night light was switched on in the corner. She gently bent over the cot and laid Bobby down, pulling a cot blanket over him. He snuffled a little and turned his head to one side.

'Asleep already,' Sarah whispered, looking pleased. 'You've got the knack, Jackie. One day you'll be a wonderful mother.'

'Just not quite as soon as I'd thought I would,' Jackie replied, turning away so that Sarah wouldn't see that her comment had provoked a fresh bout of tears. She followed Sarah back downstairs, composing herself as she did so. Another glass of wine would deaden the pain, and then she'd make her way home.

# Chapter 12

## Madeleine, 15 April 1912

In the steerage section of the ship, a couple of decks further down, *Carpathia*'s crew had managed to squeeze in extra bunks, camp beds and piles of blankets on the floor to accommodate the new passengers. People lay in corridors and stairwells, and each cabin was full to bursting. In some, people were sharing narrow single beds. But they were alive and they were safe. They were the lucky ones.

Madeleine approached a group of women who were sitting on a bed in one cabin, the door propped open. They were chatting loudly and smoking, and one of them had smiled and nodded at her as she'd passed. She'd taken that as an invitation.

'Hello, ladies. Do you mind if I come in?'

'Please do, lovey, plenty of room in here, ain't that right, girls?' The woman who spoke had a broad Cockney accent. The others agreed, in a variety of different English accents.

'Thank you. My name is Mrs Meyer, and I'm helping my husband who's a reporter. He is hoping to write a piece about the sinking of the *Titanic* for his newspaper, and wants to capture as many stories from survivors as he can. I wonder if I can ask you a few questions about your experiences?'

'Ooh, would I be in the paper? Me?' the Cockney woman said.

'You would, although of course we can leave out your name if you prefer.'

'Oh no, duckie, put my name in! I'll have to buy meself a copy of the paper when we get to New York, won't I? Be somefink I can show me grandkids. When I have 'em!' She cackled with laughter and the rest of the women joined in. It was infectious, and Madeleine couldn't help but chuckle too.

And then she stopped herself, reminding herself that these women had probably suffered losses just like the others she'd spoken to. They'd also spent a night in a lifeboat in the freezing ocean.

'Sorry, lovey. We shouldn't laugh, not when so many have lost their lives, the poor souls. But it helps us a bit, don't it, girls?' They all agreed, and Madeleine nodded to show she understood.

'Of course. May I take your name?'

'Nancy Smith. You want my story?'

'Yes, please.'

'Well, we was all abed, when we 'eard the bang and the scrape and the terrible noises when we hit that iceberg. I grabbed my friend and we dashed up top. There was one officer what tried to send us back down but we wasn't 'aving any of that, was we, girls? So we went up another way and they was loading women and children onto the lifeboats, so on we got.'

She leaned closer and spoke confidentially to Madeleine. 'I 'eard a gunshot, I did. Wondered if they was firing at some man who'd tried to push 'is way through.'

'A gunshot!'

'It was into the air. Don't listen to her,' said a woman with startlingly red hair.

'And you were all on the same lifeboat?'

'We was. It was packed. We didn't all know each other before, but we made friends, like, while we wondered if we was all going to die.'

'Were you travelling alone?' Madeleine braced herself for the answer. Who had Nancy lost?

'I was, yes. On me way to join me 'usband. He went to New York last year, got 'imself a job and a place to live, then he wrote me a letter what said I should come an' join 'im. Good job I survived, innit? He'd 'ave been devastated if I 'adn't.'

'He'll certainly be pleased to see you. What about the rest of you? Did any of you . . . lose anyone?' Maddy looked around the group but they all shook their heads. These women here were the fortunate ones, it seemed. Though Madeleine couldn't help but wonder if the extent of the tragedy might hit them later on, when they'd had time to process it.

'Fink we're lucky, ain't we all?' Nancy said, as though she'd heard Maddy's thoughts. 'There's some what have lost husbands, friends, children. Tragic, innit.' She shook her head sadly and there was a moment's quiet while they contemplated it all.

'It is, yes. I've been talking to women who've lost husbands. And one who's looking for a child, a baby, who she thinks was pushed onto a lifeboat by her husband, who was sadly lost.'

'Well, I ain't seen any babbies crawling around down here all alone, that's for sure,' Nancy said. 'But I'll come and find you if I do. That poor woman.'

'Yes, indeed. And thank you.' Maddy scribbled some more notes and left the group. Her mind was still on the missing baby. 'All alone,' Nancy had said. The one Violet had brought on board couldn't be classed as alone.

As she left the group of women, she decided to do a thorough trawl of the communal areas in the steerage section, searching everywhere for the woman in brown and her baby. She had no idea what she would say or do if she found them, but she'd promised Lucy Watts she would do all she could to search for her lost child. Further interviews for Ralph could wait. This search was more important.

But there was no sign of either the woman or her child. Madeleine could hardly knock on closed cabin doors, but she checked public areas and peeked into all open cabins. She did the same in second class, and also checked the public first class areas. All to no avail.

'How did you get on?' Ralph asked Madeleine when she returned to their cabin. 'With the women, I mean?'

'All right, I think. I've written a lot of notes.' She waved the notebook in front of him.

'That's my girl.' He looked delighted. 'Any good stories so far?'

'Yes, some. But one woman doesn't want her name in the papers. She'd run off to marry and her husband's family don't know and don't approve of her. And now he's dead.'

Ralph's eyes lit up, but he quickly replaced his expression of delight with one of sympathy. 'That's awful, and, of course, I don't need to use her real name. You're doing well, Maddy.'

Something occurred to her, a question she had to ask. 'How are you going to get the story to the papers? You'll have to wait until we are back in New York, and then there'll be other reporters swarming all over the ship. Your story will already be written, but isn't it possible that . . .'

'That someone else will get the scoop if they're quick? I've thought of that, Maddy, darling.' He looked pleased with himself, and patted her hand. 'Remember I made friends with the Marconi operator? Harold Cottam, his name is. Well, I'm going to take my story to him, once it's complete. And then as soon as we're within range of a wireless station on shore I'll get him to send it to New York. So my story will reach the papers before the ship reaches New York, and the scoop will be mine. It'll make my name, Maddy.'

She felt torn. It was good that he was so fired up about this and that he'd get the scoop, but how terrible that it was all because of such an awful tragedy and the loss of so many lives.

He must have seen the conflict on her face, for he reached

118

out to her and gently stroked the side of her face. 'It's the right thing to do, remember, Maddy? It's what we can do for these poor people. It isn't only about me getting the scoop. It's important to get the truth, the full story, told. I am a writer, I'm here on the spot, I can tell their story, tell the world what has happened. People have a right to know the truth of it as soon as possible, don't they? Especially the friends and families of *Titanic*'s passengers.'

'Yes, you're right.' She smiled at him. She considered telling Ralph about the baby, and Lucy Watts. But it wasn't the right time. Not until she had the full story, whatever it was. 'I'll go now, and talk to some more of the survivors.' And of course she could keep her eyes open for the baby and the woman in brown as she moved around the ship.

'Thank you. I'm off to find out what I can from more of the crew members.'

'Should you go and talk to Harold Cottam, make sure he knows what you will be asking him to do.'

'I already went up to the Marconi cabin and had a quick word with him. The captain has prepared a brief message, saying only that *Titanic* has gone down and that *Carpathia* has picked up all survivors, and Cottam's instructed to send that as soon as possible. Even though we're not within range of a land-based receiving station, a short message could be relayed from ship to ship. The world needs to know what's happened. It'll be at least three days before we're back in New York, and probably two days before we're within range of a wireless station on land. At that point I hope my story might be sent too.' Ralph pulled a face. 'Poor Cottam's exhausted. I believe he was up all night and the captain's sent him off for some rest. Apparently, the *Titanic*'s Marconi operator survived and is on board. He'll be an interesting person to interview too, if I can find him.'

'I expect he's resting too. Good luck, Ralph.'

'You too.'

She kissed him and left the cabin, wondering how best to

continue searching for the baby. *Titanic*'s survivors had been accommodated all over the ship, many in private cabins, and she'd already checked all the public areas. Perhaps her best chance now was to look for that stewardess, Violet Jessop, who'd brought the baby on board. She might know something more. She might have seen the woman who took the baby again.

She headed off on another tour of the ship, keeping her eyes open. In a saloon she came across the chief steward, and asked him if he knew where the *Titanic* stewardesses had been housed.

'There are two or three of them in a cabin along there,' he replied, pointing. 'Third one on the left.'

She thanked him but he'd already turned away to deal with some other query. He, like all of *Carpathia*'s crew, looked exhausted. They'd all been up most of the night.

Madeleine headed towards the cabin he'd indicated and tapped on the door. A woman's voice answered and she went in. Sitting on the beds were three women in White Star Line stewardess uniforms, an older woman and two younger. One of whom was Violet Jessop.

'Oh, I hoped for a moment it'd be Ruby at the door,' the younger woman said with a sob, and the third, the older woman, put her arm around her to comfort her.

'Ssh, Emma. We'll keep looking. If she's on the ship I'm sure we'll find her soon.'

'Emma, this is the kind passenger from this ship who helped me and many others as we came on board. I'm sorry I don't know your name?' Violet looked at Madeleine questioningly.

'I'm Mrs Madeleine Meyer. I hope you are feeling better, Miss Jessop? And your friends?'

'We're all right. Emma has poorly feet from sitting with them in cold water for so long, and she cannot find her sister, another stewardess, named Ruby Higgins. So if you come across her on your travels around the ship please send her here.'

'Yes, please do,' added Emma.

'Of course. Miss Jessop, I came to see if you had seen that baby again, or the woman who took her? I was talking to a passenger from *Titanic* who's searching for her baby, who she was sure she saw being handed to someone on the last lifeboat by her husband, who is sadly lost.'

'That does sound like the baby I looked after. But I thought the woman who took it was the mother?'

'I'd assumed so too, but this other woman, Lucy Watts, seems so distraught.'

'Oh dear. Well, no, I haven't seen the baby or the woman again. I've been in here mostly. I wish you luck, Mrs Meyer.'

'Thank you.' Now was the time to ask them if they wished to tell their stories, but something about the sobbing Emma with her sore feet made the words freeze in her mouth. These women had been through enough. 'I shall look for Ruby for you. Best wishes, to all of you.'

She left them then, to continue a tour of the ship, looking for Ruby Higgins, or Norah, or the woman in brown and her baby. If only she could reunite someone with someone else, how wonderful that would be! And what a story it would make for Ralph. She remembered then Evelyn and her cousins – they'd been reunited and that was a good story but, of course, Ralph already knew it. Even so it'd be worth interviewing the Marshall women if they'd agree to it. Perhaps there were more such stories, if she found the right people to talk to. She wanted more and more to play a part in the telling of the *Titanic* story.

Heading back towards the first-class dining room, she came upon Dr McGee. 'Excuse me, Doctor. I'm trying to help a woman who's lost her baby. Are there any orphans on board? She's given me a detailed description of what the child was wearing.'

'Well, there are some children in the second-class lounge, being fed and nursed there. Only two are orphans – two little boys who don't speak a word of English. Who is the poor mother you are trying to help?'

'Her name is Lucy Watts, Doctor.'

'Ah, Mrs Watts. Yes, I know of her. She is in fact in the lounge now, with her baby. She came on board with him in her arms.'

'Her son? He is an older child, I think? She said she's looking for a very young baby girl.'

'It was a child of two or three months she brought with her. Boy or girl, whatever. I'm sorry, there are so many and I'm probably getting confused. Anyway, go in there and speak to Mrs Watts by all means. I must dash.'

He then took his leave and Madeleine followed the passageway along to the lounge and went in. In a back corner, sitting on an armchair nursing a baby, was Lucy Watts. Madeleine smiled and walked over. 'Mrs Watts! You have found your baby. I am so pleased for you.'

But Lucy looked up at her with frightened eyes and shook her head. 'No, not this one. I'm looking for my little girl. Norah, as I told you. She's gone.'

A nurse who'd been bottle feeding another baby nearby touched Madeleine's elbow and leaned in to whisper to her. 'Take no notice of that one. She's been ranting about having lost her baby but as you can see, she hasn't. I think the trauma's affected her head, the poor dear.'

And as if to prove the nurse right, Lucy began rocking back and forth, moaning. As she rocked forward, she was squeezing the child on her lap, and soon it was crying with discomfort. 'There now, Mrs Watts,' said the nurse. 'You'll hurt your little one. Give him here and we'll put him in a crib, how about that?' She took the baby from Lucy and laid him into an empty crib nearby. As she tucked a blanket around the child, Madeleine caught a glimpse of a tiny silver bracelet on its wrist, just as Lucy had described to her.

'Mrs Watts, would you like to lie down and rest? Over there on that sofa, perhaps, so that you're not far from your baby.' The nurse gently raised Lucy to her feet and led her to the couch.

Madeleine watched as Lucy lay down and allowed herself to be covered with a blanket. A moment later her eyes were closed and she appeared to be sleeping.

'Is she going to be all right?' Madeleine asked the nurse.

'I expect so. I think she's traumatised from losing her husband and it's made her confused. Rest and time will work wonders.' The nurse smiled kindly at the sleeping Lucy and then returned to her duties with other patients.

Madeline looked down at Lucy and nodded. What the nurse had said made sense. Lucy had her baby, wearing the bracelet she'd described. The other baby, the one Violet had brought on board, must belong to the woman who'd snatched it from Violet. It was the only explanation. But Lucy had said she had two children, Norah and Frederick. And she hadn't seemed confused when Madeleine spoke to her earlier. Traumatised, distraught, yes, but not confused. Madeleine had assumed the other child Lucy had mentioned was older, but this baby she was holding now looked to be just a couple of months old, the same age Lucy had said Norah was. Twins, then, perhaps.

She turned to look at Lucy's baby, now sleeping in the crib. So Lucy had given birth to two healthy babies, while she, Madeleine, had failed to keep even one. It seemed so unfair. She couldn't help the wave of jealousy that surged through her, even though at the same time her heart broke for Lucy who had lost a baby she loved.

# Chapter 13

## Jackie, 2022

'Buy it at once,' was Henry's reply to Jackie's email asking if he was interested in the antique Marconi equipment she'd found for sale. He phoned the next afternoon from New York, to set a budget for it. 'And if you get it, could you write me a piece explaining how it worked and the impact it had on communications, especially the role it played in the *Titanic* story? I don't need *War and Peace* on it, just a couple of sides.'

Jackie smiled. 'So you can impress people with your in-depth knowledge? You could always read up on it on Wikipedia.'

Henry laughed. 'Well, yes. Precisely that. But I prefer the way you write. You'll pick out the salient points for me, I know. I'd do the research myself if I had time. When I retire.' He coughed. 'You'll be out of a job, then, you realise?'

'You'll never retire.' He enjoyed the cut and thrust of business too much, Jackie had always thought.

'You're probably right.'

'Anyway, yes, of course I'll research it and write it up. It's an interesting topic. Oh, by the way, that notebook in the

*Carpathia* box seems to be interview notes with *Titanic* survivors. I'm transcribing it all, and following up on the names mentioned.'

'Nice. Anything juicy?'

'Possibly . . .' She was thinking of Lucy Watts's lost baby, with the engraved silver bangle. 'I'll write it all up for you.' She was pleased at the prospect of the work. Anything she could get stuck into would help take her mind off the miscarriage.

'Thanks. OK then, got to dash. Be back next week for a couple of days. Then Clarissa is dragging me off to the Maldives.'

'Oh, Henry. It's a tough life.'

He laughed 'It is. I mustn't complain.' But there was something in his voice that told her he'd much prefer to come home to his Berkshire estate and live quietly there for a few weeks, rather than go on yet another trip.

'How is Clarissa?' Jackie asked.

'Oh, you know. Needy.' Henry sighed. 'Well, I must go.'

'See you then,' she said, as he hung up.

Jackie was thankful to have interesting work lined up once again. Tim had come home late, a little drunk, and had barely spoken to her. She was sleeping in the spare room – she'd been there since the miscarriage, since Tim's reaction to the news. She knew he hated that – he wanted her back beside him – but until she'd seen some sort of understanding from him, a little compassion, she didn't want him near her. Also, oddly, because the spare room had been intended as the nursery, she somehow felt closer to their lost baby in there. She'd lie awake at night, gazing around in the gloom, picturing the room the way she'd planned it for when the baby came. Then she'd relive the miscarriage and cry a little, until sleep eventually came.

She turned her attention to the website offering the Marconi equipment for sale, and soon after had secured the purchase. It would be delivered within a few days, and no doubt Henry would want to display it in the room in his country house that she called the 'museum'. With the purchase made, the next job was to do that write-up that he wanted.

She spent a few interesting hours over the next couple of days reading around the subject and making notes. It was odd to think that before Marconi invented wireless telegraphy there was no way to contact a ship at sea unless it was within sight. It was hard to imagine such limitations now that news travelled around the world almost instantaneously. Now people expected to be in immediate contact with each other at all times. Phones, communications satellites, the Internet, Google, social media and the rest had all meant that information such as what had happened to *Titanic* would now be known around the planet within hours, minutes even, of it happening. Back then, relatives of *Titanic*'s passengers had to wait days before they found out the truth. She read about how Captain Rostron of the *Carpathia* had managed to send a brief message to say that they had picked up all survivors but then it was days before any more details were known about the disaster. How frustrating must that have been!

She read through the newspaper articles relating to *Titanic* that had been stored in the box. It was clear that newspaper editors had been prepared to print anything, any rumour they heard, as fact, in the days while the world waited for details. Papers reported that *Titanic* was crippled but being towed to port, with all passengers surviving. Another said that she'd sunk with the loss of all on board. The *Times Despatch* complained that *Carpathia* was not giving out any details.

The papers dated after *Carpathia* reached New York were the first that reported the truth. Jackie read interviews with surviving officers from *Titanic*, and with the Marconi operator. The article by journalist Ralph Meyer was the most interesting, as there were details which chimed with what was written in the notebook. He'd been on board *Carpathia* and had interviewed survivors as they were picked up. Her hunch had been right, then, that the Ralph mentioned in the notebook was Ralph Meyer. She Googled his name and found a brief mention of him having been on *Carpathia* with his wife Madeleine.

'Madeleine Meyer. M.M. I have you now,' Jackie said, pleased to put a name to the writer of the notebook. The woman who'd suffered a miscarriage and who'd found herself moved by Lucy Watts's story, just as Jackie was, over a hundred years later.

The story was gradually falling into place. One thing was confusing, however – why had Madeleine's notebook been in the possession of a *Carpathia* crew member? The uniform and cap pointed to the box having belonged to a steward, but somehow a reporter's notebook, belonging to a passenger, had come into their possession and been stored in the box by the steward's descendants. There were still so many questions.

But she needed to get back to the write-up of early Marconi equipment, as Henry had requested. She wrote up all she'd found out, putting together a page on how early Marconi equipment was installed on ships and how it worked, and then a page detailing the part it played in the *Titanic* story. She was intrigued to discover that the distress sign 'SOS' was not yet in common usage in 1912, and instead, *Titanic* had sent out the sign 'CQD'.

'I wonder what that stood for,' she pondered. 'Come Quickly, Dammit! perhaps.' She Googled it and discovered that 'CQ' simply indicated an incoming message, and the D stood for Distress. Later, 'SOS' was adopted as it was easier to remember and transmit the Morse code for it – dot dot dot, dash dash dash, dot dot dot.

'I am becoming as much of an antiquarian techno-geek as Henry,' she muttered, as she made a note of that fact too.

The memoirs of *Titanic* stewardess Violet Jessop had arrived, and Jackie read that book quickly, skimming over the early parts but reading in detail the chapters relating to *Titanic*. Her mouth dropped open when she read that as Violet was boarding the last lifeboat, a man had pushed through the crowds and thrust a baby into her arms. She'd cradled it during the long dark hours of that night. When she'd come on board *Carpathia*, a woman had rushed forward and taken the child from her. She'd never seen it again.

Jackie turned back to the journalist's notebook and reread the notes on Lucy Watts. The name Violet Jessop was there with a question mark. Madeleine Meyer perhaps must have known something of Violet's story and had made the same connection Jackie was making now, 110 years later. Had that child been the one Lucy Watts was searching for? Who, then, had taken it? According to her memoir, Violet had assumed she was the baby's mother, but what if she wasn't? Clearly, it hadn't been Lucy.

'Ooh, we've got a real mystery here!' She made another note, then glanced at a clock on the wall. It was well after six. She normally didn't stay in the office beyond six. Tim would be home before her, wondering where she was. Well, let him wonder. He'd been cool towards her for days. She was still waiting for some sort of apology, some acknowledgement of the trauma she'd suffered. And the longer she spent immersed in her research, the less time she spent reliving the miscarriage or fretting about their future. Instead of thinking of her own loss, she could think about poor Lucy Watts and Madeleine Meyer, who'd both also lost a child. These two women, so long ago, to whom she felt a deep connection.

As the days wore on and summer arrived, Jackie realised that she and Tim were slipping into a new pattern. They were housemates, no longer really 'living together' as they had been. More like ships in the night, passing each other without really communicating. She'd stayed in the spare room, and Tim seemed to accept it. Only once had he asked her when she was coming back into their shared room. She'd simply shrugged in answer and he hadn't pushed the question any further. She didn't feel ready to move back. Not until he realised how devastating the miscarriage had been for her. Not until she was confident they wanted the same things for their future. Her loss had changed everything.

A fortnight after the miscarriage, the follow-up scan confirmed the pregnancy was over. It was no surprise, but even so the news made Jackie feel flat and bereaved once more. She'd hoped Tim might come with her, but the date clashed with his school's sports day, so in the end she hadn't even asked him.

That evening, telling Tim the miscarriage was confirmed was a chance for him to take her into his arms and show his own sadness at their loss, at last. She watched him carefully as she told him the news. But his reaction was simply to shrug and turn away. 'Well, we knew that anyway, didn't we?' he said.

'Yes, but I suppose there was still a nugget of hope . . .'

He turned away from her, opened the fridge and took out a can of beer. 'Hmm,' he said, as he opened it. 'So let's put it all behind us now, eh?'

'I'm trying to.' But Jackie felt tears pricking at her eyes once more. Not at the loss of the pregnancy, for which she'd already grieved and accepted as much as she'd ever be able to. But for the lack of understanding, the absence of sympathy, from Tim. It cut to her core. She had to leave the room, go to what she now thought of as 'her' bedroom and lie down, staring at the ceiling, wondering how it could all have gone so wrong.

It was as though, Jackie thought, their long relationship was reaching a natural end. If she hadn't miscarried, they'd be needing to cement their relationship, perhaps marry and make it 'official', to ensure a stable future for their child. But she had miscarried, and in losing the baby it seemed she was now losing Tim. Or he was losing her. She was sad about this but resigned to it. Tim's reaction to the pregnancy and miscarriage, his unwillingness or inability to talk about it now – it all made her feel that perhaps they no longer wanted the same things from life. Perhaps their relationship had run its course. They were at a crossroads and were each eyeing up different directions for their future.

One evening, she returned from work to find Tim had laid out all his Italian maps and books across the living room floor once more. She stepped over them, on her way to the kitchen to make herself a cup of tea.

'Thought you were out tonight?' she said, as she passed.

'No, I cancelled on Alfie. Need a free evening to finally pin down our route through the mountains.'

She stared down at the maps and realised something she'd been avoiding thinking about. How could she spend a few weeks living in a tent with Tim, when she could barely even look at him, since seeing his reaction to her miscarriage?

She said nothing for the moment, and went to make herself the tea. 'Make me one, please?' Tim called to her, and she grudgingly did so, without answering. Returning to the sitting room she placed his tea on a side table and sat on an armchair, as far from the maps and books as she could.

'Jacks? Move over here so you can see, and I'll show you the route,' Tim said, picking up his tea and taking a sip.

'Tim, I don't think we should go. We barely talk any more. How can we spend weeks in the mountains together?'

'What?' He put down his cup and stared at her.

She stared back. How could this have come as a surprise to him? 'Well, we don't, do we? Not since . . . you know.' The tears would come if she said, 'Not since we lost the baby', and right now, she didn't want to cry.

'I know we've been going through a rough patch. I understand that you needed time, on your own in the spare room, to get over what happened. But I thought the Abruzzo trip would be a kind of reset? A way to bring us back together this summer? Like the old times, when we had so many adventures, so much fun . . .' He tailed off, frowning, as she shook her head.

'I don't think so. I think we've gone beyond that, Tim.'

'You promised though, one last big trip. Then afterwards, if you're up to it, we try for a baby, like you wanted . . .'

That was exactly the problem, she thought. He saw a baby as something *she* wanted. Not something they both wanted.

130

How was that any basis for starting a family? They needed to both want the same thing, and for something as important as children, for her it was fundamental that they were absolutely on the same page.

'That agreement was before. Now, I'm not so sure,' she said.

There was a flash of something that looked like hopefulness that crossed his face. 'You mean, you're not sure about starting a family?'

'No! I don't mean that at all! For goodness' sake, Tim! I mean this Italian trip. I'm not sure about going on it.'

He stared at her. 'Why not? I thought you were excited about it. You were when we first talked about it.'

'That was before.' She was exasperated with him. Why was he being obtuse? He must have noticed the change in their relationship.

'Before your troubles? I thought you'd recovered from all that.' There it was again – him dismissing the miscarriage as something that had happened to her, that didn't directly affect him. Her 'troubles'. He made it sound like a bad period.

'Physically, yes, but . . .'

'Well, then.'

She sighed with exasperation. He still didn't understand a miscarriage was so much more than a physical problem for her. 'But . . . Tim. We're not getting on like we used to, are we? Maybe we need a break from each other.' There. She'd said it. She watched carefully to see his reaction.

'A break? How do you mean?' He looked stunned, winded, as though she'd punched him in the gut.

'I mean . . . you go. By yourself, or with one of your mates, whatever. Leave me here alone to sort myself out. You'll have your adventure, I'll have some space and headroom to get over the miscarriage. Then when you're back . . . we see where we are and what we want to do next.'

'Go by myself?' He repeated the words quietly. Jackie felt hurt

131

all over again, that from all she'd said, the part he was picking out was the idea of a holiday on his own. Not the hint she'd dropped that maybe their relationship had run its course. Truth be told, she didn't know whether it had or whether this was just a blip, something they'd get over in time, a period they'd look back on in years to come and laugh about how daft they'd been. All she knew was she needed some time away from him, to work out what she really wanted from life now. Perhaps she was being selfish, but then, as Sarah had told her, sometimes you had to put yourself first. Your own needs – what you needed to do for your own health, physical and mental – sometimes had to take priority over everything and everyone else, including those you loved best. And she did still love Tim. Very much. But it had been hard these last few weeks, and she knew she needed time apart from him.

'I'd thought,' he was saying now, 'that the trip would help us become closer again. I mean,' he ran a hand through his hair, 'I realise things haven't been quite right lately. And I suppose some of that is my fault. Maybe I didn't, I dunno, empathise enough with you? Maybe I didn't realise how hard you were taking losing that pregnancy. And I guess I'm sorry. It all seemed so distant, like it was just a . . . thought experiment or something. Because it happened sooner than we'd planned, I hadn't really got my head round it.'

Hurray, Jackie thought. He had noticed. He was apologising, kind of, for his distant manner lately, for his lack of understanding. Still, it didn't change the fact that he hadn't engaged fully with the idea of them starting a family, or with the subsequent loss of what, after all, was his child too.

He cleared his throat and continued. 'So . . . you think I should go to Italy on my own? Leave you alone? It'd be four weeks on your own . . .'

'Yes, I think you should. I think it'll be good for us both.'

He gazed at her for a moment, then nodded slowly. 'If it's

what you want. You could be right. I'll be back in mid-August, and we can . . .'

'Decide what we want to do then. Talk about our future.'

'Yes.' He glanced away, thrust his hands into his pockets, then looked back at her. 'I hope, very much hope, that this isn't the end for us, Jacks. We've been together so long, we've had great times. This can't be it.'

She pulled a tissue from the box beside her and dabbed at her eyes. 'I hope not. We'll talk about it when you come back.' But they had to want the same things, if they were to carry on together. If he wasn't sure about being a parent, then perhaps it would be the end. It would be very wrong for them to bring a child into a family where only one parent wanted it. 'You're off in two weeks, aren't you?'

He nodded. 'I need to book my flights, now I know it's just me.'

'Yes.'

'OK, then.'

And there seemed to be nothing more they wanted to say to each other. Jackie sat for a minute longer then went to her bedroom, to lie down and read a book. She heard the sounds of Tim gathering up his maps, and a few minutes later the front door opened and closed. He'd gone out. She heaved a sigh of relief, and went to the kitchen to prepare herself a meal for one.

133

# Chapter 14

## Madeleine, 16 April 1912

The following day, Ralph worked hard on writing his story. 'I've heard a lot from Harold Cottam about how *Carpathia* picked up the first distress messages,' he told Madeleine in their cabin. 'It's incredible to think he was just about to retire for the night when the signal came in. He rushed to see Captain Rostron immediately, and the captain made an instant decision to go to *Titanic*'s aid. If the message had arrived just minutes later, we'd never have received it.'

'Thank goodness for that. He's a good man,' Madeleine said. 'If he hadn't, then all those poor people we picked up would have died too.' It didn't bear thinking about.

'You're right. There was no other ship in the area. Although I have spoken to some survivors who say that early on, not long after *Titanic* had struck the iceberg, they saw another ship on the horizon. One close enough to pick up distress signals and see flares.'

'Were flares sent up? I know we saw some from one of the lifeboats.'

'Yes, *Titanic* sent up several rockets before it sank. If that other ship had come closer, it might have been able to save more people. The ones who didn't make it onto lifeboats.'

Madeleine shook her head sadly. Why hadn't the other ship responded? There'd be an inquiry, of course. She hoped the truth would eventually come out. 'You're going to put all this into your story?'

'Yes. Maybe not the first story, but I think there will be many tales to tell of this tragedy. I've spoken to *Titanic*'s Marconi operator too. He remained at his post for as long as he could, sending distress messages. He used the new signal – SOS – as well as the old distress signal CQD Only *Carpathia* responded, and he messaged us to *come at once*.'

'Thank goodness for Mr Marconi's invention then, as well as for our quick-acting captain.'

'Indeed. I'm going to write a brief story first, that can be sent by Marconi message as soon as we're within range of the shore. And an in-depth one, with all the survivors' stories, that I'll take to the *New York Tribune* office as soon as we dock in New York. It'll be the making of me, Maddy!'

His eyes shone with pride and excitement, and she had to look away. All that had been preying on her mind for days was Lucy Watts and her lost baby. And that inevitably led to her thinking of the baby Violet Jessop had brought on board, the one she'd held for that wonderful brief moment, and from there her thoughts turned to her own loss and the impossibility of her ever becoming a mother.

Something of what she was thinking must have shown on her face, for Ralph turned to her and took her in his arms. 'Oh, Maddy. Our life together has not panned out the way we thought it would, when we married. I'm so sorry we lost the baby and are never going to be parents. But we will find a new purpose in life, and this . . . this just might be the start of it. Don't you see?'

'I do see, Ralph, darling. But saying we are never going to be parents . . . might there not be a way? I mean, we could adopt a child perhaps?'

'Adopt? I don't think . . . I had not thought of it . . .' Ralph didn't look too thrilled with the idea.

'We don't have to decide immediately. But after this trip, when we're back home, we could talk about it?'

'Yes, when we're back home, we can look into it, I daresay.' Ralph nodded and then picked up his pipe and lit it. A signal, Madeleine knew, that the subject was closed for now.

She'd surprised herself by suggesting it. She had not once considered adopting a child. Not until now. But that baby snatched from her arms would not leave her thoughts. Ralph's reaction had disappointed her. They'd need to both want to do it, for it to work. That much she understood. It felt important to her that children should only be brought into a family where both parents truly wanted them.

As if there hadn't been enough emotion already, later that day, Madeleine was reduced to tears yet again. A few people had been brought on board from the lifeboats already dead, and one more had died since of his injuries. Another religious service was held and the victims were buried at sea. Madeleine attended, as did many other *Carpathia* passengers. It was the least they could do, to pay their respects.

Each body, wrapped and stitched into canvas, was tipped into the sea as the reverend spoke the words: 'We therefore commit their bodies to the deep, in sure and certain hope of the resurrection of their bodies, when the sea shall give up her dead.' Madeleine closed her eyes and sent up a prayer, to a God she was not sure she believed in any more. What merciful God would have taken all these innocent souls, for no good reason? What benevolent God would have deprived her and Ralph of the chance to be parents?

She turned away at the end of the service, knowing there were no answers.

'Madeleine? It feels like ages since we spoke. Do you have some time now, perhaps?' It was Evelyn Marshall. She looked tired and a little dishevelled. The new *Carpathia* look, Madeleine thought, now so many were sharing cabins and even beds.

'Evelyn, my dear, it's good to see you. Yes, of course. Shall we sit on deck? It's a lot warmer now that we've left the ice behind.' She took her friend's arm and led her out on deck, where they managed to find a pair of unoccupied deck chairs, and sat down.

'We're lucky to find these,' Evelyn said. 'With so many on board now, it's hard to find a space if you want to be alone.'

'Indeed, it is. How are your cousins?'

'They're well, and getting over their trauma. They realise how very lucky they are.' Evelyn leaned in closer. 'I hear you and Mr Meyer are collecting survivors' stories and writing articles? I think that's a good thing. There's never been a shipwreck quite like *Titanic* before, and I hope there never will be again. Writing people's stories is a way of remembering those who didn't live to tell their tales, if you see what I mean. When people read about the survivors it'll help them think of those who weren't so lucky.'

'Yes. That's a good way of looking at it,' Madeleine said.

'Will you stay a while in New York when we get back? Or remain on board for Gibraltar as originally planned?'

Madeleine frowned. She and Ralph had not discussed this. Perhaps he would want to stay in the city a while to get his stories written and published. 'I suppose it depends on how soon *Carpathia* sets sail again. I don't really know what we'll do.'

'We're going to postpone our Europe trip a while. Our cousins need us.'

'That's nice of you.'

'It's the least Mama and Papa feel they should do. And I am quite happy to wait and travel later. It's all put me off travelling by sea, if I'm honest.'

'But there's no other way to Europe.'

'One day, Papa says, aeroplanes will fly all the way across the ocean.'

'I think that will be a long way off. And frankly, I would feel safer on a ship on the sea rather than up in the air, wouldn't you?'

Evelyn agreed. Madeleine smiled at her friend. It was good to chat for a while. They moved on to other topics – what they had planned to do in Europe, where they had travelled to on previous trips, even which were their favourite department stores back in New York. And somehow Madeleine found herself telling Evelyn about the miscarriage, about the surgery, about the devastation she'd felt when she'd learned she would never be able to have children.

'Oh, you poor thing,' Evelyn said, her brow creasing with sorrow. 'I can't imagine how that must feel.'

'Well, it's a small thing in comparison with all this . . .' Madeleine waved her hand to encompass the *Titanic* survivors who sat on deck chairs nearby. 'But it's been hard to deal with. It's as though I'm refusing to entirely accept it.' She sighed. 'You know, I bought a soft panda toy when I was pregnant, intending it to be the first toy my baby would have. And I still have it. I have it here, with me, in my travelling trunk. Ralph doesn't know; he'd think I'm silly for keeping it. But somehow, it's as if . . .' She tailed off, not sure how to put the turmoil of her emotions into words.

'As if keeping it keeps the hope alive that one day you'll be a mother?' Evelyn said gently.

Madeleine stared at the younger woman. She understood. She got it. 'Yes, I think that's it exactly.'

Evelyn took her hand and squeezed it. 'Might you adopt? Or are there nieces or nephews you could dote on?'

'Yes, to both, but it will take me a long time to get over not being able to have our own.' Madeleine flashed a smile at her friend. 'Besides, I am not sure Ralph is keen on the idea of adopting.' She recalled the look on his face when she'd suggested it.

'I'm sure he would, if you only tell him how much you want to be a mother.' Evelyn put a supportive hand on her arm. 'Perhaps talk to him about it after this trip?'

'Yes. I will do that. Anyway, I mustn't dwell on it, it's not good for me. Thank you for listening, for being a good friend.'

'Any time.'

A thought occurred to Madeleine. 'Evelyn, do you think your cousins would let me talk to them? About their experiences as *Titanic* sank?'

'Hmm, you can ask them. Caroline would be the most likely. She has been wanting to talk of it all, whereas Charlotte and Malvina think that the less they say of it the quicker they'll forget. Lottie was never one for words, anyway.'

Madeleine remembered the terse response from Charlotte to the Marconi message that had been sent while the girls were still on *Titanic*. How long ago that seemed now! 'Thank you. Well, I shall search out Caroline, then. Perhaps I'll see you later on at dinner?'

'Yes, I hope so.' Dinners were a very different affair now that there were so many more mouths to feed. Gone were the elegant four course meals with waiter service. Now all meals were served as a buffet and the dishes were much simpler. Even so, the kitchens were doing a superb job catering for so many extra people.

They said farewell and Madeleine went in search of Caroline, finding her sitting on a deck chair, a book in her hand, but her gaze was fixed on the horizon rather than the page. 'Miss Caroline Marshall? I am a friend of your cousin Evelyn. My name is Madeleine Meyer. I wonder if you wouldn't mind telling me a little of your experiences? My husband is a journalist, you see, and he wants to capture everyone's stories, before it is too late and everyone is dispersed.'

'For a newspaper article?' There was a look of suspicion in Caroline's eyes, just as Madeleine had seen in the eyes of some of the first people she'd interviewed.

'Yes, or a book. Of course, if you don't want your name in the paper, anything you say can remain anonymous, or if you don't want to talk at all, that's fine, I'll leave you in peace . . .'

'No, no. I want to talk. But, yes, you had better leave my name out. My father might think it vulgar, me being in the papers.' Caroline took a deep breath and began her story, her eyes still fixed on some point out at sea. It was as though, Madeleine thought, in her mind she was still seeing *Titanic*, the lifeboats, and the drowning victims of the disaster.

'And the worst, the very worst thing,' Caroline said, her voice dropping to almost a whisper, 'was all the people in the water when the ship finally went down. We rowed back our lifeboat, to see if we could pick up any survivors. But they were all d-dead. All of them. So many. I saw – my God, the sight will stay with me till my dying day – I saw a baby, a tiny one, tied to an adult's life jacket, just floating there, her little face shining pale in the starlight. I reached for the child, thinking perhaps if we brought her on board and warmed her up she might somehow come back to life, but the officer on the lifeboat told me no, the baby was dead, they were all dead. And he ordered the crewman to row us away from the bodies, and I lost sight of the baby . . . and my heart broke for her. Of all those people, it was that little innocent soul, that poor little one that I will never forget, as long as I live.'

She dipped her head and covered her face with her hands, sobbing. Madeleine put a hand on her shoulder. 'I am so sorry to upset you, Miss Marshall. Please, can I get you anything? A drink, a handkerchief?'

Caroline shook her head, sniffed and composed herself. 'No. I am all right. I must learn to deal with the memory. I think that the more times I say it, the more distant it might become, as though I am recounting a story someone else told me, not anything I experienced myself. Does that make any sense?'

'It does, I think. That poor child. And her poor parents.'

'Yes. I suppose she went into the water with one of them and became separated when they . . . died. Her little face. So still, so peaceful.' Caroline brushed away another tear, and turned her gaze to the horizon again. 'She's still out there, floating on the life jacket. I wish we could have brought her here. I wish she could have been held close one more time, even though she was dead. I wish she could have had a proper burial at sea, so more people would remember her. Such a short life she had.'

'It would have made no difference to her,' Madeleine said gently. 'It is something, though, that you are thinking of her. How do you know it was a little girl?'

Caroline looked at her sadly. 'I don't, for certain, but the little bonnet that was still tied round her head, the tiny dress she was wearing, I just think she was a girl. You know, I almost hope that her parents did die too. It would be too awful to have survived but to have lost your helpless little baby.'

'Indeed.' And Madeleine thought of the agony of Lucy Watts, who was probably in exactly that position. For it was very possible that this poor dead baby might well have been Norah. Lucy might be mistaken in her belief that her husband had managed to push the baby onto a lifeboat. The infant Violet Jessop brought onto the ship might be a different one entirely, and thankfully reclaimed by its mother.

'Excuse me. Now, I think I would like to be alone for a while,' Caroline said.

'Of course. And thank you for speaking to me.' Madeleine held Caroline's hand for a moment as she took her leave. She had not taken any notes while listening to Caroline's story, and as she walked away, back to her cabin, she decided that she wouldn't. This story was too heart-rending. And if it had been Norah, the thought of Lucy reading that story in the paper and recognising her own child was unbearable. Better that this story went no further.

Ralph wasn't in the cabin, and Madeleine guessed he was off doing his own interviews somewhere. She took out the panda bear toy from the bottom of her trunk and regarded it. What a stupid little thing it was. Trying to keep alive the idea that one day she'd have a child of her own to whom she could give it, when there was so much real suffering right here on the ship. She made a snap decision, stuffed the toy into a bag and left the cabin again. There were children on board; survivors from *Titanic* with a far greater need for a stuffed panda than she had.

She trawled the public areas of the ship, looking for a suitable recipient, all the while picturing the distressing scenes that Caroline had described. Somehow the two things merged in her mind until giving away the panda felt like the only way she could help Lucy deal with her loss. At last, in a corner of the dining room with his mother, nibbling on a biscuit, she found the boy who'd cried for his lost panda when he came on board. Madeleine approached, pulling the toy out of her bag.

'Excuse me. I happened to have this, in my luggage. Would your little boy like to have it?'

'I . . . yes, he would like it very much, I think,' the woman replied. Her eyes looked sad and tired, like those of all the survivors.

'Panda!' the boy cried, reaching for it. Madeleine handed it to him with a small smile, and he clutched it to his face tightly. It would bring him some comfort, she realised. And in giving it away she felt her own grief lightening. She'd thought of the toy as a last link to the child she'd lost. But it wasn't. It was just a stuffed toy that meant nothing to her but everything to this boy who'd lost so much.

'Thank you,' his mother said. 'It will help him.' She pushed away a tear. 'We have to be strong for the little ones, don't we?'

'We do,' Madeleine agreed, 'it is all we can do.'

# Chapter 15

## Jackie, 2022

It was meant to be one of Jackie's regular nights out with Sarah, but there'd been a change of plan. Martin had invited Tim out for a curry and a few drinks, while Jackie and Sarah were due to stay home with little Bobby. Jackie had strong suspicions that Sarah and Martin were intending to sound them both out on their relationship problems, and would try to advise them on how best to work through it. She appreciated it – it was always good to talk problems through with a good friend, and no one knew her better than Sarah.

'Bring Tim round for a drink at ours first,' Sarah had said on the phone. 'Pre-drinks, the young call it, I believe. Then Tim and Martin can go out and we'll have a girls' night in together, with pizza and Prosecco.'

They'd walked to Sarah and Martin's house largely in silence. Since that evening and their decision that Tim would go alone to Italy as a trial separation, the atmosphere between them had been even more strained. It'd be better at Sarah's, Jackie thought. Having other people around to talk to, and Bobby no doubt being the centre of attention until he was put to bed, would ease the tension a little. And then when Martin and Tim went out, she'd be free to talk openly to Sarah. It would help, she was sure.

'Hey, you two! Come on in!' Sarah answered the door with Bobby in her arms. 'Martin's still in the shower. He'll be down shortly.'

'Hi Sarah. We brought a couple of bottles,' Jackie said, kissing her friend and holding out a carrier bag containing a bottle of Prosecco and a Rioja.

'Cheers! I'll put the bubbly in the fridge . . . wait . . . here, Tim, hold Bobby a moment, would you?' Sarah thrust the little boy at Tim so she could take the bag from Jackie.

Jackie watched as Sarah passed the little boy to Tim. He'd always seemed a bit reluctant in the past when offered the chance to cuddle Bobby. How would he react now, after her miscarriage, and with all that was happening between them?

'Oh, yeah, right,' Tim said, as he took Bobby awkwardly, holding him at arms' length as though he would detonate at any moment.

'Sit down there with him, it's easier,' Sarah said, as she took the wine from Jackie.

Tim perched on the edge of the sofa, sitting Bobby on his knees facing him. Bobby was babbling and smiling and reaching out, wanting to tug at Tim's beard. Altogether he was being the cutest little thing ever. How could you not melt when holding a child like that? Jackie was itching to hold him herself, but she also wanted to watch Tim's reaction. He was leaning away, out of reach of those little grasping fingers and looking anywhere except at Bobby. 'He's, uh, getting bigger,' he said.

'They do that, when you feed them,' Jackie said. 'Hey, Bobby! You bouncing on Uncle Tim's knee, are you? Go on, Tim, do "This is the Way the Ladies Ride" with him. He loves it.'

'I'm sure he does,' Tim replied, but made no move to jiggle the child at all. Bobby appeared to be growing bored of trying to reach Tim's beard, and began to squirm. 'Uh, Sarah? Think he's going to cry . . . could you take him back?'

'Yes, sure, two ticks,' Sarah called from the kitchen.

Tim rolled his eyes and sighed. Because he was having to hold Bobby a few seconds longer? Jackie couldn't believe it. She was about to say something, which she knew would come out snippy, but at that moment Martin entered the room, smelling of shower gel and shampoo. 'Hey, heard you arrive, sorry I wasn't quite ready!'

Bobby smiled and gurgled on seeing his dad and stretched out his arms. Martin leaned over and took him from Tim, whose expression was one of profound relief.

'Ah, who's my precious little man, eh? Give your daddy a kiss?' Bobby planted a huge wet kiss on Martin's cheek and grinned broadly.

'Thanks, Martin,' Tim said, brushing at the legs of his jeans as though holding Bobby had left them dirty. 'I'm not what you'd call a natural.'

'Ah, rubbish. You just haven't had the practise,' Martin said. 'You sit there and play, Bobby, while we have a glass of something to set us up?' He put the little boy down on the carpet within reach of a basket of toys. Bobby immediately pulled out a complicated-looking plastic contraption and began pushing and poking at it.

'He's such a good little boy,' Jackie said, taking a glass of Prosecco offered by Sarah.

'He's all right, aren't you, poppet?' Sarah ruffled Bobby's curls and he looked up at her and smiled.

'He's adorable,' Jackie said, sliding down from the sofa to sit on the floor beside Bobby, who offered her a bright orange octopus toy. 'Thank you, Bobby. What a lovely octopus.' Out of the corner of her eye she saw Tim's jaw clenching, and then he turned to Martin to start a conversation about the hikes he'd planned for his Italian trip.

Jackie was relieved when the men left about twenty minutes later. She'd felt unable to talk openly with Tim there, and suspected he felt the same. In any case, he'd only spoken to Martin while she'd either played with Bobby or chatted with Sarah.

'You need to talk, the two of you,' Sarah said, once the men had left. Jackie was now slouched on Sarah's sofa with Bobby on her lap drinking his supper-time milk. 'I mean, properly talk. You can't just let things tail off like this. Not after so many years.'

'I know. I don't want it to end, not really. But . . .'

'I get it, I do. Here, Bobby, pass me your cup.' The little boy handed Sarah his sippy cup and grinned at Jackie. 'Oh, you don't look the slightest bit sleepy, do you? But Aunty Jackie and I need to talk.'

'How about I read him a story?' Jackie said.

'If you like. He's rather partial to *Where's Spot?* at the moment, if you can bear to read that one.'

'Oh, I love a bit of Spot the Dog. How about it, Bobby? Let me put you to bed and read you a story?'

'Storwee!' Bobby said, and Jackie smiled, getting up from the sofa with him still in her arms.

'Oof. He's getting heavy,' she said.

'I know. While you're reading to him, I'll open another bottle and get us some nibbles. I love our girls' nights in.'

'I do, too,' Jackie said, as she left the room with little Bobby.

Ten minutes later, with Spot found under the last flap of the book and Bobby tucked in his cot, Jackie went back downstairs where Sarah had laid out olives, crisps, crackers with cheese and an open bottle of wine. 'Looks wonderful,' Jackie said.

'There's a pizza in the oven too. So, let me pour you a glass and then you need to talk to me about your long-term plans. You and Tim. I reckon Martin will be asking Tim the same questions. You know we will do all we can to help you through this.'

Jackie pulled a face, but accepted the wine and sat down in what was fast becoming 'her' place on the sofa. 'Well, he's going to Italy on Saturday. For four weeks. And then when he's back, we've said we'll see where we're at, and how we feel about things. And we'll have a heart-to-heart talk then. All I know is, Sarah, I really, really want a child. It's wonderful spending time with Bobby, I love him to bits, but . . .' She sighed, and took a sip of her wine. 'I really want my own baby. And if Tim doesn't, then . . . we can't stay together.'

'But he did want a family, didn't he? I mean, you'd made a decision to try . . .'

'We had, but I wonder now whether his heart was in it. His reaction to me getting pregnant, and then when I lost it . . . it's just made me question how committed he was to the idea. And I'm scared, Sarah, of entering into a pregnancy knowing he's not fully ready for it. What if we went ahead, and then he left me alone with a young baby? I don't know how I'd manage as a single parent.'

'He wouldn't though, would he? Not Tim. He'd stay.'

'But if he wasn't happy with being a father, that would be a terrible situation for us both to be in. Not to mention unfair on the baby. You saw how awkward he was with Bobby this evening. Couldn't wait to pass him on to Martin.'

Sarah pushed a bowl of olives closer to Jackie. 'Hmm. But I reckon once he actually held a child of his own in his arms he'd feel differently about it. Tim's not a monster, Jackie. He's a good bloke.'

'I know . . . I suppose I just want him to feel the same as I do, from the start. And I'm worried he doesn't. I honestly think he doesn't really want kids at all. Ever.' Jackie looked away, feeling tears prickling at the corners of her eyes. To change the subject, she took a couple of olives. 'These are nice. You've been so good to me through all this.'

'No problem. It's what friends are for. So, he gets back from Italy in the middle of August. Meanwhile you're on your own.'

'Yes. And to tell the truth, I'm looking forward to the space. Being able to do my own thing at home. Reading books, watching films, just sitting out in the garden with a cold drink and working out how I feel about it all.'

'It'll do you good,' Sarah said. 'And I wouldn't be surprised if those few weeks apart might make Tim realise what you two have together. It's not something to throw away. You've been together, what, twelve years?'

'Thirteen.'

'Thirteen. It's all about compromise, isn't it? He'll come back ready to change, to keep you.'

'But the decision to have children or not can't be based on compromise,' Jackie said. 'We have to both want it. Or it's not fair on anyone. It's too big, too life-changing a decision.'

'That's very true.' Sarah was about to say something else but there was a beeping coming from the kitchen. She jumped to her feet. 'Pizza's ready. Let me serve that up now.' She went out to the kitchen leaving Jackie alone for a few minutes, contemplating the next few weeks, and how she would feel without Tim around.

She'd no doubt spend a number of evenings with Sarah. And she'd catch up with her enormous pile of books to read. Her mind turned to work. She'd been busy dealing with some purchases of antiquarian books Henry had made, but the *Carpathia* notebook still played on her mind. That poor woman, Lucy Watts, and her lost child. She remembered the detailed description of the child's silver bangle.

'Sarah, do babies still have those little engraved bracelets anymore?' she asked, when Sarah returned bearing a large pizza cut into slices, and a plate for each of them.

'What? Why are you asking that? I think some get them as christening presents but people don't tend to let their babies wear them. Bobby would scratch his face to bits if he wore one, he's always rubbing his fists across his face.'

'Just something I was reading at work. But if you had one, you'd keep it for life, wouldn't you?'

'Yes. Actually, somewhere, I have the one my mother was given as a baby. She passed it on to me when I was very little. It was the expanding type and I think I wore it occasionally until I was about five and it no longer fitted me.'

'It's a kind of heirloom then.'

'Yes. Here, eat your pizza.' Sarah passed Jackie a generous slice.

'Thanks. God, I'm starving. Only had a sandwich at lunch today.' She took the plate and tucked in, thinking about the bracelet the missing baby had worn and whether it was possible someone somewhere still had it hidden away, if the baby had indeed survived the ship sinking.

After eating they moved on to other subjects and by the time she went home, Jackie felt restored, buoyed up by having had an evening with her friend. Tim arrived home an hour later, when Jackie was already in bed. Hopefully, she thought, Martin had helped him as much as Sarah had helped her.

At last, the day came when Tim was off on his trip. He left on a Saturday morning, and Jackie gave him a lift to the bus station, from where he caught a bus to the airport. He was excited but subdued. As she dropped him off, he leaned over and kissed her, briefly, and put a hand to her cheek.

For a moment she nuzzled against his hand. 'Well, I'll see you in a few weeks, then,' she said, and he nodded.

'Take care, Jackie.'

'You too. Have fun.'

And then he was gone, just like that. It had been more like saying goodbye to a brother or a friend, not a long-term partner.

But they needed this time. They needed the space, the freedom to work out what they really wanted. While Jackie hoped that Tim would come back having decided that yes, he did want children, and soon, and with her, she wasn't going to assume that would happen. Even after thirteen years together.

# Chapter 16

## Madeleine, 16 April 1912

Madeleine made her way back to their cabin to find Ralph waiting for her. 'Ah, I'm glad you've returned,' he said. 'I thought we might go together to see Harold Cottam. I have the first report all ready to send, and Harold told me that by today he hoped we might be within range, if not of land, of another ship that can relay the messages.'

Ralph was practically hopping from foot to foot with excitement, like a small boy on the eve of his birthday. Madeleine smiled at him. 'Very well, I'll come along. I must admit I'm curious to see this equipment and learn more of how it works.' She needed a distraction. She needed to put Caroline's story out of her mind. It was too distressing to think about. She could only pray that poor child hadn't been Lucy's, but knew it was quite possible they'd never know for certain.

She followed him up on deck and up the steps to the Marconi cabin. Inside, Ralph introduced her to a dark-haired young man with a serious air. The shadows under his eyes showed that he had not slept much for the last few days. Even so, he greeted them with a smile that seemed genuine. 'Mr Meyer. Good to see you again. And Mrs Meyer, delighted to meet you.'

'Well, Cottam, she's as interested in all this as I am. Will you show her what you've shown me? Only if you're not too busy of course.'

'I've got a few minutes. We're still not in range of any useful station, so I can't yet transmit these.' He laid his hand on a pile of slips of paper. 'Personal messages, they are. The captain's said that *Titanic* passengers may send personal messages, and that these are to take priority, other than in any emergency. Says people's relatives have a right to hear from them.'

Ralph nodded. 'Quite right too. I'm glad he's agreeable to getting the word out there.'

'Seems so.' Cottam then began showing Madeleine the equipment and explaining how it all worked. She gazed in awe at the polished wooden boxes from which protruded all manner of metal knobs and dials and wires. 'This here's the transmitter. It produces a radio signal by means of an electric spark. Using the telegraph key here I can switch the spark on and off, using Morse code. It's then transmitted. And this,' he pointed to another piece of equipment, 'is the receiver – a magnetic detector. I need to use earphones to hear the signal, which, of course, comes in as Morse code that I then need to translate.'

Madeleine was fascinated by it all though some of the technical detail was beyond her understanding, and from Ralph's furrowed brow probably beyond his too. Still, it was enough to grasp the principals of it all. She would never need to operate it herself, or learn Morse code.

'I think it's astounding to think that we can send messages just through the air,' she said.

'All the way across the Atlantic, when conditions are right,' Cottam said proudly. 'Mr Marconi sent the first transatlantic wireless signal ten years ago now. But on board ship, our range is more limited. We're not able to put up such tall antennas, you see.'

'And what is the range?' Ralph asked.

Cottam rubbed his chin. 'Depends on weather conditions. And time of day – radio waves travel much further at night. But we can generally reckon on a range of a hundred miles or so. *Titanic*'s system would have had a far better range.'

A message came in while they were there, and Harold Cottam broke off from his explanations to listen to the electric pulses and jot down each letter onto a pad of paper. How he could distinguish them so quickly Madeleine had no idea.

'This is important. I need to take it to the captain immediately,' Cottam said, tearing the top sheet off his pad. Ralph and Madeleine nodded their understanding and stepped back to allow him to exit the room.

'No need, the captain's here,' said a voice behind them. 'Good afternoon, Meyer, and Mrs Meyer.'

'Ah, Captain Rostron. Just had a message in from the RMS *Olympic*,' Cottam said. 'She's within range. She wants to know if she should come close and take *Titanic* passengers off us?'

Madeleine gasped to hear this. The idea of those poor people being transferred to another ship while out at sea, after all they'd been through, filled her with horror.

Thankfully, the captain seemed of the same mind. He rubbed his chin. 'Hmm. I think we've accommodated the survivors adequately. It's only a couple of days to New York. We'll manage. Besides, *Olympic* is *Titanic*'s sister ship. I dread to think what it would do to the survivors' peace of mind if they saw an identical ship draw near. They might think *Titanic* had risen from the deep. No, on balance, I think *Olympic* should stay well clear, out of sight. Message them back and tell them thank you for the offer but please to stay away.'

Madeleine was relieved to hear this. She remembered what Louis Ogden had said about Captain Rostron always doing what he felt was best for his passengers, putting their well-being above all else. This was a good example of that in action.

'Will do, sir. Thank you, sir.' Cottam jotted down the message and immediately set to work sending it, tapping away on the telegraph key at a tremendous speed. Once again Madeleine was impressed by the speed at which he worked.

The captain stayed in the cabin while Cottam worked, leafing idly through the pile of personal messages. Another passenger, a man with an impressive moustache, turned up with a slip of paper. 'Any chance of sending this?' the man asked, and Captain Rostron nodded.

'Add it to the pile there and the operator will get to it.'

When Cottam had finished sending, he turned back to the captain. 'I'll begin sending those as soon as we're within range of an onshore radio station. Tomorrow, do you think?'

'Should be, yes, if we keep up a good speed.'

'And then,' Ralph tentatively spoke, 'would you be able to send this?' He handed over a sheet of paper on which he'd written the short version of the story of the disaster.

'What's that, Meyer?' asked the captain.

'A piece for my newspaper. For all the papers. To get the truth of the disaster told. I imagine that so far there are all sorts of rumours flying around as to *Titanic*'s fate, and what's become of her passengers. I want to tell the true story, and I think it should go out as soon as possible.'

'You want to get your name in the papers, I bet.'

'I'm a journalist, sir. It's my job.'

'Not on this ship, it isn't. No. I shall not allow it. The radio is to be kept for emergency use and personal messages only.'

The moustached man was still there. 'Quite right too, Captain. My message should go ahead of his article. My brother in New York will be worried. He needs to know I was among the lucky ones.'

'You see?' The captain turned to Ralph. 'That's what's impor-tant. Not titillating details for the gossip columns.'

Ralph frowned. 'Not gossip at all, sir. Not titillating. The truth. Doesn't the world deserve that? Don't relatives of *Titanic*'s passengers have a right to know what happened as soon as possible?'

'The world will know it all when we get back to New York. That's soon enough. For now, let these people recover in peace. If you send your lurid stories back before we dock, it'll bring the world's press to our berth and the survivors will be mobbed as they leave the ship. I won't have it. They've been through enough and I won't have them suffer any more while they are under my care. You are not to send your story, Meyer, and that's all there is to it.' The captain fixed Ralph with a fierce stare for a moment then turned on his heel and left, followed by the man with the moustache.

'Oh dear, that sounded as though he meant it,' Madeleine said. Ralph, she could tell, was struggling to control his temper.

'He's wrong. The world needs to know sooner rather than later. This is too big a story to hide. Besides, the survivors I've spoken to want their stories heard. Cottam, look, it's short. Just this one side of paper. You'll send it, won't you?'

Cottam stared at the page but did not take it. 'I can't, sir. You heard the captain. I have to do what he says.'

'No, you don't. You're employed by Marconi, aren't you? Not by Cunard. You don't directly report to the captain. It's for you to judge whether to send it or not.'

'While I'm on board his ship, I have to obey the captain,' Cottam repeated.

'What if your real boss, Mr Marconi, said otherwise? Send him a message, ask what he thinks you should do. Then if he says send the story, you will have to obey him over the captain?'

Madeleine stared at Ralph. That was a clever plan, and just might work. Mr Marconi would no doubt want the story to first be told by means of his invention. It would be wonderful publicity for him.

'I'll ask, but I don't think . . .' Cottam said. He was at least sounding less sure of his decision.

Ralph put a hand in his pocket and jingled some coins that

were there. 'Listen, Cottam, if it helps, I'll make it worth your while. If you know what I mean.'

'Sir, I understand. And I understand how important you think it is. But I can't go against the captain's wishes while I'm on the ship.' Cottam had stood up and pulled himself upright. He was taller than Ralph, and now it seemed he was using his height to make his point, that he would not be swayed on this, and could not be bribed.

'Hmm. Well, the offer's open to you. Think about it. You say we'll be within range of the stations onshore tomorrow? I'll come back then, and see if you've changed your mind.' Ralph opened the door of the cabin and held it for Madeleine to pass through. And then he turned back. 'Dammit man, this is important! People deserve the truth. People deserve to know, and as soon as possible. You could do your bit here, you'll be making history. Think about it!'

Without waiting for an answer he strode off, Madeleine having to run to keep up with him. He was furious, she knew it. But what could they do? The captain had made himself clear, whether he was right or wrong.

# Chapter 17

## Tim, 2022

Tim found his allocated seat about half-way along the plane, stowed his rucksack in the overhead locker, making sure to keep his Kindle handy, and sat down with a sigh of relief. One good thing about mask-wearing – still necessary on flights – people couldn't see the stupid grin that was plastered across his face. This was it, this was the long-awaited hiking trip in Italy about to start. Two years of travel restrictions because of the pandemic, but now, here he was, on his way. A flight to Rome, a bus to L'Aquila and from then on, he'd be on foot. He had all the maps he'd need, his routes planned, campsites picked out (though some of the time he'd be wild camping in the mountains) and four blissful weeks before he had to return home.

The only downside was that he was on his own.

Through the window beside him he could see the last of the hold baggage being loaded. Soon the plane would be taxiing to the start of the runway. Jackie had offered to drive him to the airport as he hadn't wanted to leave his precious Audi in airport parking, but Tim had insisted it'd be easier to take a bus. In truth, he hadn't wanted to sit beside her for the long car journey. He hadn't wanted to prolong their time together today, when all he wanted was for the adventure to begin.

He'd been shocked when she'd suggested they have some time apart. Or had he really? Was there perhaps a tiny bit of him that had felt relieved that Jackie had been the one to suggest he go to Italy alone? She'd never been fully committed to this trip, he knew. She'd agreed to it, but only as a compromise. One last adventure and then settle down and have children. And he'd agreed to that, knowing how desperate she was to start a family. Left to him, he would have preferred to wait another few years but he understood that at thirty-five Jackie didn't think she had that many years left. So he'd agreed to it, despite his own nagging doubts about whether or not he had what it took to be a parent, to commit to eighteen or more years of looking after someone.

And then, she'd got pregnant earlier than planned, when they were supposed to be still taking precautions. He could recall the moment she'd told him in every last-minute detail; her assumption that he'd be delighted, even though it was wrecking all their plans for the summer; his fleeting suspicion she might have done it on purpose, and his stupid ill-judged questioning of her on this. Of course, it hadn't been intentional. He remembered the night she'd conceived, he remembered how they'd been caught up in the moment and taken a risk. And he'd accepted the consequence of that decision.

The plane was pushing back from its gate now, and cabin crew were working their way down the aisle closing overhead lockers, making sure everyone's seat belts were fastened and trays stowed. All the usual routines, same as always. He remembered how when the first lockdown began, planes were grounded and the skies were quiet. In the UK, you were allowed out for exercise purposes and he and Jackie had taken advantage of the quiet roads and good weather to go cycling every weekend, exploring the local countryside, enjoying each other's company, making the best of the situation they were in.

They'd always been good together. A team. Liking the same things, wanting the same things from life. This was the first time they'd been apart for more than a few days since they'd moved in together, ten years ago.

When Jackie had miscarried, Tim had tried hard not to make too big a deal of it. It had been an early miscarriage, and his understanding was that such losses were quite common and didn't affect the woman's chances of conceiving again. That's what Alfie had told him, anyway. Tim had thought that if he played it down it'd help Jackie get over the loss. And so he hadn't let her see how it had affected him. How he'd just got used to the idea of becoming a parent sooner rather than later, convinced himself that when the baby arrived his parenting instincts would kick in and he'd be able to manage. The loss had upset him, made him feel depressed, but he'd hidden that too. He'd gone out, spent many evenings in the pub, talked it all through with Alfie several times and Martin once. He'd worked so hard to get over it. Jackie, he thought, had done much the same, leaning on Sarah for support, and throwing herself into her job to take her mind off it. They each had dealt with it in their own way.

But he'd misjudged something, that much was clear.

'Cabin crew, seats for take-off please,' came the announcement over the plane's intercom, and then there was the familiar pressure as the plane accelerated along the runway, its nose lifted and they were airborne. Tim stared out of the window as roads, housing estates, fields and hills passed by beneath him.

Jackie had taken the miscarriage badly, he now understood. She must have begun to think of the embryo as a real baby already, whereas he'd been careful to think of it only as a collection of cells, to not allow himself to feel too much attachment too early. By the time Tim had realised how badly she was handling it, it was too late for them to simply talk it through. 'Hey babe, that miscarriage you had three weeks ago? Yeah, well, just wanted to say I'm really sorry you've found it hard to deal with.' He'd vaguely supposed that somewhere in the mountains of central Italy they'd have been able to have that conversation, somewhere away from the demands of their everyday lives.

And then she'd suggested they have a break from each other over the summer, so they could each have the time and space to decide what they wanted from life. He'd been shocked. Had things gone that far wrong? How had he allowed that to happen? He loved Jackie, he always had and always would. That was a given. But she wanted children now, so badly, and did he? He wasn't sure. Now that she'd lost the one she was carrying, wouldn't it be better to wait a little longer before trying again? For her health, for them both to get used to the idea and feel properly ready for it – because they both needed to feel ready to become parents, didn't they? Worst thing they could do would be to bring a child into a family where one parent wasn't fully committed to the job, yet.

Which led to the question he'd been trying not to think about, but which he needed to think about, and deeply, during these next four weeks. *Was* he committed to becoming a parent? Is it what he wanted, what he truly wanted, the way Jackie clearly did? Did he even possess the right natural instincts? He remembered with embarrassment how awkward he'd felt holding Sarah and Martin's kid, the last time he'd been there. How he hadn't known whether to pull the boy closer or hold him at arm's length. How he'd been scared that cuddling a child might bring it home to him too sharply just what they'd lost when Jacks had miscarried. He'd been trying to keep his emotions under control. What a relief he'd felt when Martin had taken Bobby from him.

No, he simply wasn't sure he could do it. He wanted children, but in an abstract way. If only you could skip straight through to the teenager stage. He'd come into his own as a parent then, after all his years of experience teaching teens. But there were a lot of years of babyhood, toddler-dom and early childhood to get through first, and that was what terrified him. There was so much he might get wrong.

Would it be better all round if . . . and he could hardly bear to consider this possibility . . . if they called it a day, and she was free to find someone else, someone who was as desperate to have a child as she was? Someone with the right instincts.

Somehow, somewhere in the Italian Apennine mountains, he needed to find some answers.

All went smoothly for the flight, his onward bus journey to L'Aquila and the start of the trek. Twenty-four hours after Jackie had dropped him off at the bus station, Tim was hiking up a track that led onto a mountain ridge. Above him the sky was a startling blue with not a cloud to be seen. The scent of pine forest filled the air, and the day was going to be a hot one. On his back his rucksack was neatly packed, containing everything he needed for the first few days, and after that he'd need to find a shop and buy more food.

There was no one else on the path, not that he'd come across so far, anyway. He had it all to himself. The entire mountain range, he liked to think. All of Italy. When he reached the top of the ridge, he'd be able to see down into the next valley and on to the ridge after that, the one he intended following for a while. It was higher than the one he was currently climbing, and he hoped he might even be able to see as far as the Adriatic Sea from the top. Certainly, he'd be above the tree line. It only depended on whether there were still higher mountains between that ridge and the sea.

He trudged onward, the track winding its way through the forest, now and then zig-zagging upwards, then following a contour for a while. Slowly but surely, he was gaining height. It was cool now in the shade, but scorching hot in open sun. Consulting his map, he saw that soon he'd be out of the forest, above the tree line. There'd be no shade then. But he'd be high enough that hopefully he'd find a bit of breeze. When he reached the summit ridge, he'd need to make a decision on where he was going to stop for the night. The forecast was for more glorious weather the next day, so there'd be no need to descend or find a campsite. All he needed was a water source to fill up his bottles, and then he could camp anywhere.

'Jackie would have loved this,' he muttered to himself. She was less adventurous than him, but once he'd got her into the wilderness, up in the mountains, away from it all, well, then she loved it at least as much as he did. She'd be grinning broadly, with her 'mountain smile', as he liked to call it, firmly in place. She'd be striding on ahead, always wanting to see the view around the next corner, or over the next rise. She'd turn back to him, arms out wide to encompass everything around her and exclaim, 'Isn't this just absolutely glorious, Tim?' And he'd have to agree that it was.

It couldn't be the case that they'd never again do this sort of thing together. It just couldn't. They'd been together so long.

As he walked, Tim thought back on all the years they'd been together. From their first meeting at the university adventure club, their hooking up in a pub after graduation, through their early hiking and camping trips, to their decision to move in together. Why had they never married? He'd never asked her, and she'd never asked him. Neither of them cared much for organised religion, and so the idea of marrying in a church hadn't appealed. 'It'd be hypocritical, as we aren't believers,' Tim remembered Jackie saying to Sarah once, when Sarah had asked if they were ever going to tie the knot.

'You can get married anywhere these days,' Sarah had said. 'Doesn't have to be a religious ceremony.'

'What's the point, then?' Tim had asked.

'A perfect excuse for a bloody great knees-up with your mates,' Sarah had replied, laughing.

But money had been tight and they'd never felt they had

enough to throw a huge wedding party. And so they'd never married. Tim wondered if that had had an impact on what was happening now to their relationship. Because they had never formally committed to each other, had that made it harder to move forward now? If they'd been married, would it have been easier for him to make that next commitment – to start a family with her?

'It's day two, Timbo,' he told himself, hearing Alfie's wise voice in his head. 'You don't need to find all the answers today. Plenty of time.'

The trees were thinning out now, and then suddenly the track twisted back on itself twice, crossed a small ravine and then he was above the tree line, in full sunshine. High above, a pair of eagles were circling, and Tim watched them, shielding his eyes from the glare of the sun. There was a flattish rock nearby and he decided to sit down for a minute, eat an energy bar and drink some water, and if there was any phone signal, he could check if there were any messages from Jacks and send her a photo or two. On a lower ridge, back in the direction he'd come from, he could see a cluster of mobile phone masts. Reception might be all right up here.

It was, and he sent her a couple of shots of the view, and a short message. '*All going well. Look at the view from here! Hope all good with you T xx.*'

She replied almost immediately, although he knew she'd be at work. '*Great pics! Have fun, be careful xx.*'

He smiled, then sighed. It was only day two, but he had to admit he was missing her.

He sent the same photos to his mum as well, then a jokey message to Alfie. '*Having gr8 time in Italy. Wish I could stay 4eva. If I don't come home you can have my collection of Marvel comics. But not the TT.*'

A reply arrived shortly after. '*Ha ha. The Alfatron has his own extensive comic collection. Srsly, mate, you need to sort things with J. Enjoy yr hol 4 now but do come back to her.*'

Tim read the message with a frown. Not like Alfie to take things seriously. He'd only meant it as a joke. Of course, he'd return to the UK at the end of the trip. He had a job, a house, a car back there.

And Jackie. If she still wanted him. Another couple of weeks and he'd be home, and they'd have the honest and open conversations they needed to have, that would, he hoped, cement their future together. Their relationship as a committed couple. And the possibility of them having a family. He wanted her, he wanted to stay with her, for them to grow old together. He knew that for certain now. He'd thought of little else. The only thing that frightened him was her desire, her need to start a family. Was he ready? Could he be a father? Was he mature enough himself? Even though he spent his days teaching sport to kids, he wasn't sure. He often felt as though he was just a bigger version of the kids he taught. Not someone responsible enough to bring a tiny baby into the world, to nourish and care for that child, to bring them up for eighteen years.

But for her, for Jacks, he'd do it. He had to, if it was the only way he could keep her. It was hard, though, with that constant nagging doubt that possibly he didn't have the right basic instincts to handle babies and small children.

# Chapter 18

## Madeleine, 16 April 1912

They ate dinner on their own that evening. No more convivial meet-ups with friends, with the captain sitting at their table engaging in conversation. Captain Rostron seemed to be taking his meals else-where, and was only now seen by passengers in the line of his duties, never socially. And the Marshall family were keeping to themselves, looking after their nieces who'd had such a terrible ordeal.

'I must admit,' Madeleine said to Ralph, as they finished their dinner, seated at a small table for two in the corner of the dining room, 'I am not much in the mood for making new friends now. It's all been so awful, and I've spoken to so many people and heard their stories – I no longer want to indulge in idle chatter over food.'

Ralph nodded. 'I know what you mean. I'm just longing to get back to New York, see my story printed, and then be on our way again.'

'And put all this behind us.' Though even as she said it, Madeleine knew that this episode would live with her to the end of her days.

'As much as we can, yes. The captain said he'll turn the ship around as fast as is humanly possible once we've discharged the survivors and re-provisioned. I won't have long in New York to get my story out.'

'We could go on a later sailing, on another ship?' She didn't want to, but it was an option, surely.

'We'd lose our money. I think we must stay on this one, Maddy, if you can bear it. There will just be time for me to dash to the offices with my story. I may not even need to, if Cottam changes his mind and agrees to transmit it. I can also ask him to send a message asking for the *Tribune* to send someone to meet us, so I can hand over the full manuscripts. As that wouldn't be transmitting the story it doesn't go against captain's orders so I think he might agree. Maybe someone else from the paper would be able to board the ship as we approach Manhattan, before we dock.'

'I hope he agrees. Do you think he will?' Madeleine watched Ralph carefully as he shrugged.

'I can't say. I'll go to see him again tomorrow, as I said, and I'll make damn sure the captain isn't in the vicinity when I do. I think he might be persuaded, if he hasn't just been told not to by the captain.' He gave her a lopsided smile and shrugged. 'All I can do, isn't it? This story must be told.' He tapped his jacket breast pocket, in which, she knew, was the typed copy of his story.

'Why are you carrying that everywhere with you?' she asked.

'Because ... it feels too important to leave it anywhere, in case it's lost.' He put his hands up, palms out. 'I know, I know. I'm possibly worrying too much. But I want to keep it with me at all times, until I know it's been safely received and printed.'

With dinner finished they headed back to their cabin. 'I've got more notes for you to write up,' Madeleine said, as they made their way along the corridors of the ship. 'I interviewed more women in steerage and they had some interesting tales to tell. You could get a book out of it, if you wanted to.'

'Hmm,' Ralph said. 'There's a thought. But my darling, books

165

take a lot of time and effort to write, and we are supposed to be travelling and enjoying each other's company. You're convalescing still, and I don't want to leave you to your own devices while I slave away at my typewriter all day. It's one thing to write and sell a few articles but not a whole book. Not now, anyway.' He took her arm and pulled her close to him. 'It's not fair on you.'

'Ah, piffle,' she said, though secretly she was delighted he was putting her needs first. 'You don't need to worry about me. If you do want to pull all this together into a book, you will have my full support. Lord knows we have gathered enough material.'

'Thank you, Maddy.' He smiled down at her. They'd reached their cabin, and he took the key from his pocket to unlock the door, then stood back to let her pass through first.

As soon as she set foot inside the room she knew something was wrong. Something felt different. She stood in the centre, frowning. Ralph must have realised too, for he immediately opened the wardrobe and checked the little safe inside. 'Your jewellery is all here,' he said. 'And our passports.'

'But someone's been here. My things have been moved.' Madeleine gestured to the little desk, at which she'd sat to write her correspondence. 'There was a pile of paper, just here.' She opened the desk drawer and gasped. 'My notebook! It's gone!'

'Your notebook?' Ralph was checking cupboards, their travelling trunk, every corner of the room.

'The one in which I've written everything from the people I've interviewed. It was in here, I know it was, and now it's not.'

'My typewriter's missing too.'

'What?!' Madeleine stared at Ralph in horror. 'Have we been burgled, while we were at dinner?'

'It rather looks like it,' Ralph said, stroking his chin. 'But look, your furs are there in the wardrobe, and one of your necklaces is on the dressing table.'

She looked where he pointed, and snatched up the necklace. It was one she'd considered putting on for the evening, and then had decided against, but hadn't put back in the safe. 'This is gold. I'm glad it hasn't been taken, but . . .'

'But the question is, *why* wasn't it taken?' Ralph finished the sentence for her.

Madeleine nodded. 'That is indeed the question. This is no ordinary burglary. Paper, my notebook, your typewriter . . .' She gasped again and clapped a hand over her mouth. 'Someone's trying to stop you writing your story, Ralph!'

'I think you are right. Good job I have it written already, and have it here.' He tapped his breast pocket, then took out a handkerchief and wiped sweat from his brow. 'I would hate to have lost this too.'

'But we've lost all my notes, all my interviews, and those you haven't yet written up!' Madeleine felt like crying. All that work, all those women's stories, all lost.

Ralph stepped forward and held her. 'Can you remember what you'd written, Maddy? If we got more paper, could you scribble down what you remember? Names, quotes, anything you can recall?'

She thought for a moment, remembering Jocelyn and Harry Marchant who'd run away to marry, the imperious Lady Hamilton who'd been upset her game of bridge was interrupted, Caroline's heartbreaking story and of course Lucy Watts and her missing baby. 'Some of it, yes. I'd probably miss some detail, but I can certainly recall a lot of what they said.' She sighed. 'After all, their stories are not ones anyone could forget in a hurry.'

'Then you must write it all down, as soon as you possibly can. Darling, it'd be better to do it tonight, before a night's sleep wipes any of it from your memory. You can dictate, and I'll write.'

'But we have no paper!'

'I'll fetch some from the library. They have a stack of *Carpathia* headed notepaper there. I'll be two ticks.' Ralph charged out of the cabin, leaving Madeleine alone.

While he was gone, she continued to check the cabin. Might she have put the notebook somewhere else? She was 99 per cent certain she'd put it back in the desk drawer, but it was worth checking just in case. She looked in all the obvious places, drawers, trunk, wardrobe and even under the mattress but to no avail. And Ralph's typewriter. That wasn't some small item one could accidentally mislay. It was a travelling model so it was smaller than some, but still a bulky, heavy item in its own case. It had been her gift to him, two years earlier. And it was most definitely not here. She tried to remember when Ralph had last used it. Earlier that day, she recalled, before they'd gone to see Harold Cottam. He'd sat at the desk typing. When he'd finished, he'd put it back in its case and stood it down beside their travelling trunk, to free up the desk space. It had still been there when they'd come back. She remembered moving it slightly after almost stubbing a toe on it.

So whoever had taken it, and the notebook, had definitely come in while they were at dinner. While they were seated in a public area, where they could be watched.

But the cabin had been locked. Whoever came in must have had a second key. And that meant . . . it was almost certainly a crew member.

Ralph returned then, breathlessly barging back into the cabin.

'Ralph, we must report this immediately to the purser. I think it must have been a crew member with a second key. Can't have been anyone else.'

'There's no paper in the library. Or in the smoking room. Or anywhere. It's all been taken away.' Ralph sat down heavily on the bed. 'You're right, we must report this. I need my typewriter back – it's a valuable item.'

'This has been done by order of the captain. He's doing everything he can to stop you writing the story.' The realisation hit Madeleine hard, and she sat down beside Ralph and took his hand. 'Nevertheless, we must report it. He can't keep your typewriter. That's theft. And there must be something I can write on, somewhere in this ship. Let's both go and look. You have your typed story?'

'I do.' Once more, Ralph patted his pocket. 'If we find nothing else, we can write on the back of it.'

'Perhaps I should take it. In case they . . . search you.'

Ralph stared at her then nodded and gave her the bundle. She opened her dress then slipped it into her corset. 'There. It's safe now.'

'Your typewriter is confiscated until we reach port, Mr Meyer.' Captain Rostron drew himself up to his full height and glared down his nose at Ralph and Madeleine.

'You can't do that. It's my personal property.' Ralph was furious.

'It is my ship, and my word is the law here. I can and have taken it away. It is perfectly safe and will be returned to you once we are docked at New York. I have told you already, I will *not* have you trying to send lurid details of the tragedy to your newspaper while you are on board my ship. I will protect the *Titanic* survivors at all costs. I have taken the typewriter, and all writing paper from your cabin and public areas, to prevent you writing up your stories.'

'But . . .' Ralph began. He was silenced by the captain who held up a hand.

'I shall hear no more about it. And if I find you have attempted to bribe the Marconi operator again, I will have you both confined to your cabin for the rest of the voyage. Do I make myself clear?'

Madeleine blinked. The thought of not being able to leave the cabin for days was awful. She put a hand on Ralph's arm. 'Darling, we must do as he says. Come away. Let's get ourselves a drink, shall we?'

'Do as your wife suggests.' The captain glared again at Ralph and left them.

'Well, that's that, I suppose,' Madeleine said.

'He's no right. I shall write to complain to Cunard. As soon as I can find some paper to write on, that is.'

'And I have an idea,' Madeleine said. 'Let's go to the bar.'

'For a drink? I'm not sure I want one,' Ralph said, but Madeleine smiled and tugged at his arm.

'Not just a drink. Come on.' She led him through the ship to the bar, and chose a table tucked into a corner. As with the rest of the ship, the area was busy, *Titanic* survivors were curled up in armchairs or lying along bench seats.

A waiter came to take their order. 'Two gin and tonics, please, and a bowl of nuts,' Madeleine said, giving Ralph a look that warned him not to say anything. The waiter nodded and left to fetch the order.

'Good job they're still managing to provide waiter service here,' Ralph said. 'Why the nuts?'

'You'll see.'

A moment later, the waiter was back bearing a tray. He placed the drinks in front of them, then a bowl of nuts in the middle of the table, and finally handed each of them a white paper napkin. Madeleine thanked him, and when he'd gone turned to Ralph. 'Pass me your napkin.'

'But I . . .' Ralph had already helped himself to a few nuts and was about to use the napkin.

'Don't wipe your greasy fingers on it! Don't you see, we can use these for paper. I need to write up what I can remember from my interviews.' She took his napkin and her own, and tucked them into her bag. 'Now then, ask a different waiter for more napkins.'

He grinned, catching on to her plan, and summoned a passing steward, who then brought a small stack of napkins which Madeleine swiftly appropriated. 'We have enough now, I think.' She downed her drink quickly, and set off back to their cabin, with Ralph following behind.

The napkins proved easy enough to write on with a soft-leaded pencil, as long as she kept it stretched taut and didn't press too hard. Within forty minutes, she had as much as she could recall from her interviews written neatly on both sides of a half-dozen napkins, which she then folded and tucked into her corset along with Ralph's story. 'There. All done. I'll keep those safe along with your other papers.'

Ralph took her face in his hands and kissed her. 'You, my darling, are a genius. Thank you.'

She smiled. 'You're welcome. Those women deserve having their stories told, no matter what the captain says. I'll go and find us a few more napkins before the captain decides to take those away too, in case we uncover more stories to write up.'

She headed out of their cabin again. On the way to the dining room to search for napkins, she passed a stewardess carrying a tray of baby bottles filled with milk. 'Excuse me,' Madeleine said, intercepting her, 'but who are those for?'

'There's a few little ones on board,' the stewardess replied, 'and some that came from *Titanic*. The mums come to the nursery to collect these, four times a day. 'Scuse me, got to hurry along now before the milk goes cold.'

'Of course.' Madeleine nodded, then as the stewardess bustled along the passageway she decided to go after her. Perhaps that woman in brown might appear, to take one of the bottles.

Madeleine followed the stewardess to the makeshift nursery. There were a few mothers with babies waiting there already, who took bottles and set to feeding their infants. None of them was the woman that had taken the baby from Madeleine. She waited, in case the woman came along later. But the last bottle was claimed by Lucy Watts.

'He needs more than I can provide,' she said, as she took the bottle and settled on a chair to feed Frederick.

'That means he's thriving,' Madeleine replied, watching as the child sucked greedily on the bottle.

'Yes. Mrs Meyer, I don't suppose you've had any luck looking for my Norah?' Lucy gazed up at her with an expression of subdued hope in her eyes.

'I'm sorry. No, I haven't. I have done all I can to look for her, but I'm afraid—'

'You think I must accept the worst. I was so sure, though, that Arthur had got her on a lifeboat.'

Frederick was wearing a little baby's bonnet, Madeleine noticed, just like the one that Caroline had described the drowned baby as wearing. She couldn't tell Lucy this. It would be too distressing for her. 'I am glad that you and Frederick have each other,' she said, gently.

But Lucy's eyes filled with tears. 'Everyone keeps saying I should be grateful that at least I have Frederick. Like he's a consolation prize. But his presence doesn't diminish my loss. I've still lost a child. It's almost more than I can bear.'

She was in agony with her grief, Madeleine could see. Her heart went out to her. 'I shall keep looking for Norah, all the time we're on board the ship.'

'Thank you. I don't understand how she wasn't handed over, by whoever Arthur gave her to. I'm certain she was saved. Someone's keeping her for themselves. But she needs her mother, she needs me!' Lucy gave way to another bout of sobbing.

'You're upsetting her. I think you should go.' The stewardess who'd brought the baby bottles approached, looking sternly at Madeleine. She had no choice but to leave then, patting Lucy kindly on the shoulder as she left.

# Chapter 19

## Jackie, 2022

'How was the Maldives?' Jackie asked Henry when she next saw him in the office.

'Oh, you know.' He grimaced. 'Too hot for me, too much sand everywhere.'

'Oh dear. More to Clarissa's liking?' The things he complained about were what most people went on holiday for, she thought.

'Ah. Clarissa and I have parted ways.' Henry reached for the coffee he'd been drinking and took a gulp.

Jackie wasn't surprised. 'I'm so sorry to hear that.'

'Don't be. She was all wrong for me, and I was wrong for her. We wanted different things from a relationship. Sooner we realised that and ended it, the better, for both of us. Gives us more time to find someone more suitable, or failing that, do our own thing without having to drag along an unwilling partner.'

He had a point, Jackie thought. Once you realise you're heading in different directions it was probably best to call it a day, before you began resenting the other person for holding you back or not going along with your dreams and desires. But surely she and Tim weren't in quite the same situation? Henry and Clarissa had only been together a few months. She and Tim had been together thirteen years. Their lives were far more entangled than Henry's and Clarissa's had been.

Henry shrugged, then smiled at her. 'So there you are. You're up to date. What have you been up to while I've been away? Did that Marconi equipment arrive?'

'Yes, and I've written up notes on it as you asked.' Jackie handed them over and also updated him on the contents of the notebook and the mystery of the missing baby.

Henry listened intently, nodding along. When she'd finished, he held a finger up. 'You know what you should do, Jackie? Write an article on what you've found, on this Lucy Watts and her babies. It's really quite a story. Then see if you can get it published somewhere.'

'Where? A newspaper?'

'Maybe a magazine, or perhaps somewhere online like the Huffington Post or the MailOnline. It's the type of thing they'd go for, I reckon.'

'Hmm, they might.' Jackie had never seen herself as any kind of journalist, but she knew this story inside out now, after all the research she'd done for Henry. She'd be able to do this, she thought.

'Feel free to write it on my time,' Henry said, with a grin. 'And you can mention that the notebook is part of my collection.'

'Well, all right then,' Jackie said. 'I'll do that.'

'Pour all the emotion you can into the story,' Henry advised. 'It could be quite a tear-jerker.'

'I will.'

She went back to her own office, pleased to have a new challenge ahead of her. Make it emotional, Henry had said. And that is what she set out to do. Using the Violet Jessop memoir, as well as numerous other sources, she painted a picture of Lucy Watts climbing aboard a lifeboat with a baby in her arms, having to leave her husband and other child on *Titanic*, yet being sure she'd then seen her husband give the baby to someone else. And then she switched to Violet Jessop's viewpoint, and wrote about how it might have felt having an unknown baby thrust upon you, keeping that baby warm and safe on the lifeboat while wondering what would happen to it, to you and the rest of the survivors. Being brought aboard *Carpathia*, safe at last, and then having someone snatch the baby from you. Back to Lucy Watts's point of view, Jackie wrote a section on how Lucy must have scoured *Carpathia* for her missing baby, helped by the reporter and his wife, pleading for information, for help finding her child. And all the while with her other baby to look after.

What had she done when the ship had reached New York? Would she have continued to search for the baby? How might that have worked? And where would Lucy Watts have lived, how would she have looked after herself and her remaining baby, with no husband?

Jackie put herself into Lucy's place, and poured her heart and soul into the piece, tapping into her own feelings of loss. She spent a couple of days editing it, refining it and adding more emotion. Then she researched likely places to publish it. Online newspapers, as Henry had suggested, seemed to be the best choices and indeed, after pitching it to the Huffington Post they responded within a couple of days to say yes, please, naming a fee which delighted Jackie.

'Well, that was easy,' Sarah said when Jackie told her of her success. 'Your first article and it's accepted straight off. I know writers who've been able to paper the wall with rejections before they get a single hit. You must be a fabulous writer.'

'Or a lucky one, with a great story to tell,' Jackie replied with a laugh.

'Yes, maybe that as well. Pleased for you, mate,' Sarah said. 'You should write a follow-up, you know. Track down this woman and her child, see what became of them.'

Jackie smiled. 'Good idea. I might just do that.'

'Have you told Tim your success?'

'I sent him a WhatsApp message about it.' They'd been messaging each other most days since Tim had gone away, but hadn't spoken. Since he'd been in the mountains he'd had sporadic connectivity, and sometimes wouldn't reply to messages until the next day.

'He must be pleased for you as well,' Sarah said. 'How's he getting on?'

'Enjoying it, so far.' He'd sent a few photos of craggy mountain peaks against an azure sky, of a pair of eagles circling high above, of his lightweight two-man tent pitched on a grassy slope far from anywhere, and a selfie of him in front of a dramatic view down a valley. Jackie pulled out her phone and scrolled through them to show Sarah.

'Looks amazing. Are you regretting not going with him? Kind of thing you enjoy, isn't it? All that wilderness, being miles from anywhere, awesome mountain scenery . . .'

'Yes, it is. But, no, I don't regret staying home. We needed to be apart for a while. Not sure I'd have been up to it anyway. I'm pretty unfit at the moment.'

Sarah laughed, but not unkindly. 'Rubbish. You're fit as a fiddle. Wait till you have a baby. That's when you lose your fitness, believe me.'

'I'd love to lose it for that reason,' Jackie said, wistfully.

Sarah looked mortified. 'Oh, hon, sorry. That just slipped out. But it will happen for you sooner or later. And I'll bet you anything Tim will come back from Italy having come to his senses, and desperate to start a family with you.'

'I do hope so,' was all the response Jackie could give, though what could possibly happen in Italy to change his mind she had no idea. She fervently hoped Sarah was right. She still loved Tim. She would always love him. But she needed to be a mum, and she wasn't prepared to push him into being a parent if it wasn't what he wanted.

* * *

176

The following day, Jackie was working from home. She went out at lunchtime, planning to pick up some groceries and have a quick salad in a café somewhere to make a change from her usual sandwiches. It didn't take long to do the shopping – she'd got into a terrible habit (already!) of buying ready meals for one, that simply needed to be microwaved. One reason why she'd been craving a decent salad for lunch.

She chose a café just along the road from the supermarket and picked a table near the window. She'd been there plenty of times before, and knew that they did a fabulous Caesar salad, which was exactly what she felt like eating. She placed the order, then pulled out her phone to pass the time while she waited for her meal. Perhaps there were new messages from Tim? If she was being totally honest, she was missing him. A lot. She was counting down the days until he got back. She'd moved back into their shared bedroom, and hoped when he came back that would be OK with him. And she was asking herself, frequently, whether she would agree to waiting to start a family, in order to keep Tim. Another year? Another two years? Would it matter? She at least knew that there was nothing amiss with either of them physically; her brief pregnancy had proved that everything was in working order. And plenty of people had babies in their forties.

There was nothing new from Tim. Not since a sunset photo from the day before, and a message that read: '*Heading towards the Passo di San Giacomo tomorrow, not too far from Sulmona. Need to buy food! Then up into the mountains again. Xx.*'

She'd opened up Google maps to see where those places were, and tried to picture it. From the photos he'd sent it all looked so beautiful, and he'd had good weather most of the time. There'd been just a couple of days where it had rained for a few hours, otherwise he'd had wall-to-wall sunshine. Did she regret not going with him? Probably. But at the time, her decision had been the right one. It was just that the two weeks that had passed since then had been enough for her to get her thoughts in order, for her to work out what she wanted.

She wanted Tim back at home with her. She wanted to have that talk about their future. She was ready to tell him that they could wait a couple more years before trying again for a baby, they could have another summer or two of adventures, if that was what it took. She hoped he'd be ready to accept that as some sort of compromise. He'd always said he wanted children. It had just happened too quickly for them. Yes, that was what had gone wrong – it was easy to see now that they'd had a little time apart. Time that she wished was over now.

Sighing, she clicked on a news website. Might as well update herself with what was happening in the world. The top news story was of an earthquake. She opened it up and scrolled through the news feed, which was being updated every few minutes as more details came in. The earthquake was in Italy, a mid-strength one but bad enough to cause a lot of damage to medieval buildings in some remote towns. Jackie frowned, wondering where in Italy it had occurred. There was a map showing the epicentre, which she enlarged. Abruzzo region.

'Christ. That's where Tim is,' she muttered, and immediately switched over to WhatsApp to send him a message. '*Just seen news of earthquake. Anywhere near you? Let me know you're all right xxx.*'

With a bit of luck he'd be somewhere with a decent phone signal, and he'd reply quickly. In case he had a phone signal but no data, she sent the same message by text.

Her salad arrived then, so she put the phone beside her, watching the breaking news as it was updated, and longing to hear the buzz that would alert her to an incoming message from Tim. But by the time she'd finished eating he hadn't replied.

The news was reporting that at least a dozen had died in one small town named Sorgente di Giacomo, about ten miles from Sulmona. The name rang a bell. Tim had been in that area the day before. She checked Google maps again and saw that the town was near a mountain pass, the one Tim had said he was heading towards. It looked to be a very small place – just a church, a central square where there were a handful of shops and cafés, and a few small streets of houses radiating out from there. Sorgente di Giacomo was on a road that wound its way up to the mountain pass in one direction and to the larger town of Sulmona in the other. To both sides were mountain ridges.

Jackie studied the map carefully. She couldn't remember the details Tim had told her about his planned route, but she knew he'd be staying in the higher mountains, only coming down to the valleys when he needed to stock up on food or if the weather was bad. Hopefully, he'd been somewhere safe when this earthquake had hit. He'd no doubt have felt it though. Well, that would be a story for him to tell when he returned home!

They'd experienced an earthquake once before, on a trip they'd done to the Balkans, in a borrowed camper van. They'd been in Bosnia, visiting Mostar and the Catholic shrine of Medjugorje where in 1981 some children insisted they'd seen the Virgin Mary appear. 'If you believe that, you'll believe anything,' Tim had said with a roll of his eyes. It was that night, while at a campsite nearby, that they felt the earth shake, heard a deep rumbling sound and their camper van rocked on its suspension. It woke them both up. Jackie had turned to Tim. 'Was that an . . .'

'Earthquake? Yes, I think it must have been.'

'Yikes. Are we safe?'

Tim made a show of counting their arms and legs, then nodding to her. 'Seem to be, yes. Go back to sleep.'

She hadn't, for hours, wondering if there'd be any more quakes. In the morning, the campsite owner had excitedly told them the epicentre had been just three miles up the road, but it had only been 4.7 on the Richter scale. 'We've had far worse,' the owner had said.

It had been a tale to tell the likes of Sarah, Martin and Alfie, when they got home. None of their friends had ever experienced an earthquake.

And now Tim had been in the vicinity of another one. This Italian earthquake was stronger – the news was reporting it had measured 6.3 on the scale. Enough to severely damage poorly designed buildings, though modern buildings would probably not suffer much at all. Tim would be safe, of course. He'd have been out in the countryside, far from falling masonry

Yet by the end of the day, she still hadn't heard from him, and her stomach was beginning to twist into a knot of worry. Even on a mountainside an earthquake might cause trees to fall, landslides, so many ways Tim might be injured . . .

That evening Jackie switched on the TV to watch the evening news bulletins. The Italian earthquake was mentioned but was no longer the top story, having been displaced by news of yet another instance of a government minister breaking the law. She was pleased to see this – it can't have been as bad as they'd originally feared. There were reports of a dozen dead, and the expectation that the death toll would rise as the small town of Sorgente di Giacomo had contained a number of medieval buildings that had simply crumbled. The earthquake had hit mid-morning, when the town had been bustling with people going about their daily lives.

She picked up her phone. Still nothing from Tim. She was beginning to feel anxious now, though she told herself that the most likely explanation for his silence was that he was in the mountains with no phone signal. She tried calling him. He'd said not to call him, as his phone battery and portable charger would only provide a limited amount of battery life, and he wanted to make it last as long as possible. 'I'll have my phone switched off quite often,' he'd said, 'so don't worry if I don't immediately answer messages. I'll see them eventually.'

His phone went straight to voicemail, as she'd guessed it would. Either it was switched off or he was out of coverage. 'Tim, when you get this, call me straight back, please? Any time. Just a bit worried about this earthquake that's in the news. Thanks. Hope you're having fun. Bye.' She hung up after leaving the message, and bit her lip. Yes, she was now officially worried.

The news report had been fairly brief, with more time given to the latest Westminster scandal. She turned to online news sites, where she found a few images of buildings in the centre of Sorgente di Giacomo which had been reduced to rubble. 'God, I hope no one was under there. Not much left. Come on, Tim, where are you?'

Maybe someone else had heard from him. She sent a text to Alfie asking if he'd been in contact with Tim and received a quick reply saying Alfie had heard nothing since a photo of some mountains a couple of days earlier. '*He'll have run out of charge while he's up a mountain, the dipstick,*' Alfie's message said, '*so don't worry.*'

But she was worrying. Who else might Tim have messaged or called? His mum. She began composing a text then decided to call.

'Audrey? It's Jackie. I was just wondering, have you heard from Tim today?'

'No, love. Had a WhatsApp message yesterday. Why?'

'This earthquake . . .'

'Oh love, he's not in that area, is he? I must admit I'm a bit vague about what part of Italy he's been in. The only part of Italy I've ever been to is Lake Garda, and that's in the north, isn't it?'

'Yes. He's in Abruzzo and that's where the earthquake happened . . .' Jackie didn't want to worry Audrey too much but then again she was his mum and needed to know.

'Oh no, you don't think . . . Have you tried to ring him?'

'Yes, and sent messages. Most likely his phone's out of charge or he's somewhere in the back of beyond with no phone signal. I just wanted to check if you'd heard, and to ask you to let me know if he does contact you.'

'There's people killed in that earthquake and they're still pulling out bodies.' Audrey's voice sounded weak and worried.

'It wasn't too big an earthquake. He'll be all right, I'm sure . . .'

'Yes, dear. Of course he will. If you hear from him you'll call me, won't you?'

'Of course.' They were both comforting each other, but Jackie knew neither of them felt entirely reassured.

'They're not saying much on the news. Is there some other way of finding out more about what's happened?'

'Good idea, Audrey. I'll look on Twitter. Maybe people in the area will know more.'

'Let me know.'

'I will. Take care.'

Jackie hung up and opened a bottle of wine. It wasn't usual for her to drink when on her own at home, but she felt her nerves needed it. She picked up her phone and began scrolling through Twitter. People were using the hashtag *#GiacomoEarthquake* when tweeting about the event. Jackie clicked on the hashtag, and scanned the posts to see what people were saying about it.

It seemed that there were some communication problems in the area. Several tweeters suggested that phone masts near Sorgente di Giacomo had been destroyed, and power lines were down. In addition, a main road was now unpassable, meaning access to the village was difficult.

One tweeter had posted: *'Hard to understand in this day and age, but the village is now almost entirely cut off. Thoughts with all those affected.'*

*'Hundreds assumed dead in Sorgente di Giacomo as all buildings in the centre collapse,'* said another tweet, with a photo of a devastated town square. Jackie scrolled through the comments, feeling a rising dread. Was it worse, then, than the news bulletin had suggested? Many of the comments beneath this photo expressed shock and sympathy with victims, but then came one that said *'Fake news. Photo is of L'Aquila earthquake in 2009. Not #GiacomoEarthquake at all.'*

Fake news. Jackie sighed. That was all she needed, for the

truth to be muddled up with fake news. Had that tweeter known they were putting up a photo of an older earthquake or was it a genuine mistake? Had they simply done it for clicks?

She scrolled on. That wasn't the only fake news tweet. It was as if the communication problems with the town had created an information vacuum, that was being filled with dubious claims and comments. People were simply making up stories. 'Thousands dead,' she read, then realised she was looking at that same photo of the L'Aquila earthquake. 'Well, that's rubbish, then.'

'*No roads in or out of Italian town, all communications down*,' screamed another headline. Was that one true? It was hard to be sure.

Jackie glanced at her phone, willing it to ring. If she could just hear that Tim was out of the area, safe and well, she'd be happy. But until she heard from him she couldn't help but worry that he might be caught up in it.

It was the not-knowing that was excruciating. Her thoughts turned to the newspapers that had been in Henry's *Carpathia* memorabilia. The ones from before *Carpathia* reached New York, that had carried all sorts of incorrect reports of the tragedy. All souls lost, all souls saved – fake news, it existed even back then before the term had been invented. It must have been terrible for the friends and family of *Titanic* passengers, waiting for definitive news. She now knew exactly how that felt, even in these days of instant global communication, and it was horrible.

# Chapter 20

## Madeleine, 17 April 1912

Another day dawned, a day closer to land but also another day during which Madeleine felt they should keep out of Captain Rostron's way. Despite the captain's warning the previous day, Ralph still set off to the Marconi cabin in the morning to try once more to reason with, or bribe, Harold Cottam. He returned with interesting news.

'It wasn't Cottam on duty. It was the Marconi operator from *Titanic*. A young fellow, with frostbitten feet from sitting so many hours in a lifeboat with his feet in water. Apparently, Cottam is exhausted from being on duty almost constantly and the captain asked the other fellow to take over to give him a break.'

'And would he send your messages?' Madeleine asked.

'Not a chance. He said Rostron's been clear about that. So we must wait.'

They strolled together around the ship, peering at the horizon ahead to see if they could sight land yet. Madeleine was also keeping an eye out for the woman in brown and the baby that might or might not be Lucy's. But although there was news that they were getting close to shore, and the operator had said they would soon be in radio contact of land and would be able to send the dozens of personal messages from *Titanic* survivors, there was no hope of seeing land yet.

'Mr Meyer? Mrs Meyer? I am glad to find you.' Charles Marshall had caught up with them as they passed along the boat deck. 'There is a subscription set up, to raise funds for those of *Titanic*'s steerage who have been left destitute by the disaster. Some of them, of course, were on the ship to start a new life in the United States. They had all their worldly possessions on the ship and have lost everything.'

'We will of course subscribe,' Ralph said, and Madeleine nodded her agreement. 'Surely there will be some compensation paid out?'

'Hmm. Maybe, maybe not. But those poor people will need money to get themselves settled, to buy the necessaries. There's also talk of buying medals for the crew and some sort of commemorative item – there's suggestion of a "loving cup" – for the captain as a mark of thanks for all he's done. He has looked after the *Titanic* survivors so well.'

Madeleine saw Ralph open his mouth as if to say that the captain had been no friend to them, even if he had acted well and decisively in going to *Titanic*'s rescue. But he clearly thought better of it, saying nothing, simply nodding.

'Say, have you seen Mr Ismay around the ship at all?' Charles Marshall went on. 'I heard he was definitely on one of the lifeboats. There are people blaming him.'

'Bruce Ismay? But why?' Madeleine asked.

'As the chairman of White Star Line, surely the ultimate responsibility for what happened rests with him. Look, he saved himself, despite the loss of so many others, and now he's holed himself up somewhere on this ship. Not facing anyone, not explaining himself. No wonder people are beginning to talk, to wonder if perhaps he cut corners, reduced costs, and thus made the ship less safe than it should have been.'

Madeleine frowned. 'All that talk of it being unsinkable . . .'

'Yes, and that led to it not having enough lifeboats for all the people on board. Had there been enough capacity, undoubtedly more souls would have been saved.' Charles Marshall raised his hat to them. 'Well, I'll be on my way. We're just thankful our nieces were among the survivors.'

'Of course. Give my regards to them, and to Evelyn,' Madeleine said, as he left.

'You know what I'm thinking?' Ralph said, once Marshall was out of earshot. 'If I can track down Ismay, and get an interview with him . . .'

'What a scoop that would be!' Madeleine saw it immediately. 'But you've nothing to write on other than napkins, and the captain would put you in chains if he found out.'

'The captain can't stop me talking to whoever I want to on this ship. And he doesn't need to know what we talk about, should I be able to find Mr Ismay. It's not just about the scoop, Maddy. It's about telling the truth, the full story, and that includes giving Mr Ismay a chance to speak out.'

Ralph had a determined look on his face, an expression that Madeleine knew well. There was no arguing with him. And he was right – Ismay deserved the chance to tell his side of the story. If Ralph managed to find and interview him, it could be the making of his career. 'Very well. Do you want me to come with you?'

'No, darling. I think it'd be better if just I spoke to him. He may not want to open up and be honest in front of a woman. But if you get any hints as to where on the ship he's been hiding, that would help.' Ralph smiled at her and kissed her. 'I shall see you later, then.'

'Good luck.' She watched him set off, striding along the boat deck and down some steps leading to the public areas. A couple of passengers watched him go, and muttered to each other, pointing his way and glaring at him. Madeleine frowned, considering if she should confront them and ask if they had a problem with her husband, but thought better of it. Instead, she set off back to their cabin to fetch a jacket. It was turning chilly.

She also wanted to check, irrational as it sounded even to herself, if there was any further evidence of crew members or officers going through their belongings. If the captain suspected that Ralph had already written a piece, might he not send someone to search for it in their cabin one more time?

Thankfully, there was no evidence anyone else had been in. Everything was just as they'd left it. Even the unused napkins, the ones she had not written on, were still piled on the dressing table. She supposed the officers wouldn't for a moment consider they'd be so desperate for writing materials that they'd use paper serviettes.

She picked up a warm jacket and a scarf, and went out again, up to the Marconi cabin on deck. There, as she'd hoped, was Harold Cottam, who'd relieved the *Titanic* operator. He greeted her politely but she could see at once that his guard was up.

'Mrs Meyer. If you are looking for your husband, I haven't seen him since yesterday.'

'That's all right. No, he's amusing himself at present. I thought I'd come and see how you are? It must be a lonely job, this one.'

'It is, but on this voyage, it's been a very busy one. There's been a stream of incoming radio traffic from other ships, all wanting to know what's happened and can they help at all. We were briefly in range of radio stations on land, but this fog is interfering with the signals, so it's as though we're still further out to sea again.'

She nodded, as though she fully understood the effect fog would have on Marconi transmissions. 'Have you managed to send any of the passengers' private messages?'

'Some, not all. Frankly, I don't think I'll ever get them all sent, before we reach New York.'

'What a shame. How far out are we now?'

'Another day, or day and a half, I should think.'

'Not too much longer then. I wonder, Mr Cottam, if you've had any more thoughts on whether you should send my husband's messages?'

The radio operator stroked his chin. 'Actually . . . I did what your husband suggested and sent a message to Mr Marconi while we were in range. He is keen to hear details of what happened. But I still think I cannot disobey the captain. He wants to prioritise the survivors' personal messages before any others. And as there are so many of those, I fear I will not get to Mr Meyer's messages, even if I was inclined to send them.'

'I see. Well, thank you for being open with us about this. We shan't pester you any further. My husband will wait until we dock to get his story sent to the papers. I would like to thank you, however, on behalf of everyone on board. You have worked hard and selflessly during the course of this tragedy. I hope you are well rewarded for all you have done. Good day.'

'Thank you, Mrs Meyer. Have a good day yourself.'

She left him putting his headphones back on, listening to the incoming messages and tapping out those survivors' messages that probably wouldn't reach their intended recipient before they docked. She was pleased to hear they were near land now, and only a day out of New York. She'd had enough of this voyage, and they hadn't even got anywhere!

She remembered then she had another mission. To try to find where Bruce Ismay was billeted on board. Maybe the Marshall family might know. It would be pleasant in any case to spend a little time with her friend Evelyn. She set off towards their suite of cabins.

'Lovely to see you, Maddy,' Evelyn said, giving Madeleine a kiss on both cheeks.

'And you. Would you care to take a stroll on deck? Or have a coffee perhaps?'

'Mama, can you spare me for a while?' Evelyn turned to Mrs

Marshall who was sitting in a chair in their cabin. On the beds lay the three nieces, napping.

'Of course, dear. I'll sit with the girls. You catch up with your friend.'

They headed towards the main dining room where coffee could always be found. 'I'm glad to get out of there for a while. Poor Caroline has nightmares whenever she sleeps, and has to be comforted. All of them cannot wait until they're back on dry land. I can't say I blame them.'

'Me neither. It's a terrible thing. I hear people are blaming Mr Ismay for it? As the chairman and director of White Star Line, they're saying it's all his responsibility.' Madeleine led Evelyn to a free table and signalled a steward to bring them coffee.

'I heard that too. But there are so many who could be blamed. The designer of the ship. *Titanic*'s Captain Smith, who ought to have steered away from the icebergs sooner. Whoever had the job of looking out for icebergs.' Evelyn shrugged. 'I think it's all just down to bad luck in the end. Apparently, ice is rarely found that far south.'

'You're probably right. Mr Ismay came on board from *Titanic*, didn't he? I wonder where he's been staying on the ship. I haven't seen him at all, have you?'

Evelyn shook her head. 'No. But I wouldn't know him if I saw him. Papa said that he's been given a crew member's cabin somewhere so I imagine he's stayed there, out of the way of anyone who might make trouble. I feel sorry for him. He's suffered too, and if he does feel responsible, he will have to live with that feeling for the rest of his life.'

Madeleine sipped her coffee. 'He will, yes. You are a good person to have sympathy for him. I wonder if the wider world will, once the full story is known?'

'I hope the papers are sympathetic to him.' Evelyn gave Madeleine a knowing look.

She'd guessed, Madeleine thought, that Ralph wanted to write about Ismay. But she couldn't confirm that to Evelyn, or reassure her that the papers, even Ralph's, would be sympathetic. It was out of her hands.

The conversation moved on then, to what they would do once they'd returned to New York, whether they were going to stay on *Carpathia* or make new plans, what the three cousins were going to do when they reached home.

With the coffee drunk, Madeleine left Evelyn to return to her family, while she went in search of Ralph to pass on the lead as to where Mr Ismay might be found. She found him, heading along a corridor.

'Ismay is likely to be in Dr McGee's cabin,' he told Madeleine excitedly. 'I'm going to knock on the door. I can do that, at least.'

'All right, but please don't get in trouble with the captain.' She had visions of him being clapped in irons in the hold of the ship.

'I won't. Come with me. Not into Ismay's cabin, but you could wait nearby. Maybe it'll be better – if the captain did happen to come by he might be more restrained towards me if there's a lady present.'

'Hmm, not so sure about that,' she said, but followed him anyway.

They reached Ismay's cabin, and Madeleine stood back to guard the door, to warn Ralph if the captain or other officers came anywhere near. Ralph glanced at Madeleine then tapped on the door. 'Mr Ismay?'

'Who is it?' came the reply, in a hoarse voice.

Ralph cleared his throat. 'My name, sir, is Ralph Meyer, of the *New York Tribune*. I was wondering . . .'

'The *Tribune* – why, are we at New York already?'

'No, sir, if you could open the door I will explain. I was on board *Carpathia* by chance and I wondered if you would like to tell your story . . .'

'Go away.'

190

'To set the record straight, to put across your side of things . . .'

'Go away, I tell you.'

Madeleine beckoned to Ralph to come away, leave the poor man alone, but he was clearly not ready to give up yet.

'Sir, you must know that there will be speculation, and some of it perhaps derogatory to yourself, and this is your chance to have the truth told from your point of view, at the earliest opportunity. I will, of course, be sympathetic towards you in the story . . .'

Behind Madeleine there was a cough, and she turned in horror to realise Captain Rostron had appeared. He must have crept up quietly. Once again, she wondered if the captain was having them watched and followed. 'Meyer? What do you think you are doing?'

'Ah, Captain. I was just having a chat . . .'

'I think he told you to go away. So why are you still here?'

'Mr Ismay might have wanted to tell his side of the story. I was giving him the opportunity to do so.'

The captain took a step towards Ralph, and jabbed a finger at his chest. 'You will leave him alone. I will not have you pestering my guests on this ship. They deserve peace and quiet, away from the like of you. This, Mr Meyer, is your last warning. If you disobey me one more time you will be confined to your cabin for the rest of the journey and I will have a crewman stationed at your door to ensure you stay there.'

'Captain, with respect, you told me not to bother Mr Cottam again, and I have obeyed that command. You never once told me not to speak to anyone else.'

'Ralph, please, come on. Let's go and find ourselves some coffee, shall we? Or a brandy?' Madeleine took Ralph's arm and pulled him away, flashing the captain a look that she hoped conveyed an apology and a promise that Ralph would do as he'd been asked.

'Make sure he stays away from this cabin, Mrs Meyer,' the captain said, his voice sounding deep and menacing.

She nodded and steered Ralph back to their own cabin, urging him to say nothing until they were behind a closed door. Inside, she pushed him gently into a seat. 'Darling, you really must not annoy the captain. He's furious with you. I know you think he can't stop you, but while we're on the ship he can, and he will. His word's law here.'

'He's a brute. A jumped-up little man who just enjoys flaunting his power.'

'He's only doing what he thinks is best for his passengers.'

Ralph shook his head. 'He's wrong. Well, as soon as we're on dry land he has absolutely no jurisdiction over what I do, and my story will be published. I *will* get the truth told. Not only that, I shall endeavour to interview Ismay in New York.'

'But darling, you won't have time if *Carpathia* is turned around quickly.'

'I'll use whatever time I have.' Ralph's face was set, and Madeleine realised there was no point arguing with him. He would cool down in time. She doubted he'd be able to interview Mr Ismay – the man had made it clear he wasn't open to speaking to reporters, even if they did have time before sailing again. But she'd let Ralph work this out for himself.

She reached out a hand and he took it. They'd been together a long time and she knew his ways; she knew when to assert herself (such as leading him away from the angry captain) and when to leave him alone and let things blow over. He smiled at her and squeezed her hand.

'Coffee? Or a brandy?' she asked.

'Brandy.'

'How about I fetch them back here? You stay and rest.' So you can't run into the captain again, she thought, but didn't dare say.

'Yes, please.'

She kissed him and headed out to find the brandy. A small bottle they could keep in their cabin for the rest of the voyage would be a good idea, even though, with luck, there'd only be another day or so at sea.

While she was searching for brandy, she could take the

opportunity, while alone, to have one more look for the woman in brown and the baby that were still occupying her thoughts. One last search of public areas, and trawl up and down the corridors of cabins. If she heard a baby cry in a cabin, perhaps she could knock on the door on some pretext or other. If she could find that baby, she could determine once and for all whether the woman in brown really was its mother, and set her mind at rest. Or if by some chance it did turn out to be Norah and she could reunite her with Lucy, somehow it felt as though that would help her get over her own loss, her own childlessness. She needed only an opportunity to find out if it might work.

# Chapter 21

## Tim, 2022

Earthquake. That's what it must have been, Tim told himself, as the dust swirled around him. He tried to move and felt rising panic as he realised his legs were trapped. It was pitch dark. He'd been at the back of the building when it happened. He'd first noticed everything around him moving, sliding, things crashing to the floor . . . there'd been a deep rumbling sound . . . a woman was screaming . . . the ceiling seemed to be cracking and falling and fixtures tumbled over, knocking him to the ground.

He'd screamed too then, as the ceiling came down completely in a huge crash and a cloud of choking dust rose up. He'd hit his head as he fell. Something was across his legs, pinning him down. The ground beneath him was shaking and it felt and sounded as though the building was still collapsing. He lay still, waiting for the dust to settle, waiting for the shaking to stop, trying to control his breathing, desperately trying to stay calm.

He'd wild camped the night before, halfway up a mountain in a small clearing. It was a beautiful night, clear and blessedly cool after a sweltering day. He'd set up his tent near a small stream which trickled down the mountainside and took the opportunity to sit with his feet in the water, and then he used his cooking pot to pour the cool fresh water over his head. Bliss. One of the things he loved about wild camping was the return to basics, the way it made you appreciate small, simple pleasures. The way it made you realise how little you really needed to be comfortable, happy and content.

He heaved a sigh of contentment, looking forward to a peaceful night in the mountains. He took out his phone to send a message and photo to Jackie and realised that it had died, it was completely out of charge. And so was his portable charger.

'Sorry, Jacks. No photos today,' he said, and pulled out his map. He needed somewhere to charge up both devices. A café that would let him sit for a couple of hours beside a socket. Or a campsite.

There was a campsite just outside a small town down the valley – Sorgente di Giacomo. He briefly cursed himself for not realising his phone was out of charge – he could have pushed on for another couple of hours walking to reach the campsite that evening. But now it was almost dusk and he didn't fancy the walk down the mountain in the dark. It would have to be the next day. He could go down in the morning, check into the campsite and leave his phone to charge somewhere, and then spend the afternoon mooching around the little town, moving on the following day. 'Be nice to have an easy day tomorrow,' he told himself. Sometimes you needed a bit of a rest day, or at least a rest half-day.

With that plan in mind, he set up his Trangia cooking stove, opened a tin of sausage and beans to heat up, and ate that with a hunk of slightly stale bread for his evening meal, washed down with a bottle of beer, and a few bite-sized cannoli pastries filled with chocolate as a dessert. In the cool evening air, it had been a perfect meal.

And then in the morning, he'd packed up camp early and set off down to the town. It had taken just two hours to reach the campsite and soon he had checked in and set up his tent once more, in a shady spot under some trees. It was the kind of campsite that catered for hikers, and there was a communal kitchen and sitting room. There were a set of pigeonholes in the campsite office where you could securely leave phones to charge, and Tim made use of one of those. He decided to go into town for a look around and to buy some groceries while his phone and power pack charged.

It was a typical little town for the area, comprised of a warren of medieval cobbled streets that fanned out from a central square in front of a solid looking church. It was very pretty. The kind of place that he imagined would barely have changed in the last five hundred years. Take away the modern shop signs and glazing and you might be back in the 16th century. The buildings were made of a pale grey stone with terracotta roof tiles and no two buildings were the same – each was at a different angle to the narrow streets, a different height.

It'd be good to gaze down on it from above, he thought, glancing over at the church bell tower. It appeared to have a walkway around the outside, just below the bells. As he looked up, he noticed a pair of tourists strolling around it, taking photos.

'Perfect,' he muttered, and crossed the square to the church. Grocery shopping could wait a while longer. He fancied going up the church tower. It was just as shame he would not be able to take photos, but he could always come back later with his phone.

The church was open and free to look around, but there was an entrance fee for the tower. It was only two euros, and he was issued with a badly printed leaflet in Italian, French and English that gave a little history of the church and its tower. The church was dedicated to San Giacomo, or Saint James, which didn't surprise him, and a short paragraph explained that the town was supposedly founded when Giacomo rested on a long journey and made use of a nearby spring. So that was what 'sorgente' meant.

There wasn't much of interest in the church which was only a couple of hundred years old, replacing an earlier one that had been damaged in an earthquake. It was rather dark and gloomy inside, and one of the side chapels was hidden behind some scaffolding. Tim headed up a spiral staircase that led up to the bell tower and emerged blinking back into the sunlight. The tower wasn't particularly tall but it was higher than other buildings around and as he'd hoped, provided a wonderful view of the jumble of medieval rooftops and the mountains all around.

He made his way slowly around the tower. From one side he could see the campsite, and he spent a little time trying to pick out his tent. The views across to the mountains were stunning, and he was able to see his onward route up onto the next ridge. 'Definitely coming back up here to take some pics,' he told himself. No matter that he'd have to pay the entrance fee again, it would be well worth it.

With that promise to himself he decided it was time to buy some food for the next two or three days and head back to his campsite. There was a small grocery shop just opposite the church in the central square that would probably have all that he needed. He looked down, noticing the tourist couple now seating themselves at a table outside a café next to the grocery shop. A waiter in a white shirt was on his way out to take their order. And a woman with a pushchair was in the process of heaving it backwards up a step into the shop. Everywhere he looked, the locals were going about their daily business, life ticking over the way it always did and always had.

His thoughts turned to Jackie, and he glanced at his watch. Right now, she'd be in her office, going through emails, tracking down whatever rare books Henry was after. To tell the truth, Tim had little idea of what Jackie did at work but she liked her job and that was what mattered. He set off down the spiral steps of the bell tower, his mind still on her as he crossed the square and went into the little shop.

He was thirsty, he realised, and he had not brought his rucksack or any water. As he passed a fridge of cold drinks in the shop, he opened it and grabbed a large plastic bottle of water. He could swig from it as he walked back to the campsite.

In the next aisle was the woman with the pushchair, which held a baby of perhaps six months old. Maybe a little more. Tim was no expert on children, but this one looked younger than Bobby but bigger than a newborn. A little girl, judging by her clothing. The woman was older, probably the child's grandmother. She was tiny, and was struggling to reach something from a high shelf. Tim had smiled at her and reached up, fetching the tin she'd been stretching for, and received a *grazie* in response. He'd then turned to peruse the jars of tomato pasta sauces in front of him, and that was the moment the earthquake had struck, sending the jars and fixtures and shop's masonry crashing down on him.

Now, he wriggled a little and discovered with relief his arms were free. Somehow, he managed to pull the front of his T-shirt up over his mouth and nose to keep the dust out. The bottle of water he'd been holding was lying across his neck, accessible. That was a good thing, he thought, in case he was trapped there for a long time. Was he injured? Everything hurt but, although his legs were pinned by a shelving unit that had fallen, he didn't think he was badly injured. He could move his toes, though he dared not try to move too much in case anything fell further onto him, making the situation worse. Panic rose up in him as he realised he was trapped in what was left of the shop. He lay still, waiting for the rumbling and shaking to stop. It seemed to go on forever though a rational part of his mind told him it was only a minute or less.

Gradually the worst of the dust settled, and he began to shout out for help. What was the Italian for 'help'? He had no idea. Did it matter? Shout anything and rescuers would follow the sound. There was noise, all around, as parts of the building collapsed further, or rubble settled. And distantly, as though from outside, there were shouts and screams.

What of the other people who had been in the shop? The woman and baby? The shopkeeper? Tim could see nothing through the dust and the gloom. He felt around him, cautiously. They'd been right beside him when it happened. His hand alighted on something – flesh. The woman's arm, he thought. 'Are you all right?' he asked, but there was only a feeble groan in reply. He reached further and discovered that one end of a concrete beam that had fallen was across the woman's chest, crushing her. The baby? He gasped. An image of the child's little face, smiling at him from under her pink sun hat, came to him. She was so young, so little. Surely her life couldn't be ending now, before it had barely begun? That wasn't right. He continued groping around him. She couldn't be far away, and maybe, somehow, she'd escaped . . .

He heard a whimper, but whether it was the dying grandmother or the child, he couldn't be sure. And then his hand alighted on something – a wheel of the pushchair. He groped further and, yes, there she was. The pushchair was upside down, pinned under the fallen shop fixtures but, like himself, protected by them from the worst of the fallen masonry. He twisted around a little and realised his legs weren't pinned fast. He could move them under the shelves. He inched them out, carefully, slowly, scraping his thighs painfully against broken shelf edges until he could reach further under the pushchair, his hand checking over the child. As he did so she grabbed at his fingers with her tiny hands. She was alive! She was well enough to grab at him, and then he heard that whimper again, and it was definitely the baby. He twisted some more until he was free of the fixture, but still in a very confined space. Just enough to sit, crouched over, and reach with both hands under the pushchair. He found the clip of the strap that held the baby in place, and with one hand supporting her managed to unclip it and slowly, carefully, pull her out, praying she wasn't injured, that he wasn't making things worse.

And then she was in his arms. He felt rising panic once more. Now, as well as keeping himself alive until rescue came, he was saddled with a small child. A baby. He knew nothing about handling babies. He tried to remember how Martin held Bobby, how he spoke to him, what he did with him. He sat, bent over with his back already complaining about the position, rocking the baby as much as the confined space allowed, speaking to her in a soothing tone. She cried a little, whimpered some more, but as far as he could tell in the darkness, she was not hurt, at least not badly.

'I don't know how your grandma is, little one,' he said to her. 'I can't help her. But I can hold on to you. If I'm going to survive this, then so are you, all right?'

He received a little squeak in return, and once more the baby clutched his finger, and tried to draw it up to her mouth.

'Ah no. My hands are a bit dusty for that.' He remembered the bottle of water, and groped around for it. With one hand he managed to unscrew the top, and took a gulp of it himself so that it wasn't completely full. 'Best not drink too much, Tim. That water could be the difference between life and death. For both of us.' He screwed the top back on, but didn't tighten it completely so that when he tipped the bottle a small amount of water seeped out. By feel he held it to the baby's lips and was gratified to hear her trying to latch on to it, to suck at it. If they were trapped here for a long time, any amount of water he could get into her might help save her.

'So, kid. You and me, eh? Stuck with each other, for the time being. What are you called, I wonder? Do you mind if I give you a name? Just for use while we're in here. How about . . .' he thought hard, then remembered a conversation he'd had with Jackie, when she'd talked about her favourite names for any future children they might have. What had she favoured for a

200

girl? Amelia, she'd suggested, or Olivia. 'Olivia. That's a good one as we're in a country that produces most of the world's olive oil. I'm going to call you Livvy, all right, little one?'

The baby made a little sound as if in response. Not a whimper, Tim thought, not this time. More of a burble. She wasn't hurt then. She seemed to be perfectly content in his arms, accepting this new, strange situation, this new person who was holding her. She seemed to like him talking to her. 'So, Livvy, what shall we talk about? How's life here in Sorgente di Giacomo, eh? I mean, before this happened. Where do you live? Where will Mum and Dad be right now?' And then he realised with a jolt that the child's mother and father might also have been caught up in this too. The baby might have lost her entire family. Perhaps best not to think about that, Timbo, he told himself. There were no more sounds from the old lady, not even when he reached out and touched her once more. He feared the worst for her, but there was nothing he could do to help her. Apart from do his best to care for her granddaughter. It was ironic. He, who had no idea how to handle babies, was this baby's only hope.

'I wonder how bad this thing is, eh, Livvy?' For all he knew, it might be just this building that had collapsed, and already there could be teams of rescue workers outside digging away at the rubble. Not that he could hear anything that suggested that. Alternatively, and this didn't bear thinking about, it could have been a massive quake, with the entire town, the whole region, devastated. 'Let's hope for the best, Livvy. Let's assume it's not too bad, and we're just unlucky here in this shop. They'll dig us out. You wait and see.'

With no light, he had no idea of the time. By his reckoning it had probably been around midday when the earthquake hit. What a shame he had left his phone at the campsite. If he had it now, he could call someone, let them know where he was and that he had a baby with him. And the torch function would have been useful too.

'Let's be quiet and listen for a moment, Livvy. See if we can hear anyone nearby that might get us out.' He listened hard, but the noises were all distant. He felt around for something he might bang on, something he might use to make a noise to let rescuers know. A tin of food, perhaps, that he could hit against the masonry. But he could find nothing, just fallen plaster from the ceiling and broken glass jars. And he dared not move too much, for fear the fragile shelving units would collapse further. They were all that was protecting him and Livvy from being crushed.

'Come on, someone. Come and find us. We need you,' he muttered, and once more Livvy squeezed his finger as though she understood and was doing her best to give him strength to endure the hours or maybe days they had ahead of them, trapped in the rubble.

# Chapter 22

## Madeleine, 17-18 April 1912

Madeleine found brandy, but saw no sign of the baby or the woman in brown. She was tempted to go back to the stewardesses' cabin to see Violet Jessop who'd brought the baby on board, and ask her once more whether she'd seen the child again. She knew she would never forget the feel of that warm little body in her arms. The pursed lips, button nose, perfect smooth skin. And the agony Lucy must be going through, not knowing whether her child had survived or not, was never far from her mind.

As she passed the passenger bulletin board, she noticed a new message that had been posted up since she last checked. She read it and clapped a hand to her mouth. *Notice to Passengers: I hereby declare that no press messages have been Marconied from this ship, with the exception of a short one of about twenty words to the Associated Press, sent immediately after the passengers had been picked up, and the passenger messages have been dispatched with all speed possible. The reason for this statement is that it has come to my attention that several passengers are under the impression that the delay in dispatching their private messages is due to the instruments being used for the press. A.H. Rostron, Commander.*

So people knew of Ralph's attempts to get his story out, and thought that was preventing their personal messages being sent? Perhaps that moustached man who'd witnessed the captain telling Ralph he couldn't send his story might have spread the word. That might explain the harsh looks Ralph had been given and the distinct frostiness from some of the passengers.

She took the brandy back to Ralph and spent the rest of the day with him, talking about how he might get access to Mr Ismay once they were back in New York and whether he'd be able to quickly write up an interview with him before they sailed again. He checked and rechecked the stories he'd already written, including the details from the women that Madeleine had jotted onto napkins. 'I shall never sleep tonight,' he told her. 'Tomorrow this story will get to the *New York Tribune* despite Captain Rostron. The scoop is mine, even if it's a day or two later than it might have been.'

Madeleine smiled, hoping that he was right, and that there was no possibility of any other paper getting the scoop at this late stage.

When the morning came, morning of the day when they would finally reach New York, Madeleine looked out of their cabin's porthole to see nothing but a blanket of white fog. The ship had slowed to a crawl and all sounds were muffled.

They headed out to breakfast and learned that they were somewhere off Nantucket. 'I spotted the *Nantucket Lightship* earlier before the fog closed in,' Mr Marshall told Ralph with excitement. 'So we aren't far off. Listen, you can hear its foghorn.'

Sure enough, every couple of minutes the low mournful sound of the lightship's foghorn sounded through the mist, followed by an answering call from *Carpathia*. The closeness of the fog, the sounds, the absolute stillness of the air and the water lent the scene an eerie atmosphere. Madeleine was looking forward to seeing land, buildings, people, other ships – anything other than the dead flat of the sea and the confined claustrophobic traumatised atmosphere of the ship and its passengers.

'You been sending reports to your paper?' Marshall asked Ralph, gesturing to the message on the bulletin board.

'No, more's the pity,' Ralph replied with a grimace. 'The captain forbade it, and no amount of persuasion would change his mind. Though Marconi himself told the operator to send news stories.'

'Well, I suppose the world will know all the details soon enough,' Marshall said with a shrug, before turning away.

'He's not in the newspaper business. They don't understand the importance of it,' Madeleine said to Ralph, laying her hand on his arm in support. He smiled at her but she could still see in his eyes the fury towards the captain he still harboured, and his determination to get the story out.

The day wore on, but the fog didn't lift until the late afternoon. At last Madeleine could see land and the relief she felt astounded her. They were nearly back. The ship swung around the end of Long Island, past Sandy Hook, into New York's lower bay. And to the surprise of everyone, except perhaps Ralph, there was a flotilla of small boats awaiting them off Sandy Hook. Tugs, ferries, yachts and steamers, all jostled for position around *Carpathia*, like a gaggle of ducklings around a mother duck. One sounded its whistle and all the others around them answered. The noise of them all was astonishing after the days of silence out at sea.

Madeleine and Ralph, along with many others, were out on deck watching the boats swarming towards them. 'See that one, I think that's the pilot boat,' Ralph said, pointing out a small white boat that was heading directly towards them. The captain on the bridge must have seen it too, for *Carpathia* slowed and then stopped, to allow the pilot to come aboard.

'Ralph, what if there are reporters on board those other boats, and the captain lets them board as well?'

Ralph stared out to sea. 'That is exactly what I have been

fearing, darling. That now we are so close, I will lose the scoop, even though I was right here, on the spot.'

But as they watched, it seemed there was no danger of that happening. Only the pilot boat was allowed alongside, and only one person, the pilot, boarded. Ralph heaved a sigh of relief. 'For once, the captain's refusal to allow any news reports to leave this ship has worked in my favour.'

There was still a way to go before they reached New York's upper bay and then the docks alongside Manhattan's west side. And the small boats were flocking ever closer. On board, Madeleine could see people standing, shouting through megaphones at *Carpathia*'s passengers who were all leaning on the deck rails, watching. 'Ralph, some of those are reporters. Look, read the placards they're holding up. *New York Times*. *The Sun*. *New York American*.'

'And they're trying to get people to shout answers to their questions, aren't they?'

Madeleine frowned and listened. 'Sir, were you on *Titanic*? Is it true the ship's still afloat?' 'Ma'am, what can you tell us about the moment you were flung into the water?' 'Who can tell us how many died?' Questions were fired up, one after the other.

Some of those on deck were shouting responses, but it all sounded so muddled Madeleine suspected the reporters on the small boats wouldn't be able to make much sense of it, even if they could hear the answers. She suspected they would not be able to hear at all.

'Listen to the questions,' she said to Ralph. 'They're asking if it's true *Titanic* is still afloat.'

He nodded. 'There will have been all sorts of made-up stories published in the papers. And all because Captain Rostron refused to let me send the truth out.'

'I can't imagine how awful it must have been for relatives of those on *Titanic*, not knowing what really happened. There will be some who think everyone's been saved, who'll be waiting for their loved ones to return, yet they never will.'

'I know. That's why I've tried so hard to get the truth told, as soon as possible.' Ralph's face was set hard, as he leaned over the railings, his hand shading his eyes, peering at each small boat. He was looking for representatives of the *New York Tribune* she realised. An idea came to her. 'Ralph, if your paper has a boat here, if they came close enough you'd be able to throw your story down to them! The boat would get back to New York before we dock, and you'd get the scoop.'

He stared at her. 'I was looking for them . . . They're sure to be here. They know I'm on board. They'll have guessed I'd write a story. But what if I missed, and the story landed in the sea? It'd be lost.'

'Wrap it in something waterproof. Attach it to something that'll float. Come on, we can do this!' She ran back to their cabin and retrieved a hat made of waxed cotton. Ralph had followed her. 'Use this.' She took the story out of her corset and handed it to him.

'And how will we make it float?' he said, wrapping his precious bundle of typed papers in the hat and tying it tightly with string. He put the rest of his ball of string in his pocket.

'That cigar box,' she said, pointing to one Ralph had left out on the dressing table. He tipped out the remaining cigars. 'Fill it with corks.'

'Corks?'

'Yes, come on, quickly!' Madeleine had seen a bucket filled with champagne corks, tucked in a corner of the dining room. She took Ralph's hand and led him there, praying it would still be in place. Thankfully it was, and she grabbed a handful and filled the cigar box with them. 'Now, attach that to the story package,' she said, and Ralph nodded. He used more of the string to bind the wrapped story to the makeshift buoy.

'Will it hold?' she asked him, and he nodded, his eyes shining.

'I think so. Come on, back up to the deck.'

Up on deck, they ran from one side to the other, scanning each small boat. Eventually Ralph shouted and pointed at a small steam boat on their starboard side. Madeleine looked and saw that a man on board was holding a placard with the words 'New York Tribune' written on it. 'That's Watson!' Ralph shouted, and began waving at the man, yelling his name.

'Here! Watson, it's me! Over here! Come closer!' He waved the bundle frantically above his head. At last, the man with the placard noticed him, and turned to speak to someone else on board the little boat. Bit by bit it inched closer, almost hitting one of the other yachts.

'Is it close enough?' Madeleine said, trying to judge the distance Ralph would need to throw his bundle.

'I think so, and look, they have a boat hook.' The man, Watson, was brandishing a long stick with a hook on the end, ready to fish Ralph's story out of the water. He was gesticulating to Ralph to throw it.

Other boats chartered by newspapers were nearby, watching with interest. If the New York Tribune men didn't manage to grab the story out of the water one of the others would, Ralph realised.

'All right, then. Here goes.' Ralph took the parcel in one hand, leaned back, and lobbed it with all his might in the direction of his paper's boat.

# Chapter 23

## Tim, 2022

Tim had no way of measuring the passage of time. He and Livvy had been trapped for how long now? Hours? Days? She'd cried, with hunger, he'd thought, for a while. He'd done his best to console her, and to satisfy her with a little water, but it wasn't enough. At last, she'd fallen asleep across his chest, in his arms. He hadn't slept himself, not that there was any way of making himself comfortable in the tiny, cramped space with his legs wedged under a fixture. He had remained awake, alert, listening for signs that rescuers were nearby. He didn't want to shout if there was no chance of being heard – he needed to conserve his strength. Besides, he didn't want to wake Livvy. While she slept, the nightmare of their situation was kept at bay for her.

If they survived, if she got through this, she'd never remember anything about it. But he would remember every second, every detail of this ordeal for the rest of his life. If he survived.

All he could do to pass the time while Livvy slept was to think about his life, his relationship with Jackie, and what might happen when or if he got home. What did he want from the future? He wanted her. He wanted Jackie. She'd be amazed to see him now, cradling this baby in his arms, doing everything in his power to care for her. Jackie had always said he'd be a great father. Of teenagers, yes, he'd always thought. He was well used to dealing with teenagers at school. It was little ones, the pre-teens, toddlers and babies that scared him. How do you deal with children too young to have any sense, too young to understand what you said to them? Children so small they needed you for everything, whose lives were in your hands? He held Livvy a little tighter. She was totally dependent on him right now, he realised. Her life, her well-being, entirely depended on him.

He'd never before understood what people meant when they talked about 'bonding' with a baby. How could you feel so much for a creature that gave so little back? But now – he got it. Despite the enormous responsibility he felt towards Livvy, he knew this ordeal would be worse for him without her. Her presence, her warm little body against his, her little sounds and the way she wriggled in his arms, all of it helped him somehow.

Funnily though, Livvy seemed to have some sort of under-standing of their predicament. Even though she was most likely Italian and so very young that surely she didn't know any of the words he said to her, she did seem to listen. She quietened her crying when he spoke to her. She nuzzled for the water bottle when he offered it to her, and when he told her there was no food and suggested she go back to sleep, and reassured her they'd be rescued, she snuggled against him. He found her hand and she wrapped her fingers around his thumb. It seemed to calm her, to reassure her.

'Well, Livvy. You are teaching me a lesson, young lady. You are teaching me that I can deal with babies. That I instinctively seem to know what to do. Thank you. I only hope I will still be around to put these lessons into practice one day.' Tim shifted a little so that the baby's head was resting against his cheek, and then he twisted his face and kissed her head. It felt warm, soft and downy beneath the dust. Gently he tried to wipe the worst of the dust from her face. He dared not spare any water to clean her up. In any case, it was pitch black and he'd no doubt just smear the dirt around or get it into her eyes which would hurt her.

'We'll just have to stay dirty, you and me, eh, Livvy?' The child burbled a little in response. She seemed to understand that conversation went two ways, and he found her 'answers' comforting in an odd sort of way. They told him she was alive, she was well, she appreciated him talking to her.

And that was keeping him going. Livvy was keeping him going.

Jackie. And his mum. If the news had spread to England, they'd know about the earthquake. Would they be worrying that he was caught up in it? Would Jackie have contacted his mum, or Alfie, asking if they'd heard anything more? If he never got out of here, who would comfort whom?

Had he and Livvy spent an entire night trapped? He was hungry, and he'd felt sleepy for a while. He knew they'd been there several hours but was it a new day or was it still the middle of the night? There was no light whatsoever seeping in. He'd been near the back of the shop, and the building must have totally collapsed around him.

And then he heard something that made his heart sing. A dog, barking. Up above him somewhere. A rescue dog? Sniffing for survivors? A dog that somehow had picked up his and Livvy's scent through all the rubble above them?

He had to make a noise. If it was a rescue dog, there'd be people with it, rescuers with listening equipment. He had to bang on something. But there was nothing – he'd already felt around for something he could tap on to let rescuers know where he was. All he could do was use his voice.

'Help! Here!' Somehow the Italian for those words popped into his brain. '*Aiuto! Qui!*'

The dog barked some more. '*Qui! Aiuto! Qui!*'

In his arms Livvy wriggled and began to cry feebly. She was hungry and weakening. 'Here, have a little water,' he said. Now that he'd heard the dog, he had more hope that they might be rescued before the water ran out. He touched her lips with the bottle and let some water trickle out and was pleased to hear her smacking her lips, sucking in every possible drop. She needed it. It was hot under the rubble.

'*Qui! Aiuto!*' he called again, and Livvy cried too, gustily, as though realising it was time to make some noise.

The dog barked. Was it closer? He couldn't tell. Were those voices?

He shouted again. Yes, voices. Male voices, somewhere up above. Then everything fell silent. Why? Had they moved away? Or were they shushing each other so they could hear him and Livvy?

'*Qui! Aiuto!*'

'*Siamo qui per te!*' An answering call! Tim wasn't sure what it meant. We are here. Here for you, perhaps? But what it clearly was, was an answer to his shouts. It meant rescue was at hand!

'I am here with a baby,' he shouted, hoping they would understand a little English. '*Bambino.*' Surely Livvy's cries would have alerted them to that anyway.

'*Sì, stai fermo,*' came the voice.

And then the blessed sound of rubble being shifted. They had started the work. They would take some time, he guessed – they'd have to be careful not to bring more masonry down on him, or on the rescuers. Had they machinery? Or was it a case of moving it all by hand? There were shouts, frantic Italian being yelled from one to another above him. It sounded as though there was quite a team at work. No more barking of the dog, perhaps the dog had been taken to sniff for survivors elsewhere.

'All we have to do is wait, Livvy,' he soothed. 'They are coming. You hear those sounds? They will get to us soon.'

How long it took before a chink of daylight reached them, Tim had no idea. A few hours, he thought. His water was running low. But it happened, and that tiny glimpse of blessed, sacred sunlight was like the hand of God reaching down and caressing him. The thought surprised him. He wasn't even a religious man.

'It's you, Livvy. It's you who's brought us rescue. You're too young to die like this.' He would miss her, he realised with a jolt, when all this was over.

Then the voices were louder, shouting something to him that he couldn't understand. '*Non capisco!*' he shouted back, and there seemed to be some discussion up above. Shortly after, someone called to him in broken, accented English.

'You cover mouth and nose. Dust will fall. We get you out.'

'OK. Thank you. *Grazie,*' Tim replied. He pulled his T-shirt up over his own mouth and nose and tried to do the same for Livvy with whatever it was she was wearing but she struggled and cried. Instead, he managed to get her on his chest under his T-shirt, and wrapped his arms around her in a protective cage in case any debris fell on them.

Bit by bit, rubble was removed from above so that the chink of light became a shaft, a hole widened, and a man's face peered down, shining a torch on him. The man grinned when he saw Tim. '*Bambino?*'

'*Sì, qui.*' Tim pulled back his T-shirt to show Livvy.

'*Il bambino è vivo!*' The man shouted to his comrades and a cheer went up. Tim smiled. They were far more pleased to be rescuing a baby than him. But that was understandable.

'Is more people?' the man asked.

'A woman was here, with the baby. But I think she is dead.'

'Baby is yours?'

'No.'

The man nodded. '*Capisco.*'

Shortly after, with the hole made a little bigger, one of the men reached right down. He was wearing a yellow hard hat and must have been held by his legs above. '*Passami il bambino,*' he said, and Tim understood he was to pass Livvy up to the man. It made sense to get her out first. Quite possibly he'd then be able to climb out the hole himself.

He pulled her out from under his T-shirt, at which she

protested, crying loudly. 'It's all right, Livvy. This man's here to help us, all right? I'll see you outside in a few minutes.' He wriggled himself out from under the fixture a little, so that he could try to pass her up to the rescuer. As he did so the fixture settled a little, pinning his legs again. He cried out in pain, doing his best to protect Livvy. The man gasped and said something in rapid Italian.

And then there was more motion up above and some equipment was passed to the rescuer which he used to lever up the fixture, off Tim's legs, making a little more space. All the while Tim kept hold of Livvy, using his own body as far as possible to shield her. At last, the shelving was off him and he could move once more, thankfully the partial collapse hadn't injured him any further. He'd be badly bruised, he knew, but if that was the worst of it, he was damned lucky.

'*Bambino?*' the man said again, and now Tim could pass Livvy to him. The man was then hauled up, with Livvy in his arms.

And then Tim was alone down there, feeling bereft without the baby's warm body against him. He shuffled around a bit and got himself into a sitting position, his top half almost out in open air, in the hole the rescuer had leaned down into. Above him, more rubble was shifted to enlarge the hole and ensure nothing fell on him. At last strong arms reached down and grabbed him, and bit by bit he was hauled out, his legs picking up more cuts and bruises along the way, no doubt, but who cared?! He was out, he was saved, he was free! He breathed in a lungful of air and blinked in the sunlight. Someone thrust a bottle of fresh water at him and he drank it in one, relishing its coolness. He was half carried, half supported over the rubble remains of the building and into the town square, where several emergency vehicles awaited. Around him he could see the scale of the devastation now. The church was still standing, intact as far as he could see. The shop he'd been in was completely gone, and the buildings either side of it were badly damaged but still partly standing. On another side of the square, another few buildings had fallen or partially fallen. Hordes of people thronged the area – rescuers, emergency services. He thought he recognised the shopkeeper who stood to one side watching proceedings, cheering as Tim made his way over the rubble of the devastated shop.

He was led to the open doors of an ambulance and lifted inside, where a female medic made him sit on a gurney to be checked over.

'*Dov'è il bambino?*' he asked her. Where is the baby?

She said something he didn't understand and pointed out of the back of the vehicle, towards another ambulance. Tim wanted to see Livvy, to make sure she was all right, being cared for. But, of course, she was, there were dozens of rescuers and emergency vehicles here now, and it was no longer his job or his responsibility to care for her. He lay back, an arm across his eyes, and that was the moment when it all caught up with him. How near death he'd been. How easily he might have died trapped in that rubble, with Livvy still clutched to his chest. How Jackie might have heard news of the earthquake and wondered if he was caught up in it, and then eventually, somehow, she'd be informed that he'd died . . .

Jackie. He reached into his pocket for his phone then remembered it was still at the campsite, charging. Suddenly he wanted more than anything else to speak to her, to tell her he was all right, he'd survived. He wanted to see her, to take her in his arms, to hold her and tell her he loved her.

'*Telefono?*' he asked the medic.

'Ssh. You lie quiet. We go to hospital,' she said, and then the doors of the ambulance were closed, the engine started up, and they were on their way. Calling Jackie would have to wait until he had been discharged from hospital.

Tim was taken not to a hospital but to a medical centre on the outskirts of the town by a convoluted route to avoid damaged and impassable roads. It was a newish building, and in that area the earthquake had not had much impact. He was cleaned up, the worst wounds were dressed, and he was issued with painkillers. Bit by bit, he'd pieced together the story. It was late afternoon, the day after the earthquake had hit. So he'd been trapped for over 24 hours. News of the earthquake had, of course, reached across Europe, but some phone masts were down and a main road was blocked by a landslide which had made communication tricky. 'Everyone want to call,' a doctor told him, 'and no one can.'

'Were many people . . . killed?' Tim wanted to know.

The doctor shrugged. 'I do not know. I have only seen those like you, hurt but not in need of hospital. I work here since yesterday and I see many minor injuries. I do not know how many have gone to bigger hospitals by the helicopter or to the . . . how do you say . . . where the dead are put?'

'Morgue?'

'*Sì.* Morgue. I do not know.' The doctor turned away, busy with tidying instruments and medical supplies. There was a queue of walking wounded still to deal with.

It was evening by the time Tim had been seen and his injuries tended to. He was not badly hurt, and thankful for it. 'You have somewhere to stay?' a woman asked. She was holding a clipboard on which she had names and details of those who'd been seen by the doctor.

'Campsite,' he replied.

'OK. You go now. There is taxi outside.' She made a note and nodded curtly to him. They needed the space, Tim supposed. He was just in the way now.

He went out of the medical centre to where a line of taxis was waiting, and climbed stiffly into the first one, giving the name of the campsite. Every muscle in his body ached from being trapped in an awkward position for so long. As the car set off, he realised he'd need to pay and patted his pockets. His wallet thankfully was still in place.

'You no pay,' the driver said. 'Is free.'

216

'*Grazie*.' The community was doing all it could for those who'd been caught in the earthquake. Tim felt a wave of emotion wash over him at this small thing, this lift back to his campsite. He stared out of the window in an attempt to stop himself from breaking down and sobbing.

It was a short journey but even so Tim saw plenty of evidence of the destruction the earthquake had brought. Farms with collapsed barns, parts of roofs fallen in, large cracks along one side of the road, fallen trees. But it was clear the town centre, the square, the shop where he'd been, was the worst affected part. He'd been in the wrong place at the wrong time.

As had little Livvy and her grandmother.

At the campsite, the taxi driver pulled up, got out and opened the back door for Tim to climb out. He shook Tim's hand and patted his shoulder. '*Buona fortuna*,' he said, as he left.

'*Grazie*.' Tim walked stiffly over to his tent and crawled inside. All he wanted to do now was sleep. He pulled off his filthy clothes and lay down on top of his sleeping bag, too tired and sore to try to get inside it.

He woke early the following morning, and only then remembered that he still hadn't collected his phone from the campsite office where he'd left it to charge. He glanced at his watch. Only 7 a.m. He needed to pick up his phone as soon as the office opened, at 8.30. First thing he would do was call Jackie.

He realised he was starving. The last thing he'd eaten had been breakfast on the day of the earthquake, and now it was two days later. Rummaging around in the tent, he found a few energy bars and ate them, one after the other, then he fired up his Trangia stove and made himself a cup of coffee. It all helped.

'Shower next, and clean clothes,' he told himself. Bit by bit, he'd make himself human again. And then he needed to decide what to do. He looked at his legs. The bruises were coming out now, in all colours. A cut on one shin was oozing blood through the dressing. His muscles were excruciatingly stiff. This was the end of his hiking, he thought. There was no chance of him going any further. He needed to work out a way to get from here to home. Back to Jackie, assuming she still wanted him. God how he hoped she did!

Later, showered, dressed, with his wound redressed, he fetched his phone from the office as soon as it opened. 'We wondered where you were,' the girl in the office told him as she passed it over, 'when you did not come back yesterday. The earthquake?'

'Yes. I was trapped a while. But I'm all right.' He smiled at her to reassure her.

'It was bad. There were ten people killed. Maybe a few more. All in the town centre. I am glad you got out.' Her name badge read 'Giulia'.

'Thank you. I'll need advice on how to get back to Rome.'

Giulia shook her head. 'The road is broken. There is normally a bus to L'Aquila and from there to Roma but not now, not until the road is made better.'

'Oh. How long will that take?'

'They are working on it already. I think maybe two or three days. You can stay here for no charge.' She smiled sympathetically at him and once more he was touched by the generosity of these people.

The campsite shop had some basic supplies and Tim bought enough to keep him going. There was probably another shop in town but he couldn't face going back there. Bread, cheese, tomatoes, and some ravioli and tomato sauce for dinner – that would do. He paid Giulia for these items and slowly limped back to his tent. Time to call Jackie.

He'd barely reached his tent when there was a shout, and Giulia came running after him from the office. 'Sorry, sorry, there is someone here to see you. Can you come back to office?'

It crossed Tim's mind that Jackie might have flown out to Italy, having heard about the earthquake, and somehow tracked him

218

down to this campsite. But how could she? And in any case, the road between here and L'Aquila was out of action. It couldn't be her.

'Come, please,' Giulia said again. Tim shoved his shopping in the tent and wearily turned back and hobbled after her. At the campsite reception she showed him into a side room where a young couple were sitting waiting. They stood up as soon as he walked in, and it was only then that he realised the woman was holding a baby. Livvy.

The woman said something in rapid Italian to him, and stepped forward. With one arm she held Livvy and with the other she took his hand, shook it and then pressed it to her lips. Tears were streaming down her face.

'Please, sit,' Giulia said. 'I translate. They are the parents of this baby. They say you saved the baby. They are very happy you saved the baby. The grandmother of the baby has died. They found where you were from the *centro medico* where you were taken. They are sorry they did not see you yesterday.'

Tim smiled at them, and reached a hand to Livvy, stroking her cheek. She stared at him. Of course, she wouldn't recognise him. Most of the time he'd held her was in complete darkness. 'Hello, little Livvy. It's good to see you safely with your parents. Thank you for keeping me company.' The baby gave him a huge smile then, displaying four teeth in her little mouth. Tim was astounded. She seemed to recognise his voice! He felt his heart melt at her smile of recognition.

'Excuse me, please,' Giulia said. 'I translate but I do not know the word Livvy?'

'Ah. It's just what I called the baby while we were trapped. What is her real name?'

Giulia quickly translated. Livvy's mother smiled, and answered, repeating the name 'Livvy'.

'Her name is Sofia, but her mama like the name Livvy too. She say thank you for looking after Sofia so well. Sofia say thank you too. You want hold her?'

Sofia's mother was holding the baby out to him. It was on the tip of Tim's tongue to say no, he wouldn't hold her. It wasn't his thing. But Sofia, or Livvy, was a baby he'd held closely for over 24 hours. A baby who'd helped him through those terrible hours. They'd bonded, trapped in that rubble. That was how Jackie would have put it. He understood the concept now. And how much more must you feel when it was your own child, your own flesh and blood?

He reached out and took her, holding her up in front of him so he could look at her, really look at her little face. She had a crop of dark hair that stuck up from her head, fat chubby cheeks that dimpled when she smiled. She gurgled at him, blowing spit bubbles. Her little hands reached for his face and he held her closer so she could touch him.

The father said something, and Giulia translated. 'She knows you. She knows you saved her, he says.'

'She's beautiful. Please tell them, she saved me as much as I saved her. It would have been a lot harder for me on my own. And I am sorry about her grandmother. I reached out and touched her, but there was nothing I could do.'

Giulia translated and the parents looked away, the father biting his lip. It was his mother who'd died, Tim thought. The mother spoke again. 'They say they are comforted the old lady wasn't alone at the end,' Giulia said. 'And they hope that you will give them your email address and they will send photos of Sofia to you. If you would like.'

'I would like that very much,' Tim said.

He held Sofia for a few more minutes while they swapped contact details. It felt good cuddling her. Her warm little body against his, but this time in a safe environment. He felt a connection with this child, that wasn't his, but who had been thrown together with him in such horrific circumstances. He'd saved her, but she'd taught him that he did have what it took to care for a child. He could do this.

'They ask, do you have children?' Giulia said.

'Not yet,' he replied.

'You will make good papa.'

And Sofia's parents smiled and nodded at this, as Sofia cooed in his arms and Tim found himself looking forward for the first time, to a day when perhaps he'd hold, like this, a child of his own.

# Chapter 24

## Madeleine, 18 April 1912

Madeleine gasped as she watched the makeshift buoy and its precious cargo fly through the air towards the waiting boat. But Ralph had misjudged, and the package had too much wind resistance to fly smoothly through the air. It was not going to go far enough. He'd thrown it at an angle towards the little boat and the string had come partly undone in flight. It caught on one of *Titanic*'s lifeboats, that were still hanging suspended against the side of the ship.

'Oh no!' Madeleine screamed. 'All your work!'

Ralph was standing, hands on head, in utter despair. The lifeboat was two decks below them and too far out from the ship's side to reach, and there was no hope of shaking it or dislodging it any other way.

'What now?' Madeleine said, and Ralph just shook his head sadly. The *New York Tribune*'s boat had manoeuvred very close now, almost directly below the lifeboat. Watson and the other man on board were looking up at the parcel but they too had no hope of reaching it, or doing anything to get it.

'It's all lost,' Ralph said. 'I'll have to write it again, from memory, when I have my typewriter back.'

'Wait, look!' Madeleine had spotted a crewman from *Carpathia*. He'd seen what had happened and was now swinging himself over the railings and onto the ropes that tethered the lifeboat to *Carpathia*'s side. 'He's going to retrieve it. Maybe he'll bring it to you and you'll get another chance?'

'Not if the captain sees. He'll confiscate it.'

'The captain's nowhere near,' Madeleine said, her eyes fixed on the crew member who was almost on the lifeboat now, reaching out towards the package.

'There's an officer coming over,' Ralph said, indicating one who was making his way towards the suspended lifeboat.

'The seaman has the package,' Madeleine said, leaning as far over the side as she dared to see what was going on. The crewman glanced up at them. 'Throw it down!' she yelled at him, indicating the paper's boat below.

The man looked down, saw the boat, and must have guessed what was in the parcel. He glanced up again, and Madeleine saw him register the approaching officer who was shouting something at him, his words lost in the hubbub. It all depended now on what the man chose to do with the package. He looked up again, and then down, and then leaned over the side of the lifeboat and dropped the package. Right into Watson's waiting hands.

'He's done it!' Ralph said, as the crewman began climbing back up the ropes, back onto *Carpathia*'s deck. There was nothing the officer or captain or anyone else could do now. The story was in the hands of the press. Watson grinned and waved, as the boat he was on picked up speed and steamed off.

Madeleine flung her arms around her husband. 'You've done it! Well done! Now you can relax, my darling, knowing you've done your best.'

But Ralph's expression was stern. 'I want my typewriter back. Now.' He stormed off in the direction of the bridge, guessing the captain would be there. Madeleine followed, urging caution. Even at this late stage, so near the port, the captain was still in charge of the ship and might order Ralph to be restrained.

She caught up with him at the door to the bridge where he was arguing with an officer who would not allow him entry. 'I need to speak with Captain Rostron,' he was saying, jabbing a finger at the officer's chest. 'And I need to speak with him now.'

'Sir, he is busy with the pilot, I am sure you understand that . . .'

'Tell him I want my property back.'

'Ralph, come on, there will be time later . . .' Madeleine urged, but Ralph shook her off.

'There won't be. Maddy, you know I will have very little time and there may well be more stories to write. I need that typewriter, and I need it now.'

'What's all this commotion? Ah. Meyer. It's you.' Captain Rostron had come to the door.

'Rostron, I want my typewriter back. We're almost back, we're in New York's waters now. I demand my property be given back to me now. I need that typewriter immediately.'

The captain looked Ralph up and down as though he was no more than a turd on his shoe, and then nodded slowly. 'I suppose you cannot do any harm having it now. We'll be docked before you'll have the chance to write anything more.'

'I've already written my piece, and handed it to my paper.' Ralph lifted his chin defiantly, as though daring the captain to say anything more.

Madeleine put a hand on Ralph's arm. 'Ralph, please . . .' she said, hoping he would say no more. He'd succeeded, there was no need now to get in any more trouble.

'So I heard,' the captain said. 'But I suppose your paper will not be able to print your story before we get back now. The survivors will be able to tell their own tales first, those that want to.'

'That's just it, you see? My story *is* their own tales. In their own words.'

'Hmm.' The captain waved a hand as though dismissing him, and turned to go back to the bridge.

'Ahem. My typewriter,' Ralph said, and the captain turned back to stare at him, then spoke quietly to another officer who nodded and left the area.

'It will be brought to your cabin. Now, if you'll excuse me, I have duties to attend to if we're all to make it safely back to port.'

'Thank you.' Ralph led Madeleine away, back to their cabin. A few minutes later a steward tapped at the door and handed in the typewriter. Just the typewriter, Madeleine noted wryly. There was no sign of her notebook. But that didn't matter. Ralph had already written up all she could recall of her interviews with the women.

'At last.' She smiled and wrapped her arms around Ralph. 'Now we can put it all behind us.' Although, even as she said this, she knew she'd never forget the survivors' stories, Lucy's missing baby, or the harrowing tale that Caroline had told her.

'Not quite yet,' Ralph said. He kissed her, then placed the typewriter on the little desk in the cabin and opened it up. Tucked into the typewriter's case was some paper which he fed into the machine, and then he began to type. 'A follow-up story. I shall start it now, and complete it when I have seen the papers for the last few days, that no doubt contain nothing but speculation as to what happened to *Titanic* and her passengers.'

'A story about the story?'

He smiled. 'Precisely that. A story about how, in today's world with Marconi equipment on every ship of any size, there is no longer any need for speculation or uncertainty after a calamitous event at sea. The truth, the full story, can be transmitted around the world within hours of the event. It is a changing world, and the likes of Captain Rostron need to change with it.'

Madeleine put a hand on his shoulder and squeezed, as Ralph began to type.

* * *

Madeleine left Ralph to it, while she went back on deck to watch while the ship made its way through New York's Lower Bay, inching its way towards its destination. As she made a tour of the promenade decks she spotted Lucy, holding baby Frederick tightly wrapped in a blanket. She was standing near the ship's railing, gazing at the coastline as they slowly passed by. Madeleine went to stand alongside her, watching the coast of New Jersey as the ship sailed by.

'You'll be glad when we dock, I think,' she said.

Lucy shook her head. 'I am not sure I will be. You see, all the while we're still on *Carpathia* there's a chance I might find Norah. Once we dock and everyone leaves the ship, that chance will be gone. And I don't know how I'll bear that.'

'Oh, Lucy.' Madeleine put a hand on her arm. She did not know what to say, how to comfort the other woman. 'Where will you go, when you leave the ship?'

'I don't know.' Lucy sighed. 'I have not considered it at all. I have only thought of Norah and my poor Arthur. I don't know what I will do or where I will stay.'

'There will be help, for the survivors. I have heard there are subscriptions and collections. I am sure there will be people in New York ready to help everyone.'

'I suppose so.' Lucy's voice was flat and lifeless. 'How can I go on, without Norah and Arthur?'

Madeleine regarded her with sympathy. 'You must. For Frederick.'

Lucy looked down at the baby sleeping in her arms and nodded. 'Yes. For Frederick.' He squirmed in her arms and began to grizzle. 'I must take him inside now and feed him. And then tour the ship one more time searching for Norah. If I don't see you again, goodbye and thank you for trying to find my baby.'

'I'm only sorry I couldn't find her for you,' Madeleine replied. 'Goodbye then, and good luck.' She watched Lucy go back inside, her head bowed, shoulders slumped as though the weight of the world was on them.

# Chapter 25

## Jackie, 2022

It was almost 48 hours since the earthquake had struck and still Jackie had not heard from Tim. She'd spent the previous day, thankfully a Saturday so she had not needed to work, frantically scouring news sites and social media, trying to build up a picture of what had happened. It had been extremely difficult. It seemed that some communication masts had been brought down by the earthquake which meant that many people in the affected area had little or no phone signal. And what little there was, was clogged by friends and relatives trying to get through to their loved ones.

As she was too. Not knowing. Fearing the worst but hoping for the best. Just as relatives of *Titanic* passengers must have, just as Lucy Watts must have, as she searched for her baby.

And now it was Sunday morning. The longer time went on, the harder it was for her to convince herself there was no problem. She knew he turned his phone off in the mountains to save battery life, but not for this long. And surely he must have been somewhere that there was mobile coverage over the last two days? She was seriously worried now. As each day, hour, minute passed she realised more and more how much she loved him, she missed him, and she wanted more than anything for him to be found safe and well. That was the most important thing.

The news reports she'd scoured, from both British and Italian websites, told of a relatively minor earthquake. It had been enough to demolish a number of buildings in the centre of Sorgente di Giacomo and buildings within a five-mile radius had sustained damage. The death toll was fourteen, with several in hospital. Bad, but not totally devastating. It was older buildings in the historic town centre that had suffered the worst. There were stories of people running outside as soon as they felt tremors – one man, a shopkeeper, had breathlessly reported that he was the luckiest man alive. He'd felt a shaking and immediately run outside into the town square. 'And now look what has become of my shop!' he said. The camera panned around to show an enormous pile of rubble where once his shop had stood.

'Were people in your shop when the earthquake struck?' the reporter asked him.

'Sì, sì. Two or three. One died, I am so sad. And one was pulled out, along with a baby.'

Jackie watched this report with a hand over her mouth. It wasn't beyond the bounds of possibilities that Tim might have been shopping there when it happened. Someone died. What if that someone was Tim? She was glad the person with the baby had been saved – no baby should ever have to die in that way. But the other person . . .

How could she find out if that had been Tim? All she knew was the rough area he'd been in.

She needed to talk to someone. Anyone. Audrey would be as worried as she was. Sarah. It had to be Sarah. She grabbed her phone and called her friend.

'Sarah? It's Jackie. This earthquake in Italy . . .'

'Have you heard from Tim?'

'No. And he was in that area, last I heard. Sarah . . . I'm getting frantic here with worry. What do I do?'

'Oh, Lord, Jackie. Want me to come over?'

'Not sure . . . I want something positive I can do, something proactive, you know? I want to find out . . .'

'Try the Foreign Office? Don't they have a number you can call if there's a catastrophe somewhere abroad?'

'Yes . . . I haven't seen a number advertised for this one. But maybe it's not a big enough event for it.'

'Even so, there'll be a number. Google it.' Sarah sounded as though she was multi-tasking. Jackie could hear Bobby chattering away in the background and sounds of breakfast being prepared. 'Look, Jackie, I bet you anything he's perfectly all right and it's just a badly-timed phone problem he has. Try to relax, OK? But meantime, call the Foreign Office to set your mind at rest. Let me know what happens. And I'm coming over this afternoon.'

'Thanks. OK. I'll do that.'

She hung up then searched online, where she quickly found a number for the Foreign Office that she could call for help and advice. It was an advice line for people with relatives who'd died abroad. Maybe, if Tim had been affected and was in hospital, or, God forbid, a morgue, they would know. Maybe even now they were trying to track down his next of kin. She called, her voice shaking as she explained the situation to a sympathetic sounding woman.

'We have not been informed of any UK nationals killed by that earthquake,' the woman said. 'But let me take your details and your partner's details. If we do hear anything, I will call you back. No news is usually good news, in these situations.'

'It's just that I haven't been able to get through to him. He normally messages me at least once a day.'

'I am so sorry. But as I understand it, there have been some communication problems with that area since the earthquake. I'm sure as soon as he can, he'll be in touch.'

'I hope so. Thank you.'

Jackie made herself a cup of tea and went back to her laptop and her constant scrolling of news. The hashtag *#GiacomoEarthquake* was still in use, though there wasn't much new information. Still, she kept at it, and kept glancing at her phone, willing it to ping into life with a message or call from Tim.

Did she feel better or worse having spoken to the Foreign Office? She wasn't sure. On the one hand, someone in charge now knew that Tim was missing. On the other hand, that made her worries official.

Her phone rang and she pounced on it, but the name displayed was not Tim. It was his mother. She'd spoken to Audrey several times since the earthquake and like her, Audrey was becoming more and more worried as time went on.

'Jackie? Any news?' Audrey was sounding frantic. Jackie wanted to play down her own fears, but on the other hand, she too was worried sick.

'No, sorry. But that might not mean anything, Audrey. They say no news is good news, eh?'

'It's just so difficult . . .' Audrey sounded as though she was choking back tears.

'Yes. Look, I called the Foreign Office. They have had no reports of any British casualties. So we have to assume that he is just out of signal, or out of charge or there's a problem with phone masts in the area or something like that . . .'

'Yes . . .' Audrey didn't sound convinced.

'I'll let you know as soon as I hear anything.'

'Likewise. All right then, I'll get off the phone in case he's trying to call you.'

'OK. Let's stay positive, eh?'

Jackie hung up, biting her nails. She was tempted to call Sarah again for a bit of support. But as Audrey had said, what if Tim was trying to call?

Instead, she went back to her laptop and scrolled for the hundredth time through the news websites. The latest reports suggested the Italian authorities weren't expecting the death toll to rise much more, if at all. No missing persons. That was a relief, at least, but again, why no call from Tim?

The longer this went on the more she realised that whatever happened, she wanted him back. She wanted him here, living with her, for good. His safety was the most important thing. She should have been on this trip with him. Rather than sitting here worrying where he was, she'd have been with him, whether or not he'd been caught up in the disaster. That would be better than this not-knowing.

Before the earthquake she'd decided she would agree to another couple of years before trying again for a baby, if that's what it took to save their relationship and keep Tim. Now she knew beyond any doubt that if he came back to her and wanted her still, she'd accept him back on any terms. Children or no children. Travelling six weeks every summer or not. Whatever compromise was necessary. She loved him, she wanted him back, and she felt sorry, mortified in fact, that she'd hinted to him that if he didn't want children any time soon then she didn't want to stay with him. How could she have thought that for even a second? She knew now that she wanted Tim first, children second. She wanted children still; she felt that need, that urge within her. But she wanted Tim more, and if keeping him meant giving up the chance to be a mother – well it was a difficult choice but she knew now that she'd choose Tim first. She just wanted him safe and well and back home with her. Funny how it was only when you thought you might have lost someone for good that you realised how much you loved them and wanted them.

She picked up her tea and drank a mouthful. It was cold. Should she make another? She was facing another long day of sitting by the phone, checking news and social media.

She sighed. And then the phone rang, and the caller display showed it was Tim, at least Tim's phone, and her heart gave a leap.

Her hands were shaking as she pressed the 'accept call' button. What if his phone had been found but not him? 'Tim, is that you?'

'Jackie? Yes, it's me, I'm sorry I'm only just calling you back . . .'

'Oh Tim, Tim!' She gulped back a sob. 'You're all right? There's been an earthquake . . .' Maybe he didn't even know about it, if he'd been somewhere inaccessible with no phone signal. The relief she felt on hearing his voice was immense. He was alive! Thank God, he was alive! Her legs were shaking and she sat down heavily, cradling the phone in both hands as though it was Tim himself.

'Yes, I know . . .'

'Did you feel it?'

He gave an odd kind of snort in response. 'Er, yeah, I did. Look, I know you wanted a few weeks on your own, but I'm planning on coming back to the UK sooner than expected.'

'When?'

'Soon as I can get back to Rome and get a flight.'

'Why are you coming back early?' Jackie was delighted to hear it, she was longing to see him again, but she couldn't work out his tone. He sounded as though he was keeping something back from her. Had his two weeks hiking led him to a conclusion he no longer wanted her in his life? Was he coming back early to break the news to her?

'Things haven't quite worked out. I've hurt my leg a bit and . . . well . . .'

'Hurt your leg? How?'

He coughed. 'Not sure I should tell you on the phone. Anyway, I need to call Mum as well.'

'Tim, can I ask why there was such a long gap? Audrey and I were both messaging you and calling you but . . .'

'I was out of charge, then I left my phone in a campsite office to recharge, and then . . .'

'Then?' Don't make me guess, Tim, she thought.

'Um, I wasn't able to get back to the campsite.' He gave a huge sigh. 'All right, listen, and I'll tell you, but you're not to worry,

232

I really am all right. I was caught in that earthquake. Kind of trapped. Actually, no, not kind of, I definitely *was* trapped. For a day. They dug me out, me and the kid that was with me. They patched me up and now I'm trying to find a way to get back to Rome for a flight home but a main road is blocked so it's hard to get out of here.'

'You're in Sorgente di Giacomo?' she said, unable to believe what he was telling her.

'Yes.'

'You were in one of those collapsed buildings?' She whispered the words, not wanting them to be true.

'Yes, a shop.'

'Oh, my God.' Jackie clapped a hand over her mouth. 'I saw it, on a news website. You were in there and you got out?'

'Er, yes. That's basically it.'

'Oh, Tim. Thank Christ you got out.' Tears began to stream down Jackie's face. Tears of relief, as the pent-up worry of the last two days was released. Something he'd said came back to her. 'You and a kid? What kid?'

'A baby.'

'Why were you in a shop with a baby?'

'I wasn't. Well, she was there with her grandmother who sadly died, but the baby was all right. Kind of protected by her pushchair, I think. Anyway, I held her while they worked to dig us out. Look, I'll tell you the full story when I get back. If you want to see me, that is.'

'Oh . . . yes, I want to see you.' He had no idea how much she wanted to. 'If you want to see me?'

'Of course, I do.' His tone was quiet, gentle, and it gave her hope. 'Well, I need to call Mum and then try to get on a bus out of here. I'll message you as soon as I have any details of when I'll be back.'

'All right.' Should she say 'love you' as she always used to? Or would that be too presumptuous that he still wanted to be with her? They had a lot of talking they needed to do, and it wasn't right to do it over the phone like this. They needed to wait until he returned.

At least she knew he was coming back, and he was alive, merely a little injured. And traumatised by his ordeal, no doubt. He was alive, he was coming home, and she hoped with all her heart that somehow they could reset, start again from there.

'Good to hear from you, Tim. Take care,' she whispered.

'Yes. You too.'

And then he hung up, and he hadn't said he loved her but she hadn't said it either, so everything was all a little unclear. But he was alive and coming back as soon as he could, and surely they could build everything else from that starting point?

'Love you, Tim,' she said, to the empty room. 'Love you so much.'

# Chapter 26

## Madeleine, 18 April 1912

The weather was dismal as *Carpathia* made her way up through the Narrows, past Staten Island, Ellis Island, Governors Island. Ralph had finished his writing and had come out to join Madeleine on the deck. Regardless of the poor weather, many passengers were out there, leaning on the railings, watching as they passed each landmark. Lightning lit up the sky, silhouetting the Statue of Liberty against the now darkened sky. Rain was streaming down but it was as though no one cared, everyone wanted to be on deck as they arrived in New York.

'Weather seems fitting, given what's happened,' Ralph said gruffly, and Madeleine nodded.

The ship slowed as it passed Staten Island, and then they were met by a tug as they passed Liberty Island. The flotilla of press boats had mostly dispersed now, the reporters realising they would not be allowed on board and the rain making it impossible for questions to be shouted up to the ship, or the answers heard. Just a few stalwarts continued alongside and the occasional shout through a megaphone was heard.

And then they reached the tip of Manhattan itself. 'Look, Ralph,' Madeleine said, pointing. Thousands of people were lining the sea wall, the mass of humanity silently watching *Carpathia*'s progress.

'All of them there, and none of them know the full truth,' Ralph muttered. Madeleine could not believe how many people had turned out, late at night, to watch the ship return. People were wearing dark clothing, she saw, and flags were flying at half-mast on many buildings. The city was in mourning. It was a sombre experience, seeing all those people not cheering, not waving, just standing, watching and quietly grieving for people they hadn't known.

Slowly the ship made its way up the Hudson River, and still crowds were gathered on shore at every possible location, despite the rain. 'There's the Cunard pier,' Madeleine said, pointing ahead to where a green neon sign spelled out the word 'Cunard'. It was the same pier they'd sailed from, just a week earlier.

Only a week, and yet the world had changed, Madeleine thought. The world would never be quite the same again. She knew, deep down, that what had befallen *Titanic* would never be forgotten. And for herself and Ralph, along with so many others, these few days would define the rest of their lives.

The ship began to turn, but not into the Cunard pier. It went on past. Madeleine could see hundreds more people on the pier, and heard a collective groan as the ship went past.

'Why are we not docking? Where are we going?' she asked, but Ralph shrugged.

'Perhaps we're going to the White Star line's pier.'

'The one *Titanic* would have docked at?'

'Yes.'

As she continued to watch, it seemed he was right. A few piers further upriver *Carpathia* stopped her engines, and lowered *Titanic*'s lifeboats into the water. They were tied together and towed away by a steam tug. Everyone on *Carpathia*'s decks watched in silence, some mouthing prayers. The last time those boats had been lowered into the water was from the stricken *Titanic*, Madeleine realised. Now they were all that remained of that 'unsinkable' ship. As they were towed away, she could just make out the name *Titanic* painted in white on the side of each one.

'I suppose those needed to be dropped off, to allow us to dock properly,' Ralph said. 'We'll be going back now to the Cunard pier.'

He was right, once more. The ship turned and went back, to Pier 54, to the hundreds, perhaps thousands, of waiting people. As they drew closer, Madeleine could see ambulances – dozens of them! And hordes of waiting medical staff, nurses, doctors, stretcher bearers. Dozens too of hearses and men in black suits who could only be undertakers. 'They don't know. They think we might be carrying hundreds of dead or injured. Look at them all,' Ralph said. 'And yet, if I'd been able to send my story, they'd have known the state of the survivors. Those ambulances are all unnecessary, as are the hearses.' He said the last sentence through gritted teeth. He was still so furious with Captain Rostron.

'Better that they're here and not needed, than the other way around.' Madeleine tried to soothe him. 'The captain was only doing what he thought was best for the survivors.'

'Hmm,' was Ralph's only answer.

At last they docked. The captain had decreed that *Titanic*'s survivors were to disembark first. Any *Carpathia* passengers who wished to go ashore must wait. They were informed that the ship would sail again the following afternoon. Less than a day for Ralph to visit the paper's offices.

Ralph and Madeleine found a position on deck from where they could see the gangplanks put into place. The first person to leave the ship was a crewman wearing yellow oilskins, and then *Titanic*'s passengers left one by one. The first fifty yards or so leading away from the ship was fenced off, keeping the various customs officials, medical staff and reporters back. Beyond that, Madeleine could see hundreds of people waiting behind a cordon, each of them anxiously scanning the faces of those leaving the ship. 'They must be relatives of the survivors,' she said to Ralph, and he nodded.

'Some will be relatives of the deceased. Many of them, I fear.'

Her heart went out to those waiting people, all hoping that their loved one, their friend or family member, would be among those saved.

She recognised some of the women leaving the ship. The Marshalls' nieces. Then the stewardesses from *Titanic* she'd spoken to. There was Lucy Watts, carrying Frederick wrapped in one of *Carpathia*'s blankets. 'I hope those poor people are given some clothes to wear,' she said to Ralph.

'I am sure New York will have arranged that. The city seems well prepared for all eventualities.'

As she watched, she spotted another woman carrying a baby, walking with a man beside her. This one was wearing a brown coat and a distinctive wide-brimmed hat in a vibrant shade of red. Madeleine leaned over to get a closer look. Could that be . . .

'Look at that couple,' Ralph said. 'They are *Carpathia* passengers. Obviously wanting to leave the ship early.' He was pointing at the same woman Madeleine was watching.

'*Carpathia*? Are you sure?'

'I remember that woman's hat, from when we boarded the ship. Yes, pretty sure. Is that a baby she's carrying? I don't remember her having one when we boarded.'

'She's . . , I'm sure she's . . .' Madeleine began, but how could she tell Ralph the whole story quickly, now? 'Ralph, we must catch that woman. That couple. If she's a *Carpathia* passenger, and you say they didn't have a baby when they arrived—'

'Not that I noticed . . .' interrupted Ralph, frowning at her.

There was no time now to explain it all. 'Come on, we have to catch up with them.' She grabbed hold of Ralph's arm and began tugging him back into the ship, down the stairs towards the gangway. It was all clear to her now. That woman, who'd pulled the baby out of her arms, must be someone who'd been desperate for a child, so desperate that when she saw what she assumed was an orphaned baby rescued from *Titanic* she'd taken her chance and snatched the baby. Just as Madeleine herself might have, if the woman in brown hadn't been quicker than her. She must have kept the child in her cabin, and persuaded her husband to go along with it. Maybe she'd even suffered a loss herself, just like Madeleine had.

'Maddy, what's going on?' Ralph said as she dragged him after her to the ship's exit. But there were crowds of *Titanic* passengers still waiting to disembark, blocking the entrance. There was no hope of pushing through. In any case, the captain himself was standing there to see people off, and he had made it very clear that *Titanic* survivors were to leave the ship first. They would not be able to get past, and by now the couple with the baby would surely be lost in the crowds. As would Lucy.

'Darling, please explain to me what's going on,' Ralph said again.

Madeleine looked from him to the gangway and back again. It was too complex a story to be summarised, and now surely there would be no chance of finding the woman. She shook her head, unable to find the words.

'Are you all right, Maddy?' Ralph put a hand on her shoulder and gazed at her, frowning. 'You look unhappy.' He led her back up to the deck, away from the crowds around the gangway.

She couldn't tell him. Couldn't explain. 'It's all been so harrowing. I just thought . . . something seemed odd but I must be mistaken. I'm just . . . so very sad for all those people waiting, whose loved ones weren't saved. Finding out only now, after holding out hope for days.'

Ralph nodded. 'I know, I know.' He sighed. 'Look, when the survivors are all off the ship and we're allowed to leave, I want to run over to the *Tribune* offices as soon as possible. I should think they'll be open all night, getting the story out. I'll hand them what I've written today. The sooner the truth of it all is printed, the better. You can stay on board if you prefer.'

239

She shook her head. 'No, I'll come with you. It'll be good to get off the ship for a little while.'

'I know. It's kind of claustrophobic. A weird atmosphere. Especially when it's been so crowded. Not that I begrudge those poor people a thing, of course.'

'Of course.' It would be her last chance – it was just possible she'd come across the woman in the red hat and brown coat. *And do what?* A little voice at the back of her mind asked. Snatch the child from her arms then search the city for Lucy? No. There was no chance of it. She needed to forget that baby now.

Maybe that woman in the red hat and her husband had always had a baby on board. They might have had a nursemaid with them who'd carried it when they boarded. Maybe the bundle she was carrying had not been the baby Violet Jessop brought on board anyway. After all, from this distance above the gangplank, how could she be sure that it was the same woman, the same baby? She needed to find something else to focus on, something that would be better for her state of mind. Put the child, and *Titanic*, and all the rest of this horror, firmly behind her.

'There are people coming on board now,' Ralph said, breaking into her thoughts. 'Oh! I do believe . . .'

'What?'

'See those two gentlemen, there? One is Mr Marconi, unless I am very much mistaken. I have seen his picture in the paper often enough. And the fellow with him . . .' He broke off, rubbing his chin.

'I suppose they're letting Mr Marconi on board because without his invention none of those people would have been saved,' Madeleine said.

'You are right. I have written about that in the piece I need to deliver tonight.'

'Who's the other man with him?' Madeleine glanced at Ralph. It had sounded as though he knew the man.

'I think it's Russell. A reporter, with the *New York Times*, I believe.'

'Surely the captain won't allow a reporter on board?'

'We're docked now. And look, it seems he's gained entry. Presumably because he's with Marconi. Come on, let's see what he's up to.'

As they turned away from the ship's railings, they saw the two men coming up onto the deck. Ralph took a step forward, and Russell nodded at him in recognition. 'Meyer. I heard rumours you were on board. Quite the story, isn't it?'

'Certainly is. Are you here to . . .'

'Interview the Marconi operators, if they'll talk. Mr Marconi here was hoping they'd transmit their stories sooner, but they didn't.'

Madeleine glanced around to see if the captain was anywhere near, but thankfully he wasn't, and the crew member escorting Marconi and Russell looked uninterested in the conversation.

'The captain wouldn't allow any news to be sent,' Ralph said, carefully. 'I did try.'

Russell grimaced. 'That's too bad. Well, I must go and see what I can get out of the operators. I hear *Titanic*'s operator is here too. I'm authorised to offer him a substantial amount. He'll have quite the tale to tell.'

'He has. I have already heard much of it,' Ralph said, with a triumphant smile. 'I must be off too. Business to attend to, at the *New York Tribune* offices.' He walked away, leaving Russell staring after him, clearly wondering if he'd lost what he, Russell, no doubt had thought of as a golden opportunity for a scoop. Madeleine smiled. If anything could improve Ralph's mood, it would be knowing he was one up on his rival reporters.

She hurried to catch him up. 'I think we'll be allowed off the ship now. Do you have everything you need?'

'Yes, right here,' he said, patting his breast pocket. 'Let's go, then. We have an obligation to get the truth told before any more misinformation is spread.'

* * *

241

They made their way back to their cabin to pick up coats and wallets, and then left the ship by the same gangplank the *Titanic* survivors had just used. The pier building was heaving with people. Signs directed survivors to an area where they could find clothes, donated by the people of New York, and at a row of desks people were being allocated accommodation. It seemed that every hotel and lodging house in Manhattan had freed up rooms and was offering them to survivors, for no payment. At another desk a man was taking names of *Titanic*'s steerage passengers. 'We've held a subscription,' Madeleine heard him explain to someone, 'and have substantial funds available to help those poor souls who lost everything.' That would be useful for Lucy Watts, Madeleine thought, as she scanned the crowds for her.

But there was no sign of Lucy, or the couple with the baby. And there were so many people it would be nearly impossible to find one individual. She gave it up and concentrated on staying within touching distance of Ralph, as they battled their way through the crowds.

There were dozens of reporters there too, as she'd guessed there would be. All brandishing notebooks, asking everyone if they were a survivor and what were their stories. Asking if there were more rescue ships to come, if it was true that officers from *Titanic* had shot themselves, whether they held Bruce Ismay entirely responsible, or whether steerage passengers had indeed been thrown off lifeboats to make more space for first-class passengers. Madeleine felt sick to the stomach hearing yet more of the rumours that must have been circulating around the world regarding the disaster.

As they made their way through the pier buildings and out onto the street, where thousands more people were gathered, they were accompanied by one overriding sound, that Madeleine knew she'd never forget. The wails and cries of relatives who'd come there in the vain hope they might spot their loved ones among the survivors, but were now beginning to face the fact that they were lost.

# Chapter 27

## Jackie & Tim, 2022

Jackie messaged Audrey, Alfie and Sarah immediately after the phone call with Tim. She got relieved replies immediately from Alfie and Sarah, and a message back from Audrey a few minutes later to say that Tim had also thankfully just called her too, to say he was safe and would soon be on his way home. *'Now we can both breathe a sigh of relief, and not let him out of our sight again,'* the message ended.

'Too right I won't, Audrey,' Jackie said, as she read this last bit. She smiled to herself. Tim was coming home. He was safe. They could start from there, she hoped, to rebuild their relationship. She'd do whatever it took, to keep him with her. She'd compromise on *everything*, if she had to.

It was a long couple of days until she got the news she'd been waiting for – Tim's flight details. He'd messaged her several times during that period – at night, first thing in the morning, and several times throughout the day. Sometimes, he had nothing to say other than *'Hi, all is well, road still closed.'* But then there were updates saying he'd managed to get a lift to L'Aquila via back roads, and then he was on a bus to Rome, and then a message arrived with the flight details. He would arrive at Heathrow the following evening, and would catch a bus home.

'No, you won't catch a bus,' Jackie muttered. 'I'll pick you up.' The man had been trapped in an earthquake for hours and was injured. No way was she leaving him to make his own way home. Besides, she couldn't wait to see him, sooner rather than later.

She worked from home the next day and finished early, then set off in her car in plenty of time to drive to the airport where she parked in a short stay car park. In the arrivals hall, she positioned herself close to the barrier where she'd be able to scan all the faces coming through. She found herself wondering whether anyone else was here to meet people from the Rome flight, whether anyone else had loved ones who had been caught up in the earthquake. It was possible, but improbable. The death toll remained at fourteen, and as far as she'd been able to find out, all the casualties were Italian nationals. Sorgente di Giacomo was a very small town in a remote spot in the mountains, not often visited by tourists other than a few hikers and backpackers. It was quite possible that Tim had been the only foreigner affected by the earthquake. Even so, she looked around at the others waiting to meet people, wondering what their stories were. A family with a homemade 'Welcome Home Nana and Grandpa' banner. A young man with a bouquet of flowers and a nervous expression. An elderly woman with what looked like her son and daughter who stood with their arms around her, clutching tissues with which they frequently dabbed at their eyes. All were here with their own stories to tell, their own life dramas, some happy, some not.

It made her think of *Carpathia*, and how people had thronged the New York docks when the ship returned, carrying *Titanic*'s survivors. She thought about the intense mix of emotions people must have felt then – because of the lack of definitive communications from *Carpathia* many people hadn't known whether their friends and relatives had been rescued or not. At least she knew Tim was safe; she'd spoken to him, she knew he was coming back. The last message from him had contained one simple word: '*Boarding*'. So she even knew he was on the plane. Thank goodness for modern technology! Even though there had been those awful couple of days when she couldn't contact Tim and the news reports from Italy were full of speculation and uncertainty, things were far better than 110 years ago when *Titanic* sank, but perhaps there was still a way to go.

She had a little while to wait until the plane was due, and then Tim would have to make his way through baggage collection and passport control. There was a screen announcing arrivals, and she kept an eye on it, between playing some mindless game on her phone that helped pass the time.

An incoming message alert on her phone sounded, and she checked what it was. Tim, saying simply: '*Landed*'. Her stomach flipped over. He was back on British soil. He'd soon be coming through to the arrivals hall and she'd see him again. Would he hug her? Or would he be a little distant and cold, as he had been when she'd dropped him at the bus station at the start of his trip?

She could no longer concentrate on her game. She watched as the arrivals screen changed to show the Rome flight had landed, then that the passengers were in the baggage reclaim area.

She kept her eyes on the constant stream of people dragging their cases through the barriers into the arrivals hall. There was Nana and Grandpa, hugging and kissing their family and saying yes, they'd had a lovely holiday but were glad to be home again. And there was an elderly relative of the old woman and her grown-up children, who crossed straight to her and hugged her wordlessly, his lips pressed tightly together as if to hold back his emotions. Jackie guessed he was here for a funeral. Then a young woman, looking anxiously about her, her face breaking into a grin when she saw the man with flowers. They embraced and kissed, she exclaimed over the flowers, he took her case and they walked off hand in hand, talking non-stop.

People going about their lives. None of them realising what Tim had been through.

And then there he was. His rucksack on his back, a small drawstring bag in one hand. Wearing the same hiking trousers and fleece he'd worn at the start of his trip. The only difference was that he was limping slightly, and there was an odd expression on his face. Fear, relief, anxiety – somehow all were mixed together as though he wasn't sure what he was doing or where he was. He hadn't spotted her yet. She stepped forward and called to him, and then he saw her, and he looked surprised but also, she thought, pleased and hopeful seeing her there for him.

'Tim. Welcome home,' she said as he approached.

'Wasn't expecting you to meet me,' he said, but he was smiling.

'How's your bad leg?'

'It's not too bad. I can walk to the car if that's what you're worried about.' He started walking towards the exit sign but she stopped him, putting a hand on his arm.

'It's you I've been worried about. I'm so glad you're safe, Tim.'

He turned to face her, and she saw in his eyes that he'd been worried too, about her, she supposed, about what kind of reception he'd be met with. 'Jackie, I—' he started saying, but broke off as she, without realising she was going to do it, pulled him into her arms, reaching up around his neck above the rucksack.

'Oh, God, Tim. I've missed you. I was worried sick.'

He was clinging to her, a hand on her head stroking her hair, the other round her waist. 'I know, I know. I missed you too, Jacks. We've got so much to talk about.'

'Yes, we have. So much. Tim, I was so frightened I was losing you.' She hadn't wanted to cry, but now he was here and she was in his arms, the tears fell and there was no stopping them.

'It . . . could have been worse . . . I'll tell you the story when we're home.'

On either side of them people streamed past, heading to the

car parks, bus stops and taxi rank. They had no idea that today was one of the most important days in her life. What they said to each other now and at home would shape their futures. 'I mean, not just the earthquake. You being away.'

He gave her a small smile. 'It worked, having time apart. Even before the earthquake. I had plenty of time to think. And trapped in the rubble helped make everything clear to me. But hey, let's get home, let me have a shower, and then . . .'

'We'll talk.'

'Yes, we'll have a proper talk and sort ourselves out, eh?'

'Yes.' She took his arm as they walked arm in arm across the concourse and into the car park. He was leaning on her a little, his leg injury must have been paining him. And it felt good to be able to support him like that. It meant they were a team, didn't it? If they kept that in mind, then whatever life threw at them – miscarriages, earthquakes or anything else – they'd be all right. At least she hoped he'd reached the same conclusions she had.

Tim stood awkwardly under the shower, trying to keep his wounded leg dry. He was relishing the warm water flowing over the rest of his body, enjoying being back home where he could relax and unwind and allow his body time to recover from the ordeal. And he'd have the time and opportunity to speak to Jackie, to have that heart-to-heart that they needed to work out their future.

He rubbed shampoo into his hair and tipped his face back so that the water pounded directly onto it. He'd been heartened to see her waiting at the airport for him. He hadn't dared hope that she would do that. She'd have had to take some time off work to be there to meet the flight. It was a good sign. There was hope for their relationship.

They just needed to find the right way to talk about it, to decide together what they wanted from each other.

He rinsed off the shampoo, turned off the shower and stepped out. From downstairs, laid-back jazz music was playing, and something smelled amazing, making his stomach gurgle in anticipation. Towelling off, he put on loose pyjama trousers and a T-shirt. He'd been pleased to see evidence Jackie had moved back into the master bedroom, it was another good sign. As he went downstairs, oddly, he felt anxious. Nervous about approaching his long-term girlfriend in their own house – it was crazy to feel that way, but he knew this evening was a make-or-break moment. They wanted to be together, but they had a lot to discuss. He needed to tell her the whole story of what had happened in Italy, and lead from there into a talk about their future.

Downstairs, Jackie had candles already lit, a pasta bake just coming out of the oven and wine poured. Tim felt loved and looked after, and it felt good. He watched her, smiling as she laid out cutlery.

'What are you grinning about?' she asked, and there was a little smile at the corner of her mouth that told him she was pleased to have him home again.

'Just happy to be here. Can I help?'

'No, you're injured. Sit there. Let's eat and then you can tell me your story.'

He sat at the table opposite her, wincing as he lowered himself into the chair, then picked up the glass of wine she'd poured for him, clinked it against hers, and took a sip. They ate in companionable silence and it was the best meal he'd had in a long time. 'Two weeks in Italy and I've come home to pasta,' he said, and Jackie clapped a hand over her mouth.

'Oh God, I didn't think. Stupid choice!'

'No, I don't mean that. It was delicious. Remember, I've been living off what I could prepare on a Trangia stove for most of the time away. Thank you for cooking this evening.'

She wouldn't let him clear the table, insisting he sit in an armchair and drink his wine while she did it. At last she came to join him, looking at him expectantly. And then he told her the entire story, of leaving his phone at the campsite, going into the church and then into the grocery shop, seeing the woman with a baby in a pushchair, and the earthquake hitting. Realising there was nothing he could do for the woman, but tugging the child out and into his arms as he lay in the darkness beneath the rubble. Trickling water into her mouth, and holding her while she slept on his chest. Calling her Livvy and discovering that she responded well to his voice.

Jackie listened intently, looking as though she was reliving it all alongside him. Tears streamed down her face as he told her how he'd felt lying there trapped, with only a small baby for company. Tim could barely look at her. She needed to know the whole story, all the details, and he needed to tell her, now. He needed to share everything with her, before they could work out their way forward.

'And you know,' he said, 'I felt as though it was Livvy keeping me going rather than the other way round. I had to stay positive for her, had to keep thinking of her needs rather than my own. It helped, in an odd sort of way.'

He looked up then, at her, and realised she was sobbing. 'Oh, Jacks. I didn't mean to upset you. But you wanted to hear the story, and . . . I guess it's good for me too, to talk it through, to know that someone knows the whole story. I wouldn't be able to tell it to Mum in this much detail.'

'No, that wouldn't be good for her. But I'm here, and I want to hear it all, if you want to tell me.'

'I do.' He took another gulp of his wine, and went on to tell her about the moment he'd heard a dog barking and then the sound of rescuers, and the glorious moment when daylight finally reached them, shortly followed by a rescuer's grinning face.

'That was a good moment. I knew then that we'd get out all right. And we did.'

'They pulled you out together?' She frowned as she asked, and he guessed she was imagining Livvy still in his arms as they were hauled out of the ruins.

'Not quite.' He told her how the baby was taken first and it was a little while before he himself was extricated. He'd got this far in the story, but now his voice broke a little as he told her how he felt being on his own for those extra minutes under the rubble. 'I thought then that I might never see her again, and that was hard, you know? We'd been through so much together, and yet I'd barely seen what she looked like, although I'd recognise her burbling and cries anywhere.'

He went on to tell her of the visit to the campsite by Livvy and her parents. 'I should call her Sofia really. That's her real name.'

Jackie smiled. 'That's a nice name, though I like your choice of Olivia more.'

If they stayed together, if they had a child and it was a girl, they could call her Olivia, or Livvy, Tim thought, surprising himself by how much that idea pleased him.

'They sent me some photos of her. Look.' He pulled out his phone and scrolled through the half-dozen photos he'd received from Sofia's parents.

'She's beautiful,' Jackie said, a wistful tone to her voice

'Yes, she is,' he agreed. 'Such a happy child. And clever too, I think. I know it sounds fanciful but when I held her and spoke to her at the campsite, I think she recognised me by my voice.'

'She probably did, yes.'

He went on to tell her the final part of his story – how he'd finally made his way home. She'd know all this already, he realised, from the many messages he'd sent, but he wanted to complete the tale.

When he was done, she reached across and took his hands in hers. 'God, you've been through a lot. I am so proud of you, Tim, for what you did for that baby. Without you, she'd never have been rescued.'

'She might have been . . .'

'You gave her water, held her safe.'

He swallowed, and nodded. She was right, he had saved her, and he was proud of himself.

It was time to move on to the other conversation they needed to have. The one about their future together. It was getting late and the wine was two-thirds gone, but even so. Now was the time. He was about to speak when Jackie cleared her throat. 'Tim, before you went away, I'd been talking about . . . us. Our future. Whether we wanted the same things.'

He gazed at her and nodded slowly, trying to read the expression in her eyes. It was one of sadness, and his heart gave a lurch. She'd said at the airport she'd missed him, but did she still want him to be part of her life? Did she perhaps not trust that he felt the same way? He needed to tell her, to convince her that he wanted her, that he'd worked it out up in those Italian mountains, and under the rubble with Livvy. He'd realised that she was the most important thing to him, and that he needed her, he wanted their relationship to become rock solid, so that they could bring children into it in time. For he now knew that he was ready and able to become a parent. But there was a necessary step before that, and he just needed to say it, to come straight out with it.

'I've been thinking—'

'I had a lot of time—'

They both spoke at once, and then laughed, nervously. 'Go on,' Tim said. 'You first. But be gentle with me, Jacks.'

'I was going to say, this whole episode, well it's made me realise—'

'That you don't want me here?'

She stared at him and shook her head, and for a horrible moment he thought that was it, it was all over. 'No, no. The exact opposite. It's made me realise I love you, Tim Wilsher. I want you in my life more than ever. More than anything else. As long as you want that too?'

'I do! Oh, Jacks, I do!'

She grinned. 'And we'll go on adventures and do lots of travelling again. Whatever you want.'

'But you want a family?'

She waved a hand dismissively, as though saying yes, that was what she wanted, but only if he wanted it too. This was his moment. He slid off the armchair and on to his knees in front of her, trying to hide his grimace as pain shot up from his bruised legs.

'Well, I—' she began, but then she stopped talking and stared at him in surprise as he took her hands in his.

'Jackie, what I want more than anything, what I was thinking about all the time in Italy even before the earthquake, is to be with you. I love you. Now and for always. I don't want anything to tear us apart. I think it might help if we made it more difficult to split up, in case we ever have a moment of madness again. So with that in mind . . . Jackie, will you marry me?' There. He'd done it.

'Marry you?' Her voice emerged as a squeak. She hadn't expected a proposal, he realised. But even before the earthquake, this was what he'd decided to do, as soon as he got back. What he should have done years ago. They *should* be married. They loved each other so much, they should make it official. They should have a wedding, a party, invite everyone and show the world they were a team, no matter what life threw at them. They'd have ups and downs, like any couple, but they'd weather them together.

'Yes. Please? Will you?'

She smiled. 'Tim, I would like nothing more.'

She pulled him towards her, off his knees and onto the sofa beside her. He winced a little, unable to hide it this time. 'I probably shouldn't have knelt on my injured leg but it seemed the right thing to do, given the occasion.'

'Oh, you silly thing,' she said, and took his face in her hands and kissed him soundly. He snaked his arms around her and breathed in her scent. And now he knew he really was home, in a place of safety, of love, of belonging. A place he never wanted to leave again.

\* \* \*

Jackie hadn't expected his proposal, but now that he'd asked and she'd accepted and she was in his arms, it felt so right, so good, so perfect. She held him tight, trying to stop the tears of happiness that were running down her face. It had been an emotional evening, listening to his story of the earthquake and the baby – the child that had brought him back to her, in many ways. She sensed too, that caring for that baby, little Livvy, might have somehow changed the way he felt about having a child of his own. He hadn't said so outright, but she'd seen the look in his eye when he showed her the photos on his phone. He'd bonded with that baby and it meant, she dared to hope, that in time he'd feel confident that he could bond with a baby of their own. She wouldn't push it. She had Tim back, and that was what she wanted. And if he never wanted a child of his own, then she'd accept that.

For now, being engaged to him, knowing he was fully committed to their relationship and feeling content just to be with him, whether or not they tried for a family, was enough.

More than enough. It was perfect. She tipped her face back and found his lips, kissing him deeply and soundly, reclaiming him and reaffirming to him that she was his, and always would be.

# Chapter 28

## Madeleine, 18 April 1912

It was as they left the pier that Madeleine caught sight of a familiar figure, standing near the edge of the crowd, a shawl wrapped around her and the bundle she was carrying. She looked lost and alone, despite the crowds. Around her, people hurried past on all sides, but no one stopped to see if she needed help.

Madeleine tugged on Ralph's arm to stop him. 'Ralph, you go on alone to the office. I have something I need to do.' She waved vaguely about her, hoping Ralph wouldn't ask for details. She wasn't sure what she was going to do herself, yet. She hadn't told him much of Lucy's story. It had seemed too raw, too close to home, and she'd known she would not be able to talk to him about it without breaking down.

Ralph stared at her, and then looked ahead, towards the street. 'What? But I can't leave you on your own in this crowd!'

'I'll be perfectly all right. There's . . . someone I need to speak to. Then I'll go to our apartment – there's . . . something I want to pick up from there. I won't be long. See you back at the ship. Go on, hurry, you have work to do.' She was counting on him wanting to waste no time in reaching the newspaper offices and handing over his other stories.

'If you're sure . . .' he said, and she nodded.

'Go.'

He stepped away and was swallowed by the crowds in no time at all. Madeleine looked back to where she'd seen the woman. She'd been near the railings somewhere. Madeleine made her way over, thanking God that she was tall and able to see over the heads of at least some of the people. But the figure she was seeking was tiny, dressed in dark clothing, blending in so well with everyone else around her. The crush of bodies, the clamour of so many people all trying to get somewhere, or work out where they needed to go – it was all so intense. A part of Madeleine wanted to give up before she'd even begun, to go back to her cabin and lie down on the bed to rest, to begin the process of putting it all behind her. But another part told her no, she must do this. It was the only way she'd be able to move forward with life, she was sure of it.

She caught a glimpse, about twenty feet away from her, the flick of a shawl, the hunched shape of someone holding a precious bundle close to her chest, protecting it. The woman was moving away, battling through the crowds, towards the street as though she'd decided at last where to go, what to do.

'Wait! Please, wait!' Madeleine shouted but her voice was lost in the general hubbub around her. And why would any one person think that the random call of 'wait' applied to them? No, Madeleine knew she must catch up with her, grab her arm and then . . . Then, she didn't know. She didn't know what she'd do, or why she was doing it. Only that she had to do it, or else risk living a life of regret and unfulfilled longing.

The woman had reached the street and was looking left and right, clearly still undecided about where to go. In her arms, the baby was wrapped in one of *Carpathia*'s blankets. Madeleine stopped and watched her for a moment, unnoticed. There was now no danger of losing her, the crowds were thinner here. The woman bent her head and lifted the child closer, kissing its head, then used a corner of the shawl to wipe her face as though she was rubbing away tears. Her shoulders heaved. She was sobbing, Madeleine realised. Sobbing, yet trying to control herself, for the sake of that child in her arms. The child she probably had no means of supporting, no money, nowhere to go.

The child that Madeleine could provide for. She could help. She could help them both. As the woman began to walk down Tenth Avenue, Madeleine made her decision and once more hurried after her. A little further along where the street grew dark and empty, she caught her arm.

'Wait, please. I want to help you.'

She stopped and turned. In the dim street lights, Madeleine could not make out her expression. She was holding the child close to her, as though afraid she might lose it. That precious child.

'I want to help,' Madeleine said again, and Lucy gasped, her eyes widening as Madeleine stepped forward.

'How?' She sounded suspicious, as well she might be. Hadn't Madeleine promised she'd help her before, on *Carpathia*, and yet she'd failed.

'My husband and I, we are . . . well off. We have an apartment here in New York. It is warm and comfortable. There are things for babies there as well. We'd thought . . . we were expecting to have a child sooner or later. We kitted out a nursery in readiness.' Madeleine took a deep breath. 'That will never happen now, and besides, we were on our way to Europe for a few months, when the ship turned back after . . . well, you know.'

'What are you suggesting?'

She was holding the baby so tightly, protectively, Madeleine saw. She did not want to lose him. And in a rush, Madeleine understood her fear. That agonising sense of loss she'd felt herself, when her last pregnancy had failed so catastrophically. That sense of loss that she still felt, that she would always feel. How much worse must it be for Lucy who had lost a living child? Or thought she had. There was still a chance . . .

'I'm suggesting, Lucy, that perhaps you and your baby could live in our apartment for the next few months, while we are away. You would be safe and secure there, and it would give you a chance to find your feet in this city. I would also leave you some money for food, things for the baby and so on. When we return, we can help you find your own place.' There. She'd said it. She'd put the offer out there.

'You would do that for me?' Lucy frowned. 'Why?'

'Because . . . because . . .' How was she going to explain it? She could barely make sense of her emotions and needs herself. 'Because you lost everything. Your husband, your other child, your belongings.'

'So did so many other people. Why me?' Lucy's voice was a whisper.

'Your story touched me,' Madeleine said simply. 'I can't help everyone. But I can help you. I wanted so desperately to find your other child on the ship, but I failed.' And here in New York, if that woman in the red hat did indeed have Norah, she'd be impossible to find. 'But this, I can do for you. Will you accept? I must go back to *Carpathia* very soon, so we don't have long.'

Lucy was staring at her, as though trying to look deep inside her to find out if the offer was genuine, if there would be a catch somewhere. And then as Madeleine watched, willing her to agree, she slowly nodded. 'Yes. I accept. It's a very kind offer. And as you say, I have nowhere else.'

'Then come with me. We don't have much time before I am due back on the ship.' Madeleine led her along the street and managed to flag down a cab. She gave her address and soon they were outside her apartment building, that overlooked Central Park. Madeleine let herself into the building and ushered Lucy into the elevator and up to the fifth floor, where her apartment was situated.

257

'I've never been in a lift before,' Lucy said, as Madeleine showed her how to operate it.

'You need it here. Otherwise it's a lot of stairs. So, here we are.' She showed Lucy into the apartment. It was only small, with two bedrooms, a little kitchen, a bathroom and a living and dining area. She pointed to the smaller bedroom, the one that should have become a nursery. 'In there, you'll find some baby items tucked away in the cupboard. Use anything you like.'

Lucy was standing open-mouthed in the centre of the room, gazing about her. 'Are you sure? I mean, are you really sure I can stay here?'

'Yes, I'm sure.' Madeleine smiled at her. 'Come, take a look at the view from the window. It's better in daylight, but you'll get the idea now.' She led Lucy to the large window that faced Central Park.

'That is beautiful,' Lucy whispered. She turned to Madeleine and there were tears in her eyes. 'Do you mean it? Can Frederick and I stay here while you are away?'

'Yes, you may.' It felt good, Madeleine thought, to be doing this practical thing for Lucy. She glanced down at the baby who was beginning to wake up, snuffling and wriggling in her mother's arms.

'Would you like to hold him?' Lucy asked.

Madeleine gasped. Oh, how she wanted to hold a child again, but if she did, would she be able to give the baby back? Could she trust herself after that reaction she'd had holding the other baby?

'Here, hold out your arms. Elbow out for his head. There. That's right.'

Madeleine had held out her arms instinctively, almost without meaning to, and now little Frederick was in them, warm and soft against her chest, rooting around as though expecting her to feed him. The little mouth opening and closing, a bubble of spit on his lip. His eyes, wide open now, dark blue with long lashes. A tiny hand escaping from the blanket, grasping at the edge of it.

And then a smile as the child's eyes focused on her and somehow Madeleine's face pleased him.

'He likes you,' Lucy said. 'He's right to. You are doing so much for us.'

'He is beautiful,' Madeleine whispered. Would her own child have been as beautiful as this one? She would never know. As she held him she made a decision. Lucy needed to know about the woman in brown. It was only right. She looked up at her. 'Lucy, there is something I must tell you. About Norah. I am not sure of this but . . . there is a small chance that she did survive and was taken by a couple that were *Carpathia* passengers.'

'What? My Norah? But . . . but how?' Lucy sat down heavily, a hand across her mouth.

Madeleine explained what had happened, stressing over and over that she could not be certain of anything.

'I must search for them! They left the ship, you say? They're in New York then. There is hope for my Norah!'

'Lucy, it will be very difficult for you to find them, if they don't want to be found.'

'But there's a chance. And even if I don't, knowing she's alive . . .' Lucy gulped back a sob, 'that's better than thinking of her still out there, in the cold dark ocean. Far better.'

'Yes.' She was right, it was. Frederick was beginning to grizzle. 'I think he wants to come back to you now,' Madeleine said.

Lucy stared at Frederick, frowning a little as though forcing herself to refocus on the child she still had. 'He is due a feed,' she agreed, and held out her arms to take the baby.

Madeleine looked at his little face, the eyes beginning to screw up, the puckered mouth, and knew that it was all right, that she could hold a baby and then hand him back and feel good about it. 'There you go, little one. Back to Mama.' She passed back the baby and her arms felt lightened but they did not ache, not like before. The experiences of the last few days had helped her, she realised. She knew now she should count her blessings. She'd had

259

a glimpse of what real loss was and what it did to people, and she understood how lucky she and Ralph really were. She watched as Lucy took the child then went to sit on a chair, opening the front of her dress so she could feed him. It felt like a privilege to see, an insight into what motherhood meant.

'Thank you for telling me,' Lucy said, once Frederick was latched on and feeding hungrily. 'There is some comfort in knowing my little girl is alive. It was the not-knowing that hurt the most. And I will search for them. I will do all I can.'

'Of course.' But how could Lucy find them now, in a huge city where she was a stranger? She had enough to contend with, looking after herself and Frederick, making a life for them both without her husband. As for the other child, Madeleine could only hope that the woman would take good care of her.

'I shall leave you some money on the table, and a set of keys to the apartment. We will be away for three months. I will speak to the concierge of this building when I leave, and let him know you are here. If you go to see him, he might be able to find work for you.'

'But how can I work, with a baby?'

'There might be something. Ask him anyway, he's very resourceful and helpful.'

'Thank you.' Frederick had finished feeding and had fallen asleep, his head lolling back and an expression of pure contentment on his face. Lucy buttoned up the front of her dress with one hand, then laid him carefully on the sofa, setting a cushion between him and the edge. Satisfied Frederick could not roll off, she stood and held out a hand to Madeleine. 'You have been so very kind. I don't know how I can ever repay you.'

'Just look after the apartment for us while we are gone. And take very great care of that precious little one.' Madeleine nodded at Frederick who was fast asleep on the sofa. She would never give birth to a baby herself, but she would stay in touch with Lucy, and perhaps she could be a kind of aunt to Frederick. Yes, that was it. She would buy the child presents at Christmas and on his birthday, visit frequently, take him out on excursions when he was older. It would be enough. A child in her life – not her own child and not living with them, but in easy reach.

'Of course I will. And you . . . take care. Have a good trip.'

'Thank you.' With one last look at Frederick, Madeleine crossed the room to the dining table where she emptied her purse of money, and laid down her key. 'There. I must go now. Good luck.'

'Thank you,' Lucy said once more, as Madeleine left the apartment and took the elevator back down to ground level. She felt lighter, as though telling Lucy about the woman in brown had lifted a weight from her.

She was crossing the building's lobby, deciding how best to tell Ralph about their lodger, when she spotted him coming in, elated and excited.

'Maddy! I remembered you said you had to pick something up.' There was a collection of armchairs for visitors at one side of the lobby and they sat down there.

'How did it go?' she asked him, although she could already see by his expression he had good news.

'They managed to publish my story, the one I threw down to them, as an Extra edition. The paper sold out everywhere really quickly. They've bought all my other stories too, and will publish them in the morning edition. It'll make my name, Maddy, just as I hoped. We got the truth of the disaster told.' He grinned at her, and then became suddenly serious. 'They asked why no detailed news was transmitted from the ship, and I told them of Captain Rostron's refusal. And then they showed me newspaper front pages from the last few days, including from the *Tribune* itself. It's shocking, Maddy, the way the lack of real news meant papers simply made things up.'

'What sort of thing were they reporting?'

Ralph sighed. 'Some said that *Titanic* had gone down and everyone on board had perished, and others said that she'd hit an iceberg but was under tow, and no lives were lost. There was much speculation about the rich and famous on board the ship but nothing at all about the hundreds of ordinary people. Can you imagine how that made friends and relatives of those on board *Titanic* feel? All these days since the tragedy when they have not been able to find out the truth?'

'It's so wrong, that those reporters made up stories like that,' Madeleine said, but Ralph shook his head.

'I don't blame the reporters, who were leaned on to write something, anything. I don't even blame the editors or newspaper owners. There was a public demand for information, so in the absence of real news, they had to print something. Whatever rumours were flying around had to be turned into stories.'

'And that would have just spread the rumours still further.'

'Yes, but for all they knew, those rumours might have been correct.'

'It still seems wrong.'

'Maddy, my love, what is wrong is that despite modern technology, we were not allowed to get the truth sent out sooner. That is what we must focus on.' He sighed. 'Imagine in the future, Maddy, when ship to shore wireless telegraphy works worldwide, no matter the distance? Imagine information about a disaster such as this one being almost instantaneously transmitted around the world, for all to hear? No more made-up headlines, no more scare stories and people wondering what has really happened and what is the truth of it all.'

She nodded. 'That would be a perfect world.'

'It would indeed. And it will come to pass. The *Tribune* has commissioned me to write one more article on that subject, an in-depth analysis of how the spread of news has sped up in recent years, with predictions of what will happen in the future. I am excited for this, and will begin investigating even while we are travelling, with a view to writing it soon after we return. There may even be a book in it.'

'That's marvellous!' Madeleine smiled at Ralph. And now she needed to tell him about their house guest. She swallowed, hoping she'd find the right words that would make him feel as she did, that this was the right thing to do.

Before she had a chance to begin, Ralph caught her arm. 'Say, shall we stay in our apartment tonight? As we're both here now. It'll be a kind of reset, before we sail again. We can have a breakfast out tomorrow, before returning to the ship.' He stood and began pulling her over towards the elevator.

'Wait. Sit down again for a moment. There's something I must tell you.' Hesitantly, she recounted her meeting with Lucy and her sudden desire to do something good for the poor woman. She was not sure how Ralph would react. When she finished talking, Ralph leaned forward and took her in his arms, kissing her forehead.

'Maddy, that is so kind of you. I am happy that you have done this. If you trust the woman then so do I, and as you say, she deserves a chance in life after losing so much. You are the kindest soul. It will be good to know the apartment is not left unoccupied while we are away too.' He gazed at her with love in his eyes. 'I should like to meet her. Let's go up.'

And this time she let him lead her back up to their apartment, where she tapped on the door. 'Lucy? It is only me, and I have brought my husband to meet you.'

Lucy opened the door looking nervous, but she relaxed when she saw they were both smiling. 'Pleased to meet you, Mr Meyer. I hope that . . .'

'I am very happy for the apartment to be occupied while we are away, Mrs Watts, and from what my wife says you are a very deserving tenant. May I meet your baby?'

Lucy nodded and went to pick up Frederick from the sofa where he still lay. She looked unsure as to whether to pass him to Ralph or not, since Ralph hadn't held out his arms the way

263

Madeleine had earlier. He didn't know what to do with babies, she realised. Lucy looked a little uncertain, so Madeleine stepped forward and held out her own arms. 'May I hold him again?'

'Of course.'

And then there was that glorious feeling once more as she cradled baby Frederick and breathed in his soft milky scent. He woke, and she sat down with him in an armchair and gently rocked him back to sleep, crooning softly to him. Behind her she was vaguely aware of Ralph giving Lucy practical instructions – how to set the heating controls, what to do if there was a problem with the electricity, what hours the concierge of the building worked.

At last Ralph finished speaking and he and Lucy stood beside her. 'Darling, I think we should go back to the ship now, and leave Lucy in peace. It has been wonderful to meet you, Mrs Watts, and I hope you are able to settle in quickly here.' There was a thoughtful look in his eyes as Madeleine stood and handed back the baby. As Lucy took him, Madeleine wiped a dribble of spit from the corner of his mouth with her thumb.

'Best wishes, Lucy. We'll see you in a few months. Look after that little fellow.'

'I will. And thank you, so much.'

They left the apartment and took a cab back to the ship, for the most part in silence. But when they reached their cabin Ralph turned to Madeleine and took her in his arms. She was astonished to see tears in his eyes. 'You have done a good thing there. In the morning, before the ship sails, let's pop round with some groceries to start her off. We'll have time.'

'And while we are out, we can buy the morning papers,' Madeleine added, and Ralph laughed.

'You have seen my ulterior motive. Yes, of course. Then when we sail again, it will be with plenty of reading matter and the knowledge that we've done some good, after such a tragedy.'

# Chapter 29

## Jackie, 2022

The next weekend, Tim took Jackie out on a tour of local jewellery shops, and by the end of the day she was sporting a gorgeous white gold and diamond ring on her left hand. She couldn't stop herself from looking at it every few minutes, admiring the way it looked on her hand, the way it caught the light and sparkled, how it proclaimed to the world that they'd made a commitment to each other at long last. Tim's leg was improving and now he was barely limping at all, though one wound still needed to be kept covered.

They hadn't yet discussed whether or not they would try for a baby. It was too soon since Tim's ordeal, and Jackie didn't want to raise the subject and risk Tim thinking she was starting up all the old arguments again. She'd made her decision – she was committing to Tim, whatever that meant. He'd made it clear back in the spring that he wasn't ready to have children. And now, that was fine by her. She wanted Tim, and if that meant no children, then so be it.

For now, she was happy to have Tim home. He was off work – not due back in school until September, and was spending the days while she was at work in the garden, either resting with a book and a beer, or gardening. He had also taken over all the domestic work, house cleaning and cooking for the next few weeks. 'Only fair, since you're at work and I'm not,' he said, and she was appreciating being looked after. Usually, they shared all the jobs evenly, with no changes during the school holidays. But this year he took on all the work willingly; which was good, since she was kept very busy at work with Henry acquiring more and more books and other collectibles, all of which needed cataloguing, and she hadn't been able to work many days from home.

One day at work, she received an unusual email, forwarded by the *Huffington Post*. It was a response to her piece about Lucy Watts and the missing baby, and it was intriguing.

*Please forward to Ms J Summers.*


*Dear Ms Summers,*
   *I was fascinated to read your article about the mystery missing baby rescued from Titanic, and the woman Lucy Watts who saved her other child. I was particularly drawn to your description of the silver bangles that each baby had. You see, my grandmother had a bangle just like that, with her name and date of birth inscribed on the inside. Her married name was Norah Frances Franklin, and her date of birth is exactly the one you mentioned in the article. She is long gone, sadly, but the family story that has been passed down is that she was orphaned when Titanic sank, and then adopted by passengers on Carpathia, who had cared for her when she was first brought on board.*
   *Your article makes me wonder; was she perhaps not orphaned at all? It certainly sounds as though she was Lucy Watts's missing baby, and had a twin. I wonder why Lucy couldn't find her on board Carpathia? Did my grandmother's adoptive mother keep her hidden for some reason?*

*You have certainly raised some questions within my family.*
*If you can spare me a little time, I would very much like to*
*have a chat with you about this.*
*Yours,*
*Neil Franklin*

Jackie read the email twice. Neil had given an address, and it
was in the UK, a couple of hours' drive away. It would certainly
be fascinating to talk to him and hear his family stories about
Norah's rescue. And he was right – this certainly raised a heap
of questions. It occurred to her – if she could trace any descendants of Lucy Watts's other child, the boy, Frederick, they'd be
relatives of Neil and his family that he wouldn't know about.
She'd meant to do exactly that, she recalled, but then the earthquake had happened and her research had taken a back seat. It
would make for another story that, no doubt, *Huffington Post*
would publish as a follow-up. In fact, and here she went into
a daydream, there might be an entire book in it. A TV docu-
mentary, even. Before she knew it, she was dreaming of award
ceremonies and Netflix dramatisations of the story, with a top
actress, perhaps with someone like Millie Bobby Brown playing
the part of Lucy Watts . . .

'Pull yourself together girl,' she told herself sternly. First thing
was to reply to Neil and email her phone number so they could
have a chat about it. And then . . . she'd see what she could do
to track the other side of the family, the other twin's descendants. Frederick would have kept the name Watts. He'd be listed
somewhere as a *Titanic* survivor.

She emailed a reply to Neil and within an hour of sending the
email he was on the phone to her. 'Wow, it is good to hear from
you! It was my son who alerted me to your article. He always
reads the *Huffington Post* and he recognised the description
of the little bracelet. I inherited it when Granny died, and my

daughter has the bangle now. She's pregnant and says that if it's a girl, she'll call her Norah and have her wear the bangle at her christening.'

'That's wonderful! I love the idea that she wants to call her child Norah.'

'Yes, and if I know Chloe, once she hears this story, she'll decide that Frederick is the perfect name if her baby is a boy. Of course, the child will be a descendant of Lucy Watts. She would have been my great-grandmother, so for Chloe's baby, she'd be the great-great-great-grandmother. Have I got that right?'

Jackie chuckled. 'Yes, I think so. So can you tell me a little about your grandmother's life?'

'Well, she always knew she was adopted. Her parents were Charles and Estella Simpson, and they made no secret of the fact she'd been on *Titanic* and saved by a stewardess who brought her on board *Carpathia*. They'd always longed for a child, and Granny used to say she was lucky she'd landed in their lap, as it were.'

'Violet Jessop was the stewardess.'

'Yes. Since reading your article I have ordered a copy of her memoir, but it hasn't arrived yet.'

'It's a good read!'

'I look forward to it. Anyway, the Simpsons were an English couple who'd travelled to New York for a holiday, and were heading back to Europe when they were caught up in the *Titanic* rescue. They stayed in New York for a few more days when *Carpathia* got back there, buying up baby items. They adopted Norah and brought her home to England on a different ship. She grew up in Leicestershire, married my grandfather John Franklin, and had two sons. My father was the eldest.'

Jackie was jotting down notes as Neil spoke, trying to piece together the story of what had happened to baby Norah. If the Simpsons had kept Norah in their cabin as the ship sailed back to New York that could be why Lucy had never found her. It must have been all a muddle on board the ship, with hundreds of *Titanic* survivors in every available space. And then they'd sailed back to England while Lucy had remained in New York.

'I'm thinking the Simpsons must have been a bit . . . well . . . underhand with their adoption of Norah,' Neil said, carefully. 'I mean, they clearly cared for her. She had a wonderful childhood, she always said, and she was grateful to them for adopting her. But they must have kept her hidden. Or Lucy Watts would have found her on the ship.'

'Yes. Maybe they were longing for a child. Maybe they'd lost a child themselves and . . .' Jackie was thinking of her own miscarriage. Her own longing for a baby. It was a strong emotion – it had nearly ended her relationship with Tim. Could it be strong enough to drive a woman to do something so desperate as to abduct a child? Or was it entirely innocent? They might not have been hiding the baby as such, and somehow never realised her mother was searching for her? They might have genuinely believed Norah was an orphan.

'But they . . . abducted her? That's what it was, really.'

'It was a long time ago,' Jackie said. 'And we will never know all the details of what happened.'

'You're right. Lucy's other child was Norah's twin, wasn't he?'

'Yes, that's right.'

Neil sighed. 'It's comforting to know that at least Lucy wasn't left entirely alone. Do you know anything of what happened to her afterwards?'

'Not yet . . . but I thought I might research it,' Jackie replied.

'That would be marvellous. And you'll stay in touch; let me know what you find out?'

'I will, yes.'

Jackie lost no time getting on with researching what had become of Lucy Watts and her other baby. First stop was to check the various websites dedicated to the *Titanic*. From these she confirmed that an Arthur Watts was listed among those who went down with the ship, and Lucy Watts, aged twenty-five, and Frederick Watts, aged three months, were listed as among the rescued. There was no one else listed with the surname Watts, and no babies named Norah listed. Jackie was unsurprised. This did point to her theory that the child Violet Jessop had brought on board had been kept in secret by someone on *Carpathia*, for unknown reasons. And now she knew that the unknown persons were Charles and Estella Simpson.

After some time browsing websites, she came across the Encyclopedia Titanica, which listed all the survivors and if you clicked on the name, there was a short article about each person, detailing where they'd boarded the ship, which lifeboat they'd been on, and what became of them after arriving in New York. Absolutely perfect, Jackie thought, as she checked the articles on Lucy Watts and Frederick Watts. They'd been third-class passengers, an English family leaving Southampton to start a new life in America. After reaching New York, it appeared that other *Carpathia* passengers, Ralph and Madeleine Meyer, had provided Lucy and Frederick with a home for a few months.

'Ah-ha, the Meyers!' Jackie said to herself, pleased to see names she recognised. Another piece of the puzzle had fallen into place. Lucy's story must have really touched Madeleine, as was evident from the notes at the back of the notebook. How kind it had been of her and Ralph to give Lucy and Frederick a home.

Lucy had stayed in New York and, in time, had married again, and had two further children. 'More relatives for Neil,' Jackie noted. And more names for her to follow up on. But the names of her later children weren't given on the website – after all, they had no connection with *Titanic*.

She did better when she looked up Frederick's entry on the website. He'd grown up in New York with his mother and later step-father and half-siblings, and had become a manager in a department store on 5th Avenue. He'd married and had five children, four girls and a boy. Later, he'd set up his own clothing store in New York, which was still in existence, owned by family members.

Jackie couldn't believe her luck. It took just minutes to find a website and contact details for the store Frederick Watts had opened. It took rather longer to decide how to word an email to them. And then more time to decide to talk to Neil first, and see if he would prefer to be the first to make contact, as they were his relatives, after all.

'Oh my God, that is wonderful,' Neil said, when she phoned him later that day. 'And so soon! I thought I'd hear from you in about a fortnight, with just a few sketchy details. I would very much like to initiate contact with the Watts family in New York. It might be that they're not interested, but we shall see. Thank you so much for all you've done.'

'No problem at all,' Jackie said. She passed on all the details she'd found, and this time it was Neil who promised to stay in touch and let her know what happened.

She went home that evening with a smile on her face and a story to tell Tim. He listened carefully as she recounted it all, from the moment Henry had asked her to go through the box of *Carpathia* memorabilia. 'He was hoping there'd be a medal in there. Apparently, all the crew members received one for their part in rescuing *Titanic* survivors. There wasn't one, but the notebook I found more than made up for that.' She told him the story of Lucy and the two babies, her write-up of this, and Neil's subsequent contact.

'So while I was away you became a journalist?' Tim said, sounding proud.

'Not quite! Just one article published. Though I think, if Neil agrees, I'll write a follow-up when we see what, if anything, comes of him contacting his distant cousins.'

'I'm imagining some sort of reunion, of the two sides of the family. This Neil, and then Frederick Watts's descendants, each comparing their baby bangles.'

'Assuming the American side still have theirs,' Jackie said, but she agreed. What an amazing event that would be!

# Chapter 30

## Tim, 2022

'I can't believe it's September tomorrow. Means I'll be back at work next week,' Tim said, flicking through the pages of their house diary. The last day of the summer term felt like yesterday. And yet so much had happened over the summer months – from losing a baby to nearly losing Jackie to nearly losing his life. And then gaining a fiancée. He looked over at Jackie, who was bent over her laptop, working from home. 'The holidays have gone so fast.'

'You poor sausage,' she said, pulling a sad face. 'Six weeks off work, all gone. Never mind. Soon be half-term. You teachers have it so easy.'

'We work blimming hard in termtime, as you well know!'

'But since you're still off today, you can make me a cup of tea.' She batted her eyelashes at him and he laughed.

'All right. You know I can't deny you anything when you look at me like that.' He went out to the kitchen, still grinning. It was so good to feel their relationship was back on track. More than that: it was better than before. They'd made tentative wedding plans for the following spring, and every day felt as though they were cementing their partnership. Building a strong, sure foundation for a future family.

As he flicked the kettle on and took mugs out of a cupboard, Tim pondered their future. Back in April, before any of the year's momentous events, they'd agreed to start trying for a baby in September. Since his return from Italy, Jackie hadn't brought the subject up, and he had the feeling she wasn't going to. Perhaps she was still unsure of whether he really wanted children. She'd been so perceptive back then, seeing the fear and reluctance that he hadn't been able to stop himself feeling.

But things were different now, thanks to Livvy. He pulled out his phone and looked at the latest photo he'd received of her, which showed her sitting on a colourful rug in a garden somewhere, holding a pink teddy bear high above her head and grinning toothlessly. He smiled. She was beautiful. And he made a decision.

A few minutes later, Tim took a mug of tea to Jackie and placed it on a coaster beside her. He sat with his own mug on the sofa. 'Jacks? Can you spare a moment?'

'Sure.' She turned to face him and picked up her tea. 'Thanks for this.'

'You're welcome. So . . . um . . . it's September tomorrow.'

'Yeah, you said. Back to work, and I'll have to make my own cuppas when working from home.'

'Mmm. Do you remember, back in the spring, before . . . all of it . . . we agreed that—' He broke off as she was staring at him wide-eyed. Had she changed her mind? '—we agreed that around now we'd start trying for a baby?' He finished in a rush.

'Of course I remember.' She spoke quietly as if afraid that too loud a voice would break the spell.

'So . . . you still up for it?'

She simply stared at him, her expression one of delight tinged with disbelief. 'You want to?'

'I do, yes. Since . . . being stuck in that rubble with Livvy, I've realised I really do want a baby. With you.'

'That's . . . amazing. Yes. I'm still up for it, if you are.'

'I am. I said I am, and I really am.'

She smiled then, and reached a hand out to him. He took it and kissed it, holding her gaze, trying to reassure her that all his misgivings around parenthood really had left him for good. But she wasn't quite certain of him, he realised. There was a smidgen of doubt in her eyes. His reactions back in the spring had left her mistrusting him when it came to parenthood. He didn't blame her, but he was different now, he'd learned something about himself in Italy. He somehow needed to prove that to her and make her believe in him again.

The following evening was a regular pub night with Alfie. Jackie was also going out, with Sarah. Tim met his friend at the Rising Sun as usual. It was just the two of them – Marco and Niall were both on holiday abroad somewhere.

'Evening, Timbo. How's the leg?' Alfie greeted him, as Tim entered the pub.

'Better. Look, no limp now! Cheers.' Tim took the pint that Alfie had already bought him.

'Glad to hear it. You had us all worried back then, you know.'

'I was pretty worried too. Can't tell you the relief I felt when I first saw a chink of daylight and heard a rescuer shouting to me.'

'You were quite the hero, old man. That baby, eh?' Alfie raised his pint glass in a salute.

Tim shrugged. 'Just did my best. Glad to have saved her. She's a darling. She helped me get through that ordeal as much as I helped her, I reckon.'

Alfie cocked his head to one side. 'Well, you've changed, haven't you? The Alfatron detects a more mature Timbo, who's now discovered he *can* look after babies when he needs to. Does this mean anything for Timbo's future, I wonder?'

'Yes, well, Jacks and I are going to try for a baby, now,' Tim said, feeling suddenly a little shy.

'That's excellent news! And this time you're properly on board with it, aren't you?'

'I am, yes.' Tim took a pull of his pint. 'Though I am not sure that Jacks fully believes me. She'd guessed, last time, that I had misgivings. And so now, however hard I try to convince her that I do, really, want a baby, I suspect there's a little part of her that doesn't quite trust me.'

'Man, that's hard,' Alfie said, pulling a face.

'Yes. Can't blame her though. I look back and I'm ashamed. I should have got over myself. And when she had the miscarriage, I should have put my own feelings aside and comforted her more. The baby we lost was as real to her as Livvy – the Italian baby – was to me, under the rubble. I didn't realise that at the time.'

'You do now.'

Tim nodded. 'Yes, I do. But how do I convince her to trust me again?'

'Actions, buddy.'

'Actions?'

'Speak louder than words.' Alfie nodded sagely and took a long draught of his pint. 'Anyway. The match on Saturday. What are our chances?'

'Slim to none,' Tim replied. As Alfie chattered on about Reading FC's forthcoming match, he pondered the advice. What could he do to convince Jackie that, at last, he was on the same page as her, regarding starting a family? What actions could he take? He had absolutely no idea.

# Chapter 31

## Madeleine, August 1912

Here they were once more, sailing into New York, passing Ellis Island, the Statue of Liberty and Staten Island. Just as they had done over three months earlier. Only this time they were on a different ship. Not *Carpathia* – Ralph had said he never wanted to sail on a Cunard ship again for fear of running into Captain Rostron. On the way over, after leaving New York the second time, they'd taken care to stay out of the Captain's way. Returning to New York at the end of the trip, they'd chosen to sail with the White Star Line, and were on *Olympic*, *Titanic*'s sister ship. It was strange, sailing on a ship that was the twin of the one that had so tragically sunk earlier in the year, but they'd enjoyed its size and opulence, and it had certainly been much faster crossing the Atlantic.

As Madeleine stood on deck with Ralph's arm around her waist, watching the familiar landmarks pass by one by one, she reflected on the journey they'd undertaken, the adventures they'd had. From Gibraltar they'd travelled along the coast of Spain and into southern France where they'd spent a month on the Côte d'Azur. Then they'd journeyed north, first to Lyon and then Paris, exploring the beautiful city in the summer sunshine, soaking up the art and the atmosphere. And then they'd crossed the Channel from Le Havre to Southampton and journeyed to London for a month, before returning to Southampton in time to sail back across the ocean.

Ralph had written articles and sent them to his paper, and had also outlined a book on the history of communication around the globe. He planned to work on it once they returned home, before their lives were turned upside down by the arrival of a little one.

Madeleine smiled as she remembered how and where Ralph had suggested tentatively that they might adopt a child, if she felt ready to. They'd been at the very top of the Eiffel Tower, gazing out across the Parisian landscape, marvelling at the twists and turns of the river Seine, the golden dome of Les Invalides, the towers of Notre-Dame and the distant dome of Sacré-Cœur at Montmartre. She'd been about to point out the Louvre when he'd turned towards her and stroked her face. 'My darling, this journey has done you good. And me. It's given me time to think, space to contemplate our future. I am ready now, where I wasn't before – and for that I apologise – to take steps to adopt a child. A baby, a toddler, an older child, boy or girl – whatever you want.'

She'd gasped, unable to answer him immediately, and he'd continued speaking. 'When I saw you holding Lucy's baby, I could see how very much you wanted a child, and how wonderful a mother you would be, given the chance. And so, let's give you – give ourselves – that chance. I wonder often, as I expect you do, how Frederick will have changed since we left. I imagine him sitting up now, playing with toys, putting his little fist in his mouth, being offered new foods, laughing and babbling at his mother. I find myself looking forward immensely to seeing Lucy and Frederick again when we return, and asking Lucy's advice on parenting if or when we do adopt our own child. What do you say?'

'Oh Ralph,' was all she could say, but she knew the smile on her face said it all. He pulled her close and kissed her.

'We'll be a family at last,' he whispered, and she nodded, too overcome to be able to say anything else. Yes, of course she had been thinking frequently about Lucy and Frederick. They'd received a handful of letters *Post Restante* and had sent one home almost every week. They knew Lucy had found work babysitting for other residents in the apartment block, where she was able to take Frederick with her. Through that work, she'd met a well-off couple who were expecting a baby, and had been interviewed for a position as a full-time nanny when the baby arrived. She'd got the job, and had excitedly written to say that the job was live-in, and there'd be a separate room for Frederick as well. It was just a few blocks further up the avenue from the Meyers' apartment. *I expect to have moved out before you come home*, she'd written, *and I promise I shall leave the apartment spick and span. Thank you once more, and I look forward to seeing you when you return. I will have one day off a week, and I would love to occasionally spend it with you.*

It was such good news, and just what Madeleine had hoped might happen. She pictured herself pushing an adopted baby in a pram around Central Park, alongside Lucy pushing her charge and Frederick in a twin pram. What a future she had to look forward to!

She'd often thought too, about the other baby, Frederick's twin, Norah, and the couple who'd taken her. Lucy had written in her letters that she had searched, she had left her details with the police, with every hospital or doctor's surgery, every shop selling goods for infants that she could find, but she'd had no joy and was beginning to conclude they must have left the city. *I think of her often*, Lucy had written, *and I feel within myself that she is alive and prospering, and it is a comfort to know she is with a woman who must have longed desperately for a child of her own, and who will give her a good life. It is the next best thing. I will, of course, never forget her and who knows, one day I may see her again or perhaps she and Frederick will be reunited in later life. Even if I am not there to see it, I like to believe that somehow it will come to pass.*

Madeleine also wondered how the couple were getting on with Norah, whether that woman too had found safety and security, and fulfilment as a mother. Lucy was right; perhaps they weren't even in New York. They might have travelled to a different city or state to start a new life with the stolen baby. Or a different country, maybe somewhere in Europe.

What the woman had done was wrong, but Madeleine didn't have the heart to condemn her for it. She must have assumed the child's parents were both dead. If that woman hadn't snatched the baby and Madeleine hadn't met Lucy, she might well have tried to keep the child herself. She'd still never told Ralph that part of it, and knew that she never would. She was in a better place now, able to face their future – no, not just face it, look forward to it. Immensely. She was privileged, comfortably off, married to a man she loved and who adored her, with a prospect of adopting a baby to love as well as being an honorary aunt to Lucy's child. She had everything to live for.

'Look, we're nearly at the White Star Line pier,' Ralph said, pointing to the Manhattan shoreline. He was right, they were almost at Pier 59. The last time she'd seen this pier was when *Carpathia* was dropping off *Titanic*'s lifeboats. That seemed like another lifetime now.

'We're nearly home,' she said, and he pulled her close against him.

'I'm glad we had this trip. I think it's helped.'

'Oh yes. It has. Immeasurably. Thank you.'

'Thank you, my darling, for taking this journey with me. Not just the one to Europe, I mean the one through life.'

'Now you're getting sentimental,' she said, laughing, and he laughed too, as they leaned on the railings, watching the tugs manoeuvre the great ship into its berth. New York, Lucy and Frederick, and their shining future awaited them.

# Chapter 32

## Jackie, 2022

It was late September, and life had settled down into the usual termtime routines. The only difference this year was that they were actively trying for a baby. When Tim had suggested it, back at the end of August, Jackie had been cautiously delighted but also a little worried. If or when she became pregnant, how would he feel then? How would he react? Would it be like last time, when he'd briefly allowed fear and regret to cross his face when he'd heard her news? She wondered how she would deal with that. Even though this time it had been Tim who'd broached the subject, she still could not shake the feeling that he was uncertain of the idea of becoming a father. He'd insisted he felt ready for it now, but did he? Did he really? She'd never forget his look of relief when she'd had the miscarriage back in early summer.

And then she realised it was more than four weeks since her last period. Add to that, tender breasts and a slight queasiness in the morning – she recognised the signs. She took a test at work one day, and when it showed up positive, she was not surprised. She had to sit quietly in her office for a while, staring at the opposite wall, working out her own feelings. Delight, yes. She still wanted a family. Fear, that she might miscarry again. Having been through that once she did not want to experience it again. And worry, about what reaction Tim would have to the news this time.

There was only one way to find out. That evening, which was supposed to be one of their date nights, when they went out for a meal and shared a bottle of wine, she would tell him. She briefly wondered if it was wise to tell him while they were out, given his reaction last time, but this time it should be different. He'd suggested to start trying. He'd said he was ready.

At the restaurant, a cosy Italian they'd always liked, she waited until they'd ordered their food. Tim had ordered their usual bottle of wine. 'And I'll have a sparkling water too, please,' Jackie told the waiter. 'I'm thirsty,' she said to Tim.

When the wine arrived, Tim poured out two glasses, but it was the water Jackie picked up. 'Well, cheers,' she said, with a smile.

Tim looked from her to the untouched wine, to the water, and back to her face. She kept a smile in place throughout, and as she watched him, she saw the exact moment the penny dropped and he guessed. His face split into a wide grin and he gasped. 'Jackie . . . are you . . . it isn't just thirst, is it?'

'Not just thirst,' she said. She picked up her wine glass and poured its contents into Tim's. 'Got a good reason for not drinking.'

'Tell me it's the reason I hope it is?' He was still grinning.

'If you're hoping that I'm pregnant, then yes, it is.' She said the words slowly, watching him carefully, and his reaction was all that she could have wished for.

'Wahey! That's fantastic!' He pushed back his chair and stood, coming round to her side of the table where he leaned over and wrapped his arms around her. 'Oh Jackie! I thought it might take months, after . . . what happened before. I'm so glad it's been quick. So glad for you, and for me too.'

'I'm happy you're so pleased.'

'You are too, yes?'

'Yes, I've just learned to be a bit more restrained this time, until we're certain it's going to keep. I'm not going to get quite so excited so soon.'

'Of course.' He went back to his chair but his grin remained. 'Even so, quietly inside, I am whooping for joy. But we won't tell anyone until you are ready to. God, Jacks, you're going to be a mum. I'm going to be a dad.'

'Last time you seemed unsure . . .' she said.

'That was before . . . before Livvy. Before I realised that I would be able to care for a baby. That I could do it – I could handle that level of dependency. I was scared, before, that I wouldn't have the right instincts. But now I know I do, thanks to Livvy.'

Jackie smiled. 'She's a lot to answer for, that one.'

'She certainly does.'

Jackie picked up her water glass and clinked it against Tim's wine. 'Here's to Livvy, then.'

'And to our little one,' Tim added.

Jackie nodded, and took a sip of her drink. His reaction had been genuine, and now she felt she could look forward to all that was to come, as this pregnancy progressed.

A few weeks later, after a successful 12-week scan that showed her pregnancy was progressing well, Jackie and Tim felt confident enough to share the good news with friends and family. Sarah was over the moon, as was Alfie. 'This time, mate,' he said to Tim at one of their pub nights, 'you're properly ready for it. I can see it in the way you told me about it. None of that nonsense about not being grown-up enough to handle it. The earthquake did you some good. Shook some sense into you. Well done.'

And Sarah simply hugged Jackie tightly, tears glistening in the corners of her eyes. 'Couldn't be more pleased for you, Jackie,' she said. 'It'll all go well this time, you'll see.'

Jackie even told Henry, warning him she'd need to take maternity leave the following year. He was delighted for her. And while she had his ear, she decided to update him on the latest news about the *Carpathia* baby mystery.

'I heard back from Neil Franklin yesterday,' she said. 'He's been in touch with various members of the Watts family in New York. And they're arranging a get-together. Neil and his daughter are going over to New York to meet their distant cousins, and compare baby bangles.'

'That is wonderful!' Henry beamed. 'And you're going too? As the person who started all this?'

Jackie shook her head. 'They invited me but no, I'm not going. I've run out of holiday days, and can't really afford it.'

Henry slapped his hands on the desk. 'Both problems are within my power to resolve. When is this reunion?'

'Week after next.' She wondered what he was going to suggest.

'I have a meeting in New York, that I can bring forward to that week. How about you accompany me on that business trip? I'll pay for everything, and you won't need to use up your holiday allowance. You'll just need to help Lisa out with some of her work on the trip otherwise she'll be jealous.'

Jackie stared at him, unable to believe what she was hearing. 'I would love to go!'

'You want to bring your fiancé too?'

'It's termtime. He can't take the time off.'

'Then it's definitely a working trip, but you, of course, will have the day free to go to this reunion. I will be very interested to hear afterwards how it all goes. In fact, if you can wangle me an invite too, I'd like to attend – as the owner of the notebook that started it all off. You know how I like to meet new people, and they're business people, so that's right up my street. Right then, check in with Lisa and then book us the flights, plus rooms at my usual hotel. Lisa has the details. And while we're there, we'll pop into Sotheby's auction house and see what goodies we might be able to pick up. I should have a reasonable amount of spare time as there's no Clarissa to demand I take her shopping for a thousandth handbag or whatever.' He pulled a face and Jackie gave him a sympathetic smile.

'That all sounds wonderful. I'll get straight on to it.' She left his office with a grin on her face. First task was to contact Neil and tell him she'd be able to make the reunion party after all, and ask if Henry could come too.

The business trip was slotted into a week, travelling to New York on a Monday and back on Friday. Jackie was pleased not to be leaving Tim for a weekend – they were making the most of their weekends together, knowing that everything would change once the baby came along. She'd taken a taxi to the airport. 'Put it all on expenses,' Henry had said. And they flew business class, which was a treat for her. She spent much of the flight chatting to Lisa, who was accompanying them in her usual capacity as Henry's personal assistant.

The reunion party was on the Wednesday of that week. Jackie arranged to meet Neil and his daughter Chloe in a café in downtown Manhattan beforehand, so they could arrive together.

She entered the café nervously, scanning the tables for a middle-aged man accompanied by a red-haired daughter as Neil had advised. She saw them immediately. It was hard to miss Chloe who was six months pregnant and had dyed scarlet hair – Jackie had pictured auburn. Neil looked out of place in the surroundings, wearing a fleece jacket and looking as though he'd be happier half-way up a mountain rather than in the middle of the city. He'd get on well with Tim, she thought. Neil stood up with a smile as she approached.

'Jackie Summers? I'm Neil Franklin and this is Chloe. Pleased to meet you!'

'Yes, that's me.' She shook his hand and sat down. 'Good to meet you too. And thanks for inviting me to this get-together.' Jackie ordered a coffee from a passing waitress. The other two already had cups in front of them.

'Well, it's all happened because of you,' Neil said.

'We think it's awesome that after 110 years, the two parts of the family will reunite,' Chloe put in. 'I hope they have their bangle still. I've got ours. I'll use it at the christening of this little one.' She patted her sizable bump. Soon, Jackie thought, she too would be that size. The idea was terrifying and exciting in equal measure.

Jackie chatted happily with them until it was time to make their way to the party, which was to be held in a conference room above the Watts store. Henry met them outside, his yellow taxi turning up just as they approached the entrance.

'Lisa's off running an errand for me. You looking forward to this?' he asked, once Jackie had made the introductions and they were threading their way through the store to the lifts they'd been advised to use.

'Oh yes!' All three answered together. In the conference room, the family had laid on champagne and canapés, and invited all members of the Watts family plus senior staff from the store. They greeted Neil and Chloe warmly, while Jackie hung back a little. Neil tugged her forward, and introduced her to a middle-aged woman named Leonora Watts who he'd been corresponding with and who'd arranged the party.

'We have you to thank for all this,' Leonora said, shaking Jackie's hand. She was immaculately made-up, wearing a neat black dress and heels. 'How did you come across the story?'

Jackie explained about her job and Henry's purchase of *Carpathia* memorabilia, and the reporter's notebook inside. Henry stood alongside her, chipping in now and again as she told the story.

'I bet that was Ralph Meyer's notebook,' Leonora replied. 'It was he and his wife, Madeleine, who provided my great-grandmother, Lucy Watts, with a home when they reached New York. I remember my grandfather talking about them, especially Madeleine, in the warmest tones. My grandfather – that was Frederick, of course – said Madeleine Meyer was always like an extra mother to him. Madeleine never had children of her own but she and Ralph adopted two and fostered dozens of children over the years. Ralph was a journalist. I'm guessing it was his notebook.'

'No, I think it was Madeleine's,' Jackie said, and then explained about the initials and the note at the end. 'I expect Ralph sent her out to interview female survivors. They'd be more likely to open up to another woman, I suppose.'

'How sad about her own loss,' Leonora replied. 'It explains why they adopted and fostered so many children, if they couldn't have their own. Well, thanks to them, and the little baby bangles Lucy had given her children, we now know the whole story.'

'Hey, Jackie? Come and look.' Chloe Franklin was waving at her. Jackie went over to see what she wanted, followed by Leonora. On a table there was a velvet cushion, and on it lay two bangles. Tiny, silver, engraved bangles.

'Oh! May I have a closer look?'

'Of course,' Chloe said.

Jackie picked up one of the bracelets and looked closely at the little garland of flowers that ran around it. A pretty thing, and what a story behind it! Inside, the engraving read Frederick Arthur and his date of birth, 27 January 1912.

'That was my grandfather's,' Leonora said with a smile.

The other read Norah Frances, and the same date of birth.

'To think,' Henry said, 'that the last time these two bangles were in the same room was 110 years ago on *Titanic*.'

He may have been talking about the bracelets, Jackie thought, but his attention seemed to be mostly fixed on Leonora Watts. She smiled to herself and put a hand on her bump. Her pregnancy was barely showing yet, but she could just feel the slight swelling below her waist.

'When's yours due?' Chloe Franklin said quietly, a half-smile on her face.

'Not till early summer. Is it that obvious?'

'Only to another pregnant woman. The way you put your hand there. Congratulations, anyway!'

'Thank you. And to you!'

'We must stay in touch, Jackie. And get together after our babies are born.'

'I'd like that.'

Across the room, Leonora was calling for all descendants of Frederick and Norah to arrange themselves for a group photograph. Jackie watched, smiling, as Henry and Leonora stood side by side flirting a little, and Neil Franklin put an arm around Chloe, and various other people joined the group with the little bangles in front. Those bracelets that had once been around the wrists of two babies who, by their parents' actions, were rescued from *Titanic* but then brought up separately. And now, as she gazed around the room, their descendants were back in touch with each other over a century later. What a legacy. Lucy Watts would have been delighted to see it happen.

# Chapter 33

## Jackie, 2022

Jackie arrived home from the New York trip exhausted but elated. It had been marvellous to spend time there, to meet Neil and Chloe and Leonora and the other members of the Watts family. Chatting to them all at the reunion had made Lucy's story truly come alive. She'd asked for permission to write more articles about them, and all had agreed and were willing to help where possible. The *Huffington Post* had expressed interest in follow-up articles too, and she'd spent the flight back across the Atlantic scribbling notes ready to be written up later.

She said goodbye to Henry and Lisa at the airport. It was Friday so there were a couple of days off before she'd see them again at work. 'Take care now,' Henry said to her, kissing her cheek. 'Mind that baby bump of yours.'

'I will, thanks, Henry.'

'And next week, I'll be asking you to renew the search for a *Carpathia* crew medal. I haven't given up on that yet, you know. If you can spare the time after writing up the story of the lost baby.' He smiled, and then was gone. He was already planning another visit to New York soon, and had been muttering something about a business venture with Leonora Watts. Those two had definitely hit it off.

Jackie took a taxi home. Tim would be home from work but as Henry was happy to pay the expenses there seemed no point in dragging Tim out to the airport. She texted him en route to say she'd soon be back, and got a simple thumbs up in reply. What did that mean? Was he not excited she was coming home? The thought crossed her mind that perhaps a few days without her might have raised doubts in his mind once more about becoming a father. You're being stupid, she told herself. After all these years, after all they'd been through that summer with the miscarriage and the earthquake, surely now she should feel confident in him? What would it take to make her finally feel secure that yes, he really wanted this baby growing inside her?

At last the taxi pulled up outside her house and Jackie climbed out, paying the driver. She wheeled her suitcase through the front garden. Tim's Audi TT was not on the driveway in its usual spot. Was he out, then? That surprised her. He knew what time she was expecting to be home. He wouldn't have gone out with the lads, knowing she was returning that evening, would he? Was that the reason for the lack of a reply to her text?

But as she fitted her key in the front door lock and turned it, she realised he was at home, after all. There was a delicious smell coming from the kitchen. Some sort of shepherd's pie, if she wasn't mistaken. And the table was set for two, with a vase of red roses in the middle.

Tim appeared from the kitchen, wearing an apron. He crossed the room to her and kissed her, squeezing her tight. 'So glad you are home. I missed you.'

'Nice to be back. You've cooked something?'

'Yes. Shepherd's pie and there's a fruit crumble and custard for dessert. But first I want to show you something. Up there.' He nodded at the stairs, picked up her suitcase and went up.

She followed, wondering what it was he wanted to show her. She was also wondering where his car was, but decided to ask him about it later, when she'd seen whatever was upstairs.

He was standing at the door to the spare bedroom. He'd bought some new piece of outdoor equipment, she guessed. A new wetsuit, or a pair of hiking boots, or a new climbing rope. 'What is it?'

'Go on. Go inside.' He pushed the door wider open and she gasped.

Gone were the boxes of old stuff from his parents' loft. Gone was the collection of outdoor gear. The room was almost bare, but had been painted a pale lemon colour, with white woodwork. A new grey carpet covered the floor, and white blinds covered the window. A rocking chair, newly painted white and with yellow and blue cushions on its seat, was in a corner by the window.

'So I thought, we can get a white cot, put it over there.' Tim pointed to the side of the room. 'And some sort of storage for baby clothes and nappies and whatever. A few pictures on the wall . . .'

'Oh, Tim. It is perfect.' Jackie's eyes filled with tears as she pictured the room finished, and their child in it. She flung her arms around him and hugged him. 'But when on earth did you find time to do all this?'

'Ahem. Alfie helped me with shifting the stuff out, and the painting. I've been at it every evening this week. Just about got it done in time, but I wouldn't touch the windowsill if I were you. Paint's still tacky.'

'Where did all the stuff go?'

Tim shrugged. 'Threw out some of it. Gave the old bed away on Freecycle. Bought a garden shed, which Alfie put together for me one day when I was at work. The outdoor gear is in that. Grandad's old stuff is in the loft. Mostly.'

'Mostly?'

'Well, I kept a few things out, thinking you might want to look at them.'

Jackie remembered the car at that moment. 'And Tim, where's your Audi?'

'Sold it.'

'You *sold* it?'

'It'll be no good when the baby comes along. I'll buy a Ford Focus or something sensible like that, to drive to school in.'

'You sold your car, cleared out your stuff, and painted this room to be a nursery . . .'

'Yes, well, we are having a baby, aren't we? Things have to change . . .'

She nodded, and he kissed her, and as he did so she knew for certain that he definitely was ready for all this now. She felt absolutely certain of it, at last. He'd proved it beyond any doubt by his actions.

'And I need to show you something else,' he said, and pulled her back downstairs. In a corner was a box that she vaguely recognised as one of the old ones that had been stacked for too long in the spare room. 'Take a look inside,' he said, lifting it onto a chair. 'This was a surprise to me too.'

She opened it up, and gasped. It was like looking inside a box that Henry might have picked up at an auction. Old books and framed photos were on top. She lifted one photo, of a man in some sort of naval uniform.

'My great-grandfather,' Tim said. 'This is mostly his stuff. I knew he was in the merchant navy, but I didn't know Mum had kept all his stuff. Apparently, he worked for Cunard for a while.'

'Ooh! When are we talking about?'

Tim had a teasing little smile playing at the corners of his mouth. 'Oh, you know. Early twentieth century.'

'What ships?'

'I don't know all of them, but there's a cap with a ship's name on it, bit further down in the box . . .'

She rummaged through and pulled it out. 'RMS *Carpathia*. Wow. Really?'

'Yes. And something else. Open that little box.' He pointed to a moth-eaten small velvet box. She picked it up and carefully opened it, feeling a rush of excitement surge through her. Inside was a bronze medal that showed an engraving of a ship on one side. She turned it over, and read out the inscription on the reverse. '*Presented to the Captain, Officers and Crew of RMS* Carpathia, *in recognition of gallant and heroic services, from the survivors of the SS Titanic, April 15th, 1912.* You're telling me your great-grandfather was a crew member of *Carpathia*? When it went to Titanic's rescue?'

'It seems so. I didn't know. Well, I knew he'd been a sailor, that was all.'

'This,' she held up the medal, 'is what Henry's been searching for.'

'I know. You told me. And I will sell it to him, for the right price.'

'Sell it? Don't you think it should stay in your family?'

'No one else wants it. I checked. Mum's happy for me to sell. And assuming he gives us a fair price for it, it'll fund all the baby gear we need to buy.'

'Don't you want to keep it?'

Tim looked at the medal in her hand and shrugged. 'Not really, no. I'll keep that photo. Not bothered about the rest of it. Just old tat, isn't it?'

Jackie laughed. Tim had never understood the appeal of 'old tat'. 'Well, I'll go through it first, if you don't mind, and let Henry have first dibs on the rest. He will be over the moon about the medal.'

'Good. So, did I do well, while you were away?'

She put the medal down and stepped into his arms once more. 'You did brilliantly, my darling. All we need to do now is arrange our wedding.'

'Give me a chance! But yes. Sooner the better, eh?'

'Sooner the better.' She kissed him again, and knew that their future together would be bright, happy and loving.

# Author's Note

While researching my earlier novel, *The Lost Sister*, I came across
the story of Violet Jessop, a stewardess from *Titanic*, and read
her memoir *Titanic Survivor*. She tells the story of the baby that
was thrust into her arms as she boarded the lifeboat, and then
snatched from her by a woman when she boarded *Carpathia*.
That tale stayed with me, and I always wondered who the baby
was and what happened to him or her afterwards.

And then, after *The Lost Sister* was published, book blogger
and reviewer Cindy Spear got in touch to tell me about the book
*Carpathia* by Jay Ludowyke, which tells the story of this ship from
when it was built right through to when it was torpedoed in
World War I, and also tells the tale of how its wreck was discovered and explored in recent years. As you might imagine, this
book goes into a lot of detail of *Carpathia*'s role in rescuing the
*Titanic* survivors. I read it on Cindy's recommendation and as I
turned each page, I knew there was another novel to be written.

Many of the historical characters in this book are real people,
including Captain Rostron, Harold Cottam and the Marshall
family. The Marconi message sent to *Titanic*, and the story of
the reunion of the Marshall cousins is all based on facts. There
was also a real journalist, Carlos Hurd, on board *Carpathia*, but

I decided to use a fictional character and his wife – Ralph and Madeleine Meyer. But the details surrounding their attempts to get the story transmitted from the ship, Captain Rostron's ban on sending it and confiscation of their typewriter and paper, and the desperate measure of throwing their articles down to a small boat are all inspired by Carlos Hurd's story as told in Jay Ludowyke's book. Lucy Watts and her family are fictional, as are the couple who took the baby Violet Jessop brought on board *Carpathia*.

Some years ago, my husband and I travelled in our motorhome through the Abruzzo region of Italy, a very beautiful part of the country. I remember seeing evidence of earthquake damage in small towns in the L'Aquila area – ruined medieval towers and churches. I wanted to contrast the speed at which news of disasters gets around now and a hundred years ago, and using an earthquake seemed to be a good way to do this. The town of Sorgente di Giacomo is fictional, as is the earthquake depicted in this novel.

Thank you so much for choosing to read The Lost Child. I hope you enjoyed it! If you did, please consider leaving a review. I always love to hear what readers thought, and it helps new readers discover my books too.

Kathleen McGurl

https://kathleenmcgurl.com
https://twitter.com/KathMcGurl
https://www.facebook.com/KathleenMcGurl
https://instagram.com/KathleenMcGurl

# Acknowledgements

Thanks to my editor Abi Fenton for all her insights and wisdom which helped make this book the best it could be. Thanks too, to Kate Mills, Rachael Nazarko and copy editor Teresa Palmiero for their input in the later stages of producing this novel.

It wouldn't have existed at all without writer and reviewer Cindy Spear who recommended the book which sparked the idea, so thank you for that, Cindy, and thanks for being such a wonderful supporter of so many writers.

Thanks to my husband Ignatius as always, for putting up with me while I moan about the sticky middle and being there to make dinner, pour wine, and generally encourage me to get on with it.

And finally thanks to all you wonderful readers without whom there'd be no point in me writing. I appreciate you all, and all reviewers and book-bloggers, immensely!

# Keep Reading . . .

## The Girl with the Emerald Flag

### A country rebelling

It's 1916 and, as war rages in Europe, Gráinne leaves her
job in a department store to join Countess Markiewicz's
revolutionary efforts. It is a decision which will change her
life forever. A rebellion is brewing, and as Dublin's streets
become a battleground, Gráinne soon discovers the personal
cost of fighting for what you believe in . . .

### A forgotten sacrifice

Decades on, student Nicky is recovering from a break-up when a
research project leads her to her great-grandmother's experiences
in revolutionary Ireland. When Nicky finds a long-forgotten
handkerchief amongst her great-grandmother's things, it leads to
the revelation of a heartbreaking story of tragedy and courage,
and those who sacrificed everything for their country.

**Inspired by a heartbreaking true story, this emotional
historical novel will sweep you away to the Emerald Isle.
Perfect for fans of Jean Grainger, Sandy Taylor and Fiona Valpy.**

# The Storm Girl

**1784.** When Esther Harris's father hurts his back, she takes over his role helping smugglers hide contraband in the secret cellar in their pub. But when the free traders' ships are trapped in the harbour, a battle between the smugglers and the revenue officers leads to murder and betrayal – and Esther is forced to choose between the love of her life and protecting her family . . .

**Present day.** Fresh from her divorce, Millie Galton moves into a former inn overlooking the harbour in Mudeford and plans to create her dream home. When a chance discovery behind an old fireplace reveals the house's secret history as a haven for smugglers and the devastating story of its former residents, could the mystery of a disappearance from centuries ago finally be solved?

**Sweeping historical fiction perfect for fans of Lucinda Riley, Kathryn Hughes and Tracy Rees.**

# The Girl from Bletchley Park

**Will love lead her to a devastating choice?**

**1942.** Three years into the war, Pam turns down her hard-won place at Oxford University to become a codebreaker at Bletchley Park. There, she meets two young men, both keen to impress her, and Pam finds herself falling hard for one of them. But as the country's future becomes more uncertain by the day, a tragic turn of events casts doubt on her choice – and Pam's loyalty is pushed to its limits . . .

**Present day.** Julia is struggling to juggle her career, two children and a husband increasingly jealous of her success. Her brother presents her with the perfect distraction: forgotten photos of their grandmother as a young woman at Bletchley Park. Why did her grandmother never speak of her time there? The search for answers leads Julia to an incredible tale of betrayal and bravery – one that inspires some huge decisions of her own . . .

**Gripping historical fiction perfect for fans of *The Girl from Berlin*, *The Rose Code* and *When We Were Brave*.**

# The Lost Sister

**Three sisters. Three ships. One heartbreaking story.**

**1911.** As Emma packs her trunk to join the ocean liner *Olympic* as a stewardess, she dreams of earning enough to provide a better life for both her sisters. With their photograph tucked away in her luggage, she promises to be back soon – hoping that sickly Lily will keep healthy, and wild Ruby will behave. But neither life at sea nor on land is predictable, and soon the three sisters' lives are all changed irrevocably . . .

**Now.** When Harriet finds her late grandmother's travelling trunk in the attic, she's shocked to discover a photo of three sisters inside – her grandmother only ever mentioned one sister, who died tragically young. Who is the other sister, and what happened to her? Harriet's questions lead her to the story of three sister ships, *Olympic*, *Titanic* and *Britannic*, and a shattering revelation about three sisters torn apart . . .

**Return to drama on the high seas with this captivating historical novel.**

# The Forgotten Gift

**What would you do to protect the ones you love?**

**1861.** George's life changes forever the day he meets Lucy.
She's beautiful and charming, and he sees a future with
her that his position as the second son in a wealthy family
has never offered him. But when Lucy dies in a suspected
poisoning days after rejecting George, he finds himself swept
up into a murder investigation. George loved Lucy;
he would never have harmed her. So who did?

**Now.** On the surface Cassie is happy with her life: a secure job,
good friends, and a loving family. When a mysterious gift in
a long-forgotten will leads her to a dark secret in her family's
history she's desperate to learn more. But the secrets in Cassie's
family aren't all hidden in the past, and her research will soon
lead her to a revelation much closer to home – and which will
turn everything she knows on its head . . .

**Discover a family's darkest secrets in this
beautiful dual timeline novel.**

Dear Reader,

We hope you enjoyed reading this book. If you did, we'd be so appreciative if you left a review. It really helps us and the author to bring more books like this to you.

Here at HQ Digital we are dedicated to publishing fiction that will keep you turning the pages into the early hours. Don't want to miss a thing? To find out more about our books, promotions, discover exclusive content and enter competitions you can keep in touch in the following ways:

### JOIN OUR COMMUNITY:

Sign up to our new email newsletter: http://smarturl.it/SignUpHQ

Read our new blog www.hqstories.co.uk

🐦 https://twitter.com/HQStories

📘 www.facebook.com/HQStories

### BUDDING WRITER?

We're also looking for authors to join the HQ Digital family!

Find out more here:

https://www.hqstories.co.uk/want-to-write-for-us/

Thanks for reading, from the HQ Digital team